Eden HALL

VERONICA HELEY

GRAND RAPIDS, MICHIGAN 49530 USA

ZONDERVAN.COM/
AUTHORTRACKER

We want to hear from you. Please send your comments about this book to us in care of zreview@zondervan.com. Thank you.

ZONDERVAN™

Eden Hall

Requests for information should be addressed to:

Zondervan, *Grand Rapids, Michigan 49530*

Library of Congress Cataloging-in-Publication Data

Heley, Veronica
Eden Hall / Veronica Heley.—1st ed.
p. cm.
ISBN-10: 0-310-24963-5
ISBN-13: 978-0-310-24963-4
1. Young women—Fiction. 2. Administration of estates—Fiction. 3. Fathers and daughters—Fiction. 4. Cancer—Patients—Fiction. 5. Stepmothers—Fiction. 6. England—Fiction. Title.
PR6070.H6915 E34 2004
823'.92—dc22
2003023565

Interior illustration by Clint Hansen
Interior design by Michelle Espinoza

Printed in the United States of America

05 06 07 08 09 10 • 18 17 16 15 14 13 12 11 10 9 8 7 6 5 4 3

Eden HALL

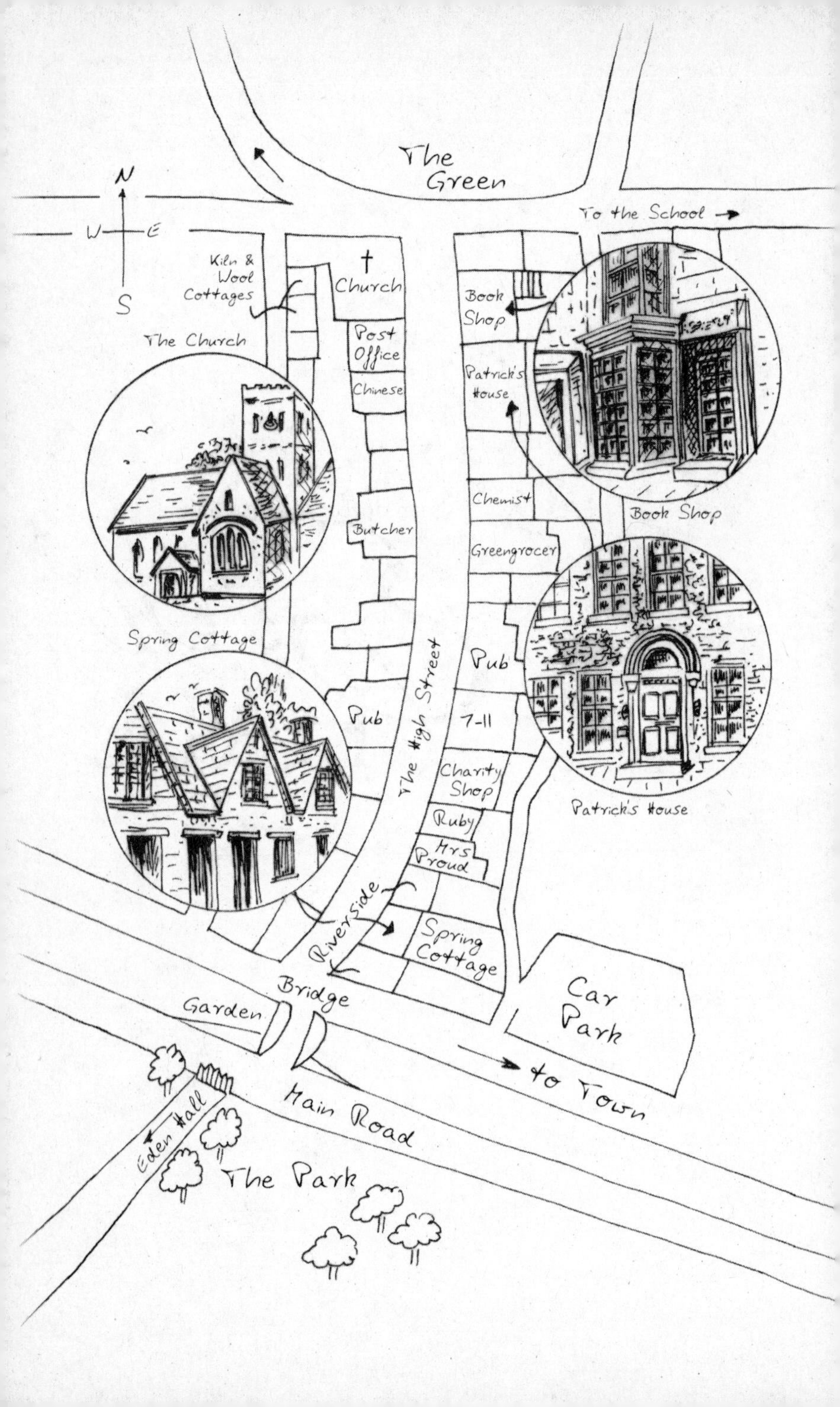
The Green
N
W
E
S
To the School
Kiln & Wool Cottages
Church
Post Office
Chinese
The Church
Book Shop
Patrick's House
Chemist
Book Shop
Butcher
Greengrocer
Spring Cottage
Pub
The High Street
Pub
7-11
Charity Shop
Ruby
Mrs Proud
Patrick's House
Riverside
Spring Cottage
Bridge
Garden
Car Park
to Town
Main Road
Eden Hall
The Park

Chapter One

She was being watched.

No one had come to meet her, but Araminta Cardale—Minty—could feel eyes upon her. The little country station seemed to be in the middle of nowhere. Three other people had alighted from the train, got into cars, and driven away. A number of vehicles remained in the car park, probably those of commuters who'd gone to the far-off city for the day. An ancient man dozed in a disreputable estate car. That was all.

The midday sun lay heavily over the trees and fields before her. The only road leading from the station car park twisted out of sight behind a stand of oak trees. There were no other houses or even people in sight.

Could they have forgotten to meet her? Surely not! It was only last night that Minty's half-sister Gemma had phoned, saying their father was seriously ill and Minty was needed. After all those years of banishment, her father wanted her back! Minty hadn't thought twice about it, but said she'd be on the first train next morning.

Then she had to face the aunt and uncle who had housed and fed—but not loved—her all those years. They'd been furious at what they called Minty's "desertion" of them, even though Minty had made hasty but sufficient arrangements for other people to take over her work in the parish. For once Minty had refused to give in to their appeals and threats. She'd gone back up to pack in the small, cold bedroom that had been hers for nearly twenty years—only to realise she hadn't any money for the journey. She quailed at the thought of having to face her uncle again, but summoned up her courage and did it. She said she'd hitchhike if necessary. In the end he'd agreed to lend her the exact amount for the train fare.

Ten minutes passed. No one came. Minty eased her shoulders under her white T-shirt.

It hadn't taken her long to pack her rucksack the previous evening. After all, she was going back to Eden Hall as a daughter of the house. No longer would she have to subdue her natural exuberance, be careful of what she said and whom she said it to. She was leaving behind the life of vicarage drudge and parish secretary. She was going to be herself for once! And leaving Lucas behind, too. An added bonus.

She had cast aside the severe navy blue skirts and white blouses that her aunt had decreed were the appropriate wear for Minty as vicar's niece and his parish secretary. All she took into her new life were the jumble sale and charity shop jeans and T-shirts she had worn when she helped in the youth club, a halfway decent cotton skirt, a couple of sweaters and a jacket. Her Bible, of course, went in first.

Before anyone else was up in the morning, she'd set out through the city streets to walk to the station, where she'd nearly an hour to wait for the little local train. She had no money to buy herself breakfast. She went into the ladies waiting room and inspected herself in the mirror. That morning she'd let her honey-coloured hair curl loosely about her shoulders, instead of pinning it up in the severe French plait preferred by her aunt.

She swung her hair from side to side, half alarmed and half pleased at the sensation. She fished a jumble sale scarf out of her rucksack and tied it round her head to hold her hair off her face. The gauzy blue matched her eyes, almost. Her eyelashes and eyebrows were as fair as her hair. If they'd been darker, she might have been considered pretty.

Minty smiled at herself in the mirror. If Aunt Agnes could see her now, how she'd scold! "You look like a prostitute," she'd say. "Just like your mother. Mark my words, you'll come to a bad end, just like her." Aunt Agnes could scold for the Olympics.

Minty twisted from side to side, trying to see as much of herself as she could in the mirror. Her skin was good, though lacking in colour. She touched the tiny gilt cross on its fragile chain round her neck. It was her only jewellery, apart from a cheap watch. She pulled a face at herself. Experience of life had given her a wary look, and she looked older than her real age of twenty-four.

Twenty minutes had passed since the train had left, and she'd no idea how to reach the Hall. Had there really been a gracious golden house set in a spreading park, or had she just imagined it?

Perhaps Gemma's phone call had been a terrible practical joke?

Minty squared her shoulders. She would not be put off now she had come so far. Gemma must have been held up. Her father might have taken a turn for the worse. Minty had no mobile phone, no money for a taxi, but there was only one road leading away from the station and she would follow it until she found someone who could direct her to the Hall. She picked up her rucksack and set off down the road.

The door of the estate car creaked open and footsteps sounded behind her. Ah, the watcher had surfaced, had he? Brought up in a crime-ridden city parish, Minty turned, ready to fight off a mugger.

He blinked at her, this elderly farm worker. His clothes had originally been good and his boots still were. Small, metal-framed glasses, a seamed and weathered face, brown eyes. He looked like a tortoise.

"You'll be Miss Milly's daughter?"

Minty nodded.

"You're like her."

Minty winced. How often had her uncle and aunt told her so. "All that fair hair!" they'd said. "The mark of a child of shame!" Minty hadn't known for a long time what they meant, but she knew now. Minty lifted her chin. She knew that what her mother had done was wrong, but her own dim memories of the first Lady Cardale had been of warmth and laughter. There hadn't been much loving or laughing in Minty's years in the vicarage, but she remembered those sensations from early childhood.

The old man squinted into the sun. "They're expecting you at the Hall? It would be Miss Gemma called you?"

"Yes." He seemed to know a lot. She'd heard there were no secrets in a village. He didn't seem about to mug her, but could she trust him?

"Thornby. Old Oak Farm. Taking some eggs up to the Hall. Give you a lift."

He walked, bandy-legged, over to the ancient estate car and pulled open the passenger door. After a moment's hesitation she got in, hugging her rucksack. He had to slam the door twice to get it to shut. The car smelt of something organic. The wet nose of a black and white collie investigated her neck and she nearly yelped.

"Down!" said the farmer, and the dog subsided. Minty clung to the half-open window as the farmer swung out of the car park and headed down the road. There didn't seem to be a handle on the inside of the door and the seat belt was broken. The car looked a wreck, but the engine sounded good. She'd heard that cars reflected the personality of their owners. Perhaps this one did, too.

The road gave a sudden twist as they came to the first sign of habitation since leaving the train station. Mr Thornby slowed down as they passed a clutch of run-down farm buildings. Minty thought he was going to say something, but he picked up speed again, continuing down the country lane. Mature trees overhung the road, and the verges were starred with the wild flowers of early autumn. She glimpsed a couple of cottages set back from the road.

Suddenly the trees fell away and they came out on to a village green fringed with houses. A cricket pitch was being mown in the middle of the green, and at one side was a white-painted changing room for the players.

As they snaked their way around the green, a church reared its tower against the sky and they came to a crossroads. Mr Thornby paused to look for traffic—there was hardly any—and took the road down the hill, which turned into a village high street.

The houses and shops in the high street were all shapes and sizes but nearly all were built of golden stone, glowing in the midday sun. Minty caught her breath. After the grimy brick buildings of the city, the village looked like a picture on a calendar. Window boxes adorned many of the houses and at intervals down the broad pavements stood timber planters spilling over with fuschias, trailing geraniums and petunias. A fairy-tale village.

"You remember it?"

She smiled. "It's beautiful."

Their progress down the street slowed because a coach crowded with tourists was moving along ahead of them. Minty's eye was caught by a huge marmalade cat sitting in a bookshop window. A woman with a child in a pushchair crossed the road ahead of their car and, though there seemed to be plenty of room, Mr Thornby swerved into the kerb to avoid her.

Minty's door flew open, depositing her on to the pavement and nudging a dark-haired man who stood chatting with a friend nearby.

The man staggered, letting slip the papers he was holding.

"Steady!" said the older man, grabbing his arm.

"So sorry!" gasped Minty, scrambling to regain her seat and rescue the door.

"Thornby! Can't you look where you're going for a change?"

"So-rry," sang out the farmer.

"What the . . . !" said the dark-haired man, staring at Minty. "*What* the . . . !"

"I'm so sorry," repeated Minty. She thought, *He's really ugly with that long nose, but . . . I've never met anyone so . . . why is he looking at me like that? Why do I want to cry? It's the shock. I nearly killed him, but . . . Why is he looking at me like that?*

The farmer said, "Miss Cardale, returning to the Hall."

"Yes," said the dark-haired man, short of breath.

"Seemingly they forgot to send a car for her."

"Ah," said the dark-haired man. He took a hasty step back, cannoned into a wooden bench and sat down. He was perhaps five years older than Minty, wearing conventional dark trousers, a white business shirt and dark blue tie. His eyes were light grey, his skin tanned with the summer sun. In the city Minty would have put him down as a teacher. Here he could be anything.

Why was he staring at her like that? She'd never seen him before in her life.

A stocky middle-aged woman bustled out of the bookshop and started to pick up the papers he'd dropped, scolding everyone in sight. "Norman Thornby, you ought to be ashamed of yourself! Too mean to spend money on a decent car; it'll land you in court one of these fine days. Are you all right, Patrick? No damage? Norman, you chose the right man to knock over this time, didn't you?"

Everyone laughed, except Minty and the man the woman had called "Patrick".

Patrick?

"I'm fine," said the dark-haired man, getting to his feet and reclaiming his papers. "Thanks, Mrs Wootton. Thornby, she's right. If you keep on driving like that, I'll see you in court one day."

All the time his eyes were on Minty, and she was looking at him. It was disturbing.

Norman Thornby waved them goodbye and set off into the traffic again.

"Well, that'll give them something to talk about. That was Patrick Sands. Much respected in these parts. Except at the Hall, of course."

Minty gasped. "Sands? The man my mother ran away with?"

"If you believe that! His son. Took over the practice when his father retired. And there's the Hall."

She looked where he pointed. At the bottom of the hill was a humpback bridge over a river, and beyond the bridge lay a park of mature trees and green sward, surrounded by a low wall. The shadows beneath the trees looked blue in the sunlight. Between the trees she caught a glimpse of golden stone and light reflected from windows.

She could feel her heart beating. Eden Hall at last. Soon she would see her father!

Mr Thornby slowed to take the bend on to the bridge.

"Oh, I remember this bridge!" cried Minty. "My mother used to lift me up on to the parapet to see the river."

The road divided over the bridge. Mr Thornby turned right and then sharply left through some open gates into an avenue lined with horse chestnut trees. A large sign at the roadside indicated that Eden Hall was open to the public five days a week . . . restaurant open . . . price . . .

Minty was so excited she didn't know which way to look, trying to take everything in. Her father . . . only a few more minutes and she would see him! Surely the Hall hadn't been open to the public in the old days. Had her father lost all his money? She'd understood he was a financier. Hadn't there been something about his establishing a charity to help educate children in inner cities . . . ? Perhaps that had been just a fairy-tale. She didn't mind if he were poor now. She knew all about poverty.

That man. Patrick. Why had he looked at her like that? As if . . . ? She shook her head in frustration.

The Hall overlooked a great sweep of parkland. Hadn't there been a lake? She couldn't see it. She dug into her memory for the stories her mother had told her about the house.

"Sheep!" her mother had said, holding up a model of a sheep. "The oldest part of the house was built on the money we made from wool." Then her mother had held up a toy train. "Then we went into railways and built wings on to the original house so that it became a hollow square."

That's right, thought Minty. *I remember an enclosed courtyard with a fountain in it. There were staircases in the towers at each of the four corners of the building. It was great to play hide and seek, running up one staircase, through the formal rooms and down another . . .*

Minty's head turned from side to side as they eased their way under a wide stone archway into a cobbled yard. They were directly under the original Elizabethan wing now, the one that had been built on the money made from wool. The sound of the car on cobbles brought back a fleeting memory. She had been just five when she'd been driven away.

To the right were outbuildings displaying signs with "Restaurant", "Shop", and "Toilets" on each.

Another archway, another courtyard. Expensive-looking cars housed in more outbuildings. On the right, windows opened on to a kitchen, clattering with noisy food preparation. She didn't remember that at all.

Mr Thornby parked by the kitchen door. "You won't want to go in the front door, because that's the way the tourists go in to visit the house. I think we'd best find Ms Phillips to look after you." He hopped out, relieving her of her rucksack and leading the way back into the first courtyard.

"Who's Ms Phillips?" asked Minty, trying to keep up with him.

There were several doors leading into the house. One stood open, but he ignored it. They passed another door marked "Estate Office" and eventually came to a door marked "Private" with a discreet logo on it. Mr Thornby rang the bell beside the door. He put down the rucksack and said, "I'll be in the kitchens back there if you need me."

As Minty thanked him, the door was opened by a youngish woman who looked at her curiously but did not speak as she gestured for Minty to enter.

Her father . . . in a few minutes she would see him. Would she be held by him, welcomed, loved? Was she tidy? Perhaps he wouldn't like her wearing jeans. It was too late to change.

She stepped inside. She was in a dark passage. The woman who had admitted her opened a door on the left and ushered her into a spacious reception room. The mullioned windows didn't let in much daylight, but sympathetic lighting helped to counter the darkness of the original panelling. This was a ground floor reception room, with comfortable modern chairs arranged around a low table on one side, and on the other the latest technology—and behind it a middle-aged, competent personal assistant/secretary.

Glasses flashed as the woman looked up from some papers she was studying.

"Ms Phillips? I'm Araminta Cardale. My sister phoned me to . . ."

Ms Phillips nodded to the younger woman, who disappeared through an inner door.

"We've been expecting you. Take a seat. Coffee? Tea?"

Minty shook her head. In a minute her father would come bursting through the door, holding out his arms to her . . . or perhaps he might be so ill that a nurse would lead her up to his bedroom, where he would be lying with his eyes turned to the door, waiting for her. Perhaps she wouldn't be able to hug him as she wanted to, but would be able to hold his hand and stroke it.

The inner door opened and in rushed a beautiful red-haired girl wearing designer clothing and glittering with gold chains. She was in tears, tissue in hand.

"Oh, Araminta, I'm so sorry! It's all been a terrible mistake, there's been the most awful row, and I'm so, so sorry! I tried phoning you, but you'd gone already."

Minty could hardly take in what the girl was saying. Was this her half-sister, Gemma? Minty felt the blood leave her head.

"I know I ought to have met you at the station, but mother was in such a state, and then Simon said . . . and of course we daren't tell father, so you see . . . ?"

Minty had risen when Gemma came in but now sank back on to the chair. It had been a mistake to leave without breakfast.

She said, "Sending for me was a mistake?"

Ms Phillips had disappeared. Gemma sat down beside Minty. "I can't apologise enough. Father's been gradually getting worse for weeks though mother refuses to see it, and of course Simon's been running the house and estate for some time, because there's so much to do, you can't imagine, even with all the volunteers. It's never ending. I help mother with her charity work and that's pretty well a full-time job, I can tell you."

Minty put her hand to her forehead. Wasn't she going to be allowed to see her father, after all?

Gemma misunderstood her. "Oh, you probably don't remember. Simon's our half-brother, mother's son by her first marriage. Father adopted him, of course, and—"

"Talking about me?" One of the handsomest men Minty had ever seen was leaning against the doorpost, looking down his nose at her. He was tall and blond with blue eyes. An open-necked white shirt over the latest jeans showed off an extraordinary tan. Somehow Minty knew the tan went all over.

She'd forgotten about Simon. She had a hazy memory of somebody who used to tease her and laugh. She shook her head, frustrated at her inability to remember.

"Is this Little Miss Hopeful, then?" he said. "Doesn't look much like the Old Man, does she?"

Minty recoiled.

"Oh, Simon!" said Gemma, disconcerted but also trying to hide a giggle. "How could you!"

"Very easily, my dear. Get rid of her before I lose my temper." He vanished.

Gemma was embarrassed. She tried on a laugh. "I'm so sorry. Simon is . . . well . . . you understand?"

Minty didn't, no. "Am I not to see my father, then?"

Gemma ignored that, lifting a hand with a giant emerald ring on it. "You have to laugh; I've known about you for ever, the black sheep of the family. I grew up wondering about you, thinking family feuds like that went out with the Borgias. Several times I nearly got in touch with you just to see what you were like, but I never did because . . . well, I don't know why, really. Then last week everything went pear-shaped. Simon's so busy with his new project that he forgot about the cleaners, and he wanted me to take over the holiday lets, and I just flipped! Then I came across your address, and I was so cross with Simon, and it seemed like a good idea to call you.

"I told mother and Simon this morning, but of course I'd got it all wrong and she was devastated. She explained how much it would hurt father if you came, so I tried to stop you. But I was too late. Oh, and do be happy for me! I got engaged last week, and mother says I'm to take over her duties here, opening fêtes and giving prizes at the school and all that and, well, you see how it is, don't you?"

Minty could only think of one thing. "I want to see my father. That's why I came."

"Mother says it would only upset him. So you see . . . ?" She spread her manicured fingers, with the glowing emerald on her left hand.

Minty felt the contrast between Gemma and her with a stab of pain, even while she tried to come to terms with her disappointment. Gemma was a darling—except perhaps for that moment in which she'd laughed at Minty with Simon. But that might have been nerves. Gemma was ingenuous, pampered. Much loved. Minty in her jumble sale clothes was something the cat had brought in.

Gemma touched Minty lightly on her shoulder. "I really am so sorry. I thought it would be the perfect answer to all our problems if you came and helped out—part of the family, you know. But you're not even my half-sister, my mother says.

"Perhaps we can arrange to meet up later in the year, in town, say? For lunch or something? Not for the wedding, of course, but . . . I did ask my mother if you could stay the night having come all this way, but I'd forgotten that Simon has got people staying, so it's out of the question, I'm afraid. Don't look so . . . it really is not my fault! Ms Phillips will get a taxi to take you back to the station."

Minty didn't see Gemma go, as she was putting her head down between her knees to still the roaring sound in her ears. When her faintness receded, she sat up and pushed her hair back from her forehead.

Ms Phillips was offering her a glass of water.

Minty drank. "Thank you."

"Have you eaten today?" A kindly enough voice. Ms Phillips wasn't devoid of compassion, it seemed. Or perhaps she wanted to avoid having a fainting girl on her hands. "I suggest you get yourself a square meal at the restaurant and then I'll call you a taxi."

Minty thought of the few pence she had left in her purse. She began to laugh but recognised the hysteria in her voice and made herself stop. What should she do? Tamely return to her uncle and aunt? Not to mention the problem represented by her cousin Lucas.

No, she thought. *Having come so far, I'm not going to be fobbed off with excuses.* She squared her shoulders, took a deep breath. "I can't go back without seeing my father, especially if he's as ill as Gemma says. Besides, it's not possible for me to go anywhere. I haven't the price of a taxi on me, nor the train fare. I don't even have enough to buy a sandwich!"

Chapter Two

Ms Phillips raised her eyebrows. "I can cash a cheque for you, if you wish."

Minty spread her hands. "No cheque book. No money. I borrowed the train fare from my uncle. I'll have to find some work somewhere in the village, waitressing, office work, cleaning, in order to eat. Anyway, I'm not leaving till I've seen my father."

"Did you forget your chequebook?"

"I don't have one."

"You do have a job, don't you?"

"Yes, I act as parish secretary to my uncle, but—"

"Suppose," said Ms Phillips, "you start at the beginning. I came to work for your father after you'd been sent away, and nobody wanted to talk about what had happened."

"I was sent away because my mother had been unfaithful to my father. When he found out, she ran off with her lover and was killed in a car crash. I went to live with my uncle—that's my father's brother—and my aunt in the city. They brought me up, sent me to college, and now I work as his parish secretary and look after my aunt as best I can. End of story."

"A bleak tale. Why do you want to see your father so badly, if he's rejected you?"

"I know he loved me once. I can remember running down the big staircase into his arms. He'd whirl me around, calling me Araminta. That's my proper name, only nobody else ever used it. I suppose I hope . . . perhaps it's foolish . . . that at bottom he still loves me. So if there's a chance to see him, I must take it."

"Wouldn't you be better off with your uncle and aunt?"

Minty repressed a shudder. "They took me out of duty and because I could be useful to them, but they never loved me. They told me over and over how lucky I was to have been taken in by them, after what my mother did. They were ashamed of me. Any hint that I was going to turn out like my mother and my aunt beat me."

Ms Phillips started.

Minty laughed, a hard sound. "I suppose I deserved it. I believe I was a hard, difficult child, and Aunt Agnes was not a well woman. Later, if I wanted to do anything outside the parish, form a new friendship, go on holiday with the youth group, go away to college, my aunt became ill. It was years before I worked out that her illnesses were psychosomatic, aimed at keeping me tied to her . . . useful to her.

"Sometimes I wanted to scream and break things and run away, but mostly I gritted my teeth and hung on. As I got older, they came to rely on me for everything. How would they cope without me?

"When I left school, I had to fight to go to college. They wanted me to stay at home and look after my aunt. That's when she got shingles and really was poorly. I argued that if I had secretarial training, I could help in the parish office, too. So my uncle lent me the money for it. At college I mixed with people from outside the parish and realised I could make my own way in the world if only I could break free of the vicarage. But I'd given a solemn promise to return and be parish secretary. So I did, while paying off my debt week by week. Now I'm earning I have to pay them for my keep, and as a parish secretary only gets a pittance, a pittance is all I'm able to hand on."

"You can't expect me to believe that your uncle made you pay for your keep."

"What? But he did. Look."

Minty scrabbled in her rucksack and produced a worn cash book. "This is a record of everything I still owe them."

Ms Phillips took the book over to the window and stood with her back to Minty, turning pages. The light caught her glasses as she turned round again, so that Minty couldn't read her expression.

"Let us understand one another," Ms Phillips said. "I do not work for Lady Cardale. I am Sir Micah's personal assistant, working for the Foundation."

Minty narrowed her eyes. Was Ms Phillips telling her that she was not necessarily prepared to follow the line Lady Cardale had taken?

"Has my father lost his money? Is that why the Hall is open to the public? I can earn my keep. Perhaps I can help?"

Ms Phillips seated herself. She was the sort of woman who wore skirts, not trousers, and sat with her knees and ankles neatly together. "No, he has not lost his money. It was not fitting for Lady Cardale to continue as Sir Micah's secretary once they were married, and it was her pleasure to open the Hall to the public. Three years ago she handed over the running of the house and estate to Simon."

Minty tried to follow what Ms Phillips seemed to be saying. "You mean you could get me in to see my father?"

"Perhaps. It is true he is very ill. May I ask what has been the matter with your aunt?"

"This and that; nothing life-threatening, but she has never been well enough to do the housework. And yes, I do feel guilty about leaving her . . . but not guilty enough to go back."

"What about boyfriends?"

Minty laughed. "I used to have a daydream about a knight in shining armour coming to rescue me. That was childish, of course. I went out once or twice with members of the youth group, but somehow they all seemed so young and I never seemed to attract anyone else. A few first dates, that's all. Nothing to take seriously." She studied her fingernails. "My aunt's nephew Lucas came to live with us while I was at college, and we went out together for a while. I quite liked him at first, and he seemed keen. My aunt encouraged him. I think she thought that if he married me and settled down nearby, she'd be able to call on my services for life. We did get engaged for a short time, though how that came about I'm not quite sure, because I was never happy about it. As I got to know him better . . ." She shook her head. "I broke it off some time ago. He's still around. He tries my door at night sometimes. I always put a chair under the doorknob, just in case."

"So in coming here, you are really running away from your past?" Ms Phillips could have questioned for the Inquisition.

Minty knew she'd gone red. "Yes, you're right. It does feel like an escape. But I meant that bit about seeing my father again. That really is important to me."

"Perhaps you hope he'll settle some money on you?"

"I never thought of that. Especially after what my mother did. No, Ms Phillips. I just want to see him, that's all. I'll make my own way in the world, thank you."

Ms Phillips closed the cash book up with a snap. "Miss Cardale, I'm going to take you across to the restaurant and ask the girls to give you some lunch—on me. In the meantime, I'll see what I can do about a job for you and somewhere to stay."

It was lunchtime, and Minty had expected the restaurant to be packed with tourists, but it was only a third full. The food on offer looked limp and stale. No wonder the place wasn't busy.

Ms Phillips sat Minty down and went to have a word with a sulky, bulky girl behind the counter. Some slices of tasteless ham beside an unimaginative salad duly appeared before Minty, who felt too tired to eat. Key phrases kept replaying themselves in her head. *Not even my half-sister ... it would upset my father ... very ill ...* Not wanted, Minty.

She'd never been wanted since her mother had died, that was the trouble. But ... she picked up her knife and fork ... she had survived. Ms Phillips was right: she must force herself to eat, even if the food was unappetising. She took one mouthful and chewed. The food wasn't as bad as it looked. She took another mouthful and found she'd been hungry without knowing it. She cleared her plate, following it up with a reasonable Cheddar cheese and biscuits. The coffee, however, was dreadful.

Minty forced her mind away from what Gemma had said, and found herself revisiting that weird encounter in the village street. Why had the man looked at her like that? Patrick. The name suited him. An old memory stirred—her aunt, shouting at her.

She mustn't think about that. To survive, she had had to forget some things.

She began to feel stronger. Better able to cope.

She watched the tourists. An elderly man and his wife pushed the food around their plates. "You don't get much for your money, do you?"

Another, younger couple were doing the same. "Shall I get us a Coke? What do they do to the coffee to make it taste like this?"

A woman came in with a teenage daughter. They looked at the food on offer and settled for ice creams. The girl said, "Show us that thing you bought for her birthday, then."

The woman handed over a packet and the girl undid it. The woman said, "I thought we'd be able to get something better here. We'll get something else tomorrow."

"It cost enough." They'd bought a cross on a chain. "Trash!" said the girl, and threw it back in the packaging for her mother to put away. "We'll give it to the kid next door. She won't know the difference."

Minty touched the cross round her own neck. That was cheap enough, but it wasn't trash. It meant something to Minty, if not to the tourist.

Minty wondered how many more trials Jesus wanted her to undergo. She tried to pray, begging Him to help her, to get her in to see her father . . . but as sometimes happened, her prayers seemed to disappear into a void. She almost despaired that there was anyone there to pray to.

When Minty, a bewildered child of five, had been dumped on her uncle and aunt, they'd taken her to church and handed her over to stout little Miss Tranmere, who ran the infants' Sunday school. Minty wondered if this had been arranged by God specially for her benefit.

Minty had been taught about a loving God by her mother, but her mother had unaccountably vanished from her life, and her aunt said her mother had been a bad woman. Miss Tranmere, too, believed in a God of love. She told the children that God understood when we were stupid and silly and did wrong things, but that He was eager to forgive and help us to put things right.

For four years, Miss Tranmere's class was the highlight of Minty's life and the foundation of her faith. By the time she'd left the infants' and moved up to the juniors, Minty had formed the habit of nightly prayers and Bible reading.

She'd soon realised that the junior school teachers were cast in the same mould as her uncle and aunt, who believed in a God of merciless justice and terrible punishment. Sometimes it seemed to her that the Jesus she read about in the Bible and the Jesus reflected in the services at her uncle's grimy church were two different people.

Now, sitting in the restaurant at the Hall, she panicked because she couldn't feel Jesus' reassuring presence around her. What had she done wrong? Had her uncle and aunt been right in saying it was wrong for her to abandon them and force herself on her father in this way? Had she sinned, without meaning to?

If He were to desert her now, what did she have left to cling to?

Ms Phillips reappeared, paused to have a word with the sulky girl behind the counter, and joined Minty at her table.

She put down Minty's cash book. "Thank you for letting me see this. I've been up to see your father's nurse. He has a day and night nurse now. I'm afraid he really is too poorly to see anyone today."

Minty bowed her head.

"I've also had a word with Simon and Gemma. Lady Cardale has gone into town and is not available, but I think she will agree with what I have suggested. As you may have gathered, there are a number of cottages in the village let out to holidaymakers. It is part of Simon's job to look after these cottages, to maintain them, supervise the cleaning, see that light bulbs are replaced, and so on. He is also supposed to check that everything is in order for newcomers on changeover day.

"Unfortunately Simon has been preoccupied of late, and holidaymakers have been complaining of low standards, malfunctions, cleaning not done."

Ms Phillips laid down a file, a mobile phone, a laptop computer, and a bundle of keys. "This is Thursday afternoon. All four of these cottages—there is a map here—are currently occupied, and all four occupants have complained of various shortcomings. The fifth cottage—which is Spring Cottage at the bottom of the hill by the bridge—is vacant because it was left in such a bad state that Simon had to cancel the next booking. I think you like a challenge, Miss Cardale . . ."

"Please call me Minty."

Ms Phillips inclined her head. "Very well, Araminta. Would you care to take on the management of the holiday lets for the rest of the season? All the contacts, booking forms, etc., are in this file here. The bookings finish in a few week's time, at the end of September, and after that . . . well, we'll have to see. I suggest we pay you a weekly wage plus free accommodation at Spring Cottage for as long as the job lasts. What do you say?"

Minty took a deep breath. Could she do it? She thought of all the dirty jobs she had done in the parish over the years: cooking, cleaning and redecorating at the vicarage, helping to rehouse the homeless, looking after the sick and elderly, running the Brownie pack. She could do it.

"Yes, please."

"Inside the file is a packet containing your first week's wages and a float for minor purchases you may need to make. Sign this form here for it, will you please? That's right. Connect the laptop to the mobile to send me emails. My email address and telephone number are in the file. Please email me at least once a day with a progress report. There is a housekeeper's shed by the bridge that contains cleaning materials, replacement lamp bulbs, etc., and there is an odd-job man you can contact for minor repairs—after you've cleared the work with me. Is that clear?"

Minty nodded.

Ms Phillips indicated the sulky girl behind the counter. "I have asked Gloria to fix you up with some provisions for today, and she believes her grandfather might be able to give you a lift. So if you care to collect your rucksack from my office . . . ?"

"Thank you," said Minty, standing. "You've been very good to me."

"I can promise nothing, you understand . . . about seeing your father. It really does depend on his health."

Minty gave a stiff nod. Ms Phillips was employed by Sir Micah and served his best interests. That was only right and proper.

As Minty returned to the courtyard carrying her rucksack, she had a good look at the logo on the door. It appeared to be a stylised bird flying out of a circle. Was this perhaps the logo of the charity her father had founded?

"Ready, then?" The ancient farmer was waiting for her in the yard, in his decrepit car. Minty piled in.

"So you're Gloria's grandfather?"

"I'm all sorts. Fingers in many pies. I'm also going to be late back and the missus'll have my guts for garters. Ms Phillips saw you right, did she?"

He drove back across the bridge and parked outside Spring Cottage, the middle one of three low-lying dwellings at the bottom of the high street. Though the sun still shone, they looked unkempt. The small-paned windows were unwashed, weeds marred the doorsteps, and paint was peeling off the woodwork. The front doors of all three cottages opened directly on to the pavement.

Minty found the key marked "Spring Cottage" and opened the door. A rank odour sprang out to meet them.

"Something gone bad in here?" Mr Thornby followed Minty into a low-beamed living room. Two dilapidated easy chairs had been drawn up before a fireplace that was empty but for an electric fire with a broken element. A rickety-looking coffee table was ringed with the ghosts of cups past. An oak dining table looked solid but was also ringed. There was only one dining chair, from which hung a tatty fringed lampshade. The lampstand itself appeared to be missing . . . or was that it in the corner, broken, leaning against the wall?

Minty hammered open a window. "What a stink! No wonder they couldn't let the place out again!" The place was littered with screws of paper, fast-food cartons, beer bottles, and cans.

The walls had originally been distempered, but it rather looked as if a party had been held here with a "Splash the Walls" contest being the highlight of the evening. The stench was appalling. In the corner lay an abandoned dog or cat basket, with an attendant buzz of flies.

"Let me, missy." Mr Thornby seized the basket and carried it out through a half-open door at the back of the room.

Minty stirred some filthy matting on the floor and decided it would have to be burned. She followed Mr Thornby. "Is this the kitchen? Phew!" An ancient gas stove was caked with past attempts at cooking, a Belfast sink was full of unwashed pots and pans and there was a muddle of broken crockery on the floor.

Life in the raw. She was disgusted. She'd seen the like in the city, of course, especially in houses that had been taken over by squatters, but it was disheartening to find this sort of squalor here, in a place where she was supposed to live.

Minty opened a door to the right of the kitchen and discovered a shower room and toilet. These had been installed within living memory and, though filthy, seemed to be in working order. "Hurray for progress," said Minty.

"Disgusting!" said Mr Thornby, turning the tap to wash his hands. "No hot water, of course. No soap, either."

"Par for the course," said Minty. There was one large bedroom in this tiny house, reached by wooden stairs from the living room. Its condition matched the rest. Stained bed clothing. Discarded underclothes, bottles, cans, food. A huge cupboard built into one wall contained more broken bits and pieces, this time of furniture. Probably the rest of the dining chairs. Mr Thornby followed her up.

"It's amazing they haven't been broken up for firewood," said Minty. "But there, the chimney's probably blocked." They made their way back down the stairs.

Mr Thornby dried his hands on his own handkerchief. "You can't stay here. Best come home with me. The wife won't mind."

Minty nearly fell on his neck, but the memory of Ms Phillips prevented her. "You're very kind, but Ms Phillips asked if I wanted a challenge and I accepted. A good cleaning and you won't know the place."

"Ms Phillips can't know how bad it is, and you can't get hold of the cleaner that does for these cottages as she's working up at the nursing home every afternoon."

Minty braced herself. "Well, I'm not made of paper. I'll manage. Your Gloria has put up some food for me and I can sleep in one of the chairs till I can get hold of some new bedding."

He rubbed his ear. "Happen I can get something arranged about the bedding. I'll see what the wife can do."

"You've been so kind, but you've done enough. Thank you for everything." Somewhat to her own surprise, she—who was not normally demonstrative—kissed his cheek.

He looked surprised, too. Then grinned. He lifted his hand to his forehead in a salute and departed, pulling the front door to behind him. A minute later she heard his car rev up and depart.

She went into the kitchen to see if she could find a pair of rubber gloves. There weren't any. Nor any usable cleaning materials in the cupboard under the stairs. There was a hoover, but it was broken. The carpet sweeper was brushless, and the dustpan and brush were encrusted with cobwebs.

"Some cleaner they've been using!" She looked at the rather pretty brass clock on the wall above the mantelpiece, but it wasn't working.

If she allowed herself to weaken even for an instant, she'd burst into tears and give up. Only, she was not the crying sort. She decided that she would visit the housekeeper's shed, find some basic cleaning materials and rubber gloves, take out the worst of the rubbish, give herself a cup of tea—if the kettle worked—study the file on the holiday lets, and then check up on the things that needed doing in the other houses. If they were all in this sort of condition, it was no wonder the occupants were complaining.

Three hours later she left the last cottage on her list.

It was a lovely late afternoon and she sat down to rest on a bench beside the church at the top of the high street. Nearby was a planter full of flowers and she let the scent of them drift over her. The village still looked delightful, but now she knew it had its darker side. Tourists might think this place was paradise, but people here messed things up, just as they did in the city. The woeful state of the cottages had brought that home to her.

She shuddered, remembering the appalling state of Spring Cottage. Then brightened. *I suppose I can thank God for finding me a job and somewhere to live. For the kindness of Mr Thornby. For the warmth of the sun. It's warm for early September . . .*

She opened the laptop and prepared her first report for Ms Phillips.

Spring Cottage first. She reported that it had been left in a bad way, but a good clean would help. A full report to follow. As for the other cottages, she had unblocked a sink, baited and set some mousetraps, cleared a gas meter and emptied a kettle of boiling water over an ants' nest. She had also started to make a list of minor repairs and things to be done. None of the cottages was in such a bad way as hers, but all needed attention. Riverside Cottages l and 3—the ones on either side of her—needed a thorough clean and probably new plumbing and electricity. All three cottages needed redecoration and some refurnishing.

She'd found Kiln and Wool Cottages at the back of the church on a lane that ran up the hill parallel to the high street. They both seemed to have been looked after better.

She sent the email and switched everything off.

It was a good vantage point, a place to look down on the comings and goings of the village street. Some of the comings and goings were advertised on the church noticeboard nearby. A garden fête was scheduled for the following Saturday. A lively place, this village.

She was exhausted. This time yesterday she'd been working on a letter to the Bishop for her uncle—she must remind him to post it—and had then scrambled to do some shopping for her aunt on the way home before cooking supper for them all. And now . . .

Minty could no longer put off thinking about what Gemma had said: "You're not even my half-sister . . ."

That hurt. If that was true, then Sir Micah was not her father and she had no right, demanding to see him. No wonder Ms Phillips had received her so coolly. And if Sir Micah was not her father . . . who was? Patrick's father?

No, she couldn't accept that Patrick's father was also hers.

As always, she came back to the one fact she'd held on to throughout. Her mother might have been this and that—Minty felt shame for her mother, as she always did when reminded of what she'd done—but Minty knew one thing for certain: her mother had loved her, Araminta Cardale. A small consolation, but it was real.

A couple on the opposite side of the road were looking at her. Perhaps talking about her. The gossip must have gone round that "Miss Milly's daughter was back."

She had to get out of the public eye and give herself time to think. The church was at her back and the front door was open.

She slipped inside.

Chapter Three

St Mary's was as unlike her uncle's church as it was possible to imagine. This was no grimy brick edifice with windows wired over to give protection from vandals. There were no dull tiles on the floor, no dusty, uncushioned pews.

St Mary's was a golden delight, a place of sunshine and space, with windows of greenish glass allowing glimpses of blue skies outside. The floor was of the same golden colour as the walls, slabs of stone peppered with epitaphs for the dead. Two brass plates set into the floor marked the passing of medieval merchants and their wives. In a side chapel were the elaborate tombs of long-dead Elizabethan and Jacobean notables, crowned with stiffly posed figurines of men, women, and children. Most bore her family name, Eden.

With a start Minty wondered whether she would see her mother's name on the wall, and yes, a plain tablet nearby marked her name, Millicent Eden Cardale, followed by her date of birth and the date on which she had died. Nearby were other, more elaborate tablets commemorating earlier Edens who had served their country in war and peace.

Minty remembered being brought to look at these. "That's your great-grandfather who died in the First World War . . . and that's your great-great-grandfather, the ambassador. Do you know what an ambassador is, little one?"

"Who's there?" A middle-aged woman was standing by the altar, clumsily trying to arrange some flowers on a pedestal.

A youngish man in clerical garb popped out from behind the pulpit. "Why, hello. Were you looking for me? Wait a bit. Haven't I seen you before somewhere?" He snapped his fingers. "Is it? Yes it is! Bless me, if it isn't our little Martha! What are you doing here? Visiting your fine relations at the Hall, I suppose. Are you going to be around on Sunday? We could do with a hand with the washing-up after the morning service, couldn't we, Mrs Collins?"

It took a moment for Minty to recognise him. Then she remembered. The Reverend Cecil Scott had once been a curate of her uncle's. She'd forgotten he'd obtained a living here.

He rubbed his hands and beamed. "Mrs Collins here's the mainstay of the church, aren't you, Mrs Collins? Though she's having a problem with arranging the flowers today, as she's hurt her hand. Someone on the flower rota's fallen sick or gone on holiday, and there's our Mrs Collins gallantly coming to the rescue. You can abandon your secateurs now, Mrs Collins, because our Martha is a dab hand at all that sort of thing. I was her father's curate for eighteen months, so I know . . ."

"He's my uncle, not . . ." Minty began, appalled at his mistake.

Cecil Scott was not listening. He was skinny, not tall, and inclined to optimism despite having previously failed as a teacher and a double-glazing salesman. Perhaps he'd found a country parish less stressful than an inner-city one, for now he was bouncing about like a rubber ball.

Mrs Collins was fiftyish and plump. She had frizzy gingerish hair and was wearing a black dress covered with red poppies. She also had a bandaged forefinger, which was making her clumsy. "Oh, Martha, can you really make the flowers speak to us?"

"My name's not really Martha," said Minty, going red. "And I'm not the daughter of . . ."

"I call her Martha because she's such a wonderful servant," said Cecil, beaming. "Quite the little handmaiden, aren't you, Martha? And you see, you've come to the right place."

He gestured to a small window that looked older than the rest and was also different in that it contained stained glass. A beautiful woman wearing expensive robes sat under an elaborate archway. She was reading a book and the book was inscribed with the name "Mary". Behind her stood her sister with a broom in one hand, wearing workaday clothes and an apron, a scarf over her hair. The legend "Martha" was written on her scarf.

"Behold our famous Mary and Martha window," explained Cecil. "People come from miles around to see it. Once a year it's my privilege to preach upon the story. This year I'm going to say that all women seem to have been born either as Mary—living their lives in contemplation of Christ and learning to love him more day by day, through study and reading his Word—or her sister Martha, who serves her fellows humbly but misses out on the best things in life."

"Splendid!" cried Mrs Collins.

"Our Mrs Collins is a wonderful example of a Mary, sitting at the feet of Christ, running the study group, raising funds for the deprived children in the city . . ."

"Oh, Reverend Cecil!" cried Mrs Collins. "You flatter me."

"Not at all, not at all," said Cecil.

Minty thought, *Oh yes, he does.*

"While Martha here," said Cecil, "is the perfect example of those who only live to serve others. So hand over the secateurs, dear Mrs Collins, and we can have half an hour on the arrangements for the study group."

Mrs Collins hastened to obey, saying to Minty, "Of course I don't expect you to do them as well as our own dear ladies, but any port in a storm, I say. Will you be staying long at the Hall?"

"I'm at Spring Cottage."

"Oh, a holidaymaker. Never mind, dear. Just do what you can. Coming, Reverend."

She fluted herself out of the church and Minty was left alone.

She walked over to the Mary and Martha window and said in a conversational tone, "Do you know what I would like to do to you? I would like to smash you to pieces!"

She let herself down on to the nearest seat. She refused to cry. *Big girls don't cry.* But she shook with anger and grief. Silently.

Lord God, am I really only a Martha to You? A useful pair of hands? Someone to sort out practical things and never get any closer to understanding You, to loving You? Is that to be my fate for ever?

She clenched her fists. *I could take those stupid flowers and stamp on them and pull the altar cloth off and . . .*

She sighed. *No, I couldn't. But dear Lord, I feel as if I'm in a long dark tunnel and I can't see any light at the end. I thought when I broke away, things would be different. I'd be different. But nothing's changed. I'm still being asked to do other people's dirty work. Will it ever get any better?*

Thoughts slid in and out of her mind. Resentment. Self-pity. She smiled at herself, knowing self-pity never got anyone anywhere. She sat there for a long time. Existing. Not thinking. Just being.

After a while she began to relax. She was not consciously praying. She was just laying herself and all her problems before Him. Not asking for anything. Not even hoping. Eventually she was able to say, *Here I am, Lord. Use me as You will.*

The healing began. The still, small voice whispered in her ear, "Minty, do you love me?"

"Yes, Lord. You know I do."

"Then feed my sheep."

She half laughed, imagining herself as a shepherdess, perhaps bottle-feeding a newborn lamb that had lost its mother.

She herself had lost her mother, and she had been bottle-fed by Miss Tranmere until she was strong enough to read the Bible for herself.

"Feed my sheep."

What did He mean? she wondered. She was tired of fighting, tired of working for others, heartsick because she'd been unable to see her father, and even more distressed at the thought that he might not be her father.

"Feed my sheep."

She supposed it meant doing whatever job he gave her to do, while keeping on with her prayers and . . . keeping on listening to him. That's what she'd done wrong that day. She'd been battering away at God, trying to get him to see things her way. But He took the overall view, knowing what was best for her.

She looked at the pedestal and the buckets of flowers nearby. Someone had spent a lot of money on them, and at least they'd been conditioned by being put up to their necks in buckets of water.

Lilies and delphiniums, phloxes and white carnations, all white and blue.

Mrs Collins had started to put some greenery in the oasis on the pedestal, but hadn't anchored the arrangement properly—and if that wasn't attended to, the whole contraption would fall apart. It was quite possible the woman hadn't even taken the trouble to soak the oasis. Those tall lilies were crying out for height, too. Were there any florist's cones around? She'd also need some heavy-duty wire.

Basics first. Build your floral arrangement on a firm base or it would fall to pieces. Build your house on the rock.

Minty thought it would probably take her a good hour to do the arrangement to the best of her ability, to the honour and glory of God. As if she hadn't enough to do already! But perhaps it was more important to honour God than to clean her cottage.

She sighed and set about doing the flowers.

She walked back down the high street in the early evening sun. There were still plenty of people about, though the shops were beginning to close. Of course, they would close at six here and probably even on Wednesday afternoons. Minty was used to the city, where shops would stay open much later. A probable exception would be the small supermarket just below the church, probably the busiest shop in the street. Next to it sat the post office; then a Chinese restaurant.

There seemed a good number of shops empty, and some of the open ones looked rather run down. The marmalade cat now lay curled up in the flyblown window of the bookshop. Minty crossed the road to press her nose against the window. Would her pay packet allow her the indulgence of buying a book? Probably not. She must clear her debt first.

She came to a greengrocer, now packing up and taking in boxes of onions, shallots, beans, cauliflowers. There were none of the exotic vegetables she was accustomed to seeing displayed in the city, but it was all good British produce, cheap and fresh. Minty craved some fresh fruit. Surely it wouldn't hurt to spend a little of her money on some cherries, dark red and sweet? But no. She must save every penny.

With an effort she turned away and continued down the street. There were two pubs, or were there three?

She stopped to look in the window of the charity shop. The clothing looked clean and in good condition. She had so little suitable clothing for her new life that she would have to visit the charity shop soon, even though she begrudged the money.

At the back of the shop were the usual ranks of bric-a-brac, including a battered collection of farmyard animals. Hadn't she had something like that as a child? Surely she remembered a wooden Noah's Ark, into which the animals were tidied away at night? She smiled, remembering how her mother had used the little toy sheep to impress upon her daughter that the earliest parts of the Hall had been built on the profits from wool.

There were more posters here, advertising village activities, including the garden fête due to take place in the grounds of the Hall.

The sky was a cloudless blue. She rested against the parapet of the bridge before going into Spring Cottage, feeling the need to refresh her spirit before facing all that grime again.

Sighing, she sorted out the key and let herself in.

What was that? She could smell something good cooking . . . and was that the back door closing?

Coming indoors out of the sunlight, she was momentarily blinded. She blinked and marvelled. What transformation was this?

She had removed the soiled matting to the back garden before going out, and someone had washed the newly exposed flagstones. An old but clean Turkish rug had been laid down on the floor in front of the fireplace—and where had the broken electric fire gone?

There were clean cotton throws over the two ancient chairs beside the fireplace, and on the dining table was a pewter mug with a bunch of buttercups in it.

Minty rushed through to the kitchen. Someone had washed up in the sink and left the pots and pans to dry on the side. Sudsy bubbles in the sink were subsiding even as she looked. The top of the cooker had been cleaned, and clean drying-up towels had appeared nearby.

Minty opened the oven door and saw a cottage pie inside, just beginning to brown over. The kitchen door was ajar, the key missing and the bolt loose in its socket. Mr Thornby—if it was him—must have taken the key with him and come and gone that way. Luckily she still had a duplicate key on her bunch.

Minty looked out, hoping to catch sight of her good neighbour, but only waving grass and bent fruit trees were to be seen. And more buttercups.

Hardly daring to hope, she checked the loo and shower; these had been attended to as well. She trod the squeaking stairs to the bedroom. Here the windows had been left open. Both were low down, so that she had to stoop to see out of them. One looked out over the neglected garden, and the other on to the street and the bridge. Lying in bed, you could see out in both directions.

The bed was large, an old iron Victorian affair. The old mattress and bedding had been removed. Minty laughed aloud. Her benefactor had obviously been unable to conjure up another good double mattress in the time, and had made do with a single one. But the duvet and pillows were all fresh and dainty. Blue and white again.

Minty went down on her knees and gave thanks. This must be Mr Thornby's work! Such kindness! She was overwhelmed. But what was that smell? She rushed downstairs to rescue her shepherd's pie from the oven and ate it at the table, sitting on the one remaining upright chair. She polished off the cheese and biscuits Gloria had provided, but left the sandwiches for her breakfast. Now if only she had some tea or coffee . . . and there in the newly cleaned kitchen cabinet were new packets of both—and a bottle of milk. Riches, indeed.

Dusk was settling over the landscape, so she tried to turn on the light . . . only to find it didn't work. In some alarm, she tried all the switches in the house. Dead. She had no power at all. No hot water. Ouch. The evening was still warm, but she knew old houses could be cold even in the middle of summer.

She would have to buy a paraffin stove. She bit her lip. She could see most of her first week's wages disappearing fast, with nothing left over to send her uncle and aunt.

She took the laptop out on to the back doorstep to catch the last of the light and sent off a quick email to Ms Phillips to say that some good neighbours had cleaned Spring Cottage in her absence but that there was no electricity. Advice, please.

She wondered if Ms Phillips had known how bad Spring Cottage was, and had hoped it might make Minty give up and return to the city. If so, Ms Phillips had been mistaken.

Then a thought struck her. Hadn't she seen a dusty box of candles in the cupboard under the stairs? Eureka! She lit them from the gas stove and placed them on saucers around the room. Let there be light! Marvellous! The room was bare but clean. She liked it like that.

She boiled a kettle for some hot washing-up water in her now clean sink, endured a cold shower and took a candle up to bed. She read her Bible with difficulty—the flickering light of the candle made the small print hard to read. Then she prayed for a while, pinched out the candle, and fell asleep.

There were no curtains at the windows and every now and then the headlights of passing cars lit up the room. She dreamed she was a child again, in the nursery back at the Hall. A picture in a book had scared her and she hadn't wanted to go to bed in the dark, so her mother had put a nightlight flickering in a pierced silver holder on the chest of drawers. The light danced and shimmered on the opposite wall and across the window. No one needed to draw curtains at the Hall, when the only view was across the park.

She awoke early. It was six o'clock, but the sun was up. A milk float went by and someone called a greeting to a woman taking her dog for a walk. Dressed only in a long T-shirt and sandals, Minty padded down the stairs to make herself a cup of coffee and take her sandwiches out into the garden.

A blackbird was singing on the rooftop. A curl of smoke rose from a chimney up the street, and house martins swooped and dived above her head. There were flagstones under her feet leading down the overgrown garden, and she could see that there had once been flower beds on either side of a path. A mock orange showered its petals on to the path, while a vigorous red rose thrust through a tangle of brambles, dangling free of the trellis that had once anchored it to the drystone wall behind.

Minty pulled a handful of weeds and inspected the soil. It was good rich soil, enriched with compost by some long-ago gardener. If she was allowed to stay, perhaps she could grow some vegetables here. Her uncle and aunt's dusty garden in the city had been laid to lawn, with a few shrubs around. Craving colour, Minty had filled some old tubs and pots with brilliant annuals that had given her pleasure but had made her aunt ask sourly who was going to water them. Well, who would water her tubs now? No one. The flowers would die. Ah well.

A robin cocked his head at her and then flew off with a whirring of wings. A butterfly alighted on an overgrown lilac buddleia—it was full in the sun, and now Minty could see that there were dozens of butterflies clustering around the flowers. Butterflies . . . she caught at a fleeting memory, but it eluded her. She smiled. She'd always loved butterflies.

Others had been treading this path recently. Presumably the good people who had wrought such a transformation in the cottage had come and gone this way, taking all the rubbish away with them.

How many people had it taken to remove the double mattress, replace it with a clean one, and do all that cleaning? Two at a minimum. God bless the Thornbys.

She wandered down the garden. She could see where someone had picked the buttercups that graced her table. A variety of fruit trees grew here. Apples. She picked one, took a bite . . . and spat it out. It was a cooking apple! She smiled, thinking of apple tarts and pies and chutneys . . .

Another tree had smaller round red apples. A dessert apple. Then there were a pear and two plum trees with branches so heavily laden that they were beginning to droop towards the earth. Greedily she bit into a plum, the juice splashing over her fingers, rich and heavy. How glad she was that she hadn't bought any cherries the previous day. What riches were here!

A soggy patch of ground trapped one foot, which she withdrew in haste to see her footprint fill with water. Was this a natural spring of water, which eventually trickled down to the river? It explained why the cottage had been called Spring Cottage.

She closed her eyes, feeling the morning sun warm her lids. She thanked God for all his goodness. She had not found her own father . . . or had she? Was God not truly her father in a way her human father could never be?

For a while the pain of yesterday's rebuff eased. She knew she was impatient. She knew she ought to wait on God's will, and she hadn't. She'd pushed and shoved at a closed door. She prayed for patience, and praised Him for all His glory and for His great kindness to her.

When she opened her eyes again, she saw that the garden path continued only a few more feet and ended in a wooden gate giving on to a narrow lane.

Leaning over the gate, she saw that the lane ran up and down the hill between garden walls. Towards the river it widened into a public car park. That was the way the good people must have come and gone.

From cottages to right and left she heard the pips that heralded the seven o'clock news. Time to get moving. She must check on supplies in the housekeeper's hut, and get some information about local tourist attractions apart from the Hall. One of the holidaymakers had asked for it, and surely such information should be in every one of the holiday lets. Then she must ring the odd-job man and get him to meet her at the cottages. Sticking doors and windows, cupboard doors off their hinges . . . a multitude of small jobs needed attending to.

Before she did anything else, she must ring her uncle and aunt to reassure them she had arrived safely. She would ring the parish office and not the vicarage, so she could leave a message on the answerphone and not be pestered with questions and demands for her immediate return. It was almost impossible to realise that only yesterday morning she had left the vicarage to walk to the railway station!

She shivered. She would never go back to that cold, dark house. She hoped.

Chapter Four

Twelve o'clock. Did the shops here shut for lunch? She wasn't familiar with their opening times.

She was later than she'd hoped to be, because the odd-job man recommended by Ms Phillips—Mr Fixit, No Job Too Small—had taken his time going round the cottages with her. He hadn't been obstructive, but he hadn't been much help, either. He said he had understood that the family weren't interested in putting more money into the holiday lets. Of course, if Ms Phillips gave him the go-ahead that would be all right, but Minty did understand, didn't she, that the work couldn't be done unless the holidaymakers agreed to his going in and making a mess, which he'd have to do if it meant taking doors off their hinges and replacing floorboards. And this was only the start of what needed doing, he could see that.

Frustrated, Minty agreed that they'd have to ask Ms Phillips's advice.

She was just coming out of the post office, where she'd been enquiring about information on local beauty spots, when she bumped into Mr Thornby.

"Mr Thornby, you miracle worker! How did you manage it?" She put her arms around him and gave him a hug. She, who never touched people if she could help it!

"Manage what, missy?" But he knew. The sparkle in his eyes told her so.

"Would it create a scandal if I were to kiss you in the high street?"

"The missus would hear about it before I could get home to explain."

She laughed.

He laughed, too. "Come to lunch on Sunday. One o'clock on the dot. The missus said to tell you it's roast beef and all the trimmings."

"I'll be there. And, thanks."

"My pleasure." He actually touched his cap to her before passing on up the street.

She asked the Lord for a blessing on him as she crossed the road and stopped to tap on the bookshop window where the marmalade cat slept. Except that he wasn't coiled up in sleep now. He stood with ears pricked, arched back, and stiff tail, looking back into the shop. Minty knew something about cats and realised he was alarmed about something.

A gnome of a man stormed out of the bookshop, shouting back, "Get lost!"

He cannoned into Minty but didn't apologise. He had a crumpled red face, scanty hair trained over a bald pate, and was in a tearing temper. There was a grinding crash from within the shop. Minty and the irate man turned to see what was the matter.

The heavily built woman whom Minty had seen helping Patrick with his papers the previous day had been climbing a stepladder to reach some books on a high shelf. Overbalancing, she had fallen sideways on to a table and from there to the floor, bringing down the ladder and a number of large books with her.

"Hannah!" screamed the little man.

"Are you all right?" Minty darted in, realising that the woman was far from all right. Minty remembered seeing a teenager fall like that and . . . yes, the woman had caught her foot in the ladder as she fell and now her leg was lying at a strange angle. Broken, of course. What other damage might she have sustained? She was conscious, luckily, but . . .

"Lie still!" Minty threw aside the largest of the books and tried to lift the stepladder. It was too heavy for her to shift by herself. "Don't move!" Minty got her shoulder beneath the ladder and heaved it up a little way but could get it no further. She was stuck, her arms braced against the floor on either side of the woman's head. If she crawled out, the ladder's weight would fall full on the woman again.

"Is she . . . she can't be . . ." The little man hovered, aghast.

"No. Help me get this ladder off, then phone for an ambulance, quick!"

"I was only . . ."

The woman began to make feeble movements. "Don't try to move, please," said Minty. "You've broken your leg. Just relax and keep quite, quite still . . ." The strain was beginning to tell on Minty's back. She wondered how much longer she could hold the ladder up.

The little man crumpled into a heap on a chair and began to sob loudly. "Oh, Hannah, I didn't mean it!"

Minty gritted her teeth. The weight of the ladder was pressing her down. She could feel sweat break out on her forehead. She said to the man. "I've got a phone in my back pocket. Can you reach it and dial for me?"

He wailed, "Oh Hannah, forgive me!"

You useless man! thought Minty. "Please, fetch someone . . . anyone!"

"But if she dies . . ." It was almost a shriek.

"She's not going to die, you idiot! Just fetch someone to help me . . ."

His face cleared. "I'll get Patrick!" He darted out of the shop.

Hannah groaned and closed her eyes, but at least she'd stopped trying to move. Minty's arms began to tremble. Someone came to the door, but scuttled away when Minty asked if they could help. Then—at last—the little man returned with the man they called Patrick.

"What's up, Hannah? Ah. I see." He bent down, put his shoulder to the ladder, and heaved it off the two women. Minty rolled off Hannah and lay on the floor, quivering, flexing her arms. Patrick delved for his mobile phone. "Ambulance. The bookshop. Mrs Wootton has broken her leg and maybe . . ."

He raised his eyebrows at Minty.

"Not sure," she said. "It was a nasty fall. I've told her to keep still, just in case."

The man relayed this information, snapped his phone shut, and knelt on the other side of Mrs Wootton. She had opened her eyes again and was looking scared.

"Come on, Hannah, use your head for once. Keep still, as Miss Cardale says. Just till the ambulance gets here. Understood?"

"It wasn't my fault!" bawled the little man, still howling. An amazing volume of sound was coming from such a small body.

"Yes, it was," mouthed Mrs Wootton. "Coming in here, upsetting me just as I'm fetching books down from . . ."

"Quiet, Hannah!" said Patrick. "What shenanigans you and your husband get up to after hours is one thing. Bringing the traffic in the high street to a halt with an ambulance is another."

Mrs Wootton said, in a stronger voice, "Just get him out of here."

"Out you go, Jonah," said Patrick, in a tone meant to be obeyed. And the little man went, still crying.

Minty thought, *They're husband and wife? Unbelievable!*

Hannah Wootton's breathing was regular, which was a good sign. Her colour was poor, but her pulse—Minty checked it—was reasonable, though fast.

"You know some first aid?" Patrick said.

"A little."

Now and again people passing by paused in the doorway, and peered in. One asked Patrick if he needed help. Patrick shook his head.

Minty looked across Mrs Wootton at him. Dark hair, slightly unruly. Steady grey eyes under quirky eyebrows. A thin-lipped but mobile mouth, a nose too long, laughter lines. There was nothing about him to hint that he might be her half-brother. No. Definitely not.

She thought, *I can trust him—I think.*

He asked in a low voice, "Are you all right? Not hurt?"

She shook her head.

"What brought you back here now?"

She replied in the same tone, "Gemma phoned, saying my father was ill and that I was needed. It turned out to be a mistake." Especially if he wasn't her father after all.

"Are you going back to the city?"

"No, I'm staying till I see my father."

"You don't remember . . . ? No, I can see you don't."

What did he mean? What had she forgotten?

Mrs Wootton said, "I can feel my arms and legs, so I haven't broken my neck—no thanks to that good-for-nothing Jonah."

Minty said, "Don't try to move till the paramedics have checked you out."

Mrs Wootton's eyes switched to Patrick. "You'll have to close the shop till my sister can get over to look after it. Or till Venetia gets back."

Patrick accepted this charge without hesitation. "Where can I contact your sister?"

Mrs Wootton tried to heave herself up, but was held down by Minty and Patrick together. "Address book—in my bag, bottom drawer of my desk. Shop keys in my pocket. They'll take me to the hospital in Chipping Norton, won't they?"

The cat appeared at Minty's side, looking down at Mrs Wootton.

"Poor Lady," said Mrs Wootton, tears forming at the corners of her eyes. "What's to become of you?"

"Don't worry. I'll find someone to feed him," said Patrick.

Mrs Wootton closed her eyes again. The cat gently touched her face with his paw and withdrew to watch proceedings from the table top.

"At last," muttered Patrick, as the ambulance could be heard coming down the street. Neither he nor Minty stood up till the paramedics had taken over.

Yes, the leg was broken. The hospital would examine the rest. The paramedics put Mrs Wootton on a board and took her out to the ambulance.

"Her keys!" Patrick hit his forehead. "Pocket!"

The paramedics rescued the bunch of keys and handed them to Patrick, who passed them on to Minty. "Find her handbag for me, will you? I'll take it with me, follow the ambulance on to the hospital. Can you ring her sister—and see to the place being locked up? And tell my secretary what's happened. Oh, you won't know where . . . next door. Plate on the door, ground floor. Say I'll ring her as soon as I can, but she's to cancel my appointments for this afternoon."

She found the handbag, extracted an address book and passed it over. "Sister's name?"

"Beryl something. Put a 'Closed' sign on the door. Right?"

"You'll let me know how she gets on?"

He gave her a long-lashed stare. That stare said, "Do you really care?"

She stared back, meaning, "Believe it!"

He gave his head a shake and removed himself.

Minty looked at the cat and the cat looked back at her. "Well, here's a howdy-do." The cat Lady seemed to agree. Minty liked cats. She picked Lady up and gave him a cuddle which the cat seemed to enjoy.

"Business first," said Minty.

She went through the address book till she found someone called Beryl and phoned her with the bad news. Beryl was flustered. She said she'd go over to the hospital right away; if the leg was broken, they might just put it in a cast and let Hannah out that day. But it would probably be best if dear Hannah went back home with her, and didn't try to climb those nasty stairs to the flat above the shop. Did Miss agree?

So Hannah Wootton lived above the shop, did she? Well, the hospital would no doubt advise what would be best for her. Meanwhile, Beryl was not going to come over to look after the shop and Minty had better see that it was locked up. Minty asked whom she should leave the keys with. Beryl flustered some more and said she didn't know, she really didn't. The best person would be Venetia, but she was still away, wasn't she? Otherwise, it ought to be Jonah. But, oh dear, that would hardly do.

Minty agreed. She said she'd hang on to the keys till Beryl or Hannah told her what to do with them.

Minty looked at the cat, who seemed to be listening to the phone call. When Minty had stacked the fallen books against the wall and managed to right the steps, the cat was waiting at the front door for her.

"You want to go out?" She let herself and the cat out into the high street. It was another bright sunny day, though some small white clouds sailed serenely across the sky.

Minty locked the bookshop up and went next door. Patrick's offices were in a stately red-brick Georgian house, partially covered with Virginia creeper. It was one of the few buildings in the village that hadn't been built of Cotswold stone. No doubt the original builder had wanted to make some kind of statement by building in a different material. The tall, elegant windows were covered inside with blinds. Minty noticed the brass plate on the side of the door; "Sands & Sands, solicitors". So Patrick was a solicitor, was he?

The front door was open and she stepped straight into a wainscoted hall, wide and high, with a black and white tiled floor.

"You must be Miss Cardale." A sparrow-like woman came out of a room marked "Reception". "I've heard all about the accident, of course. You can't drop a pin in this place without someone knowing. I've sent Jonah off to get a cuppa, though he'll probably end up in the pub, knowing him. He'll be back for news later—if he's still sober. You've locked up all right? What about the cat?"

"He wanted to be let out. It's a 'he', isn't it? But called 'Lady'?"

"A misunderstanding in his kittenhood, I'm afraid. Lady is short for Marmaladey. He's a resourceful animal and I expect he's already found someone to look after him. Besides, Hannah did install a cat flap, so he won't lack for shelter. You're at Spring Cottage, aren't you? It used to be a nice little place, but I gather the last tenants left it in a mess. Let me have your mobile number. Excuse me, the phone's ringing again . . ."

Another Ms Phillips, thought Minty, scribbling the number down.

She bought some bread from the baker's, who observed she was a friend of the Thornbys then, was she? He'd seen the ambulance, and was it true that Mrs Wootton had broken a leg and both arms? And then some mince from the butcher's, where they asked whether she was staying long at Spring Cottage, and would she be opening the bookshop herself? The latest information technology had nothing on the village grapevine.

She bought a tin of cat food and some milk, thinking to drop it back into the shop later that day, only to find Lady the cat was at her heels as she walked down the hill to Spring Cottage. Feeling rather foolish, she unlocked the door and said to the cat, "Well, are you coming in or not?"

Stately tail waving, the cat preceded her into the cottage and inspected the place. There was a scent of beeswax polish on the air. Someone had polished the furniture in her absence, and on the draining board in the kitchen lay a trug full of salad greens, some ripe tomatoes, and a carton of eggs. Bless Mr Thornby.

And dear Lord, please look after Mrs Wootton, who must be in shock from her fall. I pray it's only a broken leg and that she's soon mended and back at the shop. Amen.

Minty knew enough about cats to feed Lady before she fed herself. Lady settled down on one of the armchairs for a good wash and a sleep, while Minty sent Ms Phillips another email. The most pressing problem was that Mr Fixit had said the electrics at Spring Cottage were completely knackered. The place would need rewiring and he wasn't sure he could manage it, but would start on the rest of the small jobs Minty had pointed out—see next page—if Ms Phillips could confirm that the family wanted them done and guaranteed payment. Please advise or authorise—especially about the wiring.

Minty added—knowing this was probably beyond her remit—that the holidaymakers had been asking for fliers about local tourist attractions, but the post office didn't have any. She aimed to speak to both cleaners next morning, starting with Alice, who cleaned the cottages up by the church.

Minty sent the email and settled down to study the inventory for Spring Cottage.

Patrick rang Minty on her mobile while she was preparing supper. Mrs Wootton had broken her thighbone in two places. She needed an operation, as the bone would have to be pinned—which meant she would probably be kept in hospital for a couple of weeks. Mrs Wootton's sister, Beryl, had arrived and was with her now, but was unable to look after both Hannah and the shop.

Did Minty still have the keys, and if so would she collect any post that arrived in the morning, see to the cat and dump the mail through Patrick's letter box at the office? He was very abrupt, very businesslike. He rang off before she had a chance to say that the cat had taken up residence with her or to ask him about . . . well, just to have a chat about things in general, really.

Saturday morning. The sky had clouded over to a milky blue, so Minty pulled on a sweater and jeans before making herself a cup of coffee. She'd propped the tiny kitchen window open the previous night before she went to bed, so that Lady could get in and out. The cat had started the night on Minty's feet in bed, but had disappeared in the early hours.

Minty found three dead mice on the back doorstep, laid out parallel to one another. Heads to the door, tails to the garden. Lady had been busy. He came bounding up from the orchard now, panting for food. Evidently he was not a cat who ate his catch. He sounded like a traction engine when he purred.

Minty wandered down the garden path with her coffee and said her prayers with her back to the trunk of the biggest apple tree. It was mainly Thank you, today, with a spot of Please mixed in. For Hannah Wootton in hospital. For her uncle and aunt who would find life rather more difficult than usual, now that she was not there to help them. For her father, so ill . . . so ill . . . For courage to meet whatever He chose to send her that day.

But mainly thanks for the beauty of the day and for the good things He had sent her.

She spotted a disused outside toilet, which appeared to have been used as a tool shed in the dim and distant. Garden shears, rusted. An enormous spade, likewise. A trowel and hand fork. And a scythe. Goodness, what a lethal looking weapon!

She allowed herself half an hour to clear weeds from a small patch of garden near the back door, finding some herbs still growing among the weeds. Then she set to work to clean the downstairs windows of all three cottages. She thought there was a ladder mentioned somewhere in the inventories—she must study them further. And then she was off to meet Alice, the cleaner, at Kiln Cottage behind the church.

Minty's plan was to get to know Alice by working alongside her that morning.

Alice was tall, thin, and blonde—like Minty in a way—but Alice's hair colour had come out of a bottle and the roots showed. Alice had a high colour, a well-developed bust, and a blissfully sleeping coffee-coloured toddler in a pushchair. Alice was a good mother and a good cleaner, who had conscientiously cleaned her two cottages every Saturday morning even though she hadn't been paid for a month.

"If you want my opinion," said Alice as she and Minty cleaned the bathroom, "that Simon thinks it's beneath him to look after the holiday lets. But they're nice little houses and with a spot of tender loving care, a lick of paint, and some patching up of the tiles on the roofs, he could charge much more per week."

Minty finished polishing the bath taps. "If you give me your time sheets, I'll be happy to take them up to the Hall and get you your money."

Alice sniffed. "Tried that. The old vixen, sorry—Lady Cardale . . ." She stopped and looked sideways at Minty, who noted that Alice wasn't at all sorry that she'd called Lady Cardale a vixen, and was waiting to see how Minty reacted. Minty tried not to react at all.

Alice continued. "*Lady* Cardale," she said, giving the title extra weight, "caught me going into the house to find Simon. 'Can't you read?' she says, all icy cold. 'This is private property.' I said I needed to see Simon because I hadn't been paid, and she said, 'Mister Simon to you, and anyway he's not in.' I checked and his car wasn't there."

Alice gave Minty a sideways look as they started doing the floors. "I suppose you'll hold it against me, saying that. You being one of them."

"I'm only the poor relation, working for my living."

Alice said, "I heard something about . . ."

"My mother?"

"Yes." Alice reddened. "Sorry. Mum said . . . well, never mind that. If you can make that Simon . . ."

Minty smiled. "*I* may not be able to, but I know someone who can."

"You mean Ms Phillips? I thought of her because the word is she's very fair, always pays the bills on time. But she doesn't usually have anything to do with the running of the holiday lets, and there's talk in the village . . . but you won't want to know about that, will you?"

Minty laughed and threw a duster at Alice. "Alice, tell me. You know you want to."

Alice laughed, too. "All right, then. They're saying in the pubs that Simon wants to change everything. 'Move with the times,' he says. Turn the Hall into a conference centre or clinic or something. Build a motel in the grounds. Dunno that I believe half of it, but it's true he's allowed the holiday lets to slide. I've had to buy my own cleaning materials the last couple of months. What I think is that he's letting them run down to the point where it's going to cost a lot of money to put them right. Then he'll say they're not worth keeping, and he can sell them off to yuppies."

"Bring in some capital, you mean?"

Alice stopped work to make her point. "He could make a killing. Apart from the yuppies—though the villagers don't really want them moving in—there's folk here would give their eye teeth to have one of these cottages, even as they are. If they could afford them."

"You included?"

"Well, I can't afford one, can I?"

Work finished, they sat down for a welcome cuppa. One of the holiday lets was being kept on for another week. New people would be moving into the other.

Alice said, "So what were you doing, before you came here?"

Minty recognised that this was the key moment in their relationship. Alice had given out sufficient information—single parent mother, living in council house with mother, poorly paid job—to pay for information in return. In her response Minty would be judged by how much or how little she said, and whatever she said would go straight into the village gossip round.

Minty's life so far had taught her to be reserved. She was always conscious of the scandal that surrounded her mother's death. However, she liked Alice and felt Alice liked her. And was there any reason to hide anything? So she explained about Gemma's phone call and its outcome.

Alice sipped her mug of tea, watching Minty, judging her. "That old cow—pardon my French, Lady Cardale—will have you out of here in two ticks if she can."

"Possibly, but it was Ms Phillips who arranged for me to have this job overseeing the lets, and gave me the keys to Spring Cottage."

"A right dump that is, I've heard."

"I have it all to myself, though."

"One room in someone else's house, that's not much cop. I know."

They drank their tea in companionable silence. Minty considered Alice, thinking the girl intelligent and lively minded.

"What about you, Alice? Have you always been a cleaner?"

"No. I was at college in the city, doing a business studies course till I got pregnant with this little bit of nonsense, and my boyfriend didn't want to know." She indicated the toddler, asleep in her pushchair.

Minty had already noted that Alice didn't wear a wedding ring.

"Dunno how I finished the course . . . got a better grade than I deserved, to tell the truth. So I came back home. I worked in the supermarket till I was too big to manage. Now I take her round with me in the pushchair to do what cleaning I can in the daytime, and Mum looks after her most evenings, when I work in the pub just above you. Mum works in the supermarket herself, so she can't look after her in the daytime. I dread the day Marie gets too big to stay quiet in the pushchair. Dunno what I'll do then."

"No crèche in the village?"

"Chance would be a fine thing. Marie's been good as gold this morning, but when she's teething . . ." Alice shuddered. "Don't get me wrong, she's the joy of my life. But I'd plans to get out of this place, get a good job, make something of myself. Ah well."

"Is your address on the time sheets? I'll bring the money round."

"I'll be working in the pub this evening. If you could bring it there it would help."

Minty hurried across the road, sorting out the key to the bookshop. Someone was banging on the door, saying "Open up!" An irate customer. Minty explained what had happened, but the woman was not to be pacified.

"Didn't I order this book special, now? And isn't it for my husband's birthday? And didn't the woman ring me to say it had come in? So why can't you look it out for me, eh?"

"I don't have the authority to do so. I've just come to get the post and take it next door. I'll ask if they can find someone to open up this afternoon."

The woman went off, grumbling. There was no sign of Patrick next door. Minty wasn't sure whether she was pleased or relieved about that. His secretary took the letters and listened to what Minty had to say about someone opening the shop.

"Hannah's sister's been on the phone. They're not operating on her till Monday, and there's absolutely no chance of her getting back for a while. She couldn't possibly manage the stairs to her flat, for a start. The shop will have to remain closed for the time being, I'm afraid."

"I could come in this afternoon to sort out that customer's order . . . ?"

"You'll be making a rod for your own back, if you do. Look, I'll ring around, see if I can find someone else to do the job. Right?"

Minty looked at her watch and ran down the hill to Spring Cottage. By this time the two Riverside Cottages ought to be pristine, and she might be too late to meet the other cleaner. First she must dump her sweater at Spring Cottage, for the day was turning warm, and then . . .

She opened the front door . . . and saw at once that something was wrong.

Chapter Five

Minty could smell a cheap perfume. Then she saw there was no clock on the mantelpiece.

A large, gypsyish woman came out of the kitchen, carrying the eggs and salad stuffs Mr Thornby had left for Minty.

"You should've been out of here by now," said the woman, calmly putting the food in a large plastic shopping bag. Another even larger bag lay on the floor, bulging with the duvet from Minty's bedroom. "You know the rules, don't you? How am I expected to clean, otherwise?"

"I'm no holidaymaker," said Minty, wondering how she was going to deal with this. *Lord, help! Please! This is going to be difficult.* "I'm Araminta Cardale and I've been asked to oversee the holiday lets. Are you the cleaner responsible for these three cottages?"

"Are you, my pretty?" The fat woman looked around her. "What else have I missed?"

Minty saw that the buttercups had been tipped out on to the newly polished table and the pewter mug was missing. That made her angry because water marked wood worse than anything.

Minty sat in one of the easy chairs and indicated that the woman should sit in the other. "Your name is . . . ?"

"Guinness. Mrs Guinness, no relation." She seated herself with a fat smile. "As in *Guinness Book of Records*. As in the stuff the Irish drink."

"Your job is to clean Riverside Cottages on Saturday mornings? But not this one."

The woman bridled. "I wouldn't demean myself to touch this place until it was cleaned up. Which I see someone has. So I might be persuaded to include this in my rounds if we can come to some arrangement, nudge nudge, wink wink!"

Minty shuddered. The woman stank of more than perfume: there was the stink of corruption all about her. Minty thought, *If I let her get away with my food and the bits and pieces she's lifted from here, she'll have me where she wants me. Please, Lord. Help me find the right thing to say.*

Minty said, "Mrs Guinness, I've been with Alice all this morning. She cleans Kiln and Wool Cottages, as you probably know."

"Known her all her life. Disgraceful affair. I don't hold with living in sin."

"Alice has been having difficulty getting her money from the Hall. How about you?"

The woman tapped her nose. "You've to get up very early to get the better of me. I haven't been paid for a month. That Alice was born stupid. Went on working without pay. Not me. Not a hand's turn will I do till I get my rights."

"Perhaps you have an unusual sense of what your 'rights' might be." Minty looked up at the place where the clock should be.

Mrs Guinness smiled. "Taken for repair, my dear."

"According to the inventory there should also have been a pair of china dogs on the mantelpiece, plus a teapot and water jug, a brass lantern, and a barometer. Not to mention a pewter mug."

"All gone for repair, that's right."

"Then you won't mind giving me a receipt for them, will you?"

Mrs Guinness thought about that. "They might have come back from the menders by now, perhaps."

"You put them in a safe place for keeping, knowing that this cottage was not being let for the time being? You were waiting for someone to move in again, when you would of course return the items."

"Not the teapot and water jug. Those . . . well . . . they got smashed in transit."

"You were responsible for them. I'll get an estimate and have the amount deducted from your wages."

Mrs Guinness shifted in her chair, sucking her teeth. Not enjoying the turn the conversation had taken.

"If your wages really haven't been paid for a month," said Minty, "then I will personally see to it that you get a cheque . . ."

"Cash."

"Give me your time sheets and I'll see what I can do. Meantime, please replace the things that you have taken."

"Borrowed as security."

"Return the bedding, my food . . ."

"Holidaymakers always leave a little something in the fridge for Mrs Guinness."

"But I'm no holidaymaker."

"I know who you are." The fleshy eyelids squeezed tight. "You're the one they had to get rid of in a hurry in case Sir Micah tried to strangle you."

Minty stood up, holding on to the chair back for support. *Please, Lord. Don't let her see how much she's hurt me.* "I'll give you ten minutes to put everything back that you've taken this morning, Mrs Guinness. Then we'll inspect the two cottages that you were supposed to have cleaned today and see how you've got on."

"I've got to be off. I've my husband's lunch to see to."

Minty took no notice. "I'll expect all the repaired items to be returned here this afternoon by five o'clock."

"Can't be done. I need a coupla days to get the stuff back—from the menders, I mean."

Minty thought, *Has she pawned them, or given them away?* "Very well, Monday morning, first thing. Once they've been returned, you shall have your wages. Is that understood?"

"Miss Hoity-Toity. No better than she should be."

"Then that makes two of us. Mrs Guinness, do you want to keep your job or don't you?"

The woman's eyes went right and left. She licked her lips. Eventually she nodded. Minty would have preferred Mrs Guinness to decline. "Also, you'd better polish that water stain off the table before you go, and let me have your keys to this place as I'll do my own cleaning in future."

Minty felt quite weak when Mrs Guinness departed having replaced the things she tried to remove earlier. Lady the cat plopped back through the kitchen window, sniffed his way around the chair where Mrs Guinness had been and sat down in front of the fireplace to give himself a good wash.

Minty said, "Quite right, Lady. I feel like a good wash too, after dealing with Mrs Guinness."

She opened the laptop and found a message from Ms Phillips acknowledging what Minty had done, adding that the points raised would be put under consideration. Also that a qualified electrician would start on rewiring Spring Cottage as soon as feasible. Ms Phillips's language might be formal, but she did know how to get things done.

Minty visited both the other cottages and found that the cleaning had been done in slipshod fashion. Not up to her own standard, or Alice's. She emailed Ms Phillips to report on her dealings with the cleaners, with a request for Alice's wages to be sent down straight away—preferably to the bookshop.

Within minutes her phone rang and it was Ms Phillips. "Why are you at the bookshop this afternoon? What's the matter with Mrs Wootton?" So the grapevine wasn't perfect, or perhaps it only worked within the village.

"She fell and broke her leg. She'll be out of action for some weeks. Her sister's supposed to be looking after her, but there are customers who want to collect their orders and I seem to be the only person with a few hours to spare."

"What about my report on the future viability of the cottages?"

Minty thought, *Future viability?* So maybe Alice was right and they were thinking of selling the cottages. Which would put Minty out of a job.

"You really need a surveyor to do the job properly. Roof tiles are missing, some windows are cracked, one door scrapes on the floor, and some floorboards feel spongy to me. The plumbing is precarious, the electrical circuits overloaded. When that's been attended to, all the cottages need redecoration and some refurnishing ..."

"The holiday lets are supposed to bring in money, not lose it."

"Nevertheless, there must be a programme of renewal in lettings. If the cottages were brought up to date and supplied with linen and towels each week, you could charge maybe double what you do now."

"I see ..." A long pause. "Well, send me your recommendations by email and we'll make an appointment for you to come up to the Hall one morning next week, when we can discuss the matter."

"How is my father today?"

"Not so well. The doctor is coming this afternoon to see him."

Minty's throat went tight. "If ... if anything were to happen ..."

"I'd do my best to ensure that you saw him, yes."

"Thank you."

Another anxiety to add to her list. *Please, Lord, please don't let him die.*

She made herself a sandwich for lunch and finished off with ripe plums from the garden. To replace the buttercups, she cut some of the deep red roses from the garden and put them into a glass jam jar inside the pewter mug. Pewter mugs sometimes leaked and she didn't want any more stains on the table.

On her way up to the bookshop that afternoon a car drew up outside. Mrs Collins, wearing a black dress with enormous yellow cherries all over it, leaned out to speak to Minty.

"Yoo-hoo! It's our little Martha, isn't it?"

"My name isn't ..."

"Can't stop. Holding up the traffic, har har!" A hearty, mirthless laugh. "Just wanted to say, thought you made a good attempt at doing the flowers. I popped in this morning and just tweaked it here and there, added a touch more colour."

Minty felt rage build up inside her. That flower arrangement had been perfect when Minty had finished it, and now this wretched woman, who couldn't even anchor the oasis properly, had meddled with it. How dare she! What's more, she had no bandage on her finger today. Had Mrs Collins worn it as an excuse for making a hash of the arrangement? Perhaps the truth was that she was hopeless at flower arranging.

A lorry tooted its impatience and Mrs Collins put the car in gear again. "So I'll see you tomorrow. Come early to help put the coffee cups out and I'll get someone to show you how the urn works." She moved slowly off over the bridge, further enraging the traffic that had been building up behind her.

Minty set her teeth. Help that woman with the coffee? Attend to the urn? Not likely! And she'd dared to interfere with Minty's beautiful flower arrangement, which had cost her so much time and care.

Then Minty remembered she'd done the flowers not for Mrs Collins's approval, but for the glory of God. She felt ashamed of herself.

Sorry, Lord, she said. *I got things out of proportion, didn't I!*

It was her day for being stopped in the high street. Perhaps it was always like that when you lived in a village. It had been a bit like in her uncle's parish: "Minty, can you do this . . . ? Minty, can you do that . . . ?"

This time it was the Reverend Cecil, beaming as he chugged his way down the street. "Ah, Martha, there you are."

"My name isn't Martha; it's Araminta."

He wasn't listening. "I could do with a hand with the church magazine. I know you used to do it. Mrs Collins said it would be all right for you to use the parish computer, so you see it's all arranged."

"But . . ."

He was off, butterfly-like flitting across the road, hailing another parishioner.

Minty stamped her foot at him; then hastened on her way up the hill. She was late. Turning into the solicitors' office, she almost bumped into Patrick, who was showing a client out.

"Your secretary said . . ."

"Not here on Saturday afternoons. You've got Hannah's keys and are going to open up? Fine. Don't let Jonah in the shop or he'll create chaos. Oh, by the way, Hannah's fairly comfortable. Her sister's taken some things over for her. Venetia's due back this weekend, which should solve the problem of opening the bookshop, and . . . there's my next client . . . I'll call in later if I can, right?"

He ushered his client—a busty, thrusting farmer's wife by the look of her—into an office down the corridor, but before Minty was fairly out of the door, he had darted back down the passage after her.

"Forgive me, but someone said you're on affectionate terms with Mr Thornby . . . seen hugging him in the street?"

She raised her eyebrows. "He's been very kind to me."

"Yes, of course. He's by way of being a friend of mine, too. But if he were to ask you to do something for him in return . . ."

She stared. "My friendship with Mr Thornby is . . ."

"No business of mine?" His face broke up into an attractive, mischievous smile. "I handled that extremely badly, didn't I, Miss Cardale? I apologise. I will repeat after myself fifty times, 'Miss Cardale's too streetwise to make promises she may not be able to fulfil, or to sign documents she doesn't understand.'"

"No, I wouldn't, but . . ."

"Good. Just wanted to make sure. Now I must go . . . terribly behind."

He disappeared. *Like the White Rabbit down the rabbit hole in* Alice in Wonderland, thought Minty. *He probably goes around saying, I'm late, I'm late, all day long. And mislays his car keys. And drinks half a cup of tea or coffee and leaves the rest to get cold. And has the most attractive grin . . .*

She shook her head. The man was, of course, quite mad. How dare he criticise her for her friendship with Mr Thornby?

Well, not actually criticise, she supposed. Warned. Hmm. Yes.

Why had Mr Thornby been so good to her? It was a point worth considering. She unlocked the door to the bookshop and looked around. More mess. More dust.

Where to start?

Lady the cat walked solemnly into the shop behind her, waving his tail. He jumped up into the window, shoved one book this way, nudged another that, and settled down for a good sleep.

"Hullo. You're open, then. Mind if I look round?" Customers had arrived. Minty thought, *Panic, I'm going to need a cash float. Where would it be kept? In that locked bottom drawer, I suppose? Yes, there it is. But I don't know how to deal with credit cards, or anything. Help, Lord!*

No, I can't ask Patrick. He's busy.

"Have you got the latest Patricia Cornwell?"

"Can you change a £50 note?"

A cool, amused voice broke in. "Miss Cardale, I presume? You're so like your mother. I'm Venetia Wootton, by the way. Let me take your place at the desk and if you can find the crime section . . . Yes, madam. Of course we take credit cards."

A slim, fiftyish woman, with iron grey hair smoothly curving under. An expensive, understated grey dress. An intelligent face. Someone who knew how to deal with credit cards. Brilliant.

By lucky chance, Minty was able to guide the customer to the crime section straight away, but fell over cardboard boxes of second-hand books that surely ought to be put outside to attract customers. She lugged them out and set them on the pavement. Thereafter she bagged up purchases, smiled at customers and tidied books as necessary. Everything was dusty. After a while the woman behind the desk said, "I've found a duster," and handed it to Minty.

Holidaymakers came in to browse and buy. Locals came who had placed orders for books and wanted to know if they'd arrived. Children who wanted to finger everything in sight. There was a low table near the window with some expensive coffee table type books on it. Minty rescued the books from the children's sticky fingers, unearthed some children's books from the second-hand book cartons outside and laid them out on the table. The children liked that and the parents liked the peace and quiet even more.

When customers became less frequent, Minty explored the back of the shop. There was a locked door on the right that presumably led to Hannah's flat above. There was also a tiny loo and a cubbyhole with a sink and a shelf devoted to tea- and coffee-making. A door at the back of the cubbyhole looked as if it might lead to the outside world, but Minty didn't have time to explore. She took a mug of tea out to the cool lady, who stretched and rubbed her neck.

"Thanks. We only got back from holiday last night. Jonah crashed in on us this morning with some tale about having killed Hannah—Jonah's my brother-in-law, by the way. So I rang round to find out what had really happened. He didn't make her fall, did he?"

"It was an accident. They were arguing. She was on top of the ladder, reaching for some books high up. She overreached and fell."

"Jonah gets a little worked up about things," observed his sister-in-law. "So how did you come to get involved?"

"I was passing and helped Patrick—Mr Sands—with Mrs Wootton till the ambulance came. Then he followed the ambulance with her handbag, so I took the keys and promised to collect the post and drop it in to him. And somehow—I really don't know how—I got landed with opening the shop this afternoon. Oh yes, and the cat, Lady, came home with me last night and followed me back here today."

"Lucky for us. Are you staying long?"

"I don't know. I came back to see my father, but he's not well, so . . ."

"I see," said the cool lady. "At least, I think I do. So you're just hanging around, waiting?"

"Ms Phillips gave me a temporary job, managing the holiday lets. I'm living at Spring Cottage."

Venetia Wootton's eyes slid beyond Minty and considered a distant prospect. "I see," she said again. "Annie Phillips gave you a job, did she? That's interesting."

A large man in a chauffeur's uniform came into the shop, looked around, and made a beeline for Minty. He handed over an envelope, asked her to sign for it, and disappeared.

Venetia looked a question, so Minty said, "It's for Alice, who cleans Kiln and Wool Cottages. She hasn't been paid for a month, so I said I'd see what I could do."

"Your mother always used to care about other people, too. She was by way of being a particular friend of mine, and I never believed . . . well, that's all water under the bridge. Nowadays I run the team of volunteer stewards at the Hall. We—my husband and I—have been away for six weeks visiting our youngest daughter out in New Zealand. A beautiful country, New Zealand, but for life's dramas give me good old England any time. Are you going to be working full time on the holiday lets, Miss Cardale?"

"Araminta. Call me Minty, please."

"Minty, then. Can I offer you a part-time job here? At least till Hannah's able to come back. You see, I own the shop, but Hannah manages it for me. My husband retired from the army two years ago—we've lived all over the world—but now we're home for good. He's taken up fishing and gardening and, as I've mentioned, I've taken charge of the stewards up at the Hall. Simon was happy to pass that little job on to someone else. He—er—hasn't always the patience to deal with individual problems."

Minty grinned. That was beautifully phrased.

"So," said Venetia, "what about that job?"

After the bookshop closed, Minty took Alice's money round to the Pheasant Inn.

"Thanks," said Alice, who was setting out mats on tables in the dining area. "I owe you. Like a drink? On me."

Minty had never liked to go into any of the local pubs, because her uncle's views on the demon drink were well known. When she was at college she had gone occasionally with some of her fellow students, and it had been pleasant enough, though she'd not particularly liked the taste of beer. Shandy was OK. Ginger beer was best.

Should she accept Alice's offer? And be looked over by the village youth, who might try to pick her up?

"No, thanks. I have to get back—lots to do. But thanks for asking." The pub was all dark wood and shining glasses. It offered a wide range of beers and looked well cared for. Judging by the extensive menu chalked up on a blackboard and the delicious smells emanating from the kitchen, it would also do a good trade in meals.

An asset to the village, thought Minty.

She passed the charity shop and pressed her nose to the window, trying to see if there were any suitable curtains for Spring Cottage. But it was after six and the shop was closed like everything else except the small supermarket.

Chapter Six

Sunday morning. An overcast day, but humid. Minty could hear the hum of bees busy among the wild flowers in the overgrown garden. Somewhere in the hills a farmer was reaping the harvest.

She wondered if it would be all right with God if she didn't go to church. Churchgoing in the city had meant wearing either her Brown Owl outfit if it were a parade service, or her navy blue skirt and white blouse. With sensible black shoes, of course.

If she went today she'd have to wear a T-shirt over a cotton skirt that was so limp with washing that it was practically see through. And scuffed sandals. The contrast with Gemma in her designer clothes would be painful.

Lady the cat arrived and purred around her legs. Minty fed Lady and sat down on the doorstep with her coffee, to consider the matter of going to church. Surely she didn't really have to go? Her uncle couldn't shout at her if she didn't. He had a very loud voice and for many years she'd been as frightened of him as of her aunt, who not only had a sharp tongue but also a hand quick to reach for the leather belt.

The beatings had stopped when Minty went to secondary school. Soon after that her aunt had developed back trouble.

Once a schoolfriend had dared her to go to an all-night party with her. Minty had said no, she couldn't. It would have upset her uncle and aunt too much.

"They've got you where they want you. Why don't you break out, have some fun for once?"

So why hadn't she? She had wanted to. She'd fantasised about arriving drunk at a Sunday school party. Wearing skirts slit up to here and blouses open to there. Well, why hadn't she?

Minty sighed. Her uncle and aunt had been miserable, petty-minded tyrants, but she supposed she'd needed them as much as they'd needed her. By degrees they'd become dependent on her, and they were all she'd had, so she had tried to please them and ended up playing the role of Martha. And nearly been trapped for good.

No longer. She had a choice, now.

She could stay at home and do some gardening. She could make rude gestures to Mrs Collins when they passed in the street. When the Reverend Cecil came to call, she would tell him she was too busy to help him out.

Lady the cat came to sit beside her. Minty fondled him until he decided it was time for a good wash, and he didn't want any interference from Minty while he did that, thank you.

Minty thought, *I'll go to church and be quiet with God when I want to, when there's no one else around. All that stuff about going to church for the fellowship is just rubbish. There's no one there I want to see.*

Well, maybe Alice. Maybe Venetia Wootton. Perhaps Ms Phillips; yes, Ms Phillips would probably look for me at church.

There she went again. Trying to please someone else instead of trying to please herself.

Patrick might be there, of course. She considered that idea, leaning back against the doorjamb. The sun fought its way through the haze, and warmth surrounded her. She yawned.

Bother the lot of them. God didn't mind what she wore. She would go to church because she wanted to join in the service, sing a hymn or two, say a prayer or three. If they wanted her to do the washing-up or help with the coffee, then she'd make it clear this was a one-off. She was not going to be taken for granted, ever again.

She let her hair hang loose around her shoulders—how her aunt would disapprove—and walked in her clean T-shirt and much-washed skirt up the hill to the church. Her only spot of colour was the blue scarf she'd knotted loosely around her neck. Alice was wheeling her toddler down the hill, so Minty stopped to speak to her.

Alice was exhausted. "I was up all night with Marie. Teething. I've been walking round the streets with her since seven and she's finally fallen asleep . . . which is what I'd just like to do, right here in the middle of the street."

"Why don't you go back to bed, then?"

"Can't. Mum's got her boyfriend round today and he's into loud music."

The bell was pealing, calling people into church. Outside the church was a giant poster. "Welcome", it said, and gave the times of the services. In small letters at the bottom it said, "Crêche".

"Come in with me," said Minty. "There's a crêche."

Alice straightened up, stared at the poster and slowly shook her head. "I haven't been to church since I was a child. I wouldn't know what to do."

Minty said, "I'll take Marie in with me, if you like. Put her in the crêche. Then you and I can sit at the back and be quiet. You can doze off. Why not?"

Alice laughed. "If you took Marie in, they'd think she was yours and point the finger at you for being an unmarried mother, too."

"So?"

Alice stared. "You'd do that for me?"

"Of course. What would Jesus do?"

"Dunno what you mean."

"It's a slogan. We used it a lot in the youth group, trying to make the kids think about their behaviour. You know the sort of thing. If my friends ask me to shoplift with them, what do I do about it? Well, what would Jesus do?"

"That's not how they think in there. Some of the old biddies . . . You don't know what it's like to live in a village like this. No, it wouldn't be right."

"You've thought about going back to church?"

"Yes." Alice's voice was husky. "Now and then. I've tried to pray, even. But I couldn't . . . not with everyone looking . . . And anyway, I'm too tired to think straight."

Minty fished out her keys. "Here's the key to Spring Cottage. Let yourself in and have a good sleep. There's milk, bread, and cheese in the fridge, so make yourself at home. I'm going out to Old Oak Farm for lunch and won't be back till teatime. If you go before I get back, leave the keys on the table. I've got a second key. All right?"

Alice took the key in a daze.

Minty swung into the church just as the bell ceased. She remembered Mrs Collins had wanted her there early, to become acquainted with the tea urn.

"Oops!" thought Minty. "Black mark!" She grinned to herself and slid into a pew at the back of the church. Her flower arrangement didn't look too bad, even though Mrs Collins had stuck some unnecessary pink carnations into it.

She was not the last in. A beefy, youngish man in a good suit ushered in a semi-royal procession, shepherding them with a flourish down the aisle and into the front pew. First came a tall, thin woman with closely cut black hair, wearing a flame red suit. She was so thin that the suit hung on her. She looked neither to right nor left, acknowledging no one. Minty watched, fascinated. Lisa Cardale reminded Minty of Wallis Simpson, Duchess of Windsor. There was the same stylish, swashbuckling set of shoulders and masklike white face.

Simon followed his mother, casually but expensively dressed in leather; perhaps making the point that he was above having to wear a suit on Sundays?

Gemma hurried down the aisle after him, looking to right and left. Minty heard Gemma say, "She's not here . . ." before dropping into a seat beside the beefy man. Gemma was wearing very high heels and a stylish green silk suit that had certainly not come from a charity shop.

The Reverend Cecil coughed and the organist brought his hands down with a crash. The congregation rose to its feet and the service began.

No Ms Phillips. Now why had Minty thought the woman would be a churchgoer? Minty tucked herself in behind a massive pillar and proceeded to lift her voice in praise. She praised God from the bottom of her heart. He'd given her so much: new friends, a place to live, a job—maybe even two jobs. She had much still to ask for, but she was prepared to wait on God's timing for it.

She went up to receive the bread and wine with the others, but as she returned she met the combined stare of her family in the front pew and felt as if she'd walked into a brick wall. Lady Cardale was staring at her, wide-eyed with hatred. Simon was glaring at her. Gemma was frowning, anxiously turning to watch Minty as she walked back down the aisle. The beefy stranger looked puzzled and angry.

Minty wanted to put her head down and scurry back to her place, but she kept her head high.

She met the eyes of a woman wearing a superbly cut two-piece in a colour that was neither green nor fawn nor brown. Mrs Venetia Wootton, smiling at her. Beside her was a large man with a military air—the husband who fished and gardened, no doubt.

Behind them was the outraged, almost pop-eyed stare of Mrs Collins. Minty read the message in her eyes clearly: "Just you wait, my girl!"

In some confusion Minty dropped back into her seat. She seemed to have stirred up a lot of emotions in different people. She hadn't meant to. She was tempted to sneak out of the church before the service finished, to run and hide somewhere. But she didn't. She knelt and prayed for guidance. She stood and sang and was grateful that the last hymn was to a rousing, fighting tune.

The blessing . . . the procession . . .

Mrs Collins clicked her way out of her pew and down the aisle in high heels. She hissed to Minty to follow her AT ONCE and disappeared through a side door, presumably into the church hall.

Minty let out a sigh. It would be pleasant to tell Mrs Collins to do her own dirty work. How dare the woman presume that Minty would care to make coffee and wash up on her very first Sunday in the village? Mrs Collins was an overbearing, overstuffed bulldozer.

Minty joined the throng of people all going through to the church hall. This was a modern building in the local golden stone. There was a rudimentary stage at one end and a wide hatch down one side, giving access to a long narrow kitchen. Mrs Collins was in the kitchen, fussing around an urn and snapping out contradictory orders to a helper. All the time she darted poisonous glances at Minty who was, in Mrs Collins's eyes at any rate, dawdling.

The helper was an elderly, depressed-looking woman who was nervously trying to follow Mrs Collins's series of commands. "You've forgotten the sugar again, Ruby. Cups and saucers *first.* How many times do I have to tell you?"

The helper abandoned the sugar bowls she'd been filling, to set out the cups and saucers. A queue was forming in front of her.

Minty was looking for the door into the kitchen area when her wrist was caught by a furious Simon.

"I thought we'd made it clear you weren't wanted here. What's more, we've had your uncle on the phone asking for you. Your cousin's coming to fetch you tomorrow and you'd better be ready for him, understand?"

"Oh, Simon," protested Gemma, on the verge of easy tears. "You mustn't be so ... You know Annie's asked her to take on the ..."

"It's about time Annie learned which side her bread's buttered. She had no right to interfere. Anyway, it's you who were supposed to be handling the holiday lets."

"At least Annie appreciates I've got other things to do than ..."

A smooth voice broke in. "Miss Cardale, may I introduce my husband, Hugh? Hugh, this is my old friend Milly's daughter. You can see the likeness, can't you?"

Simon said rudely, "Mrs Wootton, my sister Gemma is Miss Cardale, not ..."

Venetia Wootton put steel in her voice. "The eldest daughter of the house is always Miss Cardale. Gemma is Miss Gemma Cardale. I hear congratulations are in order on your engagement,

Gemma. So pleased. Dear Hugh, you can let go of Miss Cardale's hand now. I expect we'll be seeing quite a lot of her in future. I've asked her to help me out at the shop, you know."

Minty took a deep breath, trying to assimilate all the information she was being given. Simon's news was disturbing. She supposed Simon meant Lucas, when he referred to her "cousin". Well, he was her cousin by marriage. Was he really coming over to collect her? Why? Had something dreadful happened back at the vicarage? She didn't want to go back.

Gemma drew the beefy, youngish man forward to meet Minty. "This is my fiancé, my very dear husband to be. Miles, this is my sister, Miss Cardale."

"Minty, please," she said, shaking the beefy man's hand. For some reason she took an instant dislike to him, and then scolded herself for doing so. First impressions were not always correct, even though he'd squeezed her hand so hard that it hurt and tried to stare her down. Even though there was something about his eyes she found disturbing.

"Minty?" he repeated, checking with Simon. So Miles was Simon's man, was he? Perhaps that was why Minty had taken a dislike to him. No, she'd seen that red glare before in someone else's eyes and it had meant big trouble then.

Ah, she had it. But it hadn't been a person. It had been in the eyes of a pit bull terrier a local man used to take for walks near the vicarage. A red glare of rage, barely held in check by muzzle and lead. And one day . . . she shuddered. That poor child had needed plastic surgery to his face afterward . . . and it hadn't helped much that the dog had been put down.

Simon looked over Minty's head and departed to join the small knot of people around Lady Cardale. Miles followed. So far, his muzzle and lead were restraining him.

A tap on her shoulder made Minty turn, to meet the poppy red face of Mrs Collins. "I thought you were supposed to be helping me."

Minty hoped a soft answer would turn away wrath. "Mrs Collins, it was kind of you to ask me to help you with the coffee. I'm sorry to have kept you waiting."

Venetia raised her eyebrows. "You're helping with the coffee on your very first Sunday? Oh, surely not. Can't you find someone else to help you, Cynthia?"

Cynthia Collins bridled. "You can see the fix I'm in with all my best helpers away. Why, I even had to arrange the flowers myself."

"The flowers looked beautiful," said Venetia, sincerely. "Let's all lend a hand with the coffee, shall we? Gemma, can you help, or do you have to rush off?"

Gemma shook her head. "I must go. Simon's got people staying."

Mrs Collins pushed her head through the hatch back into the kitchen. "Ruby, you've forgotten the sugar, again. How many times do I have to tell you?"

Startled, Ruby knocked a cup and saucer on to the floor and the resultant smash caused everyone to stop talking and turn their heads in her direction.

"Idiot! Now look what you've done!" shouted Mrs Collins.

Minty sped through into the kitchen, tying her hair back with her blue scarf. She knew how poor Ruby was feeling, being shouted at like that in public . . . just like her uncle had used to shout at her, before she learned how to cope.

"Let me help, Ruby." Minty picked a tearful Ruby up off the floor, where she was trying to collect pieces of broken china with her bare hands. "You fetch a dustpan and brush and I'll serve the coffees."

Minty retrieved the sugar and took over at the urn. Mrs Collins disappeared into the main body of the hall. Ruby had a little sniff in a corner and started on the washing-up. When the first rush of people wanting tea and coffee had abated, the door to the church swung open again and in came a tottery, elderly man, with Patrick helping him along.

Had Patrick been in church that morning? Minty didn't think so. She would have imagined—if she'd thought about it at all, which of course she hadn't—that he would have spent his Sundays playing cricket or at a country pub, sitting with a group of friends with a beer in his hand. Not in church.

"Late again, Patrick?" someone called out, in a welcoming, hail-fellow-well-met tone.

"I took Jonah over to see Hannah at the hospital. They can't operate till tomorrow, but she's not bad, considering. She'll be kept in for a while." He steered Jonah over towards the kitchen hatch. Minty found herself wishing she hadn't had to tie her hair back, because it really was her best feature.

How absurd to think of such a thing.

"Morning, Minty. Can you find something for Jonah to eat? He hasn't had any breakfast. Couldn't rest till he'd seen for himself that he hadn't killed Hannah."

Jonah was looking so fragile Minty hadn't recognised him at first. Minty served him coffee and biscuits and poured out some black coffee—no sugar—for Patrick. He drank it, leaning on the hatch. He was wearing an ancient, rather faded greeny-blue woollen shirt, corduroy trousers and grubby trainers.

"Forgive the clothes," he said. "Jonah caught me just as I was doing some gardening. I told him the hospital probably wouldn't let him see Hannah so early, but he was in such a state I had to take him over there. Luckily he was able to see her for a minute or two and she told him not to be such a fool, so he's feeling better now."

She expected Patrick to pass on to talk to someone else, but he didn't.

"Mrs Collins roped you in to do her dirty work, has she?"

"It was the Reverend Cecil. He used to be a curate of my uncle's."

"And here he comes, the great man himself." Patrick's expression was as bland as his tone.

Cecil bustled up, still wearing his black cassock plus a beaming smile. "Our little Martha did turn up eventually, did she? Good, good. I'll drop some stuff round to you tomorrow morning, shall I? Show you what needs doing. Patrick, you missed the last council meeting. Busy as ever, I suppose?" Even as he spoke, his eyes were quartering the room for someone more important to talk to.

"I'll be out, I'm afraid," said Minty. "And my name's not . . ."

"Ah, there you are, dear Mrs Collins. I was just saying to the Major . . ." And he wafted himself away to talk to Mrs Collins.

"Knows how to chat up the ladies, doesn't he?" said Patrick, in that same bland tone.

To her surprise, Minty found herself saying, "Mee-ow!" Then blushed at her impertinence.

Patrick threw back his head and gave a soundless laugh. "Right on. Very catty. Look, what are you doing for lunch?"

Minty looked at her watch, suddenly aware of the time and the pile of washing-up still to be done. "I'm due up at Old Oak Farm at one and I haven't a clue how to get there. Is it far?"

Patrick put down his empty cup. "It's harvest time . . ."

"And Mr Thornby's asked me to lunch. Yes, I'm ahead of you. Why is a busy farmer asking someone to Sunday lunch when he ought to be out working in the fields?"

"He's getting on a bit, probably wouldn't work right through. The other day . . ." he looked embarrassed. "I was out of order. Nobody likes being given advice, even when they've asked for it; and you hadn't asked for it. Apologies."

He took a tray and drifted round the room collecting dirty cups and saucers, chatting easily to those still left in the hall. Minty stacked dirty cups and saucers and took them over to Ruby to wash. Patrick had disappeared when she returned to the hatch, but Venetia was bringing over the last of the dirty cups and saucers.

"Minty, dear. Tomorrow at nine at the shop?"

"I will if I can, but I have some work to do for Ms Phillips."

"I'll clear it with her, right?"

"Are you sure? I don't even know how to deal with credit cards."

"I'll show you. Simon has summoned all the stewards to the Hall tomorrow for a conference at eleven and I shall have to go. The future is about to be unveiled to us in glorious technicolor, and I'm not sure we're going to like it."

"If you put it like that . . ."

"Bless you, Minty. I must dash. We're taking Jonah home with us for lunch. I wish he'd move in with us, but he won't hear of it. Leave the washing-up. Someone else will do it."

In Minty's experience, the only people who did the washing-up were those too cowed to protest when handed a dishcloth. She was amazed to find that she—who had always been one of the world's slaves—now objected to being used in this way.

"Yes, leave it," said Ruby, taking the last of the cups and saucers from Minty. "I'll finish up. You go and enjoy yourself."

"Don't be daft. You can't do all this by yourself."

Ruby flushed. "I know I'm slow, and if people shout at me I get clumsy and break things, but I'm perfectly all right on my own."

"Tough! Because I'm going to see the last cup and saucer put away before I leave."

"I thought at first you were like your mother, but you aren't really, are you?"

"Aren't I?"

"No. You're more . . . grown-up, I suppose." Ruby flushed, perhaps thinking Minty would take offence at what she had said.

Minty was interested. "You knew her? I can hardly remember her. Tell me about her." Chatting away, Minty learned that Ruby had once been a parlourmaid at the Hall and had been devoted to "Miss Milly", but had left soon after her mistress had died, and now worked in the charity shop. When Minty confided her dilemma about her wardrobe, dear Ruby said she'd look out one or two things for Minty to wear.

The hall was deserted by the time they finished. Minty stretched, pulled the scarf off her hair, and shook it out. Now she must find out how to get to Old Oak Farm.

Patrick came back into the hall, switching off his mobile phone. "All done, Ruby? Good. Minty, your carriage awaits. I rang Mrs Thornby and arranged to take you up there. The men are in the fields of course, and her granddaughter's driving lessons are not progressing as well as they might, seeing as she's spending more time in the back seat with her boyfriend than in the driving seat with her hands on the steering wheel ..."

He stopped. "Sorry," he said. "I've got into a bad habit of slagging people off, haven't I?"

He led Minty out to where he'd parked an oldish Rover and held the door for her to get in. A lingering odour of cigarettes? Did he smoke? Several fast-food cartons littered the back seat, plus chocolate bar wrappers and empty Coke tins, which had probably been thrown there when he took Jonah over to the hospital that morning.

Some parishioners waited on the pavement, watching them with interest.

"Are you sure you want to be seen with me?" asked Minty. "I'm beginning to think this village is a minefield. Every person I meet ..." She threw up her hands. "I never know whether I'm going to be handed a bouquet or a hand grenade with the pin out."

"That's about it. Best be wary."

He drove up the hill to the station; then turned into a narrow lane lined with drystone walls. The verges were bright yellow ragwort and honeysuckle. They passed twin pillars supporting a pair of wrought-iron gates. Beyond lay a short avenue of trees leading to a perfectly proportioned Georgian house.

"The manor house," said Patrick. "Hugh and Venetia Wootton's place. You'll be invited there soon, I expect."

He parked the car in a lay-by at the top of a hill. Before them the countryside lay in a patchwork quilt of colours ... a wood here, a field that had been harvested there ... bales of hay ... a clutch of farm buildings ... a winding river fringed with willows ...

"How beautiful!" Minty wondered if she ought to feel frightened because Patrick had stopped the car in a lonely place. She decided she didn't feel at all threatened.

He leaned back in his seat. "Do you remember any of it?"

"I'm not sure. It's like stepping into the frame of a picture that I've loved all my life. Familiar and yet not. I never want to leave, only ... there's so much I don't understand. I don't know why some people are so nice to me, and others . . . well, I suppose I understand why Lady Cardale dislikes me, but . . ."

He was staring ahead. "You mean that stupid tale about your mother and my father? They were not lovers and she was not running away to be with him."

"I've always understood that they were."

"Nonsense. Believe me."

Greatly daring, she asked, "So you're not my half-brother?"

"What? No, of course not! That's obscene!"

Was he speaking the truth? "I wish I knew whom to trust. I understand what some people want. Mrs Collins wants a slave . . ."

Patrick spurted into laughter.

"Well, she does," insisted Minty. "The Reverend Cecil, too. But what about Ms Phillips? Why is she helping me?"

"Yes, that's a tricky one. I'd say she has her own agenda."

"Well, what about Venetia Wootton? Is she being kind because she wants someone to help out in the shop, or because I'm like my mother, or because—I don't think I'm wrong here—because she doesn't like my stepmother?"

"A mixture of all three, I should think."

"What about Mr Thornby? You hinted he wants something from me. He's been so good to me, I can't tell you. Yet you're right: a busy farmer doesn't interrupt his harvesting to give me lunch without good reason, does he?"

"Minty, some people may think you can help them, that's true. But they may also like you and want to help you for your own sweet self."

She gaped. "You mean that?"

He turned to face her. "Of course I do."

The words were like a salve laid over a raw place. Because he did mean them, she could see that. She, who never cried, felt tears well out of her eyes and rush down her face. She dabbed at her cheeks with both hands, then sought for a handkerchief in her pockets. But of course she hadn't got one. "I never cry."

Patrick rubbed his forehead. "The gallant male is now supposed to produce a pristine, newly ironed handkerchief to hand you. I'm afraid I haven't as much as a paper tissue on me."

She began to laugh. She laughed and cried at the same time. Then sobered up.

"Thank you, Patrick. You'll think me very silly, but my life's been something of a roller coaster lately. So I must ask. Do you want something from me, too?"

"Yes! At least . . . no, not yet." He shook his head as if to clear it. "This is getting complicated. There's so much you ought to know but . . . Look, I'm your friend, if you'll have me. Not because my father and your mother were old friends—which they were, just friends—but between us. Right?"

"But you do want something from me?"

He sighed, and restarted the engine. "I have to deliver you to the farm by one or I'll be in trouble."

"What do you want from me?"

"Ask me again in three weeks—if you're still interested."

She was puzzled. Why three weeks? Did he think she would have returned to the city then? Her aunt's birthday came up in a couple of weeks; Minty made a mental note to send her something. Aunt Agnes never liked what Minty got for her, but insisted it was important to observe birthdays, even though she never troubled to do anything much for Minty's own birthday, which followed shortly after.

They swooped down a rise and into a lane off which lay a cluster of farm buildings. Old Oak Farm was trim, with roses about the front door and a black and white collie barking a welcome. Patrick opened the car door to let her out.

"Aren't you coming in, too?"

"I seem to have lost a day's work this week, so I'd better do some paperwork or I'll be in trouble tomorrow. Besides which, I haven't been invited. And besides which, again, they'll want to know what you think of me." He roared off with a faint whiff of exhaust.

Chapter Seven

Minty felt shy as she walked down to the farmhouse. Whatever was she doing here, going to lunch with people she didn't know? Surely she ought to be back in the city, running around after her aunt and uncle . . . worrying about Lucas.

Suppose Lucas made her go back with him tomorrow? Suppose something had happened to her uncle and aunt? A traffic accident, or a bad fall. Would she still be able to resist attempts to take her back to the city?

She wondered if she'd ever been to Old Oak Farm before. The farmhouse was old, with a crooked roof. Perhaps even older than Eden Hall.

The front door opened and out came not one but three women, led by a grandmotherly personage with short grey hair and a four-square figure. Next came a middle-aged woman with carefully blonded hair and a similar four-square figure. Finally came a four-square teenager, whom Minty recognised as being Gloria from the restaurant at Eden Hall.

"It's lovely to see you, Miss Cardale," said the oldest of the three, who must be Norman Thornby's wife. "This is my daughter-in-law, Florence, and I believe you've already met my granddaughter, Gloria."

"Gloria was very kind to me when I arrived," said Minty, smiling.

Gloria's somewhat heavy face lit up. A smile can do a lot for some faces, and it certainly did a lot for Gloria's.

Minty shook hands all round. "I can't thank you all enough. It was you, wasn't it, who transformed Spring Cottage? I don't know how I'd have managed otherwise."

"Think nothing of it," said the elder Mrs Thornby. "We loved your mother and were so excited when we heard you were coming, but I'm afraid the cottage is still not fit . . ."

"It was some of Simon's so-called friends who wrecked it," said Gloria. "But of course no one dares say anything to him!"

"You must tell us what else you need," said Mrs Thornby, ignoring Gloria and ushering Minty inside. "A new kettle? More bedlinen?"

"It was such fun," said Gloria. "We ran round like crazy, trying to think what we should take. Then we all piled into the two cars and drove down."

"All the while wondering if you'd come back and catch us at it," put in Florence, smiling. "My husband thought you might like a microwave, because we weren't sure whether the gas stove worked or not, but . . ."

"Dad found out the electrics were kaput," said Gloria. "So we had to bring it away again."

Mrs Thornby looked anxious. "He did look at the fuses to see if he could fix it, but he said it was hopeless: the cottage needs completely rewiring, so . . ."

"While Gran and Mum and I cleaned up a bit," continued Gloria, "Dad piled all the rubbish in the back of the car and dumped it. We'd taken the mattress from my sister's bed—she's living in the city now—and Mum and I heaved it upstairs. Only, we hadn't realised you had a double bed."

Everyone was laughing. The Thornbys had had a wonderful time, doing something for someone else. Patrick couldn't have been more wrong about their motives.

"So tell us what else you need to make you comfortable," said Mrs Thornby. "Florence and Gloria took one or two things in yesterday on their way to work, but we know it's not what you're used to."

"It's perfect," said Minty, thinking of her tiny cold bedroom in the dour, cold vicarage. "Mrs Guinness is bringing back a whole lot of stuff tomorrow that she—er—borrowed."

The three women burst into laughter. They seemed to know all about Mrs Guinness and her little ways.

Minty spotted an old grandfather clock with sun and moon dials on its enamelled face. Its tick-tock took her back to her childhood. "Oh, I remember that clock!"

"There, now," Mrs Thornby smiled. "We wondered whether you would. You used to sit on a stool and watch that clock for hours when your dear mother brought you over to tea. I was thinking, maybe we've even got a photo somewhere of the two of you together, taken the last time you came."

"I'd love to see it. I've no photos of her. Sometimes I wonder if I've remembered her properly."

"Gloria dear," said Mrs Thornby. "See if you can find the photo, will you? I need to check on the potatoes."

Florence said, in her comfortable way, "I don't remember your mother, as I'm what they call an 'incomer'. That's someone who wasn't born hereabouts but has come from 'outside'. I only met and married Ian the year after you went away."

Norman Thornby appeared, to be heartily kissed and thanked by Minty. "Now, missy! Not another word. We enjoyed it and it was one in the eye for that Simon and his crew, wasn't it. Now, is the food on the table? My son, Ian, wants to work through, but I'm more than ready to eat."

"Now tell me—how did you know I was coming?" asked Minty, as they sat down at table.

Florence explained, "I cook for the family up at the Hall. Gemma had just come into the kitchen to say she'd invited you to stay and wasn't it exciting, when Simon rushed in and tore her off a strip, saying she'd had no right to interfere and Lady Cardale was furious and wanted to see her about it. I'd only heard about you vaguely, so when I rang my father-in-law with the order for the eggs, I told him about the row, and he said wasn't anyone coming to meet you at the station, and I said that Simon wouldn't let Gemma go, so . . ."

"I said I'd pop round by the station myself," said Mr Thornby. "Just to make sure. And there you were."

"I'm very grateful," said Minty, guessing that he had waited a while to see if she would give up and get back on a train. "If it hadn't been for you . . ."

"I like to see fair play," said Mr Thornby. Which was one in the eye for Patrick.

"One thing bothers me," said Minty. "How did you get into the cottage? You got in the back way through the garden, didn't you? My guess is that you took the back door key with you when you took that horrid basket out into the garden, but didn't I bolt the back door when I left?"

"Oh, that." Mr Thornby smothered a grin. "It don't fit too well, that door. None of those back doors do. If you know how, you can lift and jiggle and the bolt slips out and there you are, in."

"Something he learned when he was courting," said Mrs Thornby, comfortably. "I was born and brought up in Riverside Cottage No. 1, next along of you."

Minty made a mental note to check the security of all the back doors in the holiday lets.

Gloria came rushing in, holding a large photograph album. "I found it!"

Minty found herself looking at a photograph of herself, holding a small child up on a drystone wall. Only it wasn't really her. It was her mother, holding the child Minty had been.

"She looks so young," exclaimed Minty. "She can't have been any older than I am now."

"That's right," said Mrs Thornby. "She was only twenty-four when she died—and don't you ever believe that wicked story about her eloping with Richard Sands, because there's no truth in it. It was all lies, made up by that woman to fool your father."

Minty felt the colour fade from her face. "Mrs Thornby, would you be so kind as to tell me what you meant by that? You see, my uncle and aunt always told me that my mother was running away with someone when she died."

Mrs Thornby looked grim. "So they told you that, did they? They didn't tell you that it was your father making her miserable that made her look for a shoulder to cry on elsewhere, did they? And there was that evil secretary of his scheming to catch his eye and turn him against your poor dear mother, who was nothing but an innocent slip of a girl for all she was married and had borne you. Richard Sands was an honourable man and a friend in need. Maybe she wasn't so wise in sending him so many little notes. They say she wrote to him or rang him up almost every day. So naturally there was talk. The truth of the matter was that she was on her way for an appointment with him at his office when she died. That wicked woman twisted the facts to cover up the fact that she herself was aiming to be the second Lady Cardale. What's more, I can count up to nine, even if she can't."

Gloria was interested. "You mean that she was already pregnant with Gemma?"

"Never you mind what I mean. We don't need to throw mud at the innocent. Now, my dear, you keep that photo if you like."

"Oh, I do like," said Minty, trying to assimilate all she'd been told. So her mother had not been unfaithful? It was her father's secretary, Lisa, who had turned her father against her mother? And then supplanted her? So why had her uncle and aunt insisted that Milly had been wholly to blame? She wanted desperately to believe Mrs Thornby, but for twenty years she'd had it dinned into her that her mother had been unfaithful. Her mind was whirling with possibilities.

Minty wanted to get away somewhere quiet and think things over, but she was a guest and must be polite. "I'm so much in your debt. Whatever can I do for you in return?" She remembered Patrick's warning, too late. But it was all right.

"Well, there is one thing, if you mean it," said Florence. "You can help me pick some raspberries after lunch. There's a big do on at the Hall tomorrow with all the stewards and the outside staff and everyone invited, and important people down from London. Chef from the restaurant will do some of the catering, but I promised to make some fruit pavlovas."

"I'd be glad to help," said Minty.

But she had to keep her wits about her, through the tasty roast beef and Yorkshire pudding, with fresh beans and new potatoes.

Mrs Thornby said, "I hear my husband did his famous trick with the car door when he fetched you from the station."

"What famous trick?" said Minty, in all innocence.

"The catch on the passenger door isn't too good, so if he twists the steering wheel quickly, the door flies open. Nearly landed Patrick Sands in hospital, I hear."

Gloria put in, "They say he saw stars."

"Nonsense," said Mr Thornby. "The merest touch."

"Oh," said Minty. "So you did it on purpose?" She was going to ask why, when she realised that she knew. "You wanted to stir things up, didn't you? See how poor Patrick would react?"

Mr Thornby didn't appear at all ashamed of himself. "Jumped out of his skin, didn't he?"

Gloria asked, "Do you like Patrick, Minty?"

"Gloria!" said her mother.

"Yes, of course I do," said Minty, in a brisk tone. She wasn't going to confide in these people—however well-meaning they might be—her complicated feelings towards Patrick. Also, she'd had first-hand experience of how the grapevine worked in the village and guessed that anything she said would go straight back to him. She said, "I think he must be the kindest man I know."

It had been the right thing to say, for everyone looked pleased.

Then, with the apple pie and cream, Gloria said she'd heard from the girl who worked for Miles in the estate office that Minty's cousin was coming to fetch her the next day. Was that true?

"Definitely not," said Minty.

"What's he like? Is he your boyfriend? Is he handsome? What does he do for a living?"

"Lucas? He looks like a rugby player and works in an estate agents." *And,* thought Minty, repressing a shudder, *he's my aunt's favourite and has a loud voice.*

Then it was on to Hannah Wootton's accident. Had Minty been there and seen it all? Had Jonah really caused the accident?

Minty explained what had happened and added, "Did Jonah have an illness to make him like he is?"

"He fell out of the wrong window," said Mr Thornby, laughing.

"Whose window?" asked Gloria. "Do you mean he was playing about with someone else while he was married to Hannah?"

"He was Jack the Lad in those days," said Mr Thornby. "Though you'd never think it to look at him now. Him and his coaxing ways. He could have married any girl in the village, but he chose Hannah of all people, who'd never so much as looked at a man till he came along. They made an odd-looking couple: she so big and he so little. He adored her, but he still couldn't resist flirting with other girls. The accident left him brain damaged. Childish, almost."

"Who was he playing around with . . . ?"

"Never you mind, Gloria," said Mrs Thornby. "Now if you're going to pick those raspberries . . ."

While picking raspberries Minty found herself working beside Gloria, and it was not long before she was telling Minty all about her driving instructor boyfriend and their hopes for the future.

"We'll have to move away to get anywhere to live, though, which is a pity. He still lives with his mum in the next town, and it's convenient me working up at the Hall, but there it is . . . story of village life: nowhere to live."

"That's enough raspberries," said Florence, with a sigh. "You'll stay for tea, won't you, Minty?"

Minty hesitated. "It's quite a walk back. Is there a short cut through the fields?"

Florence said, "No car?"

"I drove my uncle's car in the city. The parish car, really."

Gloria said, "My sister's old bike's in the shed here. Could you ride that? She doesn't need it now. She's married with two kids and lives in the city."

"I haven't ridden since I was so high." She had learned on an old bike she'd found in the vicarage shed, abandoned years before by some previous incumbent. She'd had a fine old time with it until one day it fell apart and her uncle said he couldn't afford to buy her another.

They got the bike out and checked it over. Mr Thornby pronounced the tyres good enough, with a bit of extra air pumped into them. The brakes worked, though the lamps didn't. She would have to get new lamps. Minty rode round and round the yard, with Gloria whooping it up ahead on her own bike.

Minty followed Gloria out on to the lane and then halfway up the hill. "Look at me!" cried Gloria, taking both feet off the pedals and freewheeling down the slope.

Minty yelled, "I shall fall off!" But did the same. The two girls ended up in the ditch at the side of the road, laughing so much they could hardly pull their bikes out of the hedge.

After tea Mrs Thornby packed the basket of the bicycle with raspberries and other goodies. "Come again soon."

Minty kissed them all, one by one. "I haven't had such fun for ages. Thank you so much, for everything."

"You're more than welcome, my dear. Take care how you go, now."

Minty waved them all goodbye. The sun was still high in the sky, but the shadows were lengthening under the oak trees that lined the lane. Time to go home. Time to think about what Mrs Thornby had said. And not think too much about the morrow when Lucas was coming for her.

❧

Minty groaned as she got out of bed and staggered down the stairs to feed the cat and get herself a coffee. She hadn't ridden a bicycle in years, and even though she had pushed the bicycle up most of the hills, she was feeling sore. Today she had to face Lucas and Mrs Guinness, tackle a new job in the bookshop, and fend off the Reverend Cecil and Mrs Collins.

She shuddered. Monday morning blues. Then she smiled, fingering the photo of her mother she'd put on the mantelpiece, and thinking she would find a frame in the charity shop for it. She'd sat with that photo in her hands for a long time the previous night, going over and over everything her uncle and aunt—and now Mrs

Thornby—had said. She remembered the present Lady Cardale stalking into the church. Proud, seemingly insensible of what others might think of her. She remembered that Mrs Thornby had hinted that Lisa was already pregnant with Gemma when Milly was killed.

Her father's part in this was not clear to her yet, but Mrs Thornby's defence of Milly brought healing to Minty's much-bruised heart.

The sun had come out. She praised God for all his good gifts to her, and asked for courage and common sense to deal with whatever the new day brought.

There was no email in from Ms Phillips, but she phoned Minty just before nine, sounding as if she had been at work for ages.

"Good morning, Araminta. Your father is a little better this morning. Venetia Wootton has advised me of her dilemma with regard to the bookshop, and I have agreed that you should be free to work there for the time being. Subject, of course, to your continuing to service the holiday lets. I will see that you have a pay packet for Mrs Guinness some time today. You are authorised to pay her as little or as much as you see fit."

"Thank you," said Minty, wondering if she would dare to withhold any money from the formidable Mrs Guinness, and deciding that she wouldn't.

"Meanwhile," said Ms Phillips, "I dislike interfering in personal affairs, but I understand your cousin intends to call on you today, with a view to taking you back to the city. I would be grateful if you would advise me if you do decide to return, as I shall have to make other arrangements for the cottages and collect my mobile and laptop from you."

"I want to stay, and I won't go till I've seen my father."

"That's what I thought." The phone went down.

Another test of my trustworthiness? thought Minty. Before she left for the shop, she checked the back door and found that what Mr Thornby had said was true. It was easy to wriggle the bolt free.

She jammed a chair under the door handle and set off for the bookshop, preceded by Lady the cat.

Venetia Wootton had already opened the shop and was staring around in a distracted manner. "Minty, I'm taking a fresh look at this place and it strikes me as being rather old-fashioned. If you've got time today, will you have a think about what we could do to bring it up to date? What's more, I don't think our present stock is right. Surely we need to be appealing to holidaymakers and those on a limited income? We don't have a public library in the village, only a mobile van that comes once a fortnight."

Venetia showed Minty how to operate the till and how to deal with credit cards before dashing off to the big meeting at the Hall.

Minty thought, *Am I going up in the world, or down? First I was the parish secretary and dogsbody. Then I was landed with the holiday lets, the bonus being a place of my own. Now I'm a shop assistant, and I think I'm going to enjoy it.*

Lady the cat had returned to his usual place in the window—which Minty thought looked rather grubby. She removed all the dusty books from the window, cleaned the windows inside and out—not without a few growls from Lady—and stacked piles of brightly coloured paperbacks there instead. She decided that the whole shop could do with a clean and redecoration. The bookshelves felt sticky and the carpet was worn to threads in places.

The shop bell rang, and a tourist came in for a holiday guide. Which Minty didn't have. She started to make a list of what they needed.

Turning away from the till, she found a little old man crouched down on a chair with his arms and knees sticking out at an angle. Jonah.

"Can I help? Please let me. The hospital said Hannah couldn't talk to me today because they're going to operate this morning."

Minty remembered Patrick's warning but took pity on him. "I'd be grateful if you'd help. There are lots of paperback books on the shelves towards the back of the shop and I think we can sell more if we have them at the front. If I clear the expensive hardback books from the shelves nearest the door, do you think you could bring the paperbacks forward?"

He sprang up, shedding twenty years in an instant. "I can do it! Yes, I can! And you'll tell Hannah that I helped?"

"Of course I will," said Minty. "By the way, I'm . . ."

"Miss Cardale. And I'm Jonah, of course."

Minty kept an eye on Jonah and found that he worked slowly, but thoroughly. There was a steady trickle of customers. The weather helped, being cool but sunny.

Minty stacked hardback books towards the back of the shop, setting aside those she discovered to be in a less than perfect condition. She would ask Venetia if these might be put on to a sale table.

The driver of a car leaned on his horn in the street outside the shop.

"Stupid man," observed Jonah. "The traffic warden will have him."

Someone swept into the shop, setting the doorbell ajangle. "Minty!" A loud, well-known voice. "Are you ready? Didn't you get my message? What on earth are you wearing? You'd better change before I take you home."

A book on architecture slipped from Minty's arms. "Lucas!" Her new-found confidence deserted her.

Lucas looked around him, frowning. "A bit of a dump this, isn't it? Come on, Minty. Where's your bag? Look sharp. I can't wait around all day!"

Jonah touched his arm, "If you leave your car there, they'll have you."

Lucas pulled his arm away. "What on earth are you talking about?"

"You're parked on a double yellow line," said Minty, "and the traffic warden's coming round."

"You'll have to square him then, won't you?" And to Jonah, "Go out and tell them I'm busy with my cousin from the Hall."

"It won't do, Lucas," said Minty, knowing even as she spoke that he wouldn't listen to her. He'd never listened to her before, so why should he now? "I got your message but I don't think you understand . . ."

Lucas looked around with distaste. "I suppose you've left your bag back at the Hall. I rang through this morning to tell them what time I'd be collecting you and got some idiot woman on the phone who said I'd find you here. I really don't understand you, Minty. You know how busy I am at the office and, when I take the trouble to come over to collect you, the very least you can do is be ready for me."

Jonah looked puzzled. He said to Minty, "You're not going away, are you? You've only just come. What will Hannah say?"

Just then a couple of customers came in. Minty made a helpless gesture with her hands. She was so accustomed to doing as Lucas told her that it was hard to disobey him, but she'd been left in charge of the shop and her first duty must be to serve the customers. Besides, she really did not want to leave.

Lucas gave Jonah a hard stare. "What business is it of yours? Minty, snap out of it, girl. Is your bag here, or up at the Hall?"

Jonah seemed to grow taller. "Minty, I'll deal with the customers, if you wish to have a private conversation with this . . . this gentleman!"

"Come this way, Lucas." Minty led the way to the tiny cubbyhole where the tea things were kept.

Lucas took the only stool, shooting his cuffs, looking at his Rolex. He was wearing office gear, a blue-striped suit over a white shirt, with a subdued blue tie. Minty wondered who would iron his shirts in future. Aunt Agnes hated ironing.

With a shock Minty saw that Lucas looked older than his thirty-one years. His light brown hair was lustreless and there was a frown line between his eyes. He did look as solid as a rugby player, but he took no exercise and would soon become tubby.

"Are my aunt and uncle well? I left a message on their answerphone . . ."

"What sort of message was that! 'I'm quite well, but not coming back. The buildings file is in the second drawer of my desk and you'll need it on Monday.' No apology for leaving them in the lurch."

"I didn't leave them in the lurch. I made sure someone could take over in the parish office, and Aunt Agnes can always get someone to help her in the house if she feels she can't cope."

"You know perfectly well she can't afford to pay a cleaner. They can't possibly manage without your money coming in. You know that."

"But Lucas, I . . ." Too late, she realised he'd put her on the defensive. She folded her arms and leaned against the wall. "I'm earning now, it's true, and I'll pay back what I still owe them, but it will take time."

"Get a loan from your rich relatives at the Hall."

"I'm working for them, yes. But I'm living in a tiny cottage by the bridge at the moment."

Lucas barked out a laugh. "So that's it! I said to Aunt, 'Perhaps it's true after all that she's Sir Micah's daughter and that they'll welcome her back.' But as she said, 'Why would they have sent her away in the first place if she were his child? And ignored her all this time?'"

"I don't know," said Minty, wretchedly.

"I suppose all young girls daydream of high-born relatives, but they have to wake up some day and live in the real world. The Cardales might want an illegitimate daughter around to skivvy for them, but they'll never forget what you are. It's just as well I came to fetch you home."

Chapter Eight

Minty rubbed her forehead. "Lucas, please. Whether I ever get to see Sir Micah or not, whether I am his child or not, I'm staying."

Lucas frowned. "If they don't want to acknowledge you, there's no point in your hanging around, humiliating yourself. Oh, please don't sulk. Listen, I've got some good news for you. There's a job waiting for you in my office, starting tomorrow. Now do you see why you have to come back with me?"

"You have a secretary already."

Lucas made an impatient movement. "The stupid girl made such a fuss . . . all about nothing . . . I hardly touched her, I swear! She was talking about sexual harassment and threatening . . . well, I had to let her go, of course."

Minty blinked. Was Lucas so self-satisfied that he didn't realise what he'd just said? She could well believe that he had made a pass at his secretary and been rebuffed. He'd always had wandering hands, as she very well knew. It had been one of the things that had turned her against him. Did he really believe that he could behave like that and get away with it? Ah, but he always had got away with it in the past, hadn't he? With her aunt's encouragement, he'd assume he could continue to do so. She looked at him with eyes that began to see him for what he was.

"So you see, Minty, you can be far more useful back home with me than licking the boots of the people up at the Hall, who are never going to appreciate you. If you're worried about what my aunt will say, she's promised not to hold it against you that you went off and left her in such pain. They had to have the doctor in to see her yesterday, and you've never so much as asked how she is."

He dropped his voice a couple of decibels. "Besides, there's some unfinished business between us, isn't there?"

Her aunt had had to call the doctor in? This was awful. Minty felt so guilty.

A genteel cough broke in on them. Jonah was holding up an expensive book. "Might I have a word, Minty? A customer wants to know . . ."

"Excuse me, Lucas." She followed Jonah back into the shop. There was no customer in sight.

Jonah began in a normal tone, "A customer wanted to know if you'd make a reduction on this book. He's just popped out but will be back in a minute." Suddenly Jonah dropped his voice to a low gabble, and danced around like a manic puppet on strings. "How dare that man say those things to you! I went next door to get Patrick to deal with him, but it's one of his days at his other office . . ." Then he resumed his former pose and normal tone of voice. "So I said if he'd come back in a couple of minutes . . ."

He broke off into a frantic whisper. "No one, I say again, NO ONE, can say Milly was a bad girl in my hearing."

Reverting to his normal manner, in a loud tone he said, "Now if you take into account our usual mark-up, then I think you might perhaps allow . . ."

Lucas came back into the shop, looking at his watch. "Minty, I must insist!"

Minty opened the front door of the shop. "Sorry, Lucas. I'm staying. Give my love to my aunt and uncle."

"Oh, my!" said Jonah, in a high, strained voice. "Is that the traffic warden?"

"What?!" Lucas rushed out.

Too late. The ticket had already been written out and was being stuck on the windscreen of Lucas's car. Lucas bellowed a protest, but the traffic warden took no notice. Lucas gesticulated angrily back at the shop. The traffic warden moved away. Lucas took one step back towards the shop, but with commendable presence of mind Jonah shot the bolt on the door, turned the "Open" sign to "Closed" and pulled down the blind.

Lucas hammered on the door, but Jonah took no notice. Lady the cat plopped down from the window and made his stately way towards the back of the shop.

"Yes!" cried Jonah, dancing around the shop like a manic gnome, while Minty leaned against the paperbacks and tried to hold herself together.

"Can we close the shop—just like that?"

"Early lunch. Not much doing on Mondays and you look as if you could do with a drink."

"I don't drink," gasped Minty.

"Don't you?" said Jonah, surprised. "Well, it takes all sorts. Come on."

He dragged Minty to the back of the shop and, unbolting the unobtrusive back door, drew her out into a courtyard garden. Pushing her down on to a chair, he said, "If I'd been ten years younger—even five—I'd have bopped that young man on the nose! How dare he say those things!"

Minty had not yet recovered. Everything she'd been told by her uncle and aunt was fighting with what she'd learned the previous day. "Perhaps because they're true?"

"Lies, all lies!"

He sat and put his arm around her. Minty found herself relaxing into his shoulder, even while remembering that Jonah was a man of dubious reputation and undoubtedly a filling short of a sandwich.

"There, now," said Jonah, proffering a slightly dusty but unused handkerchief.

Minty took the handkerchief, dabbed her eyes and blew her nose. She had not been crying. Certainly not. She wondered if it was a generation thing that Jonah had had a handkerchief to offer, while Patrick had not.

"Listen to me," said Jonah. "I may not be the cleverest person around, but I've lived in this village all my life and I knew your mother well. She loved your father dearly. He was much older than her, of course, but though she was as beautiful as she was kind, and many men admired her, there was never the slightest hint of scandal till after she died—and we know where that came from, don't we?"

"What about Patrick's father?"

"He was twenty years older than her, the family solicitor and her trustee after her father died. He was married and had a child long before Milly got herself hitched to Sir Micah. He cared for her, of course he did. We all did. But that's all it was."

"I was told they were eloping together."

"You Know Who put it about to save her own face. Everyone knew she was at it like a rabbit with her boss, getting herself pregnant, too, right under Milly's nose! There was no elopement. Milly was alone in the car when she took the bend into the bridge too fast and crashed."

Minty was horrified. "The bridge at the bottom of the street here? The one outside Spring Cottage?"

"Didn't you know? It was over in an instant. She wasn't wearing a seat belt, you see. She didn't have you in the car with her, or any luggage. Do you seriously think she'd have run off without you?"

Minty thought over what he'd said. She gave a great sigh. "Then why don't they want me back at the Hall?"

"You'd have to ask You Know Who that."

Minty nodded. Perhaps, some day when her courage was up, she'd be able to confront the present Lady Cardale. But not yet. Jonah's arm was a little too tight around her, so she eased away.

"Ah, if I were only ten years younger," he said.

She heard herself giggle. "Oh, Jonah, don't be silly."

"Your mother used to say it like that, too. Now, lunch is on me. Will a ham sandwich do? You sit tight. I won't be a minute."

Instead of returning through the shop, he went down the garden and out into the lane beyond. Minty put her head down between her knees and counted out twenty long, slow heartbeats. She was drowning . . . everything was going black around her. She no longer knew who she was. Her uncle and aunt had told her over and over that her mother was a wicked woman who'd been running away with her lover, and they ought to know the truth. But people here said that story was a lie.

Out of the depths I cry to you, O Lord; O Lord, hear my voice . . . Lord, help me!

Who am I? Who was my father? Whom can I trust?

My aunt and uncle say one thing . . . he's a minister of the church . . . he wouldn't lie about such a thing. No. Impossible!

So I must accept . . . I CAN'T ACCEPT IT. If there is one speck of truth in what Mrs Thornby and Patrick and Jonah have said, then my uncle and aunt were wrong, and everything I've believed in all these years, everything they pounded into me, was a lie.

Dear God! Help me! I'm drowning. I don't know which way to turn, whom to believe. The people here, or my uncle and aunt. Dear Lord Jesus, I cling to you, to the only hope I've got left in this shifting world. Help me. I don't know who I am, or what I am, and it's killing me.

Somewhere at the back of her mind words began to form. Something about everyone being equal in God's sight. There, now . . . she had it. Paul had said that "there is neither Jew nor Greek, slave nor free, male nor female, for you are all one in Christ Jesus". Which meant surely that God loved her, no matter who her father had been.

She had loved God since she was a child, but had she ever really believed that God loved her, no matter who her father had been? Did God really love her enough to send His Son to die for her?

If that was so, then He must be sorry she had put her dream of being accepted by Sir Micah before loving Him. It could not—must not—be the most important thing in her life. God was the most important thing. If she accepted that she loved Him and that He loved her, then everything else fell into place.

First she had to let go of her dream. She had to say to God, You are more important to me than knowing who my earthly father may be. At first she thought she couldn't do it. Then she forced out the words, saying them aloud. "Dear Lord Jesus. I am your child . . . and yours alone. Accept me as your child . . . and yours alone. Love me . . . let me feel your love. Let me grow in your love."

It was a struggle, but she did it. She held up her hands, offering her dream up to Him. "Take my dream. Use me as you think best. I am yours and yours alone."

The radiance of the sun reached her, warming her. Forgiving her. Releasing her. She felt worn out, but at long last she was at peace.

After a while she sat up straight and looked around her. As at Spring Cottage, a long back garden stretched in front of her. This one was bounded by drystone walls with roses, clematis, summer jasmine and honeysuckle rambling over them. Narrow beds on either side held a variety of low-growing alpines, including rock roses and pinks. Instead of a lawn there was a stretch of gravel, on which were set some solid wooden tables and chairs. To one side of the garden a wrought-iron stairway led up to the first floor above the bookshop. Presumably this was the back entrance to Hannah Wootton's flat.

Somewhere in the distance she could hear children playing. She remembered seeing a sign pointing to a primary school down one of the side roads. It must be their lunch break. Did she remember going to school here? Vaguely, perhaps.

She went down the garden, trying to get her bearings.

Next door rose the back of a three-storey Georgian house with a wisteria growing up it. This must be the back of Patrick's offices and possibly also where he lived. A pity he wasn't working there today. Jonah had said Patrick had another office somewhere? Like Jonah, she had an impulse to pour out her troubles to him.

The other buildings in sight were neither as tall nor as imposing as Patrick's.

At the bottom of the garden were a couple of parking places, and beyond that the lane that also ran past the back of her cottage. An estate car stood at the end of Hannah's garden, gleaming in the sun.

She stood on a chair to look over the wall into Patrick's garden. At the bottom was a Mini—presumably belonging to his efficient secretary—and a space where his Rover would normally be. His garden was quite unlike Hannah's, although it was roughly the same shape and size.

Patrick's was stone-flagged around an ancient sundial. The beds on either side were filled with shrubs, and butterflies were everywhere. There were three buddleias, which accounted for the butterflies. Butterflies? Some memory nudged her mind but vanished before she could pin it down. She tried to work out why he'd chosen these particular shrubs and decided that he'd included something for every season of the year. Was he indeed a man for all seasons? Probably, yes.

Between where she stood and Spring Cottage lay the backs of other houses, shops, and cottages, including the inn where Alice worked in the evenings. All roofed with blue slate. House martins wheeled and tittered above the rooftops, now and then swooping to nests concealed under the eaves. The sky was clouding over with puffs of cotton wool. Far off on the hillside she could hear the drone of harvesters.

Jonah burst through her reverie, bearing bags of sandwiches and bottled drinks he had got from the pub. He smelt of beer.

"Ham and lettuce," he said, laying out the refreshments on the table. "Beer."

"I don't drink."

"I couldn't get through the day without my bottled cheer."

Why didn't she drink, indeed? Because her uncle had forbidden it? No, because she'd seen too many down and outs lurching around with bottles in their hand in the city. Because drinking led to a loss of control. Because she didn't like the taste much.

"Thank you, Jonah. I really appreciate everything . . . and I mean everything."

He was frowning. "Look at those roses. I'll have to deadhead, or there won't be another flowering. Hannah and I laid out this garden, you know. I wanted a lawn here but she wouldn't have it. She wanted gravel." He sighed, and then brightened. "But she lets me deadhead and water in the evenings."

He wandered off to a shed under the wrought-iron stairs and came back with a basket and a pair of secateurs. "Won't she be pleased when she comes back?"

Minty said, "What about the shop, Jonah? Oughtn't we to open up again? What about the man who wanted a discount on that book?"

He was tetchy with her. "Can't you see I've got more important things to do?"

"I've other people to see this afternoon."

"Not my problem . . . ah . . . isn't this rose a beauty?" He cut off a deep red bloom and put it in his button-hole.

Minty laughed, shrugged, and went back to open the shop.

Alice was banging on the door already. She manoeuvred the pushchair into the shop, keeping it away from the books so that little Marie couldn't pull them off the shelves. "Minty, guess what! I went down to Spring Cottage to say thank you this morning, and there was this nice electrician. Did you know he was coming today? And just as he was telling me that you were working up here, Mrs Collins walked in, bold as brass. Then, if you please, Mrs Guinness drove up with her son in his truck and they started dumping stuff in the cottage. Mrs Collins got all upset because they'd parked right in front of her and she didn't want to back her car up."

Alice took a deep breath, holding back a laugh. "Then the traffic warden came up and they had a right to do. Me and the electrician, we were killing ourselves. His name's Dwayne, by the way, and he was at school with one of my mates from the tech. Anyway, by the time the stuff was all unloaded . . ."

Minty said, "However much was there? I was expecting a few things that she'd taken from Spring Cottage."

"A mountain of stuff. Rugs and cartons and no less than three clocks."

"Three!"

"Would there be things from the other two cottages as well? She didn't much like my seeing everything, so she kept saying loudly that she had been taking the stuff for repair and she ought to charge you for storage."

"Oh dear," cried Minty, wiping her eyes on Jonah's handkerchief. "I never thought of her having taken things from the other cottages as well."

"If you like, I could help you check the inventories of all three places after you close up here. Don't rush yourself. Dwayne won't be finished till quite late. He's just putting in a makeshift ring main for now, so you'll have power downstairs. He'll have to come back tomorrow and do the upstairs."

"Nice, is he?" asked Minty.

Alice shrugged, but her colour had risen. "I suppose."

The shop door burst open and in came Venetia Wootton, looking far from her usual serene self. Alice recognised storm signals and took herself and the pushchair out of the shop, mouthing to Minty that she would see her later.

Venetia collapsed into a chair by the till, dropping her handbag and an expensive-looking brochure on the floor. She ran both hands back through her hair, closing her eyes.

Minty ran for a glass of water. Venetia drank it. "They gave us champagne, far too much of it, and then some lunch. I couldn't eat anything, and neither could anyone else."

Minty thought, *Florence's raspberry pavlovas. What will happen to them?* Of her own accord Minty turned the "Open" sign to read "Closed", bolted the door, and pulled down the blind. "The meeting didn't go as planned?"

Venetia sighed. "Oh, it went exactly as they'd planned. I sat there and didn't say a thing. Not a word. I let them do it. What could I have said, anyway? Oh, and Annie Phillips gave me this to give to you." She fished a pay packet out of her pocket and handed it over.

"Thanks. It's for Mrs Guinness."

Venetia wasn't listening. "I can't think!" Again she ran her fingers through her hair. "Everyone's shattered. My poor stewards! Looking after the treasures at the Hall is their whole life. What about the little widow who's been making a new white work coverlet for the Blue Bedroom? It's taken her six months so far and . . . I can't stay and see it happen. I'll make some excuse . . . go back to New Zealand . . ."

Minty crouched beside Venetia, stroking her hands. "You won't run away."

Venetia picked up the brochure and riffled through it. "I'd better show this to Hugh. Maybe he can think of something. No. I've got to face it. It's the end. Another little bit of Old England sold to the highest bidder."

Minty felt a clutch at her heart. "The Hall is to be sold?"

"No, not exactly. I must go. I told Hannah I'd ring the hospital, see how she got through the op. Can you cope here by yourself?"

"Yes, for an hour or two. But tell me, Venetia. What's to happen at the Hall?"

"I can't talk now. I'm in such a state I can't think straight."

"Yes, but . . . if the Hall isn't to be sold, then . . ."

"Can you lock up when you've had enough? I'll see whom I can get to help you tomorrow."

Minty thought, *My job with the holiday lets? My father . . . ? What's happening?* She tried to see things from Venetia's point of view. Venetia was in a bad way. Minty mustn't be selfish and press her now. She said, trying to be sensible, "There's lots I don't know. About orders, everything."

Venetia wasn't listening. "Come round and have a bite to eat with us tomorrow evening about six-thirty. You know where we live? We can talk then."

She walked out of the shop as if she were daydreaming, hardly waiting for Minty to unbolt the door.

Minty saw a customer looming at the door and realised she hadn't turned the "Open" sign back again. Mechanically she turned the sign round and wedged the door open. It was a fine afternoon and there was money to be made if she could only keep her mind on the job . . . and not panic about the hints Venetia had dropped. If the Hall was not being sold, then . . . what?

"Have you a good local guide, and a map of the district?"

"I want something to read on holiday—Jilly Cooper? Something light?"

"Something for my little boy . . . something he can't tear up. He's just at that age . . ."

Minty made a tremendous effort to bring her mind back from where it wanted to go, speculating on the future of the Hall . . . and her father. She listened to the customers and made a note of everything they asked for that Hannah had not stocked. More paperbacks, obviously. A good local guide. Leaflets giving the opening times for the Hall. A guide to local walks in the locality. Maps showing tourist attractions.

Minty smiled and smiled and took money and promised to see if she could find—whatever it was she didn't have. And tried not to worry.

She wondered how Jonah was getting on outside in the garden, but didn't have a minute to look.

At four o'clock a woman walked into the shop as if she owned it, looked around and sniffed. She wore good but dowdy clothes, a hairstyle forty years out of date, and a long nose apt for sniffing. "Huh!" she said.

"Yes?" said Minty, coming forward with a smile. A dissatisfied customer, perhaps?

"I only heard this morning that Hannah was in hospital, so I was extremely surprised to see the shop was open. Who might you be, may I ask? And how did you get in?"

Minty disliked the newcomer's attitude but tried not to let it show. "Venetia Wootton has returned from abroad and taken charge. I'm Araminta Cardale. Mrs Wootton asked me to open up for her for the time being."

The woman treated the shop and Minty to a glare. "Opening up is one thing, changing everything around is another. Hannah always keeps the hardback books in the front of the shop, because they have a better mark-up."

Minty quailed. "Yes, but customers like to . . ."

"This shop, as dear Lady Cardale says, is an oasis of culture in the wilderness. We do not wish to attract the common tourist. What have you done with the good coffee-table books? Was it you who made a mess of the window display?"

Lady the cat woke up from her doze, yawned, surveyed the newcomer and plopped down from the window to make his stately way to the back of the shop.

The woman's nostrils became pinched. "Horrible animal! Most unhealthy to have cats around!" The newcomer held out her hand to Minty. "The keys, please."

Minty put her hands behind her back. "Venetia Wootton left me in charge."

A customer came in, tried to edge around the angular newcomer, failed and went out again.

Minty thought, *There won't be many sales made if this woman takes over*. She said, "Shall we ring Venetia and get her to sort it out?"

"Ring who you like, but remember this, you will have to answer for what you do to Hannah." Saying which, she strode back out of the shop.

Minty sank on to the one comfortable chair behind the desk. She had had enough for one day. Was it only this morning that Lucas had been pressing her to return to the city with him? How long ago that seemed. This new trouble at the Hall. What did it all mean? She wished Patrick were around to . . . no, she must stand on her own two feet.

She rang Venetia, partly to see if she were feeling better, and partly to tell her of the latest invasion.

"Yes, my dear," said Venetia. "I'm a lot calmer now. I rang the hospital and they said Hannah came through the operation very well. I gave Hugh the brochure and he's looking at it. We can have a good talk about it tomorrow, as I fear . . . well, if it has to be, it has to be. Your visitor sounds like Felicity Chickweed . . . sorry, her name's really Chickward, but there is a certain likeness . . ."

Minty laughed. "To a hen? Yes, well, she did try to gobble me up."

"And failed, I'm sure. No, my dear. Don't worry. The hospital say it's not likely that Hannah will be able to come back to work for a couple of months, and how she'll manage the stairs to her flat then, I don't know. So you see: you're an answer to prayer."

Lady the cat was waiting at the door when Minty locked up, and they walked down the street together. Minty tried to drag her mind back to the cottage and what she might find there. As she reached the bottom of the street, she averted her eyes from the little bridge that looked so charming in the sunlight. How could she ever bear to look at it again, now she knew it was where her mother had died?

She let herself in to Spring Cottage and wondered if she'd wandered into a junk shop by mistake. Alice had said Mrs Guinness had brought back a truckload of stuff and Alice had not exaggerated. Mrs Guinness herself was sitting in one of the fireside chairs, a tray of tea things beside her, busy with some paperwork.

"About time, too," said Mrs Guinness. "We've been playing at shops now, have we? Neglecting our proper job?"

Minty held her tongue. There was no sign of the electrician, but new wiring had been looped and tacked up around the room. She depressed a light switch and a centre light came on—minus lampshade. Presumably the lampshade was in one of the boxes on the floor.

"I think you'll find everything's there," said Mrs Guinness. "I would have brought everything in the back way, which would have been more convenient and avoided a parking ticket, but someone had most inconsiderately jammed the back door with a chair, so I've added the parking ticket to what you owe me. I've just been totting up all the repair bills, transport costs, and so on." She tore a sheet of paper off a pad and held it out to Minty. "Over and above my wages, I make it two hundred and fifty pounds. Cash preferred."

Minty took the piece of paper and sank on to the chair opposite Mrs Guinness. The nerve of the woman, first "borrowing" all those things and then demanding a ransom for returning them. Minty had no stomach for a fight after such a terrible day.

She thought, *I'll let Ms Phillips deal with this. No, I can't do that. Ms Phillips wants me to show her what I'm made of, so I have to deal with it myself. Only, how?*

Chapter Nine

The front door burst open and in bustled Cynthia Collins, wearing a black and green striped top over a black skirt.

"So you're in at last! I've called back twice today to see you and got a parking ticket for my pains. I told that warden I had only been there two minutes, but he said I had and that fool of an electrician backed him up. As for Mrs Guinness, such rudeness!" She caught sight of her and changed colour. "Oh, Mrs Guinness? I thought you'd be gone hours ago."

Minty hadn't a clue how to deal with either of them and, to judge by their body language, it wouldn't take much for them to be at one another's throats. The door banged open again and in came a pushchair, followed by Alice, who hadn't expected company, either.

"Come in, dear Alice," said Minty, helping Alice to ease the pushchair into the small space left by the fireplace. She turned to Mrs Collins. "As you can see, I'm a trifle busy at the moment. Perhaps we can talk some other time?"

Mrs Collins shrugged. "Oh very well. It's nothing urgent."

Nothing urgent? thought Minty. *When she admits to having called here a couple of times today already?* She showed Mrs Collins out.

Alice and Mrs Guinness were eyeing one another with barely concealed dislike. Minty felt a surge of anger at the way she was being messed around by everyone. She didn't allow herself to think about what she was going to do. She tore up Mrs Guinness's "repair" bill and, taking the woman's pay packet out of her pocket, laid it on the mantelpiece.

"Thank you for bringing everything back, Mrs Guinness. I estimate the cost of your having 'hired' all these things for so long will cover your estimate for repairs. Alice is now going to help me check the inventories for all three cottages. If they're in order, you shall have your back wages tomorrow."

Mrs Guinness went a mottled red. Too late, Minty realised she shouldn't have tried to get the better of the woman in front of a witness.

"You'll regret this!"

"Alice, would you take Marie out in the garden for a moment?"

Alice looked amused, but obeyed.

"Mrs Guinness, if you want to keep your job, you play by my rules."

The woman heaved herself to her feet. "I take my orders from Simon at the Hall and not from you. You won't last five minutes, mark my words."

"Perhaps not, but while I'm managing the lets, my word goes. Now, do you want to clean the other two cottages on Saturday, or not?"

Mrs Guinness snatched the wage packet from the mantelpiece and, with an air of triumph, stowed it in her handbag. "I'll think it over," she said and stalked out of the front door.

Minty found herself giggling weakly. Then she went out to find Alice in the garden. Little Marie was sitting in the middle of a patch of pink phlox, looking a perfect picture, while Alice herself was resting on a wooden garden bench in the shade of an apple tree. That bench had certainly not been there before. Mrs Guinness must have tried to bring her treasures in by the lane and the garden to start with, got as far as the back door before finding the way blocked, and left the garden bench there.

"Got rid of her, then?" asked Alice.

Minty confessed, "She got the better of me, and goodness knows if she'll turn up for work on Saturday."

"She will. She's doing all sorts of jobs, saving for a holiday on the Costa Brava in Spain."

For the next hour and a half the two girls checked over and sorted out the pile of stuff against the inventories. They made separate heaps to be returned to the other two cottages. The clocks, rugs, kettles, crockery and cutlery, towels, sheets, lampshades and bedside lamps that had been removed from Spring Cottage were all put back into place. Alice even helped hang curtains upstairs and downstairs before taking Marie off for her supper and bed. She didn't work at the pub on Mondays, because it was such a quiet night.

"I'll add this time to your worksheet," promised Minty. "I don't know what I'd have done without you. If there's ever anything I can do for you . . ."

"Maybe there is," said Alice, looking uncomfortable. "I heard there might be a part-time job going at the bookshop. Would you put in a good word for me?"

Minty blinked. She wanted that job herself. She temporised. "What about Marie?"

"If the job paid well enough, I could afford a childminder. There's something else, but say if you'd rather not."

Minty thought, *Patrick warned me . . . there's no such thing as a free meal . . . or a favour that doesn't have to be repaid.*

Alice stowed a sleepy Marie into her pushchair, avoiding Minty's eye. "It's just that you did say, about going back to church. I'd like it, really; only not when there's anyone else there to point at me. Or at Marie. I know I ought to have her christened. I always meant to, but Mum doesn't hold with it when there's no father. What do you think?"

"Yes," said Minty, surprising both of them. "I'd love to be godmother if that's what you want."

"Not yet, mind. I've got to get used to going into church first. I don't know what half of it means, really. Maybe there's some kind of course for beginners? But if you could just come with me one day when there's no one else there? While I just . . . well . . . see if I could cope?"

Minty kissed Alice. "Bless you, dear. I'd be proud."

Minty switched on the lights and found herself dissatisfied with the way the cottage looked. She had liked its bareness and sense of space before. Now there were clocks ticking and lampshades swinging and bric-a-brac twinkling. And the curtains were, to put it mildly, overdoing the floral bit. Minty told herself she ought to be grateful she now had a spare set of sheets and enough pots and pans, even if nothing matched and they had been chosen by someone with very different tastes. China with flowers on it was well enough, but china with red and black stripes was over the top.

She drew the curtains and read the note the electrician had left her. A night storage heater was arriving the next day, plus a water heater. Until then, he hoped she could manage. She boiled a kettle to wash out some underclothes and a couple of T-shirts. She really needed a couple of washable dresses. Perhaps she should visit the charity shop the next day, on the way to work?

She was thinking of going to bed, when there came another knock on the front door and in came Mrs Collins, breathing heavily and looking somewhat less co-ordinated than usual. "I'm sorry to disturb you so late."

Minty pushed the better of the two fireside chairs towards Mrs Collins.

"I suppose I must start by making you an apology. The Reverend told me your name was Martha and that you were Sir Micah's niece, but I understand now that . . ." She swallowed.

"Think nothing of it," said Minty, wondering what had driven the woman to call on her three times in a day.

Mrs Collins gave Minty a pop-eyed stare. "Well, I must say you might have corrected me earlier. There was I asking you to deal with the coffee, as if you were nobody in particular. Whatever will people think!"

Minty thought, *Ah-ha! So that's what rules you, is it? What other people think?*

"I couldn't work out at first why you weren't living up at the Hall, but then I realised poor dear Lady Cardale must be out of her mind, what with Sir Micah so ill, Simon wanting to change everything, Gemma getting engaged, and the charity ball to arrange. I don't wonder at her not feeling able to cope with an unknown step-daughter as well."

"It's a difficult situation for us all."

Mrs Collins's colour had risen while she reflected on her error, but subsided as she recalled the purpose of her visit. "Well, now we've got that settled, I wondered if you'd be so good as to help me out in another matter. Mrs Chickward—you won't know her—a most interfering woman who thinks she can run everything round here—over my dead body, I say. Well, she fancies herself as a flower arranger and when I ventured to criticise one of her arrangements she turned really nasty. Just to spite me for the flower arranging class at the fête. I'm entered for the flower arranging class at the fête on Saturday—the theme is 'A Rainbow'—but I'll scarcely have time to turn round, let alone arrange flowers in the morning. I've overall responsibility for the fête, you see. Quartermaster General, you might say, har, har! In charge of the setting up and supplies. Everything. So I wondered if you could just—well—start the flower arrangement for me and I could add the finishing touches."

Minty slept badly. In her dreams she was a child again, running down a long corridor, opening doors on either side to search for someone . . . for her mother? Finally she ran up some stairs and came to a locked door. She tried and tried to turn the handle, and finally it gave way under her hands and opened to reveal . . .

Minty shot up in bed, breathing hard. It had only been a dream, she told herself. As a child she'd had lots of nightmares. She'd learned very quickly that she mustn't disturb her uncle and aunt when she woke from a bad dream. "If you have to cry, then cry quietly."

It was nearly seven and though the sun hadn't yet broken through, it was threatening to do so at any minute. A blackbird was singing outside . . . no, not a blackbird. Someone outside was whistling "Amazing Grace".

She scrambled into ancient shorts, a T-shirt and sandals and went downstairs. Lady the cat had deserted her bed during the night but had been busy outside, judging by the appearance of a headless mouse on the back doorstep. Lady arrived from nowhere and rubbed his head against Minty's legs. Minty put some fresh food down for the cat, splashed cold water over her face, and stepped out into the garden. As always she was soothed by the beauty of it, the wildness, the sense of space.

A tramp was sitting on the bench under the apple tree. Patrick, wearing his gardening clothes and still whistling, though more quietly now.

She hesitated, remembering that she hadn't brushed out her hair. It didn't look as if he'd shaved, either. There was a strong dark shadow on his face—almost designer stubble.

"Ready for breakfast?" Patrick retrieved a large basket from under the garden seat. "I heard you hadn't got any hot water yet, so I thought I'd share my breakfast with you. Don't look so surprised. Of course I can cook. And do. Now and then. Proper coffee in a percolator, milk in a bottle, sugar in that glass container, butter in the pat, raspberry jam, knives, spoons and . . ." With a flourish he unwrapped a clean tea-towel, ". . . hot croissants!"

Frozen and put in the oven at the last minute, thought Minty. She also thought, *There's no such thing as a free meal.* She helped herself all the same. There was a busy silence until Patrick tossed the last crumbs out for the birds. There was a deep cleft in his left cheek when he smiled.

Minty stretched out her arms and legs, arching her back. The sun was breaking through the early morning mist and they sat in dappled sunshine.

"I hear," said Patrick, "you got the better of Mrs Guinness. Congratulations. I'd been told you were so meek and mild that you'd let everyone walk over you."

Minty was amused. "Am I hearing the authentic words of the Reverend Cecil? As for Mrs Guinness, I think honours are evenly drawn."

He crossed one leg over his knee and leaned back, closing his eyes. "I had her niece waiting for me at the office when I got back last night. She wanted to know if she could sue her aunt for taking back one valuable gift—to wit, a garden bench—that said aunt had bestowed upon her niece." The recollection amused him.

Minty was beginning to understand the way Patrick's mind worked. "I bet you warned her about receiving stolen goods?"

Patrick's eyebrows peaked and his grin deepened, but all he said was, "I doubt we'll hear any more about it."

Minty laughed. She shucked off her shoes and tucked her bare feet under her. "Patrick, I think I've done something rather stupid. Mrs Collins wants me to substitute for her in the flower arranging competition at the fête on Saturday. Apparently she's been taking the high ground, criticising everyone else's flower arrangements till they assumed she was an expert. She didn't disabuse them. When she got stuck with doing the flowers last week, she bandaged her finger to give herself an excuse for doing them badly. Only I came to the rescue and did them for her.

"Mrs Chickward has called Mrs Collins's bluff by entering her in the competition and Mrs Collins is terrified of being shown up. She threw herself on my mercy, asked me to substitute for her. She said she'd tell the organisers I was taking over. I said I'd do it but . . . I'm uneasy. Tell me I haven't made a mistake."

Patrick slid down till his neck was resting on the back of the bench. "Mrs Collins is an incomer with brilliant organisational skills. She's responsible for the fête on Saturday: marquees, supplies, side shows, stewarding, everything. Short of torrential rain, she will raise an amazing sum of money for charity. That's why the village puts up with her—ah—frailties. Mrs Collins has been seen to nick Mills & Boons paperbacks from the second-hand stall in the market. She's got plenty of money, so why nick them? It raises questions in the mind about her life with the lately deceased Mr Collins."

"You mean she cheats."

"She steals. So be careful. But . . ." He shook with soundless laughter. "You have to hand it to her, don't you? She's ousted Felicity Chickward from the chairmanship of the Women's Institute, and replaced her as churchwarden. On the other hand, Felicity ousted her as a governor of the local school. Felicity is of old county stock and right-hand woman to Lady Cardale, for whom she's organising the charity ball that follows soon after the fête. Both ladies play to win. Much more hangs on the flower arranging competition than the gaining or losing of a silver cup. You've been dropped right in the middle of it. I can't wait!"

Minty winced. Then, nerving herself for the difficult topic, said, "There's something else. Venetia went to this big meeting up at the Hall yesterday, and . . ."

She told Patrick everything she'd seen and heard. He sat upright and rubbed his ear. "You only caught a glimpse of the brochure, but it had a helicopter on the front above a photo of the Hall?"

She nodded. "The title was something like 'A Clarion Call to the Future'. What does it mean? Venetia said the Hall wasn't being sold exactly, but she was distressed, talked about it being the end of everything."

He resumed his former posture, lying almost horizontal and closing his eyes.

She waited. Eventually she said, "Is that a bubble I see above your head enclosing the word 'thinks'?"

He sat upright with a jerk, his eyes restless. "You're getting a sight of this precious document tonight? Will you ring me afterwards?" He began to stow the breakfast things in his basket.

"Yes, but Patrick—what does it mean?"

"It means that the heir apparent is trying on his dad's crown. I've heard Sir Micah's hardly fit to conduct business at the moment and, anyway, he wouldn't make major changes at the Hall now."

"What's your phone number?"

He searched through his pockets without result. "I thought I had a card on me."

She said, "Put it in my mobile phone memory."

He followed her into the cottage, almost bumping his head on a low beam. While she found her mobile, he looked around with a carefully bland expression on his face. "Do you like it here?"

She looked around, too. "It was fine when it was stripped bare, but I must confess that it's not my taste now." She handed him her mobile and he keyed in his number. She said, "I'd ask you to eat with me one evening, but the oven has only one temperature and that's too hot. Perhaps I could cook you a meal in your kitchen?"

"I thought you'd never ask. Perhaps Saturday after the fête? Or Sunday? I'll ring you." He nearly bumped his head again on the way out. She hadn't realised he was so tall. "Well, I must be off . . ."

They stood an arms' length apart in the garden under the apple tree. She thought, *I do like him so much. He's so comfortable to be with. He doesn't do anything without a reason, so why did he wear those old clothes and not shave before he came here? To show me what he was like at his worst? Though why a possible suitor would want to show himself at his worst, I don't know.*

I did the same, come to think of it, with my hair all over the place. Now why did I do that? To show him how I look at my worst? It's almost as if we were courting, but not yet ready to call it that. I wonder what it would be like to kiss him. I wonder what it would be like to . . .

She felt her face and neck grow red and looked away from him. *I wonder what it would be like*, she thought, *to have him kiss me*. And more. She'd never gone so far in her thoughts about a man before and was amazed at her body's reaction.

He cleared his throat.

She returned her eyes to him but lifted them no higher than his hands. Strong, sinewy hands, clenched round the basket. She thought, *He's ugly, yes, but very attractive. When he's old, he'll look like an eagle.*

"I must go," he said. "Do be careful, won't you?"

Something flashed in the sunlight behind his head. A reflection off glass in one of the cottages nearby? She recoiled. "We're being watched!"

"That'll be your old nurse, Nanny Proud, upstairs with her binoculars. She's housebound, but knows everything that goes on in the village. She'll expect you to visit her."

"I don't remember her." But perhaps she did. She frowned. She kept getting flashes of things remembered, or half-remembered. An opening door on to a light, blue-tinted space. A rocking horse? Someone with loving arms in a white dress . . . was that her mother, or . . . ? Butterflies?

"Do you remember . . . no, you obviously don't."

Without another word he lifted his hand in salute and walked away down the garden. As he disappeared through the trees she spotted a piece of paper lying on the grass under the bench. It must have dropped out of his pocket. She picked it up and called his name, but he'd already gone.

The paper had been folded and unfolded so many times, it was coming apart at the seams. She tried to refold it exactly as it had been, taking it into the cottage and laying it flat on the table. She hadn't meant to read it, but the first thing she saw was her own name . . . Araminta Cardale . . . written in capital letters across the top of the page. Next came two names she didn't recognise, both crossed out. Then "Mrs Proud, Mrs Collins, Jonah & Ruby." She scanned down more names she didn't recognise. Towards the bottom, in the same ink as her own name, was "Hannah". Some names were in pen and some in pencil. His writing was bold, sometimes reasonably neat, sometimes scrawling across the page.

Minty had never seen a list like it before. Perhaps it was a list of people he intended to visit? She folded the paper up again and put it behind the clock.

Chapter Ten

Tuesday passed in a busy blur. She sent an email to Ms Phillips to report on the electrician's progress, spent some time cleaning the cottage and checked on the mousetraps at Riverside Cottages—now empty. Possibly Lady the cat had seen to that problem.

On her way to work, she paid a visit to the charity shop and was welcomed by Ruby, her fellow slave of the church coffee rota. From behind the counter Ruby produced two crease-resistant short-sleeved dresses. They had high bodices and were long in the skirt, clinging prettily to Minty's figure. One was in cornflower blue, one in dull red, and both suited Minty to perfection. The dresses needed lifting at the shoulders—which Ruby insisted she would do that evening, free of charge. Ruby wanted a ridiculously small sum for the two dresses and said she'd look out a good skirt for Minty as well.

Much warmed by this encounter, Minty plunged into work at the bookshop. She spent time with the customers, asking where they came from—if they were tourists—and what sorts of books they were looking for, if they lived locally. When trade was slack, she explored the recesses of the shop, where she made some unwelcome discoveries.

A huge cupboard at the back was full of cartons, most of which had never even been opened. Inside were rolls of gaily coloured posters advertising books long past their sell-by date, bundles of pens, baseball caps, trinkets and even sweatshirts advertising various books. These seemed to be freebies from various publishers whose books—unsold for the most part—adorned the shelves.

What on earth did Hannah mean to do with them? Minty remembered Felicity Chickward saying that this bookshop was an oasis of culture in the middle of a wilderness. Did Hannah think merchandising beneath her?

An even more unwelcome discovery was an index file in the bottom drawer of the desk, together with a customer account book. The cards recorded details of customers who had ordered books but not collected them. Some of the records dated back years, while the books concerned—a motley collection—languished in a dark corner, taking up space without any foreseeable prospect of being sold.

A whole shelf was occupied by dictionaries and hotel guides, almanacs, film guides, and so on. To Minty's horror, all were out of date.

She must have made a disgusted noise, because a long nose poked itself over her shoulder, took in the situation and said, "Humph! Pulp them, what?" The comment came from a tall, thin, scholarly looking man who'd been browsing in the background for some time. Minty vaguely recalled him having visited the shop a couple of times before.

"Can I help you?" she asked.

"Going bankrupt, are we? Any first editions around? Preferably signed?"

"Are you a dealer?" She'd heard of those but not met one before.

"A collector. Not that there's much to collect here." Yet she recalled he'd been hovering around a certain section of the bookshop both yesterday, and today.

She said, "All right, what have I missed?"

He held up his hands and rolled his eyes, projecting a wonderful innocence that, in a man of fifty plus, looked faintly comic.

"New here, aren't you? You're not missing much, I'd say."

She took in his shabby but originally good clothes, the well-brushed greying hair, the long bony hands and feet. "Ex-schoolteacher?"

"I took early retirement after I was knifed by a fifteen-year-old who objected to my failing him for an exam. What's your excuse for hanging around a bookshop?"

She counted the reasons off on her fingers. "I was standing by the door when Mrs Wootton fell off the ladder; my people come from hereabouts and I like creating order out of chaos."

"Ditto, ditto," he said, his long nose pointing at different parts of the shop. "What you missed—though I bet you'd have come round to it—is a first edition of a catalogue of jazz records. I know it looks as if it ought to be in the sale box, but, believe me, it's greatly sought after. Perhaps we could come to an arrangement about the price?"

"His name is Jeremy Lightowler, widower, of this parish," said Minty, reporting to Venetia and Hugh over supper that evening. "He's forgotten more about books than I've ever had a chance to learn, and he's bored with life in retirement. He hung around the shop all morning, amusing me and the other customers, listening to my half-baked ideas for bringing the shop into the twenty-first century. He's nice—and available."

"Available?" said Venetia, frowning. "But Minty, I'd hardly thought of hiring anyone else."

Minty was firm. "Listen, Venetia. If Hannah's not returning to the shop . . ."

"No, I don't think she can."

"Then you need to do something about it. I don't know much about selling books, but I've been listening to what people want and I've used my eyes when I've visited good bookshops in the past. At the moment your shop looks to me as if it might be losing money."

"Oh!" said Venetia, exchanging glances with Hugh. "Yes, but it was a family concern and we thought perhaps Jonah might one day be well enough to . . ."

"I doubt it. Don't get me wrong. I like Jonah. He was very good to me the other day when things got me down. He's a lovely man, but he's never going to be able to run a business, is he?"

Venetia sighed and shook her head. "Oh dear. This is all terrible. You see, Minty, we can't see any future for the bookshop, so taking on someone else is out of the question. We thought maybe you could tide us over till the end of the season and then we'll have to close."

Minty swallowed. "Why? Is it because of Simon and his ideas for the Hall?"

Venetia looked miserable. "Come into the sitting room. Hugh will explain while I make coffee."

The sitting room overlooked a well-kept garden. Hugh handed Minty the brochure and invited her to take a seat in a brocade-covered armchair.

Minty's hand trembled. The brochure was a glossy affair that must have been expensive to produce. She scanned the pages, feeling progressively more shattered as she read on. She put it down and stared into a bleak feature.

"I'm so sorry," said Hugh, patting her hand. "It's your family home they're tearing up, isn't it?"

Minty took a deep breath. "They want to turn it into a private health club? A clinic? With a helicopter pad? But . . . !"

"It's bad, yes. Venetia was devastated. But we have to consider the other fellow's point of view. The Hall costs a bomb to maintain and has been losing money."

"I'm not surprised, if it's run as badly as the restaurant."

"There's a section on the restaurant at the back. It's to be turned into a fashionable, high-priced eaterie. Simon's brought in a consultant to design it, give it a new look."

Venetia set the coffee before them and said unhappily, "It makes sense, I suppose, but it's going to have knock-on consequences throughout the neighbourhood."

Minty said, "They want to strip the Hall down to a shell. So where's everything supposed to go? The family portraits, the Jacobean beds, the Regency furniture, the books, the porcelain and coin collections, the curios . . . everything that's been so carefully collected over the years?"

"Sold off through one of the big auction houses, I suppose, to pay for the necessary repairs and restructuring. You say that the holiday lets will also be sold off? It seems they're more trouble than they are worth."

Minty shivered. Her world was disintegrating around her. "When the rooms are stripped, they'll be equipped with all these machines supplied by this firm . . . what do they call themselves . . . ? Healthwise Products Inc. I've never heard of them."

"I did some digging around," said Hugh. "They're a subsidiary of a large American corporation. As a matter of interest, Simon and his mother are both directors of the company that will be taking over the Hall and running it as a clinic. So they stand to gain by this venture."

"Not Gemma?"

"Apparently not."

Minty took another deep breath. "Sorry. It's the shock. You'd think I wouldn't be able to remember much of the Hall, but I keep getting flashes of memory." She leafed through the brochure again. "'Special diets'. They propose to bring in a trained dietician? Does this mean Florence Thornby loses her job? Surely the family will still need someone to look after them?"

"Gemma's getting married and Lady Cardale plans to retire to the London flat," said Venetia. "As for Simon, it's anyone's guess. Bermuda, I should think. It isn't only Florence who's going to lose her job. There's to be a clean sweep of everyone who works there at the moment. Doris goes. She runs the shop—not that it's much cop, but it does give her a reason to go on living: her husband died three years ago and she hasn't got over it yet. Then I'm to go, and all the other stewards. I think only Miles and his staff are to be kept on to run the estate—or what will be left of it."

"What about Ms Phillips? She isn't employed by Lady Cardale but by Sir Micah. Was she at the meeting? What did she have to say about it?"

"He's past it, they say. Neither he nor Annie was at the meeting. She usually has a business conference with him first thing every morning when he's at his best after a night's sleep. She knew Simon was preparing some big plan or other, but she didn't know what it was. He presented her with the brochure before the meeting began, and told her to take it up to Sir Micah, 'as it might amuse him'."

Minty said, "You mean he knew nothing about it beforehand? That Simon broke the news to him by sending him a brochure? That's cruel!"

Venetia shrugged. "He handed the Hall over to Lisa to run, and she's handed it over to Simon. What can he say?"

Minty struggled to gain a sense of perspective. "Venetia, why did you say that this was the end of everything? Presumably the Hall in its new guise will bring in money and jobs?"

"Not for the village, it won't. The only people the Hall will employ in future will be the lowest paid, the cleaners, the people who work in the kitchens under the new dietician. Even there, Simon's talking about having contract cleaners coming in from town."

Hugh took up the story. "You see, Minty, we've no manufacturing industry here. We've no bank, no regular bus service to the next town, no library except a mobile one. The old families have grown tired and our youngsters have fled the nest. We've grown to depend on incomers like Cynthia Collins. Without them, we'd lapse into a coma. Tourism has been our salvation. The tourists come to see the Hall, they spend their money in the village and that keeps our shops open. Without the tourists . . ."

". . . the bookshop will have to close," said Venetia. "So you see, there's not much point in doing anything about replacing Hannah. I'm so sorry, Minty. So very sorry."

Minty cycled home trying not to think. What a blow! She'd returned to find that everything she'd thought she depended upon—her very roots—were to be pulled up and thrown away. She wondered a little frantically what use it had been to return at all, if there was to be no future for her—or for the village.

She stopped opposite the church and looked down at the peaceful scene. It wasn't late, but colour was fading from the landscape. Lights were beginning to come on in houses and in the flats over the shops. Someone was practising on the organ in the church.

Television and radio stations leaked their voices on to the evening air. A woman was out watering her hanging baskets.

Far down the street a pub door opened and light shot across the forecourt. Minty thought she saw Jonah making his way to the pub. It would be no kindness to tell him what was going to happen. Although he probably knew already as there wasn't much hidden in a village.

The shop window beside her sported yet another poster advertising the village fête. Venetia had said they usually took a stand to sell books and if Minty wanted to do something about it, it was all right with her, but she had no enthusiasm for it this year. Both she and Hugh were already booked by Mrs Collins, one to take money at the gate and the other on bric-a-brac. Minty thought about Mrs Collins and the flower-arranging class.

Minty hadn't paid much attention to the right-hand side of the street before. There was a very pretty galleried run of shops just below the church and the post office. Minty dragged her bike on to the pavement and walked along to inspect them.

First came a Chinese restaurant, takeaway, and dine-in. A solitary diner in the window had *The Times* propped up in front of him, concentrating on the crossword: Mr Jeremy Lightowler, retired teacher and collector of books. He didn't see her, and although she wanted to talk to him, she didn't think this was an appropriate moment. Three other tables were occupied; Minty recognised several of the diners as holidaymakers who had been in the bookshop that day.

Next came the two empty shop premises, cavernously dark. Then a cards and china shop with an overcrowded window full of ornaments Minty wouldn't want to buy.

If Hugh was right, soon there would be more empty shops in the village. She looked across at the bookshop—no lights on there. However, Patrick's office windows were lit up.

She hesitated. If anyone saw her walking into Patrick's house, the gossips would have a field day. She could phone him and give him the information he required, but was that enough?

She squared her shoulders, wheeled her bike across the road and inspected the brass plate and two bell pushes beside Patrick's front door. One bell for the office, another for the house. She had hardly touched the office bell when the door opened and Patrick motioned her in.

"Been expecting you," he said. He was wearing his office gear, white shirt and dark trousers. He strode back into the right-hand room—his office—leaving her to park her bike in the hall and follow him. A valuable old mahogany desk sat in the middle of the room, flanked by leather-covered chairs. The room was wainscoted, with what looked like a Regency fireplace behind the desk. Old photographs of the Hall and the village hung on the walls, while built-in bookcases lined the walls.

Patrick's desk was covered with sheets of paper, plus a copy of the infamous brochure.

She collapsed into a chair and told him what she'd learned.

He nodded. "Doris—she runs the gift shop—was on the doorstep when I got back home this evening. She brought me a brochure and back copies of the accounts the staff get at their annual thank you party. She wanted to know if they could sack her just like that. Unfortunately they can because she hasn't got a contract and has only received a token payment—an honorarium—every year for her services. Most of the stewards work for love, can you believe? Doris was distressed. She said that anything else I wanted to know, she'd be at home this evening."

He picked up a half-smoked cigarette from an ashtray and took a quick drag.

She rolled her eyes but he was unaware of her disapproval. He snatched up a pencil and started scratching notes on a pad. "Read the surveyor's report on what needs doing at the Hall. Then look at the accounts for the past seven years. Compare figures from year to year."

She did so. By the time she'd finished, he was striding up and down the room, smoking. "Well?"

She was shattered. "The Hall needs an enormous amount of money spent on it and they've no option but to go ahead with the clinic. They've spent money every year on re-roofing, rewiring, drains, crumbling stone walls, but obviously not enough has been done each time."

"Idiot!" he said, but in a kindly tone. "This is typical PR spin, the sort of thing a company does when they want to introduce an unpopular measure. They shake their heads and say, tut-tut! We need to spend thirty billion on . . . whatever. Everyone's horrified. Then the chairman gives a painful smile and says, well, they might get by with spending just ten billion instead. Everyone accepts the bad news with a sigh of relief. Because it's only ten billion instead of thirty. Get it?

"Those figures were inflated for a purpose, which is to frighten everyone into abandoning the idea of keeping the Hall open to the public. The surveyor they've used this year is an old pal of Simon's. I've just come off the phone after talking to the previous surveyor, the one who's done the job for the last twenty-odd years. I always advise my clients to use him on listed buildings, because he's the best. He was surprised not to have been asked to handle the usual survey this year. He assures me the fabric of the Hall shouldn't need anything like the figure Simon proposes to spend on it. He told Simon last year that the wiring in the old wings was going to need attention within the next couple of years, but apart from retiling part of the roof over the north wing, he hadn't anticipated anything drastic having to be done in the near future."

"Which means?"

"Well," he said, drawling out the word, "I think it's a try on. Simon specialises in them. It works like this. He asks his mama for something, and she says no. So he tells everyone else that she's said he can have it. When she hears about it, she's got two options: to brand him as a liar, or to pay up. So she pays up. It works with cheques, too—or so I'm told. He's overdrawn at the bank, so he issues a cheque he knows very well will bounce. He tells his mother what he's done and rather than see him get a bad credit rating, she pays up. This time, though, he's overplayed his hand, because it's not within his mother's power to give him what he wants."

He snatched up a jacket from the back of his chair. "Let's go and see Doris. She only lives around the corner."

Notepad under arm, he ushered Minty out, slammed the door behind him while leaving all the lights on, and tore off up the street. Amused and intrigued, Minty followed him to the crossroads, where he turned right. Three houses along he rang the bell of a pretty, early Victorian house.

A thickset woman with carefully bouffant hair ushered them into a pleasantly chintzy drawing room. She turned off the television and offered coffee or a drink.

"Really, it's information we came after," said Patrick. "This is Miss Cardale, of course."

"Indeed," said Doris-from-the-gift-shop, shaking Minty's hand. "We're all so pleased you've come back. Your dear mother used to bring you to tea every year when my flower borders were at their best. You loved the lilies and we used to say, 'Don't stick your nose in the lilies, Minty, because you'll get pollen all over you.' But you always did."

"Yes, yes," said Patrick, patting his pockets in turn. Probably looking for a cigarette and not finding any. "You offered to tell me about the way the Hall has been run."

"It's such a shame, it really is, and nobody's fault. After Gemma was born, Lady Cardale couldn't go travelling around the world with Sir Micah. So, really just to give her something to do, it was decided to open the Hall to the public. Sir Micah gave her the money to make the necessary alterations—the lifts, the extra loos, the tea room, and so on—but it was understood that after a while the Hall should be self-supporting. And it was, for many years.

"We thought we were doing well. There was always some maintenance being done at the Hall, which is what you expect with an old building. Only, it wasn't enough."

"So what happened?" Patrick gave the impression of crouching in his chair, ready to spring.

"Lady Cardale became so involved in charity work that Simon took over," said Doris. "He saw straight away that instead of keeping afloat we were actually losing money. Dear Simon! What a difference he made to the old place! So exciting! The parties and the beautiful people, even models, sometimes!"

"Sir Micah had kept an eye on things?"

"We hardly saw Sir Micah till he came home to die. Such a shame, and him not really that old." She patted Minty's knee. "So sorry, dear. You can't do much when cancer gets that far advanced."

Patrick was holding back impatience. "Simon took over the day-to-day running of the Hall from his mother?"

"I wouldn't say 'day-to-day' exactly, because he was up in London on business and off visiting his friends who invite him to all those places you see on the telly, small islands with just a few big houses on them, that sort of thing. We were so proud of him when he got his flying certificate. Fancy being able to pop off to the south of France for a weekend in his own plane, whenever he wishes."

"Didn't his junketing about cost a lot?"

"He's the heir and entitled to enjoy himself, isn't he?"

"How many cars has he got?"

"Well, three I think. Yes, he sold the Ferrari earlier this year. He needs a fast car to get to the aerodrome, of course."

"Wouldn't it have helped if he'd been around more?"

"You mustn't say that. He did his best. He brought in all sorts of economies, but somehow things seemed to get worse instead of better."

Patrick looked down at his notes. "Tell us about the takings at the gift shop."

"Simon took over the ordering from me, hoping to get things cheaper. He thought he could make a bigger profit by using people he knew, but somehow the goods never arrived or he'd been cheated and they were of poor quality. Over the last few years, my sales figures have fallen by half. It's really tragic. When he told us that the Hall would be turned into a clinic at the end of the season, I asked if I couldn't continue to run the gift shop for the new clientele, but he says he can't afford to run a gift shop at a loss and really I do understand. He's going to franchise a new shop out to some big French firm. So that's me out."

Patrick looked at Minty to see if she'd registered the facts. She had. They said thank you and goodnight to Doris-from-the-gift-shop.

Doris's parting shot was, "But you must remember, none of this was Simon's fault!"

Patrick and Minty walked slowly back down to Patrick's office, where the lights were still on.

Patrick collapsed into his chair behind the desk, as if his energy had suddenly run out. "You understand, now?"

"I think so. It was all in the accounts, wasn't it? After Simon took over, he reduced the budget for expenditure on the place every year, but took out more money for his own salary, expenses, hospitality, and so on. He's been milking the Hall's revenues to underwrite his lifestyle. He wants to continue doing it, but he's run the place down so far that he can't wring any more money out of it as it stands. So he's going to hand over the Hall to these clinic people and take off into the blue with yet another lot of director's fees in his pocket."

Patrick said, in a savage tone, "But remember—none of this is Simon's fault!" He hooded his eyes, leaning back in his chair. "So what happens now, Araminta Cardale?"

"We stop him. I don't know how, but I think you do."

Nothing but his eyes showed how excited he was. "Be careful, Miss Cardale. You're playing with people's lives here."

"The village depends on the Hall being kept open to the public. What Simon wants to do is wrong. Can you stop him?"

"Easily. Ought I to do so, that's the problem!"

She eyed him with misgiving. "Are you hideously expensive? I haven't any money, you see. In fact, I owe my uncle and aunt rather a lot. But perhaps Venetia and Hugh . . ."

"This would be a freebie. In fact, it would be a positive pleasure. That's what frightens me so much. I thought I'd forgiven him and I find I haven't. I detest him so much that I've got boiling oil in my guts. You don't know about that sort of hatred, do you, Miss Cardale? You, with your pretty smile and your innocence, your loving kindness to all creatures great and small."

She put her hand to her throat, disturbed by the violence that emanated from him, even though he hadn't moved a muscle. "No," she said. "I don't think I hate anyone."

He barked out a laugh. "Let me tell you how it was, Miss Cardale. When the scandal broke, my mother was just recovering from a bout of flu. She had no energy, was inclined to tears. My father had been thinking of taking her away for a good long holiday, but at that point he began to lose important, long-term clients from the county families. He didn't want to go away with my mother then, because it would look like running away. Gossip's difficult to counter, you know. You try to scotch it and it slides out from under your hand and reappears somewhere else in a slightly different form.

"I knew all about it, of course, from day one. I was at school with Simon, and he passed the word around. Oh yes! I was small and skinny and clever and I thought fighting in the playground was stupid. So I got jumped on. Again and again. There was a group of them but Simon was the leader. He's clever, you know. Never laid a finger on me himself. I didn't tell my father. He'd got enough to worry about, and my mother had developed a cough that stopped her from sleeping. I ended up in hospital with concussion and rope burns.

"That was the last straw for my father. He closed this house. We moved to the nearest town and he joined a partnership there. My mother died the following winter. Flu, again. Complications. I went away to boarding school.

"My father's still alive. He retired as soon as I was ready to take over the practice and bought a pretty house on a clifftop and gardens down in Cornwall. But something has broken inside him and he refuses even to visit me here.

"So you see, Miss Cardale, you are offering me revenge on a plate, and I'm not sure I'm big enough to put my hatred aside and be dispassionate about this."

Chapter Eleven

Minty could feel Patrick's anger reverberate round the room. She thought, *If I touch him, he'll explode. We might both end up on the floor.* She stopped that thought.

It made her feel humble, that he could admit his hate and still fight to maintain his balance. She said, "Surely it isn't only me who wants justice done?"

"You are the moving force in this business. I can't, because I know how much I hate them. Venetia and Hugh will do nothing, because they've run out of energy to fight. Mrs Collins won't think it her business to interfere. Lady Cardale thinks her son can do no wrong and will move heaven and earth to get him what he wants. Gemma is too self-centred to care; maybe she'll grow up enough one day to realise what's been done, but it won't be this side of Christmas. Anyway, they're marrying her off to a crony of Simon's, so don't look to her for help. Many people locally will say how sorry they are that the Hall is to be closed to the public, but they won't do anything about it. You are the incomer with the old name. You are the flywheel, the switch, the one who turns on the power. If you say nothing, do nothing, then Simon will sign to the Americans. The decision is yours."

"I don't understand. I'm new here. I don't have a voice. What could I do?"

"It's because you're new here that you can see the whole picture. And because of your mother—who was much loved here—you can ask people to fight."

She was not convinced. The overhead light was turning his head into a skull. He looked ill. Sallow.

She thought, *He can't be right, can he? Is it really up to me? Dear Lord, help!*

Patrick was playing with the papers on his desk. His hand trembled.

She recognised the syndrome because it had ruled the vicarage from the early years of her childhood. Her uncle would get overwrought about something and forget to eat. His temper would be ferocious. Then Aunt Agnes would say, "Minty, your uncle needs to eat. Quick, girl. Make him a sandwich!"

She had scurried to obey and, sure enough, her uncle would calm down after he had got some food inside him.

Patrick had eaten an early breakfast with her, got home late after a long day at work to find Doris on the doorstep and probably hadn't drawn breath since. Minty pushed back her chair. "Patrick, have you eaten today?"

He blinked.

"Food," she said. "Since breakfast?"

"Er . . . no, I don't think so." He sat upright in his chair, passing his hand across his eyes. "I don't think I've got anything much in the fridge, either."

"Will the Chinese restaurant still be open? Let's go, shall we?" She picked up his jacket and handed it to him. "Do you have money and keys with you?" Just as she would have spoken to her uncle, or to a child.

He patted his pockets, nodded and turned off the lights as they went out. The Chinese restaurant was still open, with only a courting couple and a foursome of holidaymakers sitting in it. Minty recognised the tenants from Kiln Cottage, and waved to them as the proprietor came forward to seat them.

"In the window, if we may," said Minty. She didn't want to sit near the others, and she didn't want to hide the fact that she was in a restaurant with Patrick.

"My usual, Willy," said Patrick. "Miss Cardale has eaten already, I think."

"Just tea for me," said Minty.

"It will be a pleasure, Miss Cardale." A perfect English accent. He'd probably been born here.

Patrick sat down with a bump. "I suppose I ought to apologise."

"Don't speak till you've eaten." He was restless, twisting in his seat, looking about him. Not looking at her.

She thought, *Perhaps he doesn't really like me at all. I'm a Cardale, the daughter of the people who put him in hospital and ruined his family. He must hate me. I was a fool to think he could care about me. No one could. I ought to have learned that by now. My aunt told me often enough how hard and unloving I am.*

Fragrant tea came, and Willy poured for both of them. She didn't look at Patrick, but watched people outside passing under the street lights. It was a fine night, a night for a stroll under the stars. That is, if you weren't always a loner. Always lonely.

A bowl of soup arrived for Patrick. She could feel him looking at her, but refused to return his gaze. She sipped tea, still looking out of the window.

Willy put a plate at her elbow. "Miss Cardale still likes these? I hope I've remembered correctly. If there is anything else you would like, just ask."

The serving plate was adorned with flowers and leaves, fashioned from radishes and carrots. A delight to the eye. Tiny delicacies surrounded the flowers, to tempt the appetite.

She cried, "Oh!" Willy vanished.

"Don't say anything," said Patrick. "Just eat."

She glared at him, picked up her chopsticks and ate.

Sizzling platters of hot food were wafted in front of Patrick and he ate, too. He used his chopsticks neatly. She remembered that her mother had brought her . . . here? . . . to this very place? A Chinese man had taught her how to use chopsticks. Perhaps it had been Willy himself, all those years ago?

Patrick poured them both some more tea. "May I speak now? What I said was unpardonable. I was planning to use you."

She nodded. She'd worked that out. Had he planned to use her from the very first day? From the moment he'd given her a lift to the Thornbys' farm? The thought hurt.

She laid down her own chopsticks. "I didn't realise you hated me, too."

"Yes, just for a second or two then, I did hate you." He shuddered. "I think I was out of my mind. I'm sorry." He patted his pockets for cigarettes and the ever watchful Willy placed an unopened packet and some matches on the table.

Patrick tore off the wrapper and she looked away. His hands stilled. "You don't like me smoking, do you? I only allow myself one a day, after supper."

She raised her eyebrows. He had been smoking when she'd arrived at his office.

"Well . . ." He lifted his hands in acknowledgement of the fib. "I know I shouldn't, but sometimes when I miss a meal, I . . ."

"I watched an old friend of my uncle's cough his lungs out. Yes, I hate the smell of it."

He took a deep breath and pushed the packet away from him. "All right. I'll stop, if it pleases you."

She did meet his eyes, then. He had banked his fires right down again, and looked his usual urbane self.

"Please forgive me," he said.

She said, "Why did you come back to the village? You didn't need to."

"I'm bloody-minded. I don't like running away. I love this place and these people. I've a case of terminal stupidity. That do?"

"What was it like, coming back after all those years?"

He shrugged. "Some people didn't remember me at all; there were newcomers who simply wanted a professional around and were prepared to take advantage of my services, whoever my father had been. Some people remembered and . . ."

"Welcomed you for your own sweet self?"

He took a moment to remember that this is roughly what he'd said to her on her return. He choked on his tea. Minty waited for him to recover. He might take umbrage and storm out of the restaurant. Or he might laugh. And if he did laugh, her bruised ego would like it very much indeed.

When he could speak, Patrick said, "You impertinent child!"

"I've been well taught," she said, dryly. He really did like her, or he wouldn't have reacted like that. He was a complex character: irascible, funny, tricky. But he really did like her. Most of the time, anyway.

Willy brought more tea. He removed the used dishes and the cigarettes. A perspicacious man, Willy. Patrick paid, she collected her bike, and they walked down the street together.

He put out his arm to guide her around a bench. "You said something just now about owing your uncle and aunt money. How come?"

"I have to repay all the money they've spent on bringing me up, my computer training, driving lessons."

"But your father . . ."

"Not a penny."

"I don't understand. Sir Micah may be this and that, and a serial adulterer, but it's not like him to . . ."

She missed a step and lost the rest of the sentence.

"Are you all right?" Patrick waited for her to catch him up.

"Sure." She thought, *A serial adulterer? Is that what my father is? I suppose it makes a weird kind of sense. If he messed around before my mother died, and after he married Gemma's mother. A SERIAL ADULTERER?*

Patrick hadn't noticed anything. "We need to work out how Simon will retaliate to being attacked. That is, if you still want to go ahead, knowing what a poor sort of ally I'd be."

"You don't see yourself as a white knight riding to the rescue of the village?"

"More like Don Quixote."

They both smiled at that. She thought, *My father was a serial adulterer? While he was married to my mother? Was that what Mrs Thornby meant when she said he made my mother so miserable that she looked for another shoulder to cry on? I need to think about this.*

Patrick said, "Let's think this through. Sir Micah did not *give* the Hall and estate over to his wife, but appointed her as his representative to run it. She in turn passed it on to Simon. But while Sir Micah lives, he's the only one who can sign such a momentous contract with the American company. Simon's signature on that contract would be invalid, but he's trying it on, knowing that his mother will back him rather than let him lose face and, yes, using the same tactics on Sir Micah.

"Now the Americans may believe that Simon has the right to sign. From their point of view it looks like a good deal, so they'll press for it to go ahead. I wouldn't put it past Simon to sign that contract even though he has no right to do so . . . and then there'll be the devil to pay. If Simon signs and his signature is shown to be invalid, the Americans will want their pound of flesh. They will take it to court. Lawsuits. Bad news. So I'll have to stop the Americans signing, which, yes, I think I know how to do.

"Now what will Simon do when he finds out his plans have been thwarted—lovely word, 'thwarted'? He can either wait till Sir Micah dies, which can't be long now . . . are you all right, Minty?"

She nodded and he went on. "Or if he feels he can't wait . . ." He stopped, patted his pockets searching for a cigarette. They were opposite a pub. He could easily go in and get some more, but he didn't. They continued to walk on down the street.

He said, "I think Simon will move on you next."

She halted, surprised. "Nonsense. He hates me and wants me out."

"I'm only guessing, but I think Ms Phillips will get you in to see your father very soon."

"Oh," she said, softly.

"I don't know what you expect to find. A sweet little old daddy figure? He's made of steel, not marshmallow. You'll win him round, no doubt. You've got guts and look like your mother. So Simon will want you on his side. He can be very charming when he wishes. So how flame-proof are you, Araminta Cardale?"

She blinked. "That's never going to happen. Listen, Patrick, can he work out who stopped him? Aren't you worried what he might do to you?"

"I'll present my bill on Lady Day. The payment . . . what shall we make it? How about a daisy chain?"

She really didn't know how to take him. Full of jokes one minute and serious the next. They had reached her front door.

"I can't ask you in," she said.

"I should think not. It would be all over the village before breakfast. See you tomorrow, perhaps. Or no, maybe not. I may have to stay in town overnight. I spend half the week working in town and half here. It can be difficult, socially. Look, whatever happens, I'll give you a ring."

He hesitated as if he would have added something, shook his head at himself, and turned back up the street. She watched him out of sight.

The cottage seemed cramped and too full of bric-a-brac. There was a note from the electrician saying there was no hot water yet, but he hoped to have it on the next day. She went up to bed, thinking now about the things Patrick had said, and now about that moment when they might both have ended up on the floor . . .

. . . and grew so hot she threw off the duvet.

A daisy chain. What on earth had he meant by that? Lady Day. Wasn't that something rural? A quarter day, when farmers' rents used to be due?

Minty asked God to look after Patrick and show her how to save the village. Then she began to laugh. She, to save the village? Ridiculous. How on earth had Patrick got her thinking that she was responsible for the village? She'd offer the whole boiling lot up to God and ask him to take care of everything. Including an irritating man who thought he was Don Quixote.

Wednesday dawned with a heavy feel in the air. It was going to rain, perhaps. The sky was dull and the bees sounded unnaturally loud in the garden. Or was that thunder?

She had no umbrella if it rained. She had a quick word with the electrician when he arrived and, followed by Lady the cat, set off up the hill with her jacket over her T-shirt and jeans. The charity shop was just opening and Ruby beckoned her in. Ten minutes later Minty was on her way again, wearing a long dull red dress with a low round neckline and short sleeves. A very becoming dress that wouldn't need ironing.

She carried some other treasures in a couple of plastic bags. At this rate she'd have spent her wages for the week before she'd be able to send her uncle and aunt any money. She decided to ring them when she got the bookshop opened up . . . but there were already three customers waiting at the door.

Correction: Mr Lightowler, Jonah Wootton, and the vicar. None was a customer, and all would demand time and attention.

Jonah was almost dancing, wanting to impart his good news. "Patrick's going to take me to see Hannah today, on his way to work. But I have to come back by bus."

Mr Lightowler pretended to study something in the window, but was all ears.

The Reverend was also fidgeting with impatience. "Martha, it's most important that I speak with you in private. At once."

Jonah trod on Minty's heels as she opened the door. "I'm going to pick Hannah some flowers from the garden. Do you think she'd like pinks or roses best?"

Mr Lightowler slid into the shop behind the Reverend and made for the shelf where the dictionaries—and his coveted catalogue of jazz records—lay.

Minty turned the "Closed" sign to "Open", switched on the lights, and propped the door open, dumping her charity shop purchases behind the desk. Lady jumped up into the window and settled down.

"Do you have to open the shop *now*?" hissed the vicar. "This is urgent and personal."

Jonah was happily scrabbling away at the bolts on the back door to let himself out into the garden. Mr Lightowler faded into the background. Minty suspected he was rather good at that.

"What can I do for you?" she asked.

"I called at your cottage twice yesterday evening to see you, and you weren't in."

"No, I was out for the evening."

"This morning when I went round again, the electrician said you'd just gone. Only then did he tell me you were working in the bookshop."

Minty reflected that the vicar was not connected to the village grapevine, or he'd have known where to find her. "So what can I do for you?"

"Not for me. Your uncle and aunt have been trying to contact you. They tried the Hall and got nowhere. Finally they remembered that I lived here and got me. They've rung me twice yesterday and once already this morning. Your aunt has had a fall and they need you back home. You're to take the train at noon, and your uncle will try to meet it."

First they sent Lucas to fetch her, and now they got Cecil to do their dirty work. Minty seated herself behind the desk and opened the till to put in the cash float. "I'm sorry Aunt Agnes has had a fall. I presume she hasn't broken anything, or you'd have said. I'll ring them later this morning but I won't be going back."

He took out a handkerchief and ran it round his neck. "You don't understand."

"Oh yes, I do," said Minty. "Perfectly. I'm sorry they bothered you. You've done as they asked and given me the message, so you can put it out of your mind, all right? They've got to learn how to get along without me. Their nephew—do you remember Lucas? Was he around in your time? He's still living at home and is far better placed than me to look after them."

She was surprised how easy it had been to say no. And banished the usual feelings of guilt.

Jonah tumbled back into the shop, brandishing a pair of secateurs and a bloodied thumb. "Minty, I've got a great big thorn in my thumb!"

Really, he was just like an overgrown child. "Run it under the tap, Jonah, and I'll have a look."

Cecil Scott wiped his forehead. "If you're really not going back, perhaps you'd like to come round to the vicarage this afternoon—it's half-day closing, isn't it?—and we can discuss . . ."

"I'm afraid I'm busy this afternoon, Cecil." Mrs Collins had arranged to pick her up at two, to get the flowers for the competition. "And my name is Minty, short for Araminta. Not Martha."

He had a surprisingly sweet smile. "Someone did tell me you weren't really called Martha. I said you were a Martha by nature, right?"

"I'm not so sure about that, either. Now if you don't mind, I've a customer and a wounded man to attend to."

Cecil seemed to have glued himself to the floor, for he didn't move. Minty asked Mr Lightowler in a low voice if he'd mind looking after the shop for a minute, and went behind the partition to find Jonah sitting on the stool with a handkerchief wrapped round his thumb, his face screwed up with pain. He looked exactly like a garden gnome.

"Minty, I daren't look!"

"Silly boy," said Minty, unwrapping the handkerchief. There was indeed a large rose thorn stuck in the ball of Jonah's thumb. She removed it in one deft movement, ran his hand under the tap, and checked that there was no dirt left in the wound. "There now. All better."

"Really?" He opened one eye to inspect his thumb and wiggled it around. "I think I'll take her a bunch of pinks, though. Not roses."

"Good idea." She packed him off back into the garden and returned to find Mr Lightowler taking some money from a customer, while Cecil Scott hovered over the paperbacks. When he saw her, Cecil sidled over. "I think I've got off on the wrong foot with you, but . . . I was misled. I was told . . . well, never mind that now."

Minty thought, *Yes, and it's never Simon's fault, either. I must remember that, if he asks me out. Which of course he won't. How stupid can Patrick get!*

Cecil was looking at her expectantly. She had missed something, obviously.

"Mmm . . . ?" she said, checking that Mr Lightowler was managing the till correctly, which he was.

"I said," he began in a louder voice, and then dropped it to a murmur, "how about coming round to the vicarage one evening? I could cook up a rice dish. I'm a devil with the rice dishes, they say." To her amazement, he blushed.

She wanted to laugh, but didn't. "That's very kind of you, Cecil. At the moment I don't know whether I'm on my head or my heels, sorting out the cottages and working here, catching up on old friends. I'll be in church on Sunday, though. It was very good of you to bring the message for me. I appreciate it."

Somehow she managed to waft him out of the door before allowing herself a smile.

Jonah erupted from the back quarters, bearing a beautifully arranged posy of pinks. "Minty, I've got a message from Patrick. He's waiting to take me off to see Hannah, so I can't stop."

"What's the message?" asked Minty, as Jonah looked as if he were about to leave without giving it to her.

"He said to say . . . er . . . what was it? That it's done. I'll drop by later and let you know how Hannah's getting on."

He was gone, and the shop was quiet.

"A cup of coffee?" asked Mr Lightowler, emerging from the shadows.

"Agreed," said Minty. "And then . . ."

"You're going to make me an offer I can't refuse?"

"Well, I did hope Venetia would," said Minty, with a sigh. "But there's a snag."

So, it was done. It was disconcerting not to know exactly what had been done. A little like watching a bomb drop in the distance and waiting for the sound to reach you. Minty wondered if she would recognise the Big Bang when it came? She didn't believe for a minute that Simon would start taking notice of her. Why should he?

She rang her aunt to find her full of complaints and bitter that Minty hadn't immediately responded to their call for assistance. Minty's suggestion that Lucas might be able to help was met with derision. Lucas was far too busy, overstretched at the office. And, anyway, it was a niece's duty to look after her relatives. Minty listened, but made no promise to return. Ending the call, she prayed a little for her aunt, asking God to look after her, to heal her, and if possible to make her understand that she must let go of her niece. If that was His will.

On her way home at lunchtime, Minty observed something rather strange happening. A man was walking down the high street away from her, and a fair number of people were stepping aside to avoid him. Minty had to think for a moment to place the man. It was Miles, who was engaged to Gemma.

"Do you know that man, Miss Cardale?" It was Patrick's efficient secretary, returning from the bakery with a roll for her lunch.

"Is it my imagination, or are they avoiding him?"

"When he's in a bad mood . . ." She shrugged.

"He's estate manager for Simon? Is he a good one?"

"His father was excellent. This one? Well, he was at school with Simon. I'm saying no more."

As Minty tried to make sense of this, her mobile phone rang. Ms Phillips. Would it be convenient for Minty to come to the Hall at ten the next day?

"Yes, of course," said Minty, hand to throat. "How is my father?"

"We had to call the doctor in again today, but he rallied. I'll see you tomorrow, then."

Ms Phillips disconnected and Minty told herself not to panic. So the doctor had been called again? Sir Micah had had a bad night, perhaps. It wasn't anything to do with the Big Bang. It couldn't be. No.

That afternoon Mrs Collins took Minty shopping for flowers and equipment. Mrs Collins talked all the way there and all the while Minty was picking out what she needed. Mrs Collins paid for everything except one exquisite white orchid plant, which Minty selected and paid for herself. Mrs Collins talked all the way back. Tiring, very.

Minty placed the flowers in deep buckets of water to condition them, and between consultations with the electrician about the placement of power points, and checks on the newly installed water heater, she worked on into the evening preparing the base for her flower arrangement. Dwayne, the electrician, said he knew of a fridge that was being thrown out because the owner wanted something bigger, and did Minty want it? "Yes, please," said Minty.

The threatened thunderstorm had still not broken, and she pushed damp hair off her forehead as she wove rushes into the shape of a boat.

After supper Minty picked up her white orchid and carried it carefully out of her front door and down to the pretty humpback bridge where Milly Cardale's life had ended.

Minty thought, *My mother was coming from the Hall, so she'd have crashed into the far side of the bridge. I can't go on avoiding the place, so I'll make a memorial there for her with flowers.*

She waited till there was no traffic passing, and crossed over. On the far side she paused, wondering precisely where her mother had died.

The river—hardly more than a stream at the moment—ran between deep banks. Between the river and the road was a cleared space of ground, no more than two metres wide. An ornamental urn had been placed there, on a stone plinth. The urn was filled with geraniums, cascading down to meet red and white begonias that had been planted at its feet.

There was already a garden of remembrance here. Minty knelt and planted her orchid amid the begonias and said a prayer.

A flash of light caught her eye. Someone was holding back a curtain and looking down on her from a house up the street. The figure was in silhouette and it was definitely a woman. It was time to pay a visit to Nanny Proud.

Chapter Twelve

Nanny Proud's domain lay above the hairdresser's, a couple of doors up from Spring Cottage. The building was early Victorian, the windows high but narrow. The stairs to her flat lay between the hairdresser's and the charity shop.

Minty pressed the bell and the door swung open. She climbed the stairs and entered her old nurse's living quarters.

"So you found the place at last, did you? Took your time! Now you're here, you can make me some cocoa. The kitchen's through there."

Minty obeyed. What had originally been two first-floor rooms had been knocked into one big bed-sitting room, with net-curtained windows overlooking the main street at the front and the gardens at the back. There were crocheted antimacassars, china knick-knacks and photographs everywhere. Mrs Proud, ex-nanny and now head of surveillance, was seated in a high-backed chair overlooking the street with binoculars at the ready.

A tiny kitchen and a shower room had been fitted in over the well of the staircase. Like everything else in sight, the kitchen was scrupulously clean and better equipped than Minty's, containing an up-to-date microwave, fridge, and freezer. Minty made Nanny Proud a cup of cocoa, as directed.

"Put it down there," said Nanny Proud, indicating a crocheted mat on the table beside her. "And tell me what you think you're doing here."

"As if you didn't know," said Minty, smiling and taking a seat on an overstuffed pouffe at the old woman's feet. Nanny Proud must have been in her late seventies to judge by her wrinkled hands and neck. Her ankles and feet bulged over her shoes, but her eyes were bright and her short cut hair still thick and grey. She wore a fresh white blouse under a light green washable two-piece and probably bought everything by mail order.

A huge television set stood nearby, with the remote control at the old woman's elbow, together with a mobile telephone. Two thriving pot plants were on a sideboard with a large bunch of bought flowers, plus fruit in a bowl. Nanny Proud was well looked after.

"You've been busybodying," said Nanny Proud, "poking your nose in where it's not wanted."

Minty smiled. She'd known old ladies like this before. They still wanted to be a power in the land, while afraid that their hold on those around them was slipping. Minty surprised herself by thinking, *Like Aunt Agnes. An onlooker on life. To be pitied, really.*

"Cat got your tongue?" asked the old woman, not nicely. Minty revised her opinion. This was no cuddly nanny, yearning to take a motherless infant in her arms and welcome her back. No. This was Porcupine Valley. And with that thought came memories she'd suppressed of an angry voice, sharp slaps and disapproval from Nanny.

Milly Cardale had never understood why Minty the child hadn't liked being with Nanny. Minty the adult knew exactly why.

She said, "You're looking well."

"No thanks to you, going around worriting folk. You were always the same even as a child, staring at everyone with those big blue eyes. Dumb as an ox."

"Was I?" Minty thought, *This woman never did like me. Why did Patrick want me to visit her, I wonder?*

"Nothing like my pretty little Gemma. Now there's a chatterbox for you," said the old woman with a fond smile. "Talk, talk, talk. All day long. She loves her old nanny, she does. And Master Simon, too. They look after their old nanny and see she wants for nothing."

Ah-ha, thought Minty. *So Simon can do no wrong here, either?*

"I'm to have a nice ground-floor flat in the new houses they're going to build behind the church, just as soon as they can get rid of those nasty insanitary old cottages. What do you think of that!"

Insurance? thought Minty. *With Nanny on their side, they're assured of the acquiescence of half the village.* "Sounds good."

"I don't know what's holding it up," said the old woman fretfully. "They promised me, ages ago. I don't want another winter up here, with no one coming to visit me." She became plaintive.

Minty noted there was no central heating, only a couple of night storage heaters. Adequate for younger people, but perhaps insufficient for elderly persons with restricted mobility. She also noticed a copy of the new brochure for the Hall lying on the table nearby.

"I'm sure you keep yourself busy and interested in everything that goes on," said Minty.

The old eyes sharpened. "Goings on in back gardens. Those country yokels the Thornbys trying to suck up to you, more fools they! My ears are still as sharp as when they caught you playing with those dratted animals instead of going to sleep at night."

Minty grinned. "I wondered if I'd imagined them. So there really was a Noah's Ark, was there? Did one side of the roof lift up so that you could store the animals inside?"

"Dratted thing. You never put them all back properly and I was always tripping over them. Dear little Gemma wanted to play with it, too, but I said "No, you play with your teddy bear instead," and she soon learned to stop crying for the moon. There's one thing I can't abide and that's an obstinate child. You never cried, even when I smacked you hard. Unnatural, I call it."

Minty wondered if the woman had ever liked children. She began to understand why Gemma was so anxious to please. She herself had been trained the same way. Nanny's charges had been taught to please Nanny . . . or else.

"Now Simon was a good boy," said Nanny, relaxing in her chair. "Such pretty, coaxing ways he did have. Just as well, with his mother so busy all the time, racketing about the world with Sir Micah. I never had any children of my own, but she made up for it, my lovely Lisa. She lived next door to me, you see. Her parents were nothing, and it was me encouraged her to go to college.

"She married far too young. I told her it wouldn't last and as soon as she got pregnant, he was off. She'd just landed the job with Sir Micah and was looking forward to travelling the world with him. 'Let me take care of the baby,' I said to her. 'This is your opportunity to fly high.' So Simon came to live with me and he was my darling, so he was.

"I thought for sure that Sir Micah would have married my Lisa then, but no: he fell for your mother's pretty face and married her, more fool he. I knew it wouldn't last, but he doted on her until she produced you—not even a boy! Then of course he began to see he'd made a mistake, but still he wouldn't hear of her staying quietly at home to look after you. He wanted her with him all the time, so Lisa arranged that I should bring Simon and look after the two of you together."

"So Simon is definitely not Sir Micah's son?"

"Of course not. The very idea! But Sir Micah adopted him right and tight and he's the heir and that's how it should be. I remember when Simon and I were driving up the avenue in the car Sir Micah sent for us, and we saw the Hall standing there, so grand and imposing after my own tiny little house, and Simon said—such a bright little boy he was—he said, 'Is that my house now, Nanny?'

"I said, 'Of course it is. And when you're grown up, you'll marry the pretty princess and live happily ever after.' That's what I said. And it'll all come true, mark my words."

Minty shivered. This was obsession, wasn't it? Had this woman's twisted thinking marked the characters of all three children brought up at the Hall? Was it she who had made Minty and Gemma too anxious to please, and given Simon a false idea of his own importance? And Lisa Cardale? Had she too been twisted by this old woman's ambition for her?

The old woman appeared to have fallen asleep. Minty turned her wrist to look at her watch. It was dark outside, nearly ten o'clock. Perhaps she could make a move now?

"That Patrick Sands," said Nanny Proud, suddenly. "I've watched him, looking up at your windows, bringing you gifts. Two-faced, just like his father. Mark my words, he'll come to a bad end and take you with him."

"Doesn't he come to visit you?"

The old woman gave a harsh laugh. "If he were to show his face up here, I'd have at him with my stick, so I would."

There was a stir on the stairs and Minty stood as Mrs Guinness heaved herself into the room, puffing at the effort.

"Come to put me to bed, have you?" said the old lady.

"I'm a few minutes early," said Mrs Guinness, staring at Minty.

"I'll go, then," said Minty. "Shall I see you on Saturday morning, Mrs Guinness?"

Mrs Guinness gave a stiff nod and Minty escaped. Once outside she shook her head to clear it. *Nanny Proud spreads poison every time she opens her mouth. So why did Patrick want me to visit her? To explain how the family has got the way they are?*

Why would Patrick have Nanny Proud on his visiting list, when she obviously hates him? Can she still do any damage to him . . . to any of us?

She couldn't go to bed yet. The cottage walls seemed to close in on her in the sultry night air. She sat on the bench in the back garden, trying to think. Lady the cat came to wind himself round her legs, but soon darted off to chase moths.

Minty watched the moon rise above the clouds. Not a full moon, yet, but adequate to guide people's footsteps as they left the back entrance of the pub and made their way down to the car park near the river. Some of the back gardens were still illumined by light spilling from uncurtained windows. She could hear the sound of television drama, game shows . . . radio announcements. Newsflashes.

A man and a woman walked down the lane and stopped to kiss by her gate. They turned to look at the back of Spring Cottage.

Then the man went on down the lane while the girl turned in at the gate and came to where Minty sat. It was Alice, finished with her stint at the pub.

Minty moved along the seat to make room for Alice.

"I saw you were still up. You don't mind my coming in?"

"Of course not. Was that Dwayne with you?"

"He's been waiting for me every night after the pub closes. He's nice. Minty, I know it's letting you down and all that, but I think I'll have to give in my notice. I've decided to move back to the city. There's no hope of getting anywhere to live around here, and if I go back I can go on the council list. There's childminders available and I can get a good job. And Dwayne wants me to."

"Also, you've heard that Simon wants to sell the cottages."

"I'll see you through the holiday season, of course."

"Do you really want to leave the village?"

Alice was an intelligent girl with a business degree. She was not just a single parent with a dead-end outlook. She knew the score, even better than Minty.

Alice said, "It'd take a miracle to get me to stay."

"Then I'd better start praying for one. Will you pray with me?"

Alice gave an embarrassed laugh. "I wouldn't know what words to use."

"Talk to God as if He were sitting on this bench next to us. He is here. He knows all our problems, our hopes, and our fears. He wants to help, but we have to ask."

Alice shook her head. "I can't do that yet. I wouldn't dare, and you wouldn't have asked me if you knew. Dwayne wants me to move in with him, and I've said I would."

"Oh, Alice . . ."

"I knew you wouldn't like it." Without another word Alice retreated to the lane, and Minty heard her walking away.

So that was that. Minty sat on for a long time, praying for Alice and Patrick and everyone. And then trying to listen to what God was telling her.

The night was hot and sullen. In the morning the clouds looked as if they were going to break up, still without any sign of rain. As Minty was going to be at the Hall, Venetia had arranged to be at the bookshop for the first part of the morning, when Mr Lightowler had promised to drop in and have a chat with her.

Minty walked her bicycle across the humpback bridge behind a large man pushing a wheelbarrow. He looked vaguely familiar. When he stopped to pick up a stray piece of paper from the garden beside the bridge, Minty stopped, too.

"Morning." The man addressed Minty in the slightly too loud voice of one who is a little deaf. And yes, he was wearing a hearing aid. "Look at this, now. Someone's put in an orchid. A beauty, too. How about that!"

Minty recognised him now. This was the man who'd been talking to Patrick outside the pub on the day she arrived, one week ago today. "Do you look after this garden?"

"I'm chairman of the village gardening society. I keep people up to the mark, get the plants wholesale. Planters, too. You could do with some window boxes for the cottages, couldn't you? Bit late for this year, though. Judging for the competition was a while back, in July. Still, think ahead, what?"

"I'm Minty Cardale."

He held out his hand. "I know. Tipped poor old Patrick head over heels, didn't you? Not that he was down and out for long. Hah! I'm Henry Piggott, building contractor, retired. The wife gets hay fever, so we've a little flat at the back of the school. But I can't sit around doing the crossword all day. Some old codger used to look after this patch of garden, but when he moved up to the old people's home, I took over."

Minty wondered if he knew that it was a memorial garden, and decided that he probably didn't. He had the look of an incomer, one of those invaluable people who kept things going in the village. He was probably on the church council and the parish council, as well. He would know the Woottons, of course.

"Only trouble is," said Mr Piggott, "this bit of land floods now and then. Every three years, they tell me. I wanted to transfer the flowers to the other side of the bridge, but they say that land belongs to the Hall and we can't have it. My dream is to get a wall of rough stonework built here to stabilise the bank. Maybe extend it along the roadside a little way. Put a wooden bench just here. Fine view of the park at all times of the year. My favourite, in fact."

He bent to pull out a weed, so Minty mounted her bike and rode on. She was wearing the second of the dresses she had bought at the charity shop. This one was blue with a deep V-neckline. Riding her bike, gardening, and eating so much fresh produce had banished the pallor of the city from her skin, and her hair shone, benefiting from being washed in the local soft water and drying in the sun. She knew she looked better than she had when she arrived, and she hoped, oh how she hoped, that her father would approve.

She turned off the main road into the avenue. The trees and grass in the park glimmered under the sun. Minty wanted to get off her bike and run and run to the horizon.

She gloried in the beauty of the day, in the clouds breaking up to show large areas of blue sky. She caught the scent of new-mown grass from where a man on a motorised mower was cutting the lawns near the house.

A bend in the avenue revealed the west front of the oldest part of the house, built in Elizabethan days from warm golden stone. She caught her breath: it was even more beautiful than she remembered. Mullioned windows rose up three stories on either side of the central porch, and there were towers at either corner. Her Georgian ancestors had added a stone portico to the front entrance, but it didn't seem out of place.

She was early, so she dismounted. Perhaps this was the place from which Nanny Proud had pointed out the Hall to the boy Simon, telling him that it was his for the taking?

Minty pushed her bicycle along the drive, past the grand entrance and round the corner to the south side of the Hall. She wanted to see if the lake was still there—and it was.

The south wing had been added in Regency days, the rooms being larger than those on the north and west "sheep" wings. Here the windows were not mullioned, but made of large sheets of slightly green glass. A broad terrace overlooked a great sweep of lawn, sloping gently down to the lake.

Minty rejoiced that the lake was still there. The waters sparkled in the sunlight and, as she watched, a pair of swans flew down and settled on the water. She thought, *Oh, I wish Patrick could have seen that!* Then: *Why did I think he'd be interested?*

She mustn't be late for her appointment with Ms Phillips. In some haste she wheeled her bike back round the house to the first courtyard. The shop was unlit and deserted. There were sounds of food preparation in the restaurant, but it had not yet opened its doors. Minty thought of Florence Thornby and Gloria losing their jobs, and sent up a little prayer for them.

She wheeled her bike through to the far courtyard, the one where the family and staff kept their cars. She imagined she could identify the owners of each car. The longest and sleekest would belong to Lady Cardale and Simon. Gemma's would be the Renault with a scraped wing. Would the estate car belong to Ms Phillips? And whose might the people carrier be? Did it belong to Miles, perhaps?

She chained up her bike and made her way to the open office door.

"Thank you for coming, Araminta," said Ms Phillips.

The girl who had ushered Minty in before was behind the desk, but rose when Minty appeared and disappeared through the inner door. Ms Phillips was seated beside the coffee table on which sat a cafetière, coffee cups and a plate of biscuits. "Would you care for some coffee?"

Minty accepted and sank into a chair, reflecting that this was a change of tone, indeed. Was it a reflection of the Big Bang, perhaps? "How is my father today?"

"A little better and looking forward to seeing you in about an hour. But first . . ."

Minty felt a warm glow throughout her body. She was actually going to see her father! "The holiday lets?" she said, in an effort to seem in control. "Even if the plan is to sell them, it would be wise to have some work done first."

Ms Phillips inclined her head. "I agree it would be sensible." She passed over a coffee cup to Minty. "We can discuss that later. Before you see your father, he would like you to study this."

She handed over a copy of a letter to a bank. The letter instructed the bank to remit a sizeable sum of money to the Reverend Reuben Cardale every month. It was dated twenty years previously.

Minty shook her head, puzzled.

"Sir Micah set up a direct debit," said Ms Phillips. "A generous monthly sum for your keep and extras. When you started school, the amount was increased to cover private school fees."

"But I went to the local state school."

"I know. I've checked. Nevertheless, Sir Micah increased the amount every year to cover all eventualities including holidays, special tuition for music and dancing lessons, and school trips. In due course he increased the amount again, to cover your college fees, driving lessons, and the purchase of a car. He cancelled the direct debit . . ." Ms Phillips laid another letter before Minty . . . "on Monday of this week."

Minty took a couple of deep breaths, fearing she might faint. Nonsense, she wasn't going to faint. Fainting was stupid.

"The bank can't have understood . . . the instructions weren't passed on . . . it's just not possible!"

But she knew it was possible. She blinked rapidly, shaking her head. If this were true . . .

Ms Phillips pushed a large file over to Minty. It contained a record of all the instructions over twenty years that Sir Micah had given his bank to ensure that his daughter was cared for. Minty turned the pages slowly at first, and then more rapidly. Every now and then there were handwritten letters from her Uncle Reuben, suggesting that the money be increased to cover private school fees, uniforms, school trips, and so on.

Minty felt sick.

Ms Phillips said, "Where did the money go, Araminta?"

"I don't know. My uncle never had any money to spare. They gave to charity, of course, but not this amount." She shook her head. "I can't believe it!" She jumped up, hands pushing back her hair. "So this is . . ."

"Fraud," said Ms Phillips, in the same even tone. "You understand now how disconcerted I was when you told me you were in debt to your uncle and aunt. When you showed me your account book, I took the liberty of photocopying the pages. I have spent a considerable amount of time on the phone since then, checking your story. I then took the lot to Sir Micah, who was very distressed. Hence the doctor's recent visits."

Minty said, "It's thousands and thousands of pounds! I could have gone to private school, to university! I could have had my own car, bought good clothes! Gone on holidays like my friends!" She shook her head. "I can't take it in. All those years of skimping and saving, working so hard for my uncle and aunt because they said they couldn't afford to pay anyone to work in the house! This is a dream and I'm going to wake up in a minute."

"Take your time. I have to go over some papers now with Sir Micah. Drink your coffee. Have a little wander around outside if you wish. The house is not open to the public till twelve today and the family are all out. I will return for you in an hour's time."

Minty stared in front of her. However, what she was looking at was not the wainscoted office, but a home movie of her childhood and youth in a threadbare vicarage. She heard her uncle's voice promising to give money for this and that good cause. She heard her aunt complaining that they must economise on hot water and heating . . . she felt the roughness of the second-hand uniform and clothes she had worn and the thinness of the old towels at bath time.

She saw herself mending her underwear under her aunt's supervision, kneeling with dustpan and brush to clean under the beds because the ancient hoover didn't have a hose attachment.

She saw herself walking home from school to save her bus fare and being praised for it by her uncle . . . and her bus fares disappearing into one of the charity boxes on the hall table. She had at least been able to choose which charity the money should go to. She saw herself declining invitations to schoolfriends' birthday parties because her uncle didn't approve of spending money on the presents she was expected to take.

Minty wanted to scream and throw something. Break a window. She sipped her coffee. It was cold, but she didn't care. She ate all the biscuits on the plate, poured herself another cup.

She would very much like to take her uncle by his scrawny neck and wrench off his clerical collar and beat him to death. Slowly. Hopefully he would beg and cry for mercy.

No, she mustn't think like that.

WHY NOT?

Well, you're supposed to forgive those who've sinned again you.

OH, YEAH!

Not this girl. She would creep up behind her aunt when she was in the kitchen, that dark kitchen with its inadequate lighting. She would pounce on her, and shake her like a terrier shakes a rat. And her aunt would squeak and scream just like a titchy little mouse.

HAH!

And then she would bury them both in the back garden and erect a beautiful stone cross over them: *Rest in peace all ye who steal from orphans.*

Well, not precisely an orphan. But near enough.

And dance on their graves. Stamp, stamp, stamp! Hurray!

She was so angry she felt she could fly. She broke out of the office into the courtyard and breathed in fresh air. Perhaps it would rain soon. She would welcome a fully fledged storm in her present mood. A tornado would do. A whirlwind to pick up her uncle and aunt and whiz them out of sight, out of mind . . . out of her mind.

Minty put both hands to her aching head and bowed it down to her knees. It was intolerable, what they'd done.

Chapter Thirteen

She didn't know how long she stayed like that, crouching over, holding herself together. She straightened up. She felt sick.

She told herself to think about something else. In a little while she'd see her father again. At the moment, she didn't particularly want to see him, or anyone. She wanted to go for a long walk and tire herself out and not think about anything at all. Least of all her family.

She walked across to the gift shop. Doris was inside, dusting. No customers. Of course, the house wasn't open till midday. Minty smiled at Doris and took a tour around. A meagre display, just as Doris had said. Hardly anything much of anything, and what there was seemed to be of poor quality.

Doris seemed to be saying something to her, and her own mouth seemed to be responding. Minty hadn't a clue what they'd talked about, but Doris didn't seem disconcerted.

Minty walked past the restaurant—still not open, but she could see Gloria inside, pushing a cloth around in desultory fashion. Gloria waved to her, and Minty gave a cheerful wave back.

It was amazing how normal you could pretend to be when all you really wanted to do was drown yourself. Or someone else.

She thought of Patrick talking about hate. She hadn't understood him then, but she understands now all right. She burned with the desire to hurt, destroy . . . kill.

She walked through the inner courtyard and out on to the terrace beyond. Now she was on the east side, which was also Georgian. There was a terrace here, too, though not as fine and wide a one as on the side overlooking the lake. She was standing above a square formal garden, surrounded by high laurel hedges.

Yes! She remembered this, too. She used to play tag around the geometric beds when she was a child, chasing someone . . . a girl? Patrick? No, how could she have been playing with Patrick? Being chased by Simon? The box edging to the beds hadn't been clipped that autumn, and were ragged.

Dissatisfied, she walked to the end of the terrace and turned the corner on to the south front. Now she could see across the lake and on to the distant horizon. She breathed more easily with so much space around her.

Great stone urns stood at intervals on the balustrade that edged the terrace. They could have done with the ministrations of a gardener, or of the genial chairman of the village gardening society, Henry Piggott. A few trailing geraniums, a marguerite or two and a bush fuschia failed to give the necessary impression of plenty. The windows behind her were those of the main reception rooms. She knew, without peering in to check, that one set of windows was for the library, the music room, the red drawing room and . . . her memory failed her.

An enormous snail had made it to the top of the balustrade. She picked it off, dropped it on the terrace and ground it under foot. There!

That made her feel better—for about five seconds.

She walked up and down the terrace, hugging herself although the day was warm. She tried not to think about the wrong that had been done her, tried not to think about what she would say when she saw her aunt and uncle again. Failed.

She was sitting quietly in her chair in the office when Ms Phillips returned.

She said, "My father ought to have checked."

"I disagree. Reuben was his elder brother and a minister of the church. Besides, you did write letters thanking your father for various gifts."

"Every birthday and Christmas my uncle showed me a five pound note that he said my father had sent me. Under his direction I wrote a thank-you letter. He said my father was a busy man and didn't need to be bothered with any chit-chat, so I was to keep it short and simple. I never got to spend the money, which went into charity boxes to help children who were *much* worse off then me."

"Clever," said Ms Phillips, appreciatively. "Sir Micah never read the letters. My instructions were to take any letters from your uncle to him, and letters from you directly to Lady Cardale. Well, Araminta, do you wish to call in the police and prosecute your uncle?"

Could she do that? The disgrace would kill her uncle and aunt, though of course they deserved it. But . . .

"I don't know yet. Ms Phillips, didn't it occur to you, even once, that anything was wrong?"

"You forget, I was not seconded to work for Sir Micah till after Gemma was born. Lady Cardale told me that you were not Sir Micah's child, but that he wanted to pay for your keep in memory of your mother. These things happen. Why should I have queried it?"

"Didn't you ever suspect the truth?"

"About your parentage? Not for many years, no. You must understand that Sir Micah has always travelled a great deal, and I with him. We were never here for long. A few weeks in the summer and then at Christmastime, perhaps. It was years before I had any real contact with anyone from the village.

"When I first heard someone—it was Mrs Wootton, actually—deny that your mother and Mr Sands had been lovers, well, I didn't believe it. When the denial was repeated by people whom I had grown to respect, I did begin to wonder. So I checked back through Sir Micah's diaries. He met and married your mother in Sydney, Australia. She was there on a gap year before going to university and he had been sent to do a hatchet job on a factory his parent company had bought. They tell me it was a whirlwind romance. I never saw her myself, but they say she made him laugh and that they adored one another. They came back to this country a year later, when she was six weeks pregnant."

Minty closed her eyes for a moment. So all those jibes from her aunt had been lies. "That bad woman's child!" How many times had she heard that? So much so that she had doubted everything about herself.

Her eyes flew open. "But when my mother died, he rejected me, saying I was not his!"

"You must understand that if a person wants something very much, sometimes they come to believe it's true. Lady Cardale had convinced herself that your mother lied about her dates. It was in her interests to believe it, since she was already pregnant with Gemma before your mother died."

"You think it was my stepmother and Mrs Proud who spread that rumour?"

Ms Phillips inclined her head. "So I believe."

"My father knew the truth. He could have stopped the gossip. He need not have sent me away."

"Your father has never taken me into his confidence on that subject, but . . ." she hesitated. "I observed from the day I started work here that he avoided Lady Cardale's company and found no great joy in her children, though he tried—he tried very hard—to be a good father to them. Husband and wife kept up appearances in public, but she stopped accompanying him abroad and busied herself in opening this house to the public." Again she hesitated. "I do not normally listen to gossip, but a member of his staff informed me that Sir Micah had been devastated by his first wife's death."

"Having been responsible for it?"

Ms Phillips inclined her head. "It may be so. He married your stepmother very soon after your mother died, hoping perhaps that the child she was carrying would be a son. She never showed any affection for Gemma, but she doted on her own son, Simon. I am given to understand that she never liked you. Perhaps because you reminded her so much of your mother? Perhaps your father thought that since he had to be away so much, you were best out of her way, and so entrusted you to his brother. I really do not know. Now if you are ready, I will take you up to see your father."

Minty didn't move. "After what you've told me? I'm not sure I want to see him." Thinking of the years of misery he'd put her through, she felt nothing but anger. Could she meet him with a smile now? No, she couldn't.

"You came here to see him. He wants to see you," Ms Phillips said. "He is dying, Araminta, and very lonely. If you could only make him laugh, just once more?"

Minty grimaced but followed Ms Phillips through the door connecting the office to the back quarters of the Hall. From down a corridor to the right came the sounds of a radio playing and the clash of pans. Florence Thornby at work?

They stepped out into the cloisters, an arcaded walk that lined all four sides of the fountain court. It was predictable, thought Minty, that the fountain was not working. A woman wearing a steward's badge scurried across the courtyard from one side to the other, disappearing through a far door in the tower opposite. Minty thought, *That door leads to the Long Gallery . . .*

Everything was so much smaller than she remembered. In her childhood it had seemed vast. Now it was merely big.

Ms Phillips led the way past signs on doors for the great hall till they reached the far end of the cloisters. She opened a door into the tower that linked the oldest and later wings. They were now in a circular room from which stairs started, running up and down. A rope had been slung across the stairway to the basement. What was down there? Minty couldn't remember.

Ms Phillips opened a door marked "Private", which Minty had expected to lead out into the fountain court, but instead revealed a large modern lift.

"Sir Micah had two lifts built within the courtyard when the Hall was opened to the public. This one is kept for family use and the one in the opposite corner is mainly for tourists." She pressed a button and the lift descended without so much as a whisper of sound. Stepping in, Ms Phillips took them up to the top floor.

The lift door opened on to a replica of the ground floor antechamber, but this room was furnished as a reception room and office. A double row of clocks on one wall were set at different times for different parts of the world. A man was working on one of the computers, and another man and a woman—professional people by the look of them—were seated at a low table by a window, studying some papers. The man and the woman at the table looked hard at Minty as Ms Phillips led her through the office, but did not speak. Ms Phillips paid no attention to any of them, but led Minty to another door, on which she tapped.

A woman in nurse's uniform came to the door, exchanged a quiet word with Ms Phillips and stood aside for them to enter the sickroom. The room was full of light and overlooked the lake, way below. A hospital bed occupied the centre of one wall, with medical equipment ranged around it. A wheelchair sat in one corner, neglected. The nurse went to the bed and adjusted the flow from a large metal container, because the man on the bed was wearing an oxygen mask.

He was not at all what Minty had expected. Her memories of her father had become so indistinct that she had confused him with her uncle Reuben, who was tall, solid, and beaky.

It was hard to tell Sir Micah's height, but his head was massive. He was big boned and had probably been something of a heavyweight till cancer pared the flesh from his bones. His short-cropped hair was iron-grey and so were his eyes. The eyes measured Minty without a flicker of a smile and she stared back.

Perhaps both stares meant, "What do you want of me?"

There was a comfortable chair by the bedside, facing the man on the bed. Minty sat, thinking, *This man is my father, my really truly father whom I have longed to see for years, and I don't feel anything. Not a thing*. She folded her hands in her lap.

"Talk to him," urged Ms Phillips, sinking on to a chair in the background. "Tell him something about yourself."

Minty thought, *Why should I?* Then she thought, *But he's dying, and what will it cost me? Five minutes of my time?*

Ms Phillips had asked her to make him laugh, just once more. Maybe she could do that.

She said, "Where shall I start? Well, I suppose when I was little and longed for a kitten. My uncle and aunt said I couldn't have one because cats were dirty and brought in fleas, and who was going to look after it and feed it? I said I'd be responsible, but they wouldn't hear of it. I said a kitten would frighten the mice away, but they said we didn't have mice. And, as a matter of fact, we didn't. So I learned to live with my disappointment. One day my Sunday school teacher found a stray cat who'd had a litter of kittens in her garden shed. I fell in love with the sweetest little black and white kitten. Her name was Chippy. My Sunday school teacher said she was going to take all the kittens down to the pet shop when they were old enough, but that if I liked, I could have one for myself.

"I knew how my uncle and aunt felt about cats, and I couldn't think how to change their minds till I saw a notice in a newsagent's window, reading, 'Wanted, Good Homes for Pet Mice'. A boy had been careless and got so many mice he didn't know what to do. His mother said they were all to be destroyed if he didn't find homes for them. He wanted just a few pence for two mice. Problem: I hadn't even got two pence of my own.

"I wasn't going to be beaten. On Sunday I kept back the money I should have put in the collection plate, and bought four mice. After that, the vicarage had mice . . . and I had my kitten."

The man on the bed gasped, his head rolled on his pillow and his hand beat on the counterpane. His colour rose. The nurse looked alarmed and hurried forward, but Ms Phillips was smiling.

The man was laughing. He laughed so much that tears stood out at the corners of his eyes. Eventually his paroxysm subsided.

Minty found she was holding one of his hands in both of hers. His hand was large, square. The skin felt a little too hot and the pulse was rapid but slowing.

Now he was breathing slowly, quietly. Still looking at her from under heavy eyebrows. She looked back, steadily.

"More," he said, or rather mouthed. His voice had gone.

She told him more about Chippy, who'd been a clever little creature. Chippy had soon learned to disappear when other members of the family appeared. She didn't like the vicarage when Minty was out, and used to find newly parked cars so that she could sit on the hot bonnets. She would move from one car to another as the engines cooled. But whenever Minty appeared, Chippy was sitting on the back doorstep. Minty had learned to beg fish skins and bones from the fishmonger, so that she could boil them up for food for Chippy. The little cat had thrived. For eighteen years she'd been Minty's dearest friend.

"She died of old age this spring," said Minty. "I missed her terribly. Lady, the cat from the bookshop, is not nearly such good company."

He nodded, but didn't try to speak again. His fingers closed around hers, and he lifted them both from the coverlet for an instant. He smiled at her. The warmth of his smile brought an echo of a smile to her face, too. He continued to smile, looking at her, while gradually his eyelids sank over his eyes.

She sat on, watching him and holding his hand. She thought, *It's amazing, he loves me! And this emotion that I'm feeling for him . . . is that love, too?*

She realised he wasn't going to apologise for his neglect of her. This was a man who had, perhaps, committed many sins of neglect in his time, but whatever he'd done, it wouldn't have been out of spite. Nothing trivial. He was, he seemed to be saying, what he was. Take me or leave me. A man of forceful character. A man worth two of Uncle Reuben. A man she could have loved wholeheartedly in other circumstances.

She could see what had attracted her mother to him: even ill as he was, even dying, he had charisma. She couldn't take her eyes off his face.

At last his fingers relaxed their hold upon hers. Ms Phillips touched Minty on her shoulder, and led the way into a pleasant sitting room next door, furnished in green. Everything was modern, cool, and expensive. Like the sickroom next door, the windows overlooked the lake.

Minty sank on to a window seat, feeling as if she'd run a marathon. Ms Phillips murmured something into a phone, and excused herself to go back into the sickroom. Minty slumped in her seat. She needed time to recover.

When Ms Phillips returned, Minty said, "How long has he got?"

"Hours, days, weeks . . . no one knows. He's been going downhill steadily for the last two months."

Minty put her hand to her throat. "Why did he come back here? He could have been treated in Switzerland or the States. Anywhere."

"When the third lot of treatments failed, he refused to try again. He had houses and flats everywhere, as you say, but they meant nothing to him any more. He said his family was all he'd got left, and they lived here. That's why we came."

"So his loving family put him in that bare room, instead of one of the state bedrooms?"

"They are dark and inconvenient for nursing. When the Hall was opened to the public, Sir Micah organised a number of self-contained flats for the family and staff. He chose these rooms overlooking the lake for himself and had them decorated to his own taste. My own flat lies above what used to be the stabling, over the restaurant. The present Lady Cardale has her apartments on the west front overlooking the main entrance, and Gemma is on the east overlooking the formal gardens. Simon is on the top floor overlooking the outer courtyard, above the offices.

"Sir Micah loves to look out at the sky. He has always loved the view over the lake. When we used to fly in by helicopter in the past, he always said, 'Now there's a bit of Old England.'"

"And do his beloved family care for him?"

Ms Phillips seated herself, knees and ankles neatly together. "Lady Cardale and he have grown apart over the years. They rarely meet nowadays, even though they live under the same roof. Gemma gives the impression of being a sweet child . . ."

A new, deep voice broke in "with the backbone of a jellyfish . . . and the sting of one, too."

Minty was surprised that the discreet Ms Phillips had been so critical. That could have been Patrick speaking.

"Besides, she's marrying a man who's got all the charm of a hyena, added to a thirst for money."

Minty's smile widened to a grin. She must remember to tell Patrick that.

The shadow of a frown crossed Ms Phillips's smooth forehead. It wasn't she who had spoken those words of criticism.

A little woman—possibly no more than five feet tall—had entered the room soundlessly, and was busying herself laying the day's newspapers on a low table nearby. She was clad in black. It was she who had voiced criticisms of Gemma and Miles.

Ms Phillips gave a little cough. "Araminta, this is Serafina, Sir Micah's invaluable housekeeper. Serafina, this is . . ."

"I know who she is. I recognised her from the portrait."

Portrait? thought Minty. *What portrait? Where? Of my mother?*

Serafina was possibly of Middle Eastern origin. She had a nutcracker face that split into a grin as she nodded to Minty.

Minty tried to get more information. "Which leaves Simon . . . ?"

Ms Phillips did not reply, but fiddled with her neat hairstyle. Serafina folded her hands in front of her and raised her eyebrows, but did not speak.

Ms Phillips said, "Sir Micah kept an eye on all of you, of course, through a detective agency. He learned that you were busy and happy working in the parish office for your uncle."

"Busy, yes. Happy, no."

"He didn't know that, did he? In fact, your uncle gave us quite the opposite impression when he came over to see Sir Micah last year. He said you were going to marry his wife's nephew, Lucas."

Minty was disgusted. "Oh, they would have liked it. I'd have been their slave for life in exchange for a wedding ring."

"We didn't know that, either. When the Reverend Cecil Scott arrived, I took the opportunity of speaking to him at some length about you. He also said that you were busy and happy in your parish work. He referred to you throughout as 'our little Martha'."

"One of these days I'm going to do something terrible to that man."

Ms Phillips said, "Hah!" which was probably her version of a laugh.

"So," said Minty, "what about Simon?"

Ms Phillips looked steadily at Minty, without replying. Serafina drifted around the room, flicking a duster at this and that.

Minty watched Serafina while she said, "Stop me if I'm wrong. Sir Micah adopted Simon after Gemma was born, hoping that the boy would in time take the place of the son he'd never had. Simon looks good. He can be charming. He was given a good education. He likes the high life and he knows how to spend money. I think Sir Micah gave him the chance to fly high in the world of finance, but something went wrong, because Simon is now milking the house and estate here instead of earning money out in the world."

Ms Phillips looked away, and didn't reply.

Serafina addressed a rather nice seascape. "And there's his debts, of course."

"Debts?" echoed Minty. "So he messed up in a big way, did he? And came home to Mummy to see what she could do to make him better? So that's why he wants to turn the Hall into a clinic?"

Ms Phillips stirred. "You've learned a lot in a short time, haven't you?"

Minty was indignant. "Simon doesn't give a snap of the fingers for anyone but himself. The village will die, but that's not important if he can still jet set around the world."

Ms Phillips stood. "Is that all you are interested in? Preserving the village as a part of Old England?"

"I love this place. I've been drawn into the lives of the people here, and I don't want them to suffer. The village depends on tourism, and if the Hall is closed to the public, most of the shops will go and so will the rest of the young people."

"Don't you love the Hall, too? Don't you want it preserved for posterity?"

Minty sighed. "Yes, but it's not my home. I think I'm the sort of person who's more interested in people than in buildings, however beautiful. If it's possible for me to get some kind of permanent job here, I'd like to stay and perhaps work up some other kind of tourist attraction. It might help to keep the village going."

Ms Phillips gave her a long, steady stare; then looked at her watch and exclaimed at the lateness of the hour. Serafina had already disappeared.

"Before you go," said Ms Phillips, "I've been instructed by your father to give you this cheque, representing the allowance you should have received for this past year. If you take it to the bank in town, they will honour it."

Minty recoiled. "After his rejection of me? After twenty years of neglect? I won't take a blind penny from him. Does he think I'm only interested in him for what I can get?"

"You haven't considered. You could get yourself some good clothes, a car . . ."

Minty took the cheque and tore it up. "Tell him I'm not to be bought. I can earn my own living, thank you very much!"

Ms Phillips didn't appear to be perturbed. "I thought you might say that. You've worked very hard this week on the holiday lets . . ."

"Part-time. Yes. You've paid me for that already. I still owe you a proper report, but that depends on what you mean to do with them. If they're to be sold, then I'll need to get quotes from builders, decorators, and the electrician to see what can be done to bring them up to scratch. If it's decided to keep them, then the same applies, but you'll also need to do some refurnishing."

"I can't take any decision on that at the moment. Suppose you continue to look after them for a week or so, doing what you can to keep them occupied until the situation is clarified? Do take the money. If you're not returning to the city, you'll need a job. Let your father help you. Don't you need things for yourself, and for Spring Cottage? About the cottage, I really must apologise for sending you there. I had no idea it was in such a bad shape."

"I can work part-time at the bookshop and part-time for the holiday lets if that's what you really want. That will bring in enough to keep me in the manner to which I have become accustomed."

"Sarcasm doesn't suit you."

"Don't you think it appropriate?"

Ms Phillips bent her head. "Very well. Part-time on the holiday lets—here's another week's wages for you in cash." She handed over a wages packet, which Minty took somewhat reluctantly. She wanted to be independent, but she did have to eat, and she had done the work for it.

Ms Phillips added, "May I ask you also to spare half an hour every day for your father? Say at half past ten? What do you say?"

"Are you trying to pay me for visiting my father?"

Ms Phillips shook her head. "No, but I am going to ask you to sit down and eat before you leave the Hall. We don't want you running under a lorry on that rackety old bike of yours, do we?"

There was a knock on the door and Serafina came in, pushing a hostess trolley before her. "Annie, the master says he could fancy some chicken soup."

Ms Phillips lit up. "Oh, that is good news. He hasn't fancied anything to eat for days. Araminta, please feel free to wander around as you wish this afternoon, but remember, he will be expecting you tomorrow at half past ten." She wafted herself out.

Minty wondered if Annie Phillips loved Sir Micah. It seemed possible. Serafina had also vanished. Obviously there were to be no more indiscreet revelations from that quarter.

Food? How could she think of eating when so much was happening?

The portrait. Where was it? She scanned the room but there were no portraits there and no photographs, either. Not even of Gemma or Simon. There were pictures on the wall, seascapes, cloudscapes. They were all beautiful, mostly modern, probably hideously expensive originals. But no portraits.

Over the fireplace hung an elegantly plain gilt-framed Regency mirror. The glass was foxed, probably original. Needing to hold on to something, Minty put her hands on the mantelpiece and bent her head. Where would a portrait of her mother be found? In another room of Sir Micah's flat? Minty guessed that the present Lady Cardale would not let it be hung where she could see it.

The tantalising odour of rich chicken soup caused her to raise her head, and as she did so she saw herself in the mirror, holding both hands over her cheeks, looking straight into her own eyes. Crying.

The hairstyle was wrong and so was the neckline of the dress.

Minty checked her own hands, which were still on the mantelpiece. She looked into the mirror again, and saw . . . what she usually saw when she looked in the mirror. Just Minty.

Breathing hard, she drew back and the image in the mirror drew back as well. Only a moment ago she had seen . . . her mother? Crying? Looking at her, asking her for . . . what? Justice?

Ms Phillips was right and she was overtired. She needed to sit down and eat, and then she would feel better. She pulled the hostess trolley over to the window and sat down to enjoy chicken soup—out of this world! A delicious salad with homemade pâté, hot rolls and butter, with a bowl of strawberries and cream. There was also a cafetiére of coffee. Presumably Florence Thornby cooked for the rest of the family, while Serafina cooked for Sir Micah.

Ms Phillips had been right and Minty did feel better after she'd eaten. The sky had clouded over and thunder rumbled almost overhead. Minty started as lightning shot across the sky, closely followed by another growl. The dark clouds overhead released a storm of rain over the land. Soon the slope was awash with water. A fine outlook for the fête on Saturday.

"Storm without and storm within," said a voice at Minty's elbow. Serafina had returned to remove the trolley. "Simon's come back in a fine old temper, demanding to see the master. Would you know anything about that?"

Was this the Big Bang? Minty said, "Serafina, where can I find my mother's portrait?" But the room was empty behind her.

The storm seemed to be directly overhead. From the sickroom Minty could hear raised voices. Well, Ms Phillips was perfectly capable of dealing with that.

Minty explored the rest of Sir Micah's suite. She found a series of beautifully furnished and decorated rooms all looking out over the lake; a dining room in dark gold, two bedrooms. Each had an inner doorway connecting to a corridor linking up with bathrooms, a kitchen and utility room, and at the end, two small rooms for someone living in. For Serafina?

Minty paused, thinking hard. She couldn't remember these rooms at all, but had a vague feeling that they'd been out of bounds before. Used only for storage?

With a leap of recognition, she came to the anteroom at the end of Sir Micah's suite and ran to the door to the chapel. Inside would be her mother and . . .

The door was locked.

She didn't understand it. That door was never locked. The tower room was a special place where her mother went every day to be quiet. "Up the pretty stairs to the golden room," her mother had said, helping her little daughter to climb the steep steps.

Grown-up Minty hesitated. She couldn't be mistaken, could she? This was the right tower? She glanced out of the windows to left and right, and yes: there was the lake on the left and on the right, beyond the formal gardens, she could see a little hill with a white folly in the shape of a Grecian temple on top. She'd been able to see the temple from the nursery windows. It had been a favourite place of hers. If it hadn't been raining so hard, she would have wanted to go there now.

She took stairs leading down to the first floor, running her fingers along the flowers that had been stencilled on the walls long before by her grandmother.

"Down the pretty stairs," her mother had said, "and then you shall choose. Shall we get out the toys in the nursery, or shall we have a bounce on the bed?"

Minty always chose the bed, because she didn't want to go back to Nanny Proud and Simon in the nursery. The bed was a giant four-poster in which her mother and father slept. It had cream linen curtains embroidered with strange plants and animals in blue and green. It had a roof and skirts and when you let the curtains fall, you were in a little house of your own.

Grown-up Minty had the same decision to make: nursery and toys? Or a bounce on the bed? She tried the door to the nurseries but it was locked. Oh.

She turned the other way . . . she must be directly under her father's apartments now. The door to the bedroom stood open and the great Jacobean bed was still there, its cream and blue curtains stiffly looped back. There was a plastic cover over the bedlinen. No bouncing permitted. Great knotted ropes of red allowed the onlooker to pass through the chamber—but not near enough to touch anything. She followed the guide ropes into the next room, and the next.

These were the great state bedrooms, the walls hung with silk, their windows shrouded with blinds to keep out the light. Eerily quiet, the furniture seemed to be aware of her as she passed through the rooms. She thought she remembered some of the furniture, but not as well as she remembered the cream and blue bed.

She turned a corner and was back in the oldest part of the house, standing on the landing above the well of the great staircase. She was a small child again, standing at the bend of the stairs, watching as the people below ran about and wept because her mother was dead . . . and her father had turned to ice.

The voices echoed back through the years.

"She can't be dead . . . she took the corner too fast . . ."

The woman with the black hair and dead white skin held on to her father's arm, pressing close to him . . . Lisa, pouring her poison into his ear.

Grown-up Minty clutched at the banisters to stop herself falling. Sightseers were crowding into the panelled hall below because this was the main entrance for tourists. A steward checking tickets looked up, saw Minty looking over the banisters and fell back, exclaiming something. A second steward, answering questions about one of the old clocks that stood at the foot of the stairs, also looked up and gaped.

Minty backed away, bewildered. What were they staring for? She wanted to get out quickly, but if she went down, the steward would ask for her ticket and she had none.

She sped back along the landing, back through the great state bedrooms, past stewards who were now taking up their positions. One or two looked at her curiously but she didn't stop. Her feet knew the way though her head didn't. She found the stairs to take her down to the ground floor. Now she was in the Long Gallery where she had played on rainy days. The floorboards shone with polish, and the marble fireplaces gleamed. From every wall her ancestors looked down upon her—but not her mother.

Small groups of people were filtering into the gallery behind her, watched by eagle-eyed stewards. Minty sped past them, looking for the small door she remembered led to the kitchen. The visitors stared at the girl flying along the gallery, but she could not stop.

At the end of the gallery was a doorway into the base of the tower. One sign pointed to a lift, and another directed tourists down stairs to the old kitchens and cellars. She ignored those to tumble through an inconspicuous door with a sign on it saying "Private". She found herself in the corridor with windows overlooking the cloisters and the inner courtyard. Nearby was the clatter of cooking pans, and there—at last—was the door into the kitchen.

Florence Thornby—kind middle-aged Mrs Thornby—looked up from her food processor and saw her. Florence had been crying.

"Florence! Oh, my dear! Are you all right?"

Florence Thornby sniffed. "I can always get another job, work at one of the pubs, probably. But Simon's told Gloria he won't be keeping her on because she doesn't fit the image he wants for the new restaurant. We've lost a son and a daughter to the city already. I don't think I can bear it if Gloria goes, too."

Somehow they had their arms around one another. Minty rubbed Florence's shoulder. Florence sniffed and hugged Minty. "I know you can't do anything," said Florence. "But, well . . . thanks for understanding."

"We can all pray," said Minty, wondering if it were right to give Florence a hint about the Big Bang and deciding that Patrick had been talking nonsense.

Florence blew her nose, washed her hands, and returned to the food processor. "Well, must get on. Come out and see us again soon?"

"I will."

Minty rescued her bicycle and fled the Hall through the last drops of rain.

Chapter Fourteen

Minty was relieved when she could at last turn the "Open" sign to "Closed" at the end of the day. She had two pay packets burning a hole in her pocket, one from working at the bookshop and the other from Ms Phillips, and she didn't have to send any part of them to her uncle and aunt. What riches! What would she buy? Clothes . . . or shoes? She would see what Ruby had in stock. Chocolates? A book?

In her absence that morning Mr Lightowler had had a long talk with Venetia. His enthusiasm had prevailed so far that Venetia had agreed after all to run a bookstall at the fête and suggested meeting after the shop closed.

The storm didn't seem to have refreshed the air, so at half past six they all—including Hugh—sat out in the garden to plan for the fête. Lady the cat supervised the meeting from the middle of the table.

Mr Lightowler began by saying that he understood the future of the bookshop was in doubt, but if he could afford to waste time doing what he liked more than anything else in the world, who was to prevent him? Neither Venetia nor Minty.

Hugh suggested, "I'll bring the Land-Rover down to the back of the shop at 1800 hours tomorrow, Friday, to load up. Entry to the grounds is at 8:30 on Saturday morning. I'll hump boxes to the stall for you, but then I'm on the gate for a couple of hours."

Minty made an effort to concentrate. "I've run stalls at fêtes since I was so high. We've got boxes of T-shirts, pens, and baseball caps doing nothing in the back cupboard. Could we give one of these away with every book we sell?"

"Brilliant," said Venetia, fanning herself. They were all feeling the heat.

"Minty and I have been routing out a lot of dead stock," said Mr Lightowler. "If you agree, we'll put nonsense prices on them, just to get shot of them. They're only taking up space we could use for new stock."

Minty said, "I can make the stall look attractive, but I'll need a little time first to set up my flower arrangement. Hugh, could you pick me up with my materials on your way to the Hall on Saturday morning?"

Hugh wagged his finger at her. "Going to outshine Mrs Chickward, are we?"

Minty giggled. "I shouldn't think so. Venetia, is what we're doing all right with Hannah?"

Venetia nodded. "I've been over to see her, poor thing. It was a nasty break and she's not young. She's actually pleased that I have someone else to take over the shop, as she'd like to retire and live with her sister when she can get about by herself again. I've cleaned out her fridge and packed up some things to take over to her, but Minty . . . would you water her pot plants for her now and then? She's fretting about them. I'll give you the keys before I go."

Minty was finding it difficult to keep her mind on the discussion. She had to decide whether to send to prison the people who had brought her up, she'd met her dying father for the first time that day, she felt all the problems of the village had landed on her shoulders, and she'd just realised that she'd fallen in love with a man who gave no sign of loving her back. *Oh, Patrick . . . !*

Venetia touched her arm. "Whatever's the matter, my dear?"

Minty tried to smile. What could she say? "I saw my father today. I was impressed."

Venetia looked at her askance. "You were wandering around the Hall today?" She started to laugh. "Is that why the stewards said they'd seen a ghost? It's all round the village. Millicent Cardale walks again, so the master's about to die. Superstitious nonsense!"

Minty tried to laugh, too. "I suppose it could have been me. I got lost and a couple of the stewards gave me funny looks, but you see, I didn't have a ticket, so I ran away."

Venetia said, "What a relief! I couldn't be doing with a ghost on top of everything else."

"I thought I saw my mother's ghost myself, but it was nothing. Just me getting overtired and thinking about her." Hugh, Venetia, and Mr Lightowler all looked hard at Minty. She raised her hands in protest. "It was only a reflection in a mirror, just for a second or two."

"Did you cross yourself?" enquired Mr Lightowler.

"I sat down and ate the chicken soup and salad prepared for me by Serafina. Who is she, by the way?"

Hugh looked morose. "Some say she's a black belt in judo. Others that she's got the evil eye. She actually prepared food for you?"

"It's more than she'll do for anyone but Sir Micah and Ms Phillips," said Venetia, mopping her neck. "Phew, is it hot, or is it just me?"

Lady streaked for shelter as lightning shot across the sky and thunder cracked overhead. They ran indoors as the rain came pelting down.

"A poor outlook for the fête," said Hugh, gloomily.

Minty had no mac or umbrella, so waited till the storm was over before leaving the shop. She spent the time finding her way up into Hannah's flat and watering the plants. Lady came up with her but didn't want to stay. Every now and then Minty looked out of the window to see if Patrick had returned, but his parking space remained empty.

She was restless, disturbed by the storm and by the decisions she had to make. She went across to the church to see if it was open. It wasn't. Then the rain came down again, so she waited on a bench in the porch for it to stop.

A large black umbrella shot into the porch, closely followed by the Reverend Cecil Scott. Minty drew back, but he'd seen her and his face lit up.

"My dear Martha! Oh, sorry. I can never remember. Minty, isn't it? So you came. I'm so glad. We're ever so short-handed this evening, but since you're early, we can have a bite to eat beforehand."

She hadn't a clue what he was talking about. He looked upset. "Didn't you get my message? It's the youth club, you see. We don't get many but . . ."

"I'm sorry. I just couldn't. Not tonight. I came here to be quiet and think."

He beamed. Sat down and patted the seat beside him. "Tell me all about it, eh?"

She shook her head. He was appealing, in a puppyish sort of way. But expecting her to unburden herself to him . . . no way!

"Is it about your uncle? I heard he was dying. I'm so sorry. He refuses to see me, I'm afraid."

Minty blinked. Dear Cecil; he'd got confused again. She was not in the least surprised to hear that Sir Micah had refused to see him, though. "My uncle is Reverend Reuben Cardale and he's not dying, so far as I know. But he is in big trouble, quite apart from being worried about my aunt, if that's what you're thinking."

"I'm sorry." He meant it. "He was so kind to me. If it hadn't been for him, I'd have given up long ago. I'm not that clever, you know, and though it did seem that God was calling me to work for him, I had my moments of doubt. Your uncle encouraged me to keep going, and when I was turned down for the first two parishes I applied to, he wrote to Lady Cardale for me. She thought I'd suit, and indeed, I've been very happy here."

Minty was silent. She hadn't known that.

"Why don't you tell me—whatever it is?"

"I have to decide what to do about . . . something. It's not easy. At first I was so angry that it seemed obvious what I should do." And here she remembered Patrick's outburst of anger. "But now, I just don't know what to do for the best."

"Have you prayed about it?"

She pulled a face. No, she hadn't, and she didn't want to. That would mean letting go of her anger and she wasn't prepared to do that yet. "This has nothing to do with God."

He said, gently, "Perhaps you've got it the wrong way round? Shouldn't it be prayer first, and decisions afterwards?" He folded his hands in prayer. "Dear Father God, you know how imperfect we are and very inclined to go our own way. Please put out of our minds all feelings of self-interest. Make it clear to us how we should act when we have difficult choices to make."

He was silent. Minty bowed her head. Perhaps he was right. Yes, she knew that he was right. She'd allowed her anger to come between her and God. So she, too, prayed.

She prayed for understanding, and guidance. She prayed that He would show her how to clear all feelings of hurt and anger from her heart, and help her to reach the decision He wanted her to make.

"There, now! That's better, isn't it?" he said, all cheerful bunny again.

Tactless man! He almost undid the calm his prayer had brought her. She grabbed back at the calm, remembering how Patrick had to fight his battle against hate time and again. And usually won.

The rain had almost stopped. "Thank you, Cecil. I do feel better. Perhaps I'll be able to come to youth club another time, but tonight I've something important to do."

He looked disappointed, and she felt him watching her as she scurried down the street. There were pools in the road and puddles on the pavements. The flowers in the planters looked beaten down. But the sky was lightening. She hoped.

"Minty! Minty! Here!" It was Ruby, beckoning to her from the door of a tiny cottage. Minty glanced at her watch. Her uncle would be leaving for a church meeting in half an hour and she wanted to catch him before he left, but Ruby was looking so pleased to see her that Minty hesitated. Also, it began to tip down with rain again.

Ruby drew her into her tiny cottage. "I've been looking out for you for ages, hoping you'd come down the street because . . . look what I got for you!"

Minty stepped into a small living room direct from the street. Everything was brown: furniture, curtains, wood, everything except the ornaments that glittered white with gold or silver trims. Ruby held up a large umbrella with a National Trust logo on it, and a long, caped green mackintosh.

"Oh, you darling!" cried Minty. "How clever of you! I did have an ancient umbrella and a horrid brown mac, but I left them in the city. How much do I owe you this time?"

Little Ruby laughed. "You wait—you haven't seen the best yet. Look!"

Something shrouded in tissue paper hung from an inner door. Ruby swept back the paper to reveal . . . a cornflower blue evening dress in floating silk chiffon. A dress fit for a princess. It was sleeveless, the neckline was low, and the bodice embroidered with crystal beads. The skirt was in layers, dipping to dozens of different points.

"Oh!" cried Minty. "Oh, what a beautiful dress! I've never seen anything so lovely!"

"Try it on. I think it's your size, but it may need a little taking in around the waist."

"For me?" Minty was bewildered. She allowed Ruby to help her into the dress. "But Ruby, a dress like that must cost hundreds of pounds, and when would I ever be able to wear it?"

Ruby turned Minty round. "At the ball next week, of course. Now, stand still and let me zip you up. The length's about right, but the bodice . . . hmm . . . I'll just take a tiny tuck in here . . . and here . . ."

"Ruby, I've not been invited."

"Don't bother me with details," said Ruby, irritated. "Of course you'll be invited. Or someone will take you. Stand still!"

Minty stood still. She looked down at Ruby's bowed head. "Ruby, you knew my mother, didn't you? I've heard such conflicting stories. Tell me what went wrong?"

Ruby sighed. "Lisa stalked him, that's what went wrong. They said she'd been after him for years. He should have sent her away but she was useful to him, and she knew how to make Miss Milly look silly and girlish. He was much older than her, had been about the world. He was used to women throwing themselves at him, and when he was a bachelor, he hadn't seen anything wrong in helping himself now and then. He was faithful to Miss Milly for a long time, in spite of the constant drip of poison coming from that Lisa. Miss Milly was no good at that sort of fighting, and she got worn down by it. No wonder she turned to an old family friend for sympathy. Still and all, it took Lisa four years to get him into her bed.

"Your father was shattered by Miss Milly's death. Went to his room and locked the door. Wouldn't come out. Lisa was frantic, tried everything to get him to let her in. Eventually she managed it. We all went to the funeral, of course. You'd disappeared by the time we got back. Lisa said you'd gone to stay with friends. Your father left with Lisa the following day and we heard they married soon after, somewhere abroad. You'll manage better than your mother did."

Minty blinked. Her poor mother. Would her daughter really manage any better? "But Ruby, tell me—"

"I told you to stand still! No more questions, now. I don't like talking about the old days. Now, take a look at yourself in the mirror. Those shoes won't do. I'll see if I can find you some gold sandals in the shop."

There was a mirror hanging over the fireplace and Minty could see herself in it, her hair hanging loose. She flushed with excitement and pleasure. She pirouetted, the skirt flaring out around her legs and the beads on the bodice catching the light. "It's so beautiful, but Ruby—even if I'd been invited to the ball, I couldn't take it. The cost—"

"Is nothing. You should have seen it when it was brought into the shop. Some pretty chit had worn it to a May Ball and ended up in the river. Or that's what it looked like. The skirt was in rags, and there were stains all down the bodice. If you look carefully, you'll see I've had to disguise them with the beads. The dress was going straight into the dustbin when I thought I might be able to do something with it. So I washed it and cut the skirt into points to hide where it had been torn. The beads I've had by me for ever. It was a pleasure, Minty. It really was."

Minty never cried. But she wanted to now.

It was Ruby who brought out her handkerchief. "Besides, you've been so good to my little old boy that I wanted to repay you."

Her "little old boy"? Prompt on cue there was a tap on the inner door. "May I come in now, Ruby?" Round the door came a well-known face. "Why, she looks just like a fairy, doesn't she, Ruby?"

"Jonah, what are you doing here?"

"Why, he's my lodger," said Ruby, with a self-conscious look. "Didn't you know?"

Minty gaped. Did this mean what she thought it meant? That it was *Ruby's* window from which Jonah had fallen, all those years ago? *Ruby?* Then did Ruby know that he still hankered after Hannah? Yes, she must do. Yet she still looked after him.

What grief that long-ago affair had led to! Hannah refusing to forgive her husband for straying, and Jonah still grieving after his estranged wife. And little Ruby still caring for a man who still loved his wife. Minty didn't know what to say, so she kept her mouth shut and made a mental note to pray for all three of them.

Ruby shooed Jonah away and helped Minty out of the dress. "I'll have it ready for you by Monday, and if you think you're going to pay me for it, you've got another think coming. Just make sure my little old boy can keep on looking after Hannah's garden, that's all. He's been doing it for thirty-odd years, and it'd kill him to stop now. There's no garden out the back here, you see. Just a courtyard."

Ruby hesitated, reddening. "Perhaps you've heard some gossip about him and me. Well, we did do it just that once. My father came back early and Jonah caught his foot and fell awkwardly out of the window. He nearly died. He was months in hospital and he was never the same, after. Hannah refused to visit him, so I used to go, now and then. He'd no memory of the accident or about being with me. He had to learn to speak and walk all over again. I used to think it would have been better if . . . but no, the Lord knows best . . . and sometimes he's almost like his old self again, though he's never been able to hold down a job since.

"Hannah wouldn't take him back, so when he came out of hospital there was nowhere for him to go. His brother was away with the army and the manor house was let. So I took him in. I don't expect you to understand, but . . ."

"I'll do my best to see that he can continue looking after the garden," said Minty.

"That's all we can do, my dear. Our best. Now the sun's out again, and no doubt you'll need to be off to see your young man."

"Ruby, I have no young man."

"Don't you, my dear? Now you could have fooled me!"

Minty dived into her own dress to hide her face.

It was now well past the hour when her uncle would have left for his meeting. Minty hurried down the hill, patting her pockets for her mobile phone . . . which she must have left at the cottage, because she hadn't got it on her . . . and wondering if Patrick had managed to do without his cigarettes.

The moment she opened the door of the cottage, she knew Mrs Guinness had been there. That sickly perfume was unmistakable. Minty felt a prickle of fear run down her back. What had the woman been doing in here? How had she got in? Had she returned to "borrow" something she felt she couldn't live without? The large teapot, for instance? Minty let her eyes wander around the room. The teapot was still there, but perhaps the photograph of her mother had been moved a little to the left?

Then the explanation came to her; it had been the electrician, Dwayne's, last day here. No doubt he'd let Mrs Guinness in when she chanced by, nosy as ever, to see what was going on. Cecil had said he'd left a message for her. So where would that be?

There was a note on the table from Dwayne to say he'd installed the fridge for her, and also an old but workable spin dryer he had no further use for.

There was no note from Cecil. Nor from Patrick. Not that she'd expected one from Patrick, of course. Not really.

Lady the cat was yowling to be let in. Minty let Lady in, and he walked warily all around the ground floor, sniffing at scents too faint for Minty to detect.

In the rubbish bin was a crumpled up note from Cecil, which did indeed ask if she'd like to help him out at the youth club that evening, with supper thrown in. He also asked—if she hadn't already got a partner for the ball—whether she would like to go with him. For a moment Minty was tempted, thinking of swishing down the stairs at the Hall in that wonderful dress. But no. It was impossible. Poor Cecil!

There was no note from Patrick even in the rubbish bin. Minty told herself that she wasn't in the least disappointed. He'd forgotten, of course. He was a very busy man.

The air was still very humid, so Minty opened the back door wide to get a through draught—and yelped with frustration. She'd left the flowers for the fête in two deep buckets filled with water, but someone had pushed or kicked the buckets over. Luckily they'd been in the lee of the back wall and so hadn't been pounded too much by the rain, but . . . what spite! Mrs Guinness again, of course.

There was also a plant pot tipped over on the bench. A plant with white flowers that hadn't been there when she last looked. Over the past week she'd gradually been clearing patches of earth outside the kitchen. Someone had brought her a plant for the garden and someone else—presumably Mrs Guinness, had tossed it out.

Who would have brought her a plant? Jonah? No. Jonah's taste was for roses and geraniums. Besides, he was fixated about Hannah's garden and it wouldn't have occurred to him to bring her a plant. She picked it up. It was an argyranthemum, a plant she had always known as a marguerite. Or a daisy.

Daisies, thought Minty. Patrick? This was a present from him? She wished she knew what it meant. He hadn't left any other message, but he hadn't forgotten her. She could phone him to say thank you, and he would explain why he hadn't been around today and perhaps confirm his invitation for her to cook their meal on Saturday after the fête.

There were no messages on her mobile. Well, the daisies were message enough. He'd recorded his number in the memory bank, so all she had to do was . . .

It wasn't there. She went through the list again and again. Think, Minty, think! He had put his number in; she had watched him do it. Would Mrs Guinness have wiped it off? But why? Because he'd warned Mrs Guinness's niece off receiving stolen goods?

There was no phone book in the cottage. A pity. If she'd had his office number, she could have left a message for him there.

Of course, the plant might not be from him, and he was perfectly entitled to go away for a few days without telling her. He'd said he might have to be away overnight.

He'd promised to ring her and hadn't. Big deal. Why was she so surprised that he'd forgotten? Why should he remember her? He had more important things to think about, hadn't he? It would be awful to thank him for his gift, if it hadn't come from him.

She looked at her watch. Her uncle would now be halfway through his meeting. Lucas would be out and her aunt would be sitting in front of the television, feeling sorry for herself. Minty tried to recall the peace she had achieved after praying in the church porch with Cecil. Some words had come into her mind then, about how to act if someone in the church did something wrong. "If a brother sins, two of you should go to him and talk to him about it."

Well, she had no one to go with to her uncle, but she could at least approach him without anger, without laying blame. Just stating the facts as she knew them, and asking for an explanation.

With the phone in her hand, Minty sent up a prayer that she was doing the right thing and keyed in the number of the vicarage. Her aunt didn't pick up the phone. She rarely did, saying that it was bound to be for her husband or her nephew. Let the answerphone do what it was supposed to do.

Minty listened for the tone and said, "Uncle, this is Minty. Ms Phillips at the Hall has shown me proof of my father's financial support over the years. You always told me I was in your debt, so I think I'm due an explanation. It's been suggested I report this to the police, as a case of fraud. I'm not going to do that. Yet. However, I would like repayment of at least some of the money you have received on my behalf."

She put the phone down, breathing hard. She thought she'd done the right thing. She hoped she had. Her anger was cooling now, though she wondered if it would resurface later—as it had with Patrick. *Don't think about him.*

She got Lady and herself some supper and worked on the base for the flower arrangement for Saturday. As she worked, she found herself praying in snatches. For the different people she had met that week . . . for her father. For poor bullied Ruby, who had turned out to have a surprising lodger . . . for the lodger himself! And here she laughed a little. Who would have thought of Jonah as a lady's man? Yet Mr Thornby had known.

She prayed for Cecil Scott. She had misjudged him; he was not as ineffective as she had thought. She prayed for Alice and her daughter Marie, that Alice would make the right decision about her future. She must also pray for Patrick, and Venetia and Hugh. Mr Lightowler.

She snapped her fingers. Patrick had made a list and lost it in her garden. She'd thought it had been a list of people to visit, but it hadn't been that because Nanny Proud would never have let him visit her. It had been a prayer list. Patrick had been praying for all sorts of people, for Hannah and Jonah and Nanny Proud. For Araminta Cardale.

So was Patrick a praying, active Christian?

She liked that thought. Some time soon she would ask him.

Then she had another, sobering thought. Since her arrival in the village, she'd been tempted several times to break her habit of prayer. At one point she had even thought of missing a church service. Several times she'd been so angry that she'd rejected the very idea of praying. But when she'd turned back to Him, He'd been there, waiting for her, loving her, helping her on her way. She thanked him aloud for that. *Thank you, Lord.*

Chapter Fifteen

Friday morning and the rain had finally stopped. A heavy mist covered the land, but if the sun broke through it would be steamingly hot.

Minty felt restless and uneasy. As she got ready for work, she glanced at the heavy bolts on the inside of the doors. She told herself that Mrs Guinness couldn't possibly get in again today because Dwayne wouldn't be there to let her in. Somehow this reasoning failed to convince.

She went into the bookshop early, so that she could take time off mid-morning to be with her father. That is, if he hadn't died in the night. She shuddered at the thought. She had only just met him again and already felt a bond between them.

Patrick's car was still not in his slot behind his office and there was no message from him at the bookshop. She shrugged. So what?

Just after ten she left the bookshop and cycled down to the Hall. By the time she arrived, there was a heavy stream of traffic all going into the Hall grounds, preparing for the fête on the morrow. They rounded the house, aiming for the slope down to the lake. Minty spotted Mrs Collins directing operations with a megaphone.

Ms Phillips was in her office, but she had someone with her. "Sir Micah is better today and looking forward to seeing you. Can you find your own way up?"

Yes, of course she could. Sir Micah was indeed better. He was still in bed but no longer wearing an oxygen mask. He was even wearing a cashmere sweater over a shirt, and he held out his hand to her as she seated herself at his side. He smiled at her. It was like the sun coming and shining on her, when he smiled at her like that.

"Tell me . . . about yourself," he half spoke, and half whispered.

She could think of half a dozen things to say that would all sound like complaints at her treatment at his hands. She didn't want that.

"Well, now . . . it was coming up to Christmas. I was five years old and like every other girl in the class I wanted to play Mary in the Nativity play. Actually, there were going to be two Nativity plays: one to be performed at church, and the other at school. The teachers cast the plays partly on the children's looks and partly on their good behaviour.

"I craved approval, so I was a model pupil. I really did love my Sunday school teacher at church, because she was a kind and loving person. She cast me as Mary. I was so thrilled! I felt I looked the part, too, with curly blonde hair and blue eyes.

"When my uncle and aunt found out, they were horrified. They told my Sunday school teacher I wasn't fit to play Mary, because of my mother. They weren't too careful about who overheard them, so very soon everyone at church knew I wasn't fit to be Mary, because of what my mother had done."

Sir Micah's hand tightened into a painful grasp around Minty's fingers, but she smiled and continued with her tale.

"I didn't cry, because Nanny Proud said big girls don't cry. I held my head high and when the other children mocked me, I pretended not to care. I got hold of my aunt's scissors and cut my hair short.

"Don't get upset, because that wasn't the end of the story. My teacher at school asked my aunt why my hair had been cut so short, and my aunt—never one to mince words—told her. My schoolteacher was shocked. She hadn't intended to cast me as Mary in the school production, because she had several children from Middle Eastern backgrounds whom she thought more suitable. She cast me as the angel instead, and gave me more words to say. I've always been grateful to her for that."

Sir Micah had a pad of paper and pencil at his side. He scribbled, "Meaning?"

"I don't know that it meant much to me at the time," said Minty, "except to endure without making a fuss. Now, I look back and see it taught me a lot. You can't make everyone like you. Life's not always going to treat you fairly, but sometimes you get what you want. And if you don't," she shrugged, "you make the best of what you've got."

He stared at her. Perhaps he was staring through her. The nurse came in, checked to see he was all right. He waved her away. His eyelids drooped, and his hand relaxed its grip on her. Minty stood up and wandered over to the window. There was a lot going on outside. Even as she watched, an enormous marquee was hoisted into the air and anchored fast. A stage was being assembled next to it, and beyond that, a giant slide . . . and a bouncy castle.

Sir Micah made a movement to attract Minty's attention and lifted his eyebrows.

She said, "You want to know what's going on outside? It's a campaign and Mrs Collins is the general, sending aides-de-camp all over the battlefield, setting up the commissariat, laying down power lines, directing the erection of the billets, bringing in the supplies. She's a marvellous organiser. You know that I'll be in the thick of it tomorrow?"

She told him about the bookstall and Mr Lightowler and Venetia and Hugh. Then she told him about the feud between Felicity Chickward and Mrs Collins, and how she'd got drawn into it.

He scrawled something on his pad and held it up for her to see. "Report tomorrow?"

"When it's all over, yes. I don't think I can get away before then." She sat down beside him again, thinking that he looked terribly frail. But his eyes were hard and bright. He held out his hand and she put her own into it. He smiled at her and again Minty felt his warmth around her.

Ms Phillips came into the room. Perhaps he had signalled for her on the buzzer that lay close to his left hand? Ms Phillips was carrying a jewellery case, which she opened and handed to Minty.

"These were your mother's. The set was designed and made for her as a wedding present in Australia. Sir Micah asked me to get these from the bank for you to wear next week at the ball."

Minty said, in some irritation, "Everyone seems to think I'm going to the ball, but I assure you I'm not."

"Haven't you had an invitation?"

"Not from anyone I would care to go with."

"Not from Simon?"

Minty stared at Ms Phillips. "Good heavens, no!"

A signal passed from Sir Micah to Ms Phillips. "I'll see to it that you get your own invitation tomorrow. Would you care to try the necklace on?"

For the first time Minty looked at the jewels, large opals set in heavy gold. There were a necklace, two bracelets, two stud earrings and two drop ones.

Minty gasped. She couldn't help thinking how well the jewels would go with the blue dress Ruby had found for her. She lifted the necklace and tried it against her neck. Ms Phillips fastened it for her.

There was only one small mirror in the room. She rushed over to see herself. The opals glowed against her newly tanned skin, bringing out the blue in her eyes and the gold of her hair.

Minty cried, "Oh! They're so beautiful!" She tried on the bracelets, and let them fall down from her wrists to her forearms, holding them up for Sir Micah to see.

"I don't think you should wear everything at once," said Ms Phillips, judiciously. "Either the bracelets and the earrings, or the necklace alone? Oh, and your father wants you to buy yourself a new dress for the ball; shoes, everything you need. The money's in this envelope."

"You're always trying to give me money," said Minty, shaking her head. "But I don't want it. I have a dress already." And she laughed to think that a charity dress was going to the ball, thanks to Ruby. "Shall I come and show myself off to you before I go to the ball?"

Sir Micah grinned and nodded, waving away the envelope Ms Phillips was holding out for Minty to take. She bent and kissed him, very gently. His skin felt slightly clammy. She was filled with sorrow for him and for herself. She thought, *He's going on his final journey. How I wish he would go into the night trusting in God . . . but he's not ready for that yet, if he refuses to see Cecil.*

His hand lay on the coverlet. She picked it up and kissed that, too. "Till tomorrow, then?"

He nodded, and she left, taking the jewel box with her. In the anteroom she took off the necklace and the bracelets and carefully put them away in the box. Ms Phillips had followed her out, so Minty asked for and got a large Jiffy bag to put the jewel case into. The opals were one more link with her mother. She'd heard that opals signified tears. Well, big girls don't cry, and she thought they were the most beautiful things she had ever seen.

"They're insured?"

Ms Phillips nodded.

"May I ask, was it you who arranged for Gemma to ask me back?"

Ms Phillips nodded again. "Sir Micah has been disappointed in the way his children turned out, only wanting money from him. They don't even visit, if they can help it. He'd talked a lot about you recently, wondering how you'd turned out, but for some reason didn't want to send for you himself. I knew that Gemma and Simon had fallen out over the holiday lets and I . . . er . . . suggested that Gemma might find you useful and supplied her with your phone number. She is a creature of impulse. She rang you there and then. She was sorry next morning, of course, but the deed was done and you came. You see now why I had to check out your claim not to have received any money from your father. It would have broken his heart if you'd been no better than the others."

"Thank you," said Minty. "And no, I don't want his money. Ever." She tried to think what else she needed to ask Ms Phillips. "There's just one other thing. I hate to bother you when you have so much else to think about, but do I have the authority to sack Mrs Guinness?"

"What's brought this on?" asked Ms Phillips.

"She was in Spring Cottage sometime yesterday without permission. A message had been left with Dwayne the electrician for me during the day and I only found it when I looked in the bin."

"Who was it from?"

Minty shrugged. "Cecil Scott, poor man. And no, I am not leading him on, nor going out with him, nor likely to do so. I know it sounds petty, and so was the tipping out of the flowers I'd left to condition outside the back door, but I'd stupidly left my mobile phone on the table and one particular phone number has been deleted from its memory. And that is rather awkward."

"Whose phone number? Simon's?"

"Of course not!"

"Was it your cousin's, or someone else from the city, from your past?"

"No." Minty half laughed. "Believe me, you don't want to know."

"The very worst scenario is . . ."

"Think it, then," said Minty. "It was Patrick Sands."

Ms Phillips ran a finger delicately over one eyebrow, a sign of severe mental distress. "He is the last person that Sir Micah would wish you to become friendly with."

"It's a bit like Romeo and Juliet, isn't it? The more we're told our families don't want it, the more likely we are to get together. I like Patrick very much and I think he likes me. So far that's all there is to it."

Ms Phillips swallowed that pill without even grimacing. "Why would Mrs Guinness want to erase Patrick Sands's telephone number from your mobile?"

"We're both in her bad books because we've stopped her petty thieving. I think she picked up my mobile out of curiosity and listened to the message on it. Patrick had promised to ring me, but there's no message there now. I think she erased it, and then erased his number so I couldn't get back to him."

"Supposition."

"I know. Patrick might not have left a message for me. But I am . . . uneasy. So do I have the authority to sack her?"

"You must have good grounds and give written warnings. Also, you'll need to find someone else to take over her job. Can you do that?"

Minty thought of Alice, who would probably welcome extra work—if she stayed. Perhaps having extra work might induce Alice to stay. She nodded.

❧

The Hall was open to visitors again that day. Minty could hear the hum as she made her way out. She would have loved to have gone exploring again, but after causing that silly rumour about the ghost, she felt she should put it off till the Hall was quiet again.

Gloria Thornby was standing by Minty's bicycle—the bicycle that had come from the Thornbys—when Minty reached the courtyard.

Gloria said, "Have you been to see Sir Micah again? Does he know what Simon wants to do? Can't you talk to him, get him to stop Simon?"

"Gloria dear! My father is not well, and I don't know that he takes any interest in . . ." Minty was aware that she sounded feeble and hated herself for it.

"Then he should take an interest. We're people. We're not just things to be bought and sold." She looked as if she was going to cry. She looked as if she had been crying already.

Minty put her arm around Gloria and thought about the good time she had had up at the Thornby farm and how kind they had all been to her.

Minty said, "I wish I knew how to help. Are you praying about it? I'll pray, too."

"You do what you like." Gloria tossed back her hair. "We're going to need more than prayer to save our jobs." She stalked off back to the kitchens.

Minty sighed. Gloria obviously didn't know how powerful prayer could be. She got back on her bicycle, and did pray about it.

She stashed her bike in the garden of the bookshop and hurried inside. Mr Lightowler had volunteered to cover for Minty and was attending to several customers. Minty made them both a cup of coffee and got on with packing up the things they would need for the fête the following day. Someone came in and Mr Lightowler called to Minty, "Special delivery for you!"

A huge bouquet of flowers wrapped in cellophane was thrust into Minty's arms. Red hothouse roses, dozens of them. There was a card with the flowers, but all it said was "Sorry!"

"Which of your young men is that from?" grunted Mr Lightowler. "I've had the Reverend in here this morning already, asking where you were. Patrick Sands is still away, I think. Are the flowers from him?"

"I don't think so." Patrick's mind was on daisies, and this overblown extravagance wasn't like him. She didn't know who it could be from . . . unless perhaps her cousin Lucas was trying to woo her back home by sending her flowers? No. That wasn't Lucas's style, either. He was a box-of-chocolates man, and a small box at that.

She thought, *What a pity . . . hothouse roses die so quickly.* She took them out to the cubbyhole where they made coffee, and shoved them in the sink.

"Surprise!" Someone put their hands around her eyes and pulled her back to his chest. She went rigid. This was not Patrick. The smell wasn't right. This man smelt of a very expensive after-shave. She thought of yelling for Mr Lightowler but decided not to do so, since he was serving another customer. She waited patiently for the man—whoever he might be—to declare himself.

He turned her round and she found herself looking into intense blue eyes, alight with mischief. He looked like a Greek god, with a tan that had to go all over. He was the handsomest man she'd ever seen close up, and he was smiling down at her. Amazingly, it was her stepbrother, Simon Cardale.

"I know," he said, teasingly. "We got off on the wrong foot, didn't we? I thought you were a gold-digger, come to see what you could get now my father's dying. If only I'd known that you were for real! And the prettiest star on the horizon! Do say you understand?"

One part of her mind reminded her that nothing was ever Simon's fault, but her mouth seemed to have a will of its own. She found herself smiling back at him, and saying, "Yes." Surely he was sincere. And truly sorry. Yes, she could see he was.

"You dear girl! I must admit that every time I've seen you, I've found it hard not to fall at your feet. How could such a beautiful, gentle creature as you have been kept from us for so long?"

From somewhere at the back of Minty's mind a dark childhood memory hovered, of Simon pinching her and then laughing. She thrust that away. He had only been a small boy then and he was all grown up now. It was true that he'd rejected her when she first arrived, but of course he'd have expected her to be after Sir Micah's money. If he was truly sorry—and looking up into his eyes, she had to believe that he was—then she must forgive him. He was her stepbrother and she'd always longed for brothers and sisters.

And wouldn't it be fun to flirt with him? Just a little? Didn't she deserve a little fun now and again?

She laughed and shook her head at him. At the back of her mind a small voice said, *How flame-proof are you, Araminta Cardale?* But she ignored it. Patrick had been wrong about Simon. He wasn't bad. He might be spoilt. Well, yes. How could he not be spoiled with those looks and charm?

Simon held her by her shoulders. His eyes were the most intensely dark blue she had ever seen in anyone. He looked like St Michael and St George rolled into one. A true knight. He was looking at her as if she were the most desirable girl in the world.

He said, "Gemma was upset, too. She wants to get to know you and be friends, but she's shy, the silly thing. She asked me if I'd make the first move, and of course I agreed. So, are you going to meet us halfway, Minty?" He glanced at the flowers, and a shadow of a frown crossed his perfect face. "You ought to have got those yesterday. I'll have something to say to the shop about that. I thought roses would be best. The most perfect flowers for the most beautiful girl in the world. You got my message?"

"Message?"

"My card. Saying 'Sorry!'"

"You didn't sign it."

"I thought you'd understand," he said with a hint of reproach. Such was his charm that she immediately felt contrite. Of course, she ought to have known who the flowers were from.

"So here I am in person to invite you to kiss and make up. Gemma wants you to come out to supper with us tonight, make up a foursome. Do say you'll come! She'll be so distressed if you turn her down . . . and I will, too."

"Why, I . . . I hadn't thought." She put her hand to her head. Wasn't there something she ought to be doing tonight? What about Patrick? No, Patrick was away. Getting ready for the fête? It was almost all done. A good dress? The one she had on might not be suitable, but she had nothing better.

"Was that a yes? Great! I'll pick you up here at half past six." He threw her a kiss and was gone.

Minty took a deep breath and put her hands over her hot cheeks. She was going out with the handsomest man in the county that night. And with Gemma, too. Simon was right, and she ought to be friends with her half-sister and stepbrother. It would also be the Christian thing to do, to reach out the hand of friendship, forgive and forget past insults. She could dress up her second-hand frock with the opal earrings, so she wouldn't look too shabby. Her sandals were scuffed, but she couldn't do anything about that. She had no suitable handbag, but she could put her keys in the pocket of her dress and didn't need to take anything else with her.

As for Patrick . . . well, his car still wasn't back and he hadn't left any message for her at the shop, which he could easily have done if he'd been serious about keeping in contact with her. So, roll on closing time.

Chapter Sixteen

At half past six Minty helped Mr Lightowler shove the last carton into the back of Hugh's estate car, washed her face, brushed out her hair and donned the opal earrings. The rest of the jewellery she replaced in its case and stowed in the office safe.

Simon arrived at a quarter to seven. A toot on a horn and he drew up in a red Lotus. "Hop in! Can't hang around here. Too many parking tickets as it is."

She was no sooner in than they were off, down the road in a powerful plunge past the shops, crossing the bridge, turning to the left and away . . .

"I thought Gemma was coming?"

"Meeting us there. Miles is taking her."

He was wearing a cream-coloured suede jacket over a crisp white shirt and designer jeans. He looked superb. Minty brushed dust from her dress, and told herself firmly that second-hand clothes didn't mean you were a second-hand person.

"How do you like the car?" he asked. He proceeded to talk about his cars, telling her their various merits and idiosyncrasies. Having put her at ease, he asked how her day had gone, made sure she was comfortable. He told her a funny joke he'd heard, asked if she liked dancing. He was good company, light-hearted, laughing.

She had hungered for this, being made much of, being cared for. All those years of endurance, followed by that strange half-wooing of Lucas's . . . and now this. The car sped along lanes, across main roads and through the evening air as if it liked to fly, rather than travel on mundane wheels. Minty was lost within the first few minutes, but didn't care. She'd never before travelled in such a superb car, beside such a handsome man. Was this the knight in shining armour of whom she'd always dreamed? This evening was a heady experience and she intended to enjoy every minute of it.

He turned at last into the extensive car park of a gabled pub. Tubs and hanging baskets of flowers added a note of gaiety, and to judge by the well-dressed clientele piling into the place, the prices would be sky high.

"Minty, oh my dear!" cried Gemma, getting out of a sleek saloon. Her fiancé, Miles, waited, scowling, while Gemma kissed Minty on both cheeks. "I can't tell you how thrilled I am. Oh, let me look at you. Have you really been working in that horrid shop all day? You look fabulous. Positively, I'm green. Those opals. My dear, where did you get them?"

Gemma was wearing an expensive trouser suit in peacock blue silk, and enveloped in a cloud of flowery fragrances. Her fingernails were polished, and the emerald glowed on her hand. Her handbag was a mere trifle on a long chain, and her sandals were of green to match her suit. She looked as if she had just come from a beauty parlour.

Minty stifled envy and thought how wonderful it was to have a sister who greeted her so kindly. It was better than her dreams to be welcomed into such a wonderful family. She kissed Gemma back. "I'm glad you want to be friends, Gemma. Especially at this time, when father is . . ."

Gemma's beautiful eyes filled with tears. "Oh, don't say it! Don't! I can't bear it. Every time I think about it, I cry . . . don't I, Miles?"

"Such a tender little heart," said Miles, sourly. He kissed Minty, too, and for the first time that evening she felt a frisson of unease. Miles's kiss was just a tad too enthusiastic, and his eyes were definitely hot. They signalled that something was going on behind his eyes, something that caused her to recoil. She thought, *He hates me. But why? Oh, surely I must be mistaken.*

Simon was impatient. "Let's go in or they'll give our table to someone else. Minty, you'll love this place. It's a sight better than the Chinese takeaway you had the other night."

That was a false step, thought Minty, frowning. So Simon knew that she and Patrick had had a Chinese meal together? Well . . . so what if he did know? Simon was right and this place *was* a cut above the Chinese restaurant. If Patrick had really been serious about her, he'd have offered to take her to a place like this, instead of asking her to cook a meal for him. If he could go off without telling her, then she was certainly entitled to go to dinner with her family.

They were shown to some bench seats in an alcove outside the restaurant area. The inn was all low beams, with huge fireplaces filled with fir cones and stands of flowers. The menus were enormous, too.

"What shall we have to drink?" asked Simon. "I vote for champagne, to seal our new relationship."

Minty said, "Not for me." But Simon was already ordering. She thought, *Well, I've only tasted champagne at a couple of wedding receptions in the parish, and although I didn't like it much, a sip or two won't hurt me.*

"To us!" cried Simon, when the champagne came.

"To a rosy future!" cried Gemma, taking a gulp.

"To us," said Minty, sipping it and deciding that no, she still didn't like the taste.

Gemma threw down her menu. "You order for us, Simon. You know best."

"Shall I? Minty, do you like red or white wine best?"

"A little of whatever you like. And some water, please." She wasn't a teetotaller and had been used to the odd half glass of wine here and there, but that was her limit.

"Nonsense, we can't be doing with that vicarage mentality here, my girl. We're out tonight to celebrate, not to attend Communion."

Gemma and Miles laughed, but Minty flushed. "Well, a little red, then."

"Not used to it, eh?" said Miles, giving her a narrow-eyed, contemptuous look. They made her feel like a schoolgirl. Miles had already finished his first glass of champagne as had the others.

"Drink up! There's plenty more to come," said Simon. He topped up Minty's glass and called for another bottle. Minty touched her lips to the glass and tried not to make a face.

Gemma made Miles move over, so that she could sit by Minty. "I'm so glad you've come tonight. I hated having to turn you away that first day, but everything's turned out for the best, hasn't it? Simon's quite happy about it now. I hear you've been good, sitting with father. How is he? I've been up to see him once or twice, but I can never think of anything to say. Then he just waves me away. Or that dragon Ms Phillips comes in and says there's papers for him to sign . . ."

The second bottle of champagne was empty before they were told their table was ready. Minty left her almost-full glass on the table. She was a trifle worried about all this alcohol. Would Simon be fit to drive home later?

A bottle of red wine was brought to the table. Simon pronounced it perfect for the starter and, ha ha, he was sure Minty would appreciate it better than the champagne, which he thought must have been on the dry side for her. He said he must remember that she had a sweet tooth. Minty smiled and didn't contradict him. It seemed simpler.

The starter was delicious, though perhaps a trifle salty. Minty asked Simon to get some water for her. He said, in a minute, and continued with an anecdote about some friends of his who were hang-gliding in Spain, and had Minty ever had an opportunity to go hang-gliding, no? What about snorkelling on the Barrier Reef? No? How he looked forward to showing her all these things.

Gemma was drinking as much as the men.

Simon put his hand over Minty's. "What else am I going to have to teach you, my little prude? You really must learn to lighten up a bit, now you're out of the vicarage."

"Yes, indeed," said Gemma, emphatically.

Minty began to wonder if she was out of her depth.

"A toast to the future!" Simon cried.

They all drained their glasses, except for Minty, who took a small sip and put her glass back on the table. She resolved to make the best of things. She was here now, and she didn't need to drink as much as they did. It was good to feel a part of this new family of hers and good to taste new things to eat. She wished Miles didn't keep staring at her, though. She moved her shoulders uneasily under her dress, and turned back to Simon, who was talking about how well his new car handled.

The main course came and another two bottles of wine. The toasts kept coming. Minty began to feel bothered because she took no more than a sip of wine each time.

"Come on, drink up, Minty. You can't be a wet blanket on a night like this."

"Come on, Minty. Here's to your blue eyes . . . and everything else!" That was Miles, following Simon's lead. Was Gemma attracted to the aura of savagery Miles carried around with him? Was that why she was marrying him?

Minty was desperate for a good long drink of cold water, but Simon insisted wine was the best thirst quencher.

He called for another bottle as the main course was cleared away. Minty got out of her seat in the slight confusion caused by the waiter taking the dishes away and made for the bar. She asked for water but the man behind the bar ignored her. Of course, they would make their money here on the wine, but . . . how could she get some water?

The bar extended around a corner, so she went round where a woman happened to be serving. An older woman, experienced. Minty asked her for a glass of water, and the woman was sympathetic. "Got to take a pill? Wait a mo', and I'll fetch you one. Ice and lemon?"

Minty waited while the woman served a couple of men who were buying rounds of drinks, and thanked the woman when the water eventually came. She drank the water and replaced the glass on the bar.

When she got back to their table, it was to find that Miles had taken Gemma off home. "He forgot something he's got to do tonight," said Simon, who still appeared only slightly merry in spite of all the wine he'd drunk. "We'll get home in our own time . . . or perhaps not get home at all, eh? I've been thinking. Got to attend to my new little friend's education. I've got the plane nearby. Why don't we go for a look at the lights of the city tonight? Or even better, I'll take you over to Deauville and we can play the tables. Are you lucky with the dice, Minty? I bet you are. You shall be my lucky lady tonight. Drink up, and we'll be off."

This brought Minty up short. What was he proposing? A night flight? To France? To gamble? He would call her a prude if she refused, but her uneasiness was growing all the time.

Only, how could she get out of it? She reseated herself at the table. Cheese and biscuits had arrived. A Stilton. More saltiness. She took a nibble of cheese and reached for the wine again. Only, something stayed her hand.

How well she remembered the lectures the youth leader at church had given them. "Don't drink and drive—it's dangerous to everyone else as well as to you. Don't drink anything that you haven't seen poured out of a bottle. Never leave your drink unattended, in case something is added to it."

Simon might merely have been playing the hospitable host when he pressed her to drink so much wine. Or not.

It might just be coincidence that Miles and Gemma had gone home early, leaving Simon to take Minty home when he chose. Or not. She wondered if she'd allowed Simon's attentions to her to go to her head. Yes, perhaps she had. She'd been foolish, but now that she knew the score, she wouldn't play his game any longer.

"I'm a bit worried about getting back late, Simon. There's the fête tomorrow, and I'll be hard at it from early morning on."

"The fête? My dear, don't be so parochial. What's the fête to me?"

So that was that.

She tried again. "Do me a favour, Simon? Let me drive your car home? I've a licence but I've never driven anything as marvellous as your car."

"Drive my car? My dear little poppet! You must be out of your tiny mind. Come on, drink up. The night's young and there's another bottle on its way."

"Do you really think you should have any more?" She hated sounding prissy, but she was becoming seriously alarmed at his intake.

"If you think I'm over the limit, we can always ask for a key to a room here. Is that what you would like? Ah, of course it is. You should have said earlier, my dear."

"Excuse me for a moment." She stood up and went to the toilet. What was she going to do now? Gemma and Miles had long since departed. She'd no idea exactly where she was and even if she could get a taxi to take her home, she hadn't any money on her to pay for it.

She went into the loo and sat there, praying. *Please, Lord. Help! I was stupid to come here, though I don't know how I could have refused. There's so much that's wrong about this situation ... and tomorrow ... I don't want to let anyone down ...*

Perhaps there was someone in the pub whom she knew, who might be able to help her? She hadn't seen anyone in their part of the dining room, but there were many alcoves in which a friend might lurk. The Woottons had been going out tonight. Perhaps by the most enormous stroke of luck, they might actually have come to this very restaurant. Or perhaps one of the holidaymakers she knew. Or even Mr Lightowler. She walked slowly through the restaurant, scanning the diners. Nothing. Nobody.

Except ... well, didn't God have a sense of humour? In an alcove she spied the village dragon, Mrs Collins's arch-enemy, none other than Mrs Felicity Chickward with a tubby little man about Minty's own age. Mother and son? Aunt and nephew?

The man spotted Minty looking at them and nudged Mrs Chickward, who looked up and saw Minty. The hatchet face remained impassive. Minty took a deep breath and went over to their table.

"Mrs Chickward, how nice to see you. Are you all ready for tomorrow?"

"I am always prepared," said Mrs Chickward. "This is my nephew, Neville. He takes me out for a meal every year on my birthday. He's a chartered accountant, would you believe, even if he does still look ten years old. Neville, this is Miss Cardale, who likes to be called by the diminutive 'Minty', though why she should choose to shorten such a lovely name as Araminta, I do not know."

The youthful looking Neville rose and bowed, pulling out a chair for Minty. "Are you by yourself? Won't you join us?"

Minty hesitated. It was a genuine hesitation. Had God really directed her into Mrs Chickward's path? Why would that old battle-axe want to help Minty? "I did come with some people but two of them have already gone home and my escort is not quite . . ."

"Too much bubbly?" said Mrs Chickward, sipping her own glass, which contained white wine. "Tut!" Minty's eyes rounded in surprise. Had Mrs Chickward actually said "Tut!" Minty would have laughed or at least giggled, if the situation had not been so serious.

"Definitely too much bubbly."

"Want a lift home?" asked Neville, polishing off a glass of what looked like water with lemon and ice in it.

"That would be perfect," said Minty, gratefully.

Mrs Chickward laid her spoon and fork down. She had, she indicated, finished her meal, even though Neville still had half a pear in wine on his plate. "It will be your first time at our little fête, won't it, Miss Cardale? I think you will be surprised by how well we do. All for a good cause, of course. Lady Cardale chooses a new charity to support every year, and this year it is my own pet charity, a hospice for terminally ill children."

"Splendid," said Minty. "I'll just go and tell my . . . escort . . . that I've got a lift home, shall I?"

Simon was waiting for her with glass upraised. She explained that she had unexpectedly run into some friends who had offered her a lift home since Simon had plans to go on elsewhere. He gave her a hard, shrewd stare, most unlike his former caressing looks. "All right, I'll take you back if that's what you really want."

"Thank you," she said, wondering if he could even stand upright after all he'd drunk. "But you haven't finished your meal and they're ready to go. On the other hand, why don't you leave your car here and come back with us?"

"You think I'm not fit to drive?" He was turning ugly.

"Goodnight, Simon." She almost ran back to Mrs Chickward and Neville, who were by now ready to depart.

Neville was driving a large and powerful car, but luckily it was a saloon and there was room for her in the back. Mrs Chickward naturally took the front seat. "May I ask, Miss Cardale, if what I hear about you is true? I heard a rumour, but of course I take no notice of rumours. Gossip, I say, is the worst sin of all in a village. Does more harm than fornication."

Minty blinked. She thought, *That's a novel point of view.* Then she noticed that Neville was adjusting his mirror to a different angle so that he could see her sitting in the back. Neville was smiling. Had he a sense of humour?

"Which particular rumour?"

"That you are a long-lost daughter of Sir Micah's. I thought his daughter by his first marriage had died. Dear Lady Cardale told me herself that she had, but I like to check my facts."

"Rumour has spoken the truth for once, Mrs Chickward. I am Sir Micah's eldest daughter but I have been living till recently with my uncle and aunt in the city."

"Don't drive so fast, Neville. You know it makes me nervous."

Minty met Neville's eyes in the mirror. Yes, the man was definitely enjoying himself. Minty sought for a safe topic of conversation, but the only topic that came to mind was not at all safe. Though perhaps, thought Minty with a sinking heart, this was what the Lord wanted her to talk about. Well, she would stick to the truth and nothing but the truth—though perhaps not the whole truth?

"Mrs Chickward, I wonder if I could ask your advice. Mrs Collins is going to be so busy tomorrow that she has asked me to substitute for her in the flower arranging competition."

Neville braked as Mrs Chickward's hand shot out and fastened on the steering wheel. "I *knew* she wasn't up to it! So she asked you to do an arrangement for her, did she? Well, we'll have to see about that!"

"She realises she can't compete with you, who are practically a professional . . ."

Neville's eyebrows signalled that the word "practically" had been a mistake.

Minty hurried on. "She thought she'd give me a chance, instead. She said she'd tell the stewards that she was handing it over to me. What I don't know—because as you say, this is my first time—is how long we've got and where we can set up."

It had been the right line to take. Mrs Chickward was flattered and pleased to impart her knowledge. She did know her flower arranging, Minty could tell. By the time they drew up on the green at the top of the high street, Minty had been given a crash course in what to expect, along with several very useful tips.

"Thank you. I really am very grateful . . . and for the lift, too."

Neville, who hadn't spoken all the way to the village, now said, "Well, Aunt, you're always on at me to help at the fête. I can be free tomorrow if you wish."

"Changed your mind, have you?" Mrs Chickward sounded sour. She was, after all, no fool.

"Yes," said Neville, blandly. "And perhaps if you can still get me a ticket—or perhaps two—for the ball next week?"

"Humph!" said Mrs Chickward, extricating herself from the car with an effort. "Don't think I can't see what's going on under my nose, because I can."

"Yes, indeed. Dear Aunt Felicity." Neville kissed his aunt on the cheek, and escorted her to the door of a large house on the green before returning to help Minty out.

"You've been very kind," said Minty.

"I'll walk you home, if I may. Where do you live? At the Hall?"

"In a little cottage this side of the bridge." She looked up at Patrick's windows and saw, with a leap in her throat, that lights were on. At last! She missed what Neville said next. "Sorry," she said. "It's been rather a long day."

"I said, I'll see you tomorrow, then? What stall are you on? Perhaps we could have a bite together at lunchtime?"

"I'd like that, but I have to fit in with other people's timetables." They had reached the cottage, which was in darkness. She got out her key. "Thank you, Neville. For everything."

She thought he might want to try for a kiss, so she let herself into the cottage as quickly as she could and shot the bolt behind her.

Then she smelt it.

If she hadn't smelt Simon's distinctive aftershave lotion so recently, she might not have recognised it. Miles had also been wearing an aftershave, but it was not as potent. Gemma had been wearing a light and flowery perfume. Neville hadn't worn any. No, this was Simon's.

So Simon had been in the cottage that day, had he? Perhaps Dwayne had dropped back for something, Simon had spotted him and asked to be let in? Or perhaps—nasty thought—Simon had retained master keys for all the cottages, since he'd been responsible for them in the past.

She put the light on. Everything downstairs looked just as it should. She'd had her mobile with her all day and left it at the bookshop, so he couldn't have touched that.

Lady was nowhere to be seen. Minty went out to the kitchen. The window was still propped open and the back door shut as it should be. Lady was sitting on the bench outside and, though pleased to see Minty, seemed uneasy and refused to come inside.

Minty sat on the bench, stroking Lady and thinking about this. Lady had been happy enough to come in after Mrs Guinness had left, but now he didn't want to do so.

Minty said, "You silly cat, there's no one there!"

Not downstairs, anyway. Fear prickled its way down Minty's back. Could Simon possibly have got back before them? Given the speed at which he drove and given that Mrs Chickward had asked Neville to drive slowly, Simon might well have done so.

If so, what was she going to do about it?

She didn't like any of the answers to that question. Eventually she collected a spade from the tool shed and went back inside. There was now a faint glow of light coming from upstairs. Minty started up, listening to the noises the old house was making. She knew all those noises by now. What she didn't normally hear was the creak of her bed.

At the top of the stairs she opened the door to the bedroom.

Simon said, "Surprise!"

The covers of her bed had been pulled back, and Simon was standing on the far side of it. He was stripped down to his trousers, bare-chested, with a bottle of champagne in one hand and a couple of glasses in the other.

She held the spade at her side. "Would you please leave?"

"Don't be such a prude! You know you've wanted to get into bed with me from the moment we met. Come over here, my darling, and let's see what you're made of under that rag you're wearing."

"I repeat, please go!"

"Don't come the vicarage miss with me! Come here and let's get acquainted . . . my way!"

"If you don't leave immediately, I shall scream!" In Jewish law, a girl would be judged to have colluded with her attacker, if she didn't scream. It seemed a sound law to Minty.

Simon's mouth turned ugly. "I said, come here!" He threw the glasses and the champagne down on to the bed. She retreated a step, remembering how strong he had been when he'd clasped her to him that morning in the shop.

"You wouldn't dare scream," he said, with a sure-of-himself smile. "No one would hear you. Anyway, even if you did, I'd say you invited me here. No one would believe you hadn't."

She feared what he said was true, but it was not going to stop her. As he jumped over the bed towards her, she threw the spade at him and turning, fled down the stairs, screaming at the top of her lungs. She wrenched open the bolt on the front door and ran into the road, still screaming.

Chapter Seventeen

A car coming down the hill braked within a foot of her. Another car crossing the bridge screeched to a halt behind her. She stood there with her arms above her head, screaming and screaming.

"What . . . !"

"Who . . . ?"

Curtains twitched, windows were thrust up, doors opened. Holidaymakers shot out of the cottages on either side of her. The drivers left their cars. She continued to scream, eyes closed, till a woman's arm went round her and she felt herself guided to the pavement.

"What is it?"

"I nearly ran her over! It would have been her own fault if . . ."

"What is it?" The woman's voice again. A kindly voice, authoritative, not young.

Minty opened her eyes, chest heaving, throat sore. She said, "Man . . . in cottage . . . !"

"Who? What did she say? Man in her cottage? A burglar? Ring the police."

The woman continued to hold Minty fast. "It's all right. I've got you."

Quite a crowd had collected. People were scurrying down the hill to see what was the matter.

Minty lifted her head, attracted by the movement of a curtain in a house above her. Nanny Proud and Mrs Guinness were standing in the window, looking down. It was late for Nanny Proud to be out of bed. Perhaps—a nasty suspicious thought—they had been waiting to see the result of Simon's latest ploy?

The traffic was moving again, but the crowd continued to collect. Minty leaned against the wall of the cottage, still with the woman's arm around her. She began to shake. Patrick was hurrying down the street. She wanted to run to him, but there were too many people watching. He stopped to ask someone what was the matter.

"A burglar in her cottage. Must have got out the back way. No one's followed her on to the street."

The woman holding Minty's arm asked, "Do you want the police, Minty?"

She gasped, "It was Simon Cardale."

"Best not, then. You've got a good screech on you. He won't try that again in a hurry."

Perhaps, thought Minty. And perhaps not. Patrick was on his mobile phone. Probably trying the Woottons, but of course they were out this evening. He wouldn't know that. He was looking annoyed, trying another number.

The woman said, "Are you all right now? I'll send my husband to look upstairs for you, make sure he's gone."

"Yes. Thank you. I threw a spade at him." She spurted into hysterical laughter, quickly stilled. Hysteria wouldn't help.

Patrick was talking to someone on the phone, looking satisfied. He'd got something moving, then.

The woman sent a bulky man into the cottage. Minty looked at her properly for the first time. "Thank you. You're from the pub, aren't you? I think I saw you there . . ."

"When you came in to pay Alice, yes. Are you all right now?"

She was shivering. "I don't know. Suppose he comes back?"

"Bolt both doors once you're in."

Yes, but the back door bolt isn't foolproof and he got in when I was out, thought Minty. *He's still got keys, hasn't he? I'm never going to feel safe there again, if he can get in whenever I'm out.*

"She doesn't want the police. Knew him, of course! Lovers' tiff, ha-ha!"

The crowd was drifting away, all except for Patrick, now on the opposite side of the street, looking over the bridge towards the park. Also Willy with a woman from the Chinese restaurant.

"All clear," said the publican, reappearing with the spade and the bottle of champagne. "I found these upstairs. You should keep your tools locked up. Burglars can prise a door open with a spade like this."

"Thanks. I'll remember."

Willy appeared at her side, and introduced the woman with him. "Mr Sands called us. Miss Cardale, my wife, Lilian. Perhaps you would care to spend the night in our daughter's bedroom? It is small but it would be safe."

Patrick was looking back at them now, nodding. He had arranged this, obviously.

Minty tried to think. "You're very kind. Would you come into the cottage with me for a moment?"

She didn't much like going back into the cottage, but she made herself do so. The place looked alien to her now. Dark and unwelcoming. It was probably all in her mind, but she shuddered at the thought of staying another night here. "Will you help me pack some things and take me to a safe place? I thought I was brave, but it turns out I'm not."

They helped her make a bundle of bedclothing and toiletries. What she couldn't stuff into her rucksack went into two dustbin bags. She'd accumulated quite a lot of things since she arrived. She also took the cat tins. The last thing she picked up was her mother's photograph from the mantelpiece.

"We'll leave the light on down here, bolt the front door, and go out the back way. Lady will follow us. I'll come back tomorrow morning early and clear the food out of the fridge."

"You will come to us, then?"

"You're very kind but I don't want to get you or anyone else into trouble." She told them where and how she intended to go, and they agreed it was as good a place as any. Minty had to stiffen her jaw to talk properly. She was beginning to discover how much the evening had taken out of her.

Willy's wife said, in prim English, "We have a daughter ourselves, oh so pretty. Mr Simon like her very much. Too much. She said no, but he wouldn't listen. She cried and cried. She said, who would believe her? So now she live with my brother in the city. We miss her very much."

"I understand," said Minty. "Is he really above the law? Perhaps I should have called the police."

"Better not. That man spreads dirt around him. Let Mr Patrick deal with him. Mr Patrick very good man. You make him laugh. He doesn't laugh enough, I think."

Minty called to Lady and the cat followed them out of the back door and up the lane. Nanny Proud's window was now curtained and dark. The pub was closing up for the night; Alice would perhaps soon be going off to see Dwayne. They passed the back of the charity shop and Ruby's little cottage, where perhaps her "little old boy" would be dreaming of visiting his Hannah again. Past Patrick's stately Georgian house. His car was out at the back, his window curtains not drawn, light pouring out over the courtyard garden.

Because Simon had collected her from work, Minty still had the shop keys on her. They turned into the bookshop garden, went up the outer stairs, and she let them into Hannah's first-floor flat.

The curtains were open here, but after a whispered word from Minty, Willy went around drawing them before they turned on any lights. It was a pretty flat, or rather a maisonette because it was on two floors. The first floor contained a kitchen-cum-dining room overlooking the street, while at the back was a sitting room overlooking the garden. Willy tested the bolts on the French windows and pronounced them satisfactory. On the top floor there was one larger and one smaller bedroom, plus a bathroom with shower cubicle.

Minty dropped everything on to the floor in the sitting room. For two pins, she would let herself cry.

"We bring over some food, some tea," said Willy.

"No, nothing," said Minty. "I'm all right now. Safe. Only the Woottons and Mr Lightowler know I have the key to this place, and Simon can't get in. I shall sleep safely here. But please don't tell anyone—and I mean anyone—that I'm here. And thank you both, so much. I don't know what I'd have done without you."

"I will ring Mr Patrick, just to tell him you are safe."

"Of course you must do that, but don't tell him exactly where I am. Please."

She saw them safely off the premises, being careful to turn off the lights and bolt the door behind them. Minty threw off her clothes and had a shower. Then she realised she must draw back all the curtains on both floors before she got into bed, lest someone notice that they had been moved and wonder who was in the flat.

She stood by the window of the sitting room, looking down over the pretty garden Jonah loved so much. The clouds had cleared away and it was a fine night.

She could pray now. She thanked God for delivering her from evil. She thanked him for the kindness of the people who had helped her. She prayed for Gemma and Miles who had left her in Simon's hands without a word. She hoped that Gemma had not known what Simon had intended, but she was beginning to understand that Gemma was as much under Simon's thumb as was Miles. She thanked God for Willy and his wife, and with sorrow she prayed for their daughter in the city . . . and for all victims of sexual assault.

She thanked God that she had not killed Simon with that spade. She found she was trembling again. She was horrified at herself. She had thrown it at him . . . she couldn't remember clearly . . . but had it hit him? Could she have wounded him, seriously? How could she have done such a thing!

She remembered Patrick looking across the bridge into the park. Had Patrick seen Simon escaping that way? Had Simon fled out of her back door, down the alley, round to the bridge and across? She hoped he'd been at least a little frightened.

Light was falling into the courtyard from a first-floor window of Patrick's house. A man's shadow appeared on the courtyard below, silhouetted against the light within. Patrick was standing at the window, leaning on it, looking down the back gardens towards Spring Cottage.

If the windows had been only a little closer together, they could have reached out and touched.

She wondered if he were thinking of her. She thought, *Patrick, I'd like to make myself small and creep into your pocket. Bless you, my dear. You worked out how to rescue me without causing gossip. Now you're probably worrying about my staying overnight with Willy and his wife.*

A mobile phone trilled. She could hear it through the walls. His shadow answered the phone, nodded. Willy reporting that Minty was safe? Yes. The shadow closed up the phone and retreated from the window, dwindling, until the light inside was finally switched off. Only then did she, too, go to bed.

Though not to sleep. Many of the things Simon had said that evening had hurt. Was she really so unsophisticated? Such a wet blanket? She banged the pillow into a different position. As for being a prude, well maybe she was if by that he meant that she was chaste. She'd never yet met a man whom she wanted to go to bed with, apart from . . .

She wondered what she would have done if she'd found Patrick in her bed. That made her laugh. Patrick would never do anything so, well, crude! If Patrick had wanted to make love to her . . . well, how would he have done it?

Eventually she slept.

She woke with a start. It was full daylight and it was the day of the fête. She scrambled into a T-shirt and jeans, fed Lady and dashed down the back lane to Spring Cottage. It looked undisturbed, thank goodness. She ate cereal and drank coffee while she packed the materials for her flower arrangement into boxes, and was ready on the doorstep when Hugh drove up in his estate car.

Evidently Hugh hadn't heard of the ruckus the night before. She told him about it briefly as they drove along. He might well hear a more lurid version during the day, and at least she could give him the facts first.

"Once I'm out of the cottage it's vulnerable because he's got keys and I can't secure both doors from the outside. I hope you don't mind, but I've moved into Hannah's flat for the time being. No one except Willy and his wife knows I'm there and I can get into it from the back garden without anyone seeing."

He was horrified. "My dear, you must move in with us at once!"

"Dear Hugh, it's so like you to offer, but it would be too much of an imposition. Hannah's flat suits me down to the ground, really."

"I still don't like it." They joined the stream of cars and vans making their way into the park.

Mrs Collins was in her element, directing operations, kitting out stewards with yellow sashes and clipboards. Today she was wearing one of her black and red dresses, topped off by an enormous hat crowned with pink roses. A sight to behold!

Two great marquees had been set up at the head of the slope down to the lake. Opposite them was a stage, where sound equipment was being tested out. There was an enclosed ring for children's sports and another for dog obedience classes. Dotted around were dozens of smaller tents and stands, with antlike figures busy setting out their wares for sale. Mrs Collins had seen to everything, including the weather, which was set fair.

Hugh led Minty into the first marquee, where the bookstall was to be. One side of the tent was open so that people could wander in and out at will. They had been given a pitch between a man who made doll's house furniture and a woman who made patchwork quilts and cushions. Hugh helped Minty carry all their boxes into the marquee and then took her along to the second tent where flowers and fruits were being displayed and where the flower arranging competition was to be held.

Minty approached a woman at the entrance and said, "Mrs Collins arranged for me to . . ."

"Over there. No. 7."

Minty felt like a squirrel between two trees. She dumped her flower arranging material in the space allocated and raced back to the bookstall. She spread brightly coloured sheets over their two tables, upended empty cardboard boxes on top, and covered them with more lengths of material—all from the charity shop. Then out came L-shaped metal stands to display the best-selling hardback books. Mr Lightowler arrived at this point, carrying cartons of coffee and some doughnuts. Minty helped him to set up the books so that as many as possible of the good hardbacks were on show, face outwards. The tattier paperbacks were stacked in front with their spines uppermost.

She left him pinning a large sign up, reading, "FREE GIFT WITH EVERY BOOK PURCHASED, As Long As Stocks Last". Munching a doughnut, she ran back to arrange her flowers. Half a dozen women were already at work in that section, very serious, very concentrated. Except that now and then they would look sideways to see what everyone else was doing.

Minty met with a gracious nod from Mrs Chickward, who was constructing a veritable firework display of varicoloured flowers on an elaborate ironwork frame, the whole being finished off with festoons of rainbow-striped silk. It was formal and impressive—rather like the lady herself.

Minty made herself quiet for a moment before she started. What she was going to do was probably far too elaborate, but it would perhaps remind some people of the age-old story of Noah's Ark.

She'd filled a deep, wide trough with blocks to form a wet oasis as the base for her arrangement. Across the back she'd fixed chicken wire in the shape of half a rainbow, securing it on the right to a clutch of tall cones, also driven into the oasis. She'd brought a dead branch from one of her apple trees, and now she wired that to the front of the cones, curling ivy around it. She tested the structure. It seemed secure.

She drove the stems of some tall lupins and delphiniums into the oasis at the base of her rainbow shape and gently bent them over to the right, securing each one at intervals on to the arc of chicken wire. The darkest blue delphinium went at the bottom, and the lightest yellow lupin at the top with red lupins between. That would do for the rainbow.

Next she placed her home-made reed boat in front of the rainbow, surrounding it with cornflower heads in blue and lilac to represent the sea.

More flowers went into the cones at the back of the apple tree branch, with the lightest yellows at the top and the deepest blues trailing down the tree. When she'd finished, it looked as if the rainbow had climbed up into the sky until it met the tree, and then tumbled down the tree to earth. She pressed moss around the base of the apple branch to simulate grass.

She stood back, biting her lip. She thought she'd been mad to try something so ambitious.

Emptying out the bag of farmyard animals she'd bought from the charity shop, she placed a plain narrow slat of wood from the boat on to the "land" under the tree, and on this set the animals leaving the Ark. Along the front of the exhibit she arranged sprays of autumn seed heads, sprays of blackberries, and glossy sprigs of flowering ivy to represent the fruits of the earth.

One last touch. She placed a tiny white orchid on to the tip of the reed boat, to show the dove signalling that the flood was over.

She cleared up, glancing at her watch. She'd taken longer than she had hoped she would. She hoped the judges would like it, but she didn't really care. She had to get back to the bookstall.

Mrs Chickward was standing in her way as she left. "My dear Araminta—inspired! I take my hat off to you. You really have taken on board the little tips I gave you last night."

"I'm very grateful to you, Mrs Chickward," said Minty. And she was. "I think your display is magnificent and I hope you win."

"Winning isn't everything," said Mrs Chickward, magnificently. "It's running the race that counts, not winning."

Minty hid a smile. "Of course you're right."

She shot out of the tent, nearly knocking over Mrs Collins who was on her way in. Minty thought, *Oh, I bet she wants to alter my flower arrangement . . . well, it can't be helped, I'm late already.*

She ran back to the bookstall. Mr Lightowler was already besieged with customers and she plunged into the business of taking cash and giving change. Mr Lightowler was wearing one of the baseball caps, back to front. He looked flushed. It was warm in the tent and getting warmer. Minty seized another cap and thrust her hair up through it.

A four-square child of indeterminate sex and age edged round the stall and stood in Minty's way. She was sucking an ice cream, which made Minty's mouth water.

"You Minty? Gotta message." She produced a much-folded sealed envelope and handed it over. "Gotta wait for a reply."

Minty tore it open and recognised the bold handwriting on the note inside as Patrick's. The note started, "Are you all right?" This had been crossed through with a heavy hand. Of course he knew she wasn't all right. "I'm on the gate till one, half an hour to eat, then children's slide till four. Want any help moving? Can you make it tonight?"

Minty was surprised that Patrick had been so open in sending her this message. Surely the child would spread it around that Patrick was corresponding with Minty?

The child said, "Did you really see off a burglar last night?"

"Well, yes," said Minty, weakly.

"It were Simon ratbag, weren't it?"

"What makes you think that?"

"He done my older sister. Poor cow. You shoulda hit him harder."

Minty didn't know how to answer that one, so borrowed a pen from Mr Lightowler and scribbled on the note. "Free at five, I hope."

The child vanished but the fruity-voiced Reverend Cecil took her place. "Take a break?"

"Daren't," said Minty, sorting out some more giveaway merchandise. "Is it always so busy?"

"If it's not actually snowing, yes. Can't you make an excuse to get away, just for half an hour? I thought you and I could just, well, steal away for a bit."

"Really, I can't. Oh, I nearly forgot, I did get your message eventually, but it had got mislaid and I didn't find it till too late to get back to you."

"So you'll come to the ball with me?"

"It was kind of you to ask, but my father's arranged something."

"Oh." He looked so downcast she was tempted to be kinder to him. But no, he mustn't expect more than she was prepared to give.

"Tell you what, though," he said. "Mrs Collins says that you helped her a lot with her Noah's Ark display and she's agreed you can show it to the Sunday school tomorrow. I thought you'd like to know."

"Mrs Collins said . . . !" But he'd gone. Minty laughed, shrugged, and went back to bagging up some more books for Hugh, who seemed to have taken the place of Mr Lightowler when she wasn't looking. Then Willy and his wife appeared. She darted out from behind the stall to thank them for all their help. They said they didn't want thanks, but clearly they were pleased she'd acknowledged their help.

She thought that at lunchtime things would slacken off a little. She was wrong. She saw Simon cross the lawn with his arm in a sling. She didn't know whether to feel pleased or guilty about that.

Neville arrived with an enormous baguette and a Coca-Cola for her. Hugh had disappeared, but Mr Lightowler had returned. He told her to sit down and eat, which she did. Neville collapsed beside her, perspiring gently in the heat. "Been in the food tent all morning. Only got away by breaking a plate. Sound practice, that, if you don't want to do the washing up. Break something."

She laughed. She liked Neville. He said, "Been worrying about you. Someone said you'd disturbed a burglar last night when you got back. Feel bad about that. Should have seen you in."

"I was all right, honest."

"Still feel bad about it. Oh well. Been to see the flower arrangements. Aunt Felicity's is stunning. The judges had a hard job, but

I think on the whole that they're right to give her second place. What's yours like?"

"Oh," she shrugged. "A bit childish, probably."

"Fancy a bite to eat this evening?"

"I don't know yet. I have to pay a visit to my father, and then . . . I'll know about five o'clock."

"I'll drop by later, then."

She nodded and off he went, back to his duties in the food tent. She looked out over the field, hoping to see Patrick, but he was nowhere in sight. She experienced a sudden loss of confidence. Suppose she'd got it all wrong and Patrick wasn't really interested in her? After all, she'd never attracted anyone like him before. After last night, she wasn't at all sure of her own powers of judgement. Perhaps she'd been mistaken in thinking him someone rather special.

Later she thought she saw Patrick crossing the lawn and looking toward the tent. If it was him, he was wearing a floppy panama hat—sensible on such a hot day.

"There you are!" A cloud of delicate flowery scent announced the presence of Gemma, ice cool in a cream linen trouser suit and wide-brimmed straw hat.

Gemma kissed Minty, who felt even more hot, sweaty, and badly dressed than usual beside the immaculate Gemma. "I hope you didn't mind us leaving early last night, but darling Miles had something he needed to do. I was a teensy bit worried because Simon does drive fast, and when I asked him about it this morning he was so grumpy, I couldn't get a civil word out of him. But there, if he will fall down the stairs and hurt his arm . . . ! You must come round some time and see my little flat. Tra-la!" she said, and wafted herself off.

Mr Lightowler grunted. "Come the revolution, her sort will be dangling from lamp-posts."

"That's unkind," said Minty, heaving yet another box of T-shirts on to the stand. "Gemma's sweet. Mostly. Just a bit spoilt, that's all."

Mr Lightowler snarled. Yes, he actually snarled. Minty took another look at him and realised he was dog tired. She said, "Go away. Take a break. Wander around. Lie on the grass. Don't come back till you feel better."

He slunk off, which left Minty in charge. She wiped sweat off her forehead and wondered how much longer she could last without a long, cool drink. Suddenly a double whopper of an ice cream was thrust in her face. "Chocolate," said the child of indeterminate sex. "He says, if you don't like it, I can have it."

"I love it," said Minty, quickly licking around the rim. "May I ask who . . . ?"

The child jerked its head towards the giant slide. Patrick. "Did he get you one, as well?"

The child nodded but waited, eyes watchful, for a tip.

Minty went through her pockets and found some odd coins. "Will these do, to get another for you?"

A nod. A disappearing act.

"Miss . . . miss? How much is this?"

"Miss, I want a red one, too!"

Another well-known face appeared, behind a pushchair that appeared to be occupied by a huge ball of pink fluff. Alice, with Marie hiding behind candyfloss.

Minty yelped. "Is that the time? Oh, Alice, I meant to come round to . . ."

Alice smiled. "No sweat. I knew you'd be up to your eyeballs. Everything's OK, except they've used the spare light bulb in Kiln Cottage. I said you'd see to it. I came past your place and Mrs G was just coming out of Riverside. She said she needed more cleaning materials, and I said I'd tell you."

"Bless you. Look, Alice. I need to talk to you . . ."

Alice mouthed "Later!" and walked away.

Venetia appeared, looking worn. "I'll spell you for a bit, Minty. Mr Lightowler's in the tea tent, talking to some crony of his. Put that man down in the middle of the Sahara and he'd find a friend. Hugh's working flat out on the candyfloss because someone hasn't turned up to do it. I was supposed to be on bric-a-brac but Mrs Collins yanked me off that to do the plant stall, and if I see another plant that I don't know the name of, I shall scream! What was all that about your fighting off a masked man with a gun?" She broke off to speak to a customer. "No, we haven't any jigsaws. This is a bookstall. Try the toy stall, three along."

Minty bagged up another couple of books plus free pens. "Get the true story from Hugh. I'm OK, honest."

"You look hot. Have you been here all morning? No, love, Barbara Cartland isn't soft porn. She's respectable, really." Then to Minty, "Take a break. Run away and play . . . or better still, the judges are about to announce the prizes. Why don't you go and see if you've won anything?"

Chapter Eighteen

Minty dusted herself down, licked her fingers, hoped the ice cream stains on her top weren't too noticeable and joined the throng making their way to the cleared space around the stage. Lady Cardale was standing at the microphone by a table of glistening silver trophies. Several people standing nearby were already holding giant cups for Best in Show, Best of Five Vegetables, and so on.

"Now we come to the Flower Arranging class," said Lady Cardale, in her hard, clear voice. "The judges had a difficult decision to make here."

"They always say that," said a woman standing at Minty's elbow.

"But after much debate, it was decided that the following were Highly Commended."

"All the toadies getting theirs," said the Voice of Experience, as three women mounted the steps to receive their certificates from Lady Cardale.

"While third prize goes to Mrs . . ."

"She's Brown Owl, Brownies, you know. Has to get something!" A pleased-looking girl went up for a tiny silver cup and a certificate.

"It was particularly difficult to choose between the two final entries, both of which, in their own different ways, deserve to win first prize."

"That woman who organises the show will get it, mark my words!"

"And in this case the very well deserved second prize goes to Mrs Felicity Chickward."

"Told you so. That Collins woman will get First." Mrs Chickward made her stately way up the steps to receive a larger silver cup and a certificate. She did it, Minty noted, with some grace. A gallant loser.

"And the first prize goes to the woman who has masterminded this whole event, giving unstintingly of her time to the community, without whom we would not be raising nearly so much money for charity . . . Mrs Collins!"

There was a scattering of applause. Minty didn't know whether to laugh or to cry. Mrs Collins bustled forward, beaming, but Mrs Chickward stepped up to the mike.

"Dear Lady Cardale, if you will allow me? I happen to know that Mrs Collins found herself unable to do the flower arrangement herself today, as she was so busy organising everything. So she asked someone else to do it for her. I am sure Mrs Collins will agree with me that her protégée—and mine—fully deserves the first prize."

"Oh? Well . . . who is it?" Lady Cardale was not amused.

Mrs Chickward smiled at Mrs Collins, relishing the moment of victory over her rival. "A newcomer to the village, but no stranger. Araminta Cardale!"

"What? No! Well, I never!"

"Who did she say? Wasn't that the girl who . . . a couple of masked men . . . ?"

Minty gaped. Someone pushed her forward and she made her way to the steps through a sprinkling of applause. Many of the people there did not know her, but knew the name. Some did know her and most of them were smiling.

Minty climbed the steps to the stage in a daze. Mrs Collins was there, grinning through rigid lips. Mrs Chickward was clapping hard and smiling. Lady Cardale looked as if she'd just spotted a wasp in her salad, but she took a large silver cup from the table and presented it to Minty. Several cameras flashed, immortalising the moment for posterity. Minty kept smiling.

Mrs Collins followed Minty back down the steps. Minty saw the woman was on the verge of tears and felt sorry for her.

"Mrs Collins, you have been so kind to me, a newcomer. To think that, in the middle of organising this successful day, you found time to help me! I am most sincerely grateful."

"Yes. Well, that's all right then." Mrs Collins was chagrined but prepared to accept Minty's thanks. She went off, her self-esteem more or less restored.

"Well done, Araminta," said Mrs Chickward. "No sense making an enemy of the woman. By the way, you'll be amused to hear that after you left the tent this morning, Mrs Collins put a couple of artificial poppies in your arrangement. Absurd. After she'd gone I took the poppies out and threw them away."

Mrs Chickward smiled graciously and went on her way. Minty stifled a giggle. Those two dames were really something!

The fête was winding down. Stallholders were packing up, loading their bits and pieces into the boots of cars and lorries. Minty saw Patrick helping to dismantle the children's slide, and Neville carrying plastic boxes away from the food marquee.

Hugh, Venetia, and Mr Lightowler had packed up their small amount of unsold stock and were already heaving boxes into the back of Hugh's car. They were delighted with the way the day had gone and told Minty they could manage well enough without her. She continued on her way to the Hall, wondering where she could get a wash and brush up before she saw her father.

Ah, the Ladies was next to the shop and restaurant, both of which were open, but doing a poorish trade. Minty tried to scrub ice cream stains off her T-shirt, but gave up in disgust. She hadn't even a comb to run through her hair. *Meet Miss Scruffy,* she thought.

She ran cold water over her arms and face, thinking about what she could say to her father about Simon. She could ignore the incident, but would that be the right thing to do?

Ms Phillips was not in her office downstairs, but another girl—a stranger—was. "Miss Cardale? They're expecting you. You know the way?"

Her father was out of bed and sitting in a wheelchair with a rug over his knees, looking down at the field of the fête below. A nurse sat quietly in a corner, flicking over a magazine.

He looked up and smiled, beckoning Minty to join him. He had a pad of paper and pen on an armrest, and his colour was perhaps better than it had been, though he still looked gaunt. Was he really better? Was he going to live for a while? Oh, she hoped so.

"Ta-rah!" she said, holding the silver cup above her head.

He grinned. "Tell me," he said, or rather, croaked.

So she told him all about her day and how Mrs Collins's attempt to take credit for Minty's flower arrangement had been foiled by Mrs Chickward. He sat with the cup on his lap, smiling. She apologised for her scruffy appearance. It had been hot in the tent and the ice creams—and probably a stray bit of tomato from her lunch—seemed to have stuck to her.

At some point Ms Phillips joined them in the room, taking a seat to one side.

Minty took a deep breath. "You may have heard from Gemma—or Simon—that they asked me to join them for supper last night."

It wasn't her imagination. Both her father and Ms Phillips stiffened to attention. "Assume we know nothing," said Ms Phillips.

Minty gave the bare facts.

"You went with one man and came back with another?" That was Ms Phillips.

"Wouldn't you?"

"If what you say is true, why didn't you call the police?"

"I didn't know his reputation then."

Sir Micah scowled.

"And I wasn't sure whether you'd want me to cover for him. Simon thinks he's God's gift to women. He may well be to some, but not to me. I'm afraid of him, a little. He may decide to punish me for refusing him, to catch me somewhere that I can't defend myself. I swear to you as Almighty God's my witness, that if he rapes me I will call the police and pursue charges. I will see him in jail no matter what he says and no matter how expensive a barrister he can afford."

Ms Phillips clapped her hands together, once, twice, three times. Sir Micah, however, was still frowning.

"Look," said Minty. "I know he's your heir and your hope for the future. He's as handsome as the day is long and very charming, but he's got no right to try to get a woman drunk or force her to have sex with him. No man has." She thought, *And that includes you!*

Sir Micah understood. His eyes went out of focus, considering some long ago affair, perhaps? Then he sighed and nodded, acknowledging the point she'd made.

Minty braced herself to go on. "What you did to my mother . . . and to me . . ."

"Enough!" he said, hoarsely. "Do you think I don't know?" His voice faded to a croak.

There was a long silence. Ms Phillips watched, immobile. The only sound was Sir Micah's rapid breathing, which gradually slowed to normal.

"Well," said Minty, leaning back against the window. "That's it. I don't know what happens next. Except that I moved out of the cottage, Ms Phillips. Simon's got keys and I can't be sure it won't happen again. I'm not telling you where I've gone."

Sir Micah seized his pencil and wrote a few words down for Ms Phillips. She looked at what he'd written, nodded and made a noiseless exit.

"Thank you for believing me," said Minty, holding out her hand to him. He took it, and held it.

He wrote a few more words. "You want to stay and work here?"

"Yes. The Hall, the village, they're everything I've ever dreamed of, and no, I'm not looking at them through rose-coloured spectacles. In the city I learned about poverty, homelessness, drugs, petty crime . . . all spiced with my aunt and uncle's sour outlook on life." She shivered. "I learned the ways of that world, but I didn't fit in. I longed to get away, but I had to pay off my debts . . ." She made a helpless gesture with her hands.

"I know now that it wasn't the poverty, but the ugliness and the lack of love that repelled me. Near the vicarage there's a street that leads due west. I used to stand on the corner and watch the sunset, and feel such a longing for . . . I didn't know what. Now I do know. Many of the city's problems are still here; the petty crime, the poverty, the lack of affordable housing. Probably there's drugs here, too, though I haven't seen them yet.

"But the beauty of it, the wide open skies! And the people here! I've grown to love them all. I've seen how the village depends on tourism and is facing a bleak future if the Hall closes to the public. Oh, I'm sorry. You won't want me to criticise . . ."

At some point Ms Phillips had returned to the room. "Suppose you were given a job helping to look after the Hall and estate, Araminta? Tell us what you'd do."

"What? That would be fantastic, but surely it's out of the question? What about the plan to turn the Hall into a clinic?"

Ms Phillips smiled slightly. "The American company has withdrawn its offer—at least for the time being."

Minty thought, *Is this the result of the Big Bang?* She tried to concentrate. "Well, to start with, the restaurant and the shop are badly run, but it wouldn't take much to put them right. The gardens look uncared for. I know it means spending money to make them look better, but it would be money well spent because it would attract gardening visitors. I've only seen part of the house that's open to the public. Everything is beautifully arranged but perhaps a little lifeless? A few personal touches might help. But above all, the publicity needs attention."

"What would you like to see happen in the village?"

"Affordable starter housing. The village has no crèche for young mothers. Oh, how can I tell what needs doing? I'm too new. It's true that people keep asking me to help them, but I don't know how.

"Yet I feel such a sense of belonging. I can't explain it, except perhaps by saying that I've made more friends here, got involved with more people's lives than I ever did before. I feel so alive now, whereas before . . . I was just going through the motions." She frowned, trying to put her thoughts into words.

"Since coming here, I've learned something else about myself. I've learned that I needn't have put up with everything that my uncle and aunt threw at me. I did it—I can see it now—I did it because I desperately needed to belong, to be loved. Well, I don't think they did love me. Not as I understand love. But I stayed because I thought I could make them love me one day.

"Yesterday I made the same mistake. I knew what Simon was like, really, but I wanted him and Gemma to accept me. I was flattered. I was stupid, and I paid for it. I'm afraid I'm a slow learner."

Sir Micah was leaning back in his chair with his eyes closed. She touched his hand.

"I'm sorry. I've tired you."

Was that a trace of a tear at the corner of his eye?

She hesitated. Ms Phillips beckoned to Minty, so she kissed Sir Micah's cheek and left the room, carrying the silver cup with her.

Ms Phillips said, "Tomorrow at half past ten?"

"I have to explain my Noah's Ark to the Sunday school. I'm sorry if I tired him too much." She tried to laugh. "All that emotion. Yuk."

"He wanted to know what you were made of. He'll expect you after church, then." She led the way to the lift, opened it and ushered Minty in. "Where did you say you were staying?"

"It's not that I don't trust you, Ms Phillips, but I'd suggest that you get the locks changed on all the holiday lets as soon as possible."

"The bookings for the holiday lets finish at the end of September and by then we'll know whether the cottages are to be sold or refurbished. In the meantime please continue to look after them as best you can."

Stepping out of the lift after Ms Phillips, Minty came face to face with Simon who still had his arm in a sling. She recoiled at the hatred in his face.

"Cow!" he said and thrust past her into the lift. Minty thought, *So much for being given a job looking after the Hall!*

"Take no notice," advised Ms Phillips, walking ahead of Minty down the corridor. Which confirmed Minty's belief that Ms Phillips had eyes in the back of her head.

Minty couldn't shake off the effect Simon had had on her so easily. She began to shiver. Ms Phillips led her into the reception room, dismissed the girl there and sat Minty down in a chair. "Coffee? Tea? Something stronger?"

"It's stupid to be frightened of him."

"Believe me, Simon won't try that again."

"I'm all right now." She looked around. "Is this your own office, or is it part of the estate office?"

"The estate offices are also on the ground floor of this wing, but this room and the whole of the floor above are rented by the Foundation. This room is a convenient reception room for visitors to Sir Micah, since it's not easy for strangers to find their way up to him from the courtyard."

Ms Phillips accompanied Minty out into the sunshine. Nearly all the evidence of the fête had been removed by now, except for two of the largest tents. "We're putting flooring into those for the ball," said Ms Phillips. "You should have received your invitation in the post this morning."

Two men converged on Minty from different parts of the field. Both looked hot, tired, and dirty, but both were smiling—until they saw each other.

Patrick said, "Is it all right then? Why didn't you return my call?"

Neville said, "Can we get away now?"

Minty gave a hand to each of them. "Patrick, your message was deleted from my phone—as was your mobile number. What did you have in mind? And you, Neville?"

The two men looked at one another and for a moment Minty thought there would be unpleasantness. Then both men laughed.

"Patrick Sands," said Patrick, extending his other hand to be shaken.

"Neville Chickward." Doing likewise. "I seem to remember you from—"

"That fraud case." Both men started to laugh. Then gave one another a high five. "You did good!" said Neville.

"Ditto," said Patrick. "Well, fancy that!"

"You know one another?" Minty was pleased.

"We met in court on opposite sides, but agreed the verdict was fair."

"What a rogue my client was," said Neville. "Though I say it as shouldn't. What are you doing here?"

"I live here and at the moment I am suffering from sunburn, heat stroke, and thirst. I don't know which to address first."

"A shower first," said Neville. "Followed by a couple of beers. Followed by something to eat in a quiet, cool place."

"My sentiments exactly," said Patrick. "Minty promised to cook for me, so I got in some steaks and salad stuffs. The beer's already in the fridge. Join us?"

Minty thought, *That's neat and solves a lot of problems. How like Patrick to think of a way out of an awkward situation. I do love him. Oh. No, it's too early to say that, feel that.*

She smiled at them both. "Shower first. Change of clothes. Long soft drink. Then I'll be happy to cook for you both."

"Minty! Oh, Minty, I've been looking for you everywhere." It was Gemma, tripping along on her high heels. "Miles has got to work and Florence isn't on duty today, so I thought you could come up and cook something for me in my flat."

Minty couldn't think of anything she would like to do less. "I'm afraid I've already been invited out for the evening."

"Oh. Well, can't I come, too?"

Chapter Nineteen

Patrick was equal even to this. "We're all having supper at my place. Do you know Neville Chickward? Why not join us?"

Gemma said, "Oh, but . . . I don't know . . ." She glanced at Minty for help, probably worried about consorting with Patrick, the family enemy. "I really need to talk to Minty."

Mrs Collins interrupted, red-faced, exhausted, and cross. "Am I tired! I can't wait to take my shoes off. Araminta, they need the Noah's Ark up at the church tomorrow, but Cecil has forgotten to arrange transport. You won't leave it here, will you? The site has to be cleared tonight."

Minty looked at the two hot and tired men. She herself felt as if she would melt if she didn't have a shower soon. Hugh and his car had gone. Crunch time.

Patrick looked down at his grimy hands. Neville sighed. To their credit both men said they would help.

Neville volunteered to bring his car to the tent while Minty walked there with Patrick. Gemma fluttered alongside. "Shall I carry the cup, Minty? My car isn't big enough, and you really need an estate car for this, don't you? I could ask Simon if we might borrow his four-wheel drive, but . . ."

"No," said Patrick and Minty together. They glanced at one another and smiled.

Minty had been afraid that Patrick would compare Gemma's elegant perfection to her own sweaty, dirty self, but he obviously wasn't doing so. Gemma looked crushed. Minty wondered if the girl had been born without any brains, or if they had been beaten out of her by Nanny Proud and Lady Cardale. Yet she could be very sweet.

It was difficult to snatch a moment with Patrick, but Minty managed it while they carried the base of the arrangement over to the car between them.

"Where were you? Did you leave a message for me?"

Patrick said, "My partner had a family crisis and I had to take over some of his urgent cases. I did leave a message for you. What went wrong?"

She told him as they manoeuvred the base into the boot of the car. "I think Mrs Guinness listened to your message out of curiosity, and wiped it out of spite."

"Give me your mobile now and I'll put the number back in." She fished it out of her back pocket and handed it over. He said, "I expected you to ring me. I kept my mobile switched on even when I was in court. Judges hate their words of wisdom being interrupted by mobile phones. An old friend rang for a chat in the middle of a case, and I nearly got sent down to the cells. You could have left a message for me at the office." He handed the mobile back to her.

"I saw the marguerites and guessed they were from you, but when I didn't find a note or a message on the phone, I wasn't sure. I didn't know what to think. You're so busy. I thought you might have forgotten me."

"I nearly did time in the cells for you!"

"Sorry." She knew she had gone red. "You were right about Simon, by the way. And about my meeting my father. He's . . . impressive."

"Is he impressed with you?"

"I don't know. There's a bond between us, very strong. I can't bear the thought of his dying when we've only just met again."

"You've forgiven him for sending you away, then?"

"Yes and no. I understand him better now. The world in which he moved was so different from anything I've ever known. That world has such different values, he probably didn't see anything wrong in what he did. No, I'm wrong there. He does know it was wrong, and I think he's suffered for it. I don't excuse what he did and he knows I don't. Forgiveness? It takes time. I think I trust him . . . more or less."

Neville came up with the apple branch, while Gemma trailed after him, carrying the reed boat and exclaiming that she had got a nasty smear of dirt on her immaculate top and must go home to change, immediately.

"My place at seven?" said Patrick.

"I can't wait," said Gemma, and went off with a wave of her hand.

"I'm staying over at my aunt's, so I'll have a wash and brush up there," said Neville. "What about you, Minty? I don't like the thought of your going back to the cottage by yourself. I'll come in with you, see there are no bogeymen under the bed?"

Patrick opened his mouth and shut it again.

Minty said, "Thanks, Neville. That would be good."

They dumped the flower arrangement in the church hall; then Neville parked on the green and walked Minty down to her front door. Spring Cottage smelt dusty and there was no sign of Lady the cat.

There were two envelopes on the floor inside the front door, which Minty scooped up and put in her pocket. Neville made a great show of looking up the chimney and into the coal scuttle before tramping upstairs to the bedroom. "All clear," he said, coming down again. He rubbed his chin. "May I ask, are you and Patrick . . . ?

"What makes you think that?"

"Your body language. You look at him when you think no one's watching, and he looks at you in the same way. If there's nothing in it, then maybe there's a chance for me?"

"Neville, you are a good kind man." Neville blushed. "Patrick and I, we've only known one another for a week. There's nothing between us yet, but . . ."

"You hope there will be? Well, I'm not going to step aside that easily, and if it doesn't work out with Patrick, I'll still be around and waiting for your call. I don't live that far away and can be over within the hour."

"Dear Neville. Thank you. Now you must be on your way, and I must wash and change."

Neville left and Minty went quickly through the cottage, picking up one or two personal items she'd left behind the previous night. Her bike was in the shed outside and would have to stay there. She hesitated about leaving by the garden path. She'd come in by the front door and maybe she should be seen leaving the same way. As she left the cottage, she checked to see if Nanny Proud was sitting at her window overlooking the street. She was. Minty guessed she'd done the right thing, even if it meant she hadn't been able to bolt the front door as she left.

The others had already been and gone from the bookshop, for there were the boxes from the fête stacked neatly at the back.

Minty went up to Hannah's flat and opened her letters. One was the promised invitation for the ball.

The other was from her uncle. It was a short note handwritten on vicarage notepaper, enclosing a cheque for two thousand five hundred pounds made out to her.

The note was short. "My dear Araminta, your aunt and I acted throughout as we thought best. This money is all we have left. We trust that one day soon you will understand, and look forward to your return. We remain, your loving uncle and aunt."

So what had happened to the rest of the money? Spent, obviously. How could he possibly think they had acted for the best? She prayed, *Lord, help me to understand them. Help me not to feel such disgust, such revulsion for them!*

An old clock on the mantelpiece ticked away the seconds. How much time did she have before she was due at Patrick's? She had nothing clean to wear, nor anything decent, really. She put all her dirty clothing into Hannah's washing machine while she had a shower and washed her hair. There was a tumble-dryer in the flat. What luxury! She pulled on the non-iron blue dress and hung everything else up on an airer in the kitchen. Lady the cat arrived through the cat flap, demanding food. He was easy to satisfy and seemed happy to be back in his old home.

Minty brushed out her hair and clipped on the opal earrings. Should she leave by the back windows and the iron staircase? Or through the bookshop?

Her mobile rang and it was Patrick.

"Shall I come round for you?"

"I'm not at the cottage, you know."

"I heard Hannah's washing machine a while ago, and realised it must be you. You'd be safer at the Woottons."

"But restricted in my movements. Simon has no keys here."

"What really happened?"

She told him. "But when I got back, Simon was in my bedroom. I threw a spade at him and ran. I might have killed him. It makes me quake, just to think of it. I meant to kill him, you know. I've discovered I'm not the nice person I thought I was. I didn't know I could hate like that."

"Join the human race. Talking of the human race, why has Gemma decided to gatecrash our party this evening?"

Minty was uneasy. "She said she wanted to talk to me. I suppose she just wants to be friendly."

"Friendly as in leaving you to Simon's mercies last night? It might be a good idea not to let her know where you're staying."

Minty was reluctant to believe Gemma could be so two-faced. She was thoughtless, certainly. But not really bad. "Surely she's just a poor little rich girl? A lost child?"

He picked up the reference to Peter Pan immediately. "Isn't she more like the crocodile? Talking of Peter Pan, you do realise that Neville's smitten with you?"

"Peter Pan? Neville? Yes, I suppose there is something boyish about him. He's nice."

"Yes." A long silence.

Minty almost giggled. Was Patrick jealous of Neville? Wow! Good! The silence had gone on too long. She said, "It's all right, Patrick. Really."

"It is?"

"Yes." It was the nearest they had come yet to a declaration of interest in one another.

He said, "Well, the other things I mentioned when I rang you. Do you need an escort to the ball? It won't help you with the family if I go with you, but perhaps . . ."

"All fixed."

"Oh." He was disappointed. "Well, would you like to go blackberrying tomorrow after church? Picnic included? Oldest clothes."

"Love it."

She could hear his doorbell ring. He suggested she exit from Hannah's via the bookshop as it would be only natural that she had gone there to see that all was in order after the fête. "Oh, and don't forget to bring the silver cup."

She met Neville on the doorstep. He was wearing the good suit he'd had on the previous night, with a clean shirt. He looked scrubbed and edible in a roly-poly way. Gemma was coming up the road in a fabulous deep blue silk cocktail dress that showed off her pretty figure . . . and didn't she know it!

Patrick opened the door. He, too, had made an effort. Minty stared. He looked taller than she remembered in a silky grey shirt with a fine dark stripe over dark grey trousers. He looked elegant. Minty realised he was staring at her, too. Of course, this was the first time he'd seen her in a becoming dress and wearing jewellery.

Gemma didn't like to be kept waiting. "Are you going to let us in, then?"

Patrick apologised and led them up the stairs to the first floor. There was a modern fitted kitchen-cum-dining room at the front of the house and a deep, wide sitting room at the back overlooking the garden. The walls were wainscoted but had been painted a pale cream, and the furniture was of all periods, mostly antique. Large chairs were covered in leather or chintz, while an enormous chesterfield took up prime position beside the marble fireplace.

"Oh," cried Gemma. "You're wearing those heavenly opals again, Minty. Do let me try them."

She snatched them off Minty and put them on. She held out her arms and twirled around, her silk skirts moving gracefully around her slender body. "Look! I think they were designed for someone with my colouring, don't you think?"

Both men looked and both then looked back at Minty, who felt drab in her charity shop dress and scuffed sandals. Minty wondered if Gemma had chosen to wear a dress from a designer label to show up Minty's shabby outfit.

"Do let me wear them for the ball!" cried Gemma. "I have the most stunning new dress, but I couldn't make up my mind whether to wear my pearls with it or not. These would be just perfect. Do say I may, Minty!"

Neither man said anything. Were they waiting for her to assert herself?

"I'm sorry to disappoint you," said Minty, holding out her hand for the earrings. "I'm so attached to them myself that I can hardly bear to let them out of my sight."

As she replaced the earrings, Patrick produced a bottle of champagne. "Let's toast Minty from the silver cup."

Gemma tossed her lovely head. "Oh, Minty doesn't like champagne, or drink of any kind, but I'm game for it."

Minty fixed a smile to her face. What was Gemma up to? Was she trying to turn the two men against her? Was Patrick right about Gemma? Was she herself not falling into the same old trap of wanting to please others at any cost? She thought of the humiliations of the previous night, and blushed. "It's true I don't like champagne much, but . . ."

"Had some paint stripper masquerading as champagne, have you?" said Patrick, with sympathy.

"Battery acid, sometimes," Neville agreed.

Minty was warmed by their understanding. "Let's put the cup to its proper use."

"Oh," said Gemma, taking off her expensive court shoe. "Isn't it supposed to be chic to drink out of a lady's slipper? I've never had anyone drink out of my slipper. Do let's try it."

"Another time," said Patrick, popping the cork and pouring some into the cup. "This is Minty's celebration. Suppose we all take a sip in turn."

"Like at Communion," said Gemma, still sparkling. "You know it's 'Mary and Martha' Sunday in our church tomorrow? The anniversary of the people who gave the window to the church? I always look forward to it. Cecil does a splendid talk about how we all ought to be Marys rather than Marthas. I must say I've always identified with Mary. Whom do you identify with, Minty?" She grabbed the cup off Patrick and gave a perfunctory toast. "Here's to Minty."

Minty thought, *You cat! You want me to say I'm a Martha, but I don't feel like Martha any more, so I won't.*

"There's a thought," said Patrick. "What character in the Bible would we most like to resemble? Neville, how about you?"

Neville took the cup from Gemma with a flourish. "I'd be Matthew. He'd been a tax collector, remember? I bet he always got his sums right and never let his clients down. What's more, I quite fancy writing my memoirs when I'm older. Plus dying in bed in comfortable fashion. Here's to your blue eyes, Minty."

Patrick took the cup from Neville. "I think I'd like to resemble Elijah. Before you all laugh and ask when I'm getting into training to be a long-distance runner, it's not about that bit of his life. It's not even about confronting an evil power, or defying the pagan priests of Baal. No, I must admit to a fellow failing. Every now and then I have to go off by myself into a quiet place to think. And listen for the still, quiet voice."

There was silence. Both men had spoken the truth about themselves at a level beyond the usual social chit-chat.

Patrick lifted the cup and toasted Minty. "To Minty, every day and always."

He passed the cup to her. "Well, Minty? Who would you like to be? How about Lydia, a 'seller of purple', who welcomed Paul to Philippi and helped found the church there? She must have been a good businesswoman, as well as a woman of God."

Minty sipped the champagne, which was not unpleasant. She had an impish thought as she handed the cup back to Patrick. "I think the person I'd most like to be is the Old Testament Deborah."

The men shouted with laughter but Gemma looked puzzled.

"Who led her troops into battle?" cried Neville.

"And defeated the foes of Israel. Here's to General Minty." Patrick lifted the cup in a toast to Minty. "Now for supper. I've got the steaks seasoned and the grill's hot. Minty, will you take charge of them? Neville, can you cut up garlic bread? Gemma, how about knocking up a salad for us?"

Gemma recovered some of her poise. "If you've got a great big apron to protect my dress, I'll set the table for you."

Chapter Twenty

What should have been a pleasant evening between friends, developed spiteful undertones.

As Patrick had guessed, Gemma—despite her beautiful face and innocent-seeming manner—was a man-eating crocodile. Minty and the two men bounced the conversation along, talking of the fête and the possibility of floods if the river burst its banks again in the winter, until Gemma started.

"What do you want to put water glasses out for? Oh, I suppose we have to humour Minty."

"I'd love a little wine," said Minty. "But water as well. Yes, please."

Patrick nodded. "I'm having some water, too. I see too many drunks in court."

Gemma took out her cigarettes and lit up as they finished their first course. She blew smoke directly at Patrick, who averted his face. *Bravo, Patrick!* thought Minty.

As they removed the first course and collected ice cream from the kitchen, Gemma helped Minty carry out the plates.

"I must talk to you, Minty." For once Gemma had dropped her airs and graces. "I don't quite know what happened last night after we left, but Simon is absolutely livid with you. I suppose I shouldn't say this, but he can be spiteful if you cross him. The thing is, he's under tremendous strain at the moment, trying to arrange everything for the future. Something's gone wrong with the plans for the future of the Hall. So, just be careful for a bit, all right?"

"You mean Simon might waylay me some dark night?"

"No. I mean that he might get Miles to . . . oh, I don't know. Let down the tyres on your bike, perhaps? Those two have always been so close. Oh, forget it. Probably nothing will happen."

Minty was deep in thought as she took in the dishes for the ice cream. She would mention Gemma's warning to Patrick later. Once back at the table, Gemma resumed her charm offensive on the two men. Cheese, biscuits, and fruit came and went. Patrick lit the candles on the mahogany dining table. Minty made her one glass of wine last, and noticed that neither Neville nor Patrick drank much. Gemma drank more than either, but it didn't seem to make any difference to the way she operated.

"Where's Miles tonight?" Minty asked.

Gemma shrugged. "Doing something for Simon." Her glance flicked to Minty and back to Patrick. "Don't let's talk about him. Are you going to make it to church tomorrow, Patrick?"

"If I can get Jonah over to see Hannah and back in time. He can't seem to take in the fact that she's not coming back."

"Oh, do try to make it. I'll look out for you," said Gemma, touching the back of Patrick's hand in an intimate way that made Minty want to scream.

Neville twinkled at Minty. "Aunt Felicity has ordered me to accompany her to church tomorrow. Minty, is there anything I can do to help you then ... apart from washing up after coffee? I've done enough of that today to qualify me for sainthood."

"Washing up?" Gemma laughed. "You haven't been doing that, surely!" She raised her beautifully white, soft hands to show them off. Hands that had never suffered from harsh soap and hard water.

Patrick said, "Minty, you do realise you might end up taking a Sunday school class tomorrow?" Gemma offered Patrick a cigarette and he took it without thinking. "That child Becky said she'd go if you were doing it. She doesn't usually."

Gemma said, "That dreadful child who looks like a boy? Probably dealing in drugs already."

"No, no," said Patrick, looking startled to see a cigarette in his hand. Without missing a beat he put the cigarette in an empty dish and said, "She's a little toughie, I grant you, but Minty will know how to deal with her."

"Shall we have some coffee?" asked Gemma. "Preferably with brandy. I just adore brandy in proper glasses, don't you? These glasses are Victorian, aren't they, Patrick? Did you inherit them? They tell me you've got brains. So what are you doing, wasting your time as a country solicitor, when you could be working at the Bar and earning millions?"

Minty had had enough. "Behave yourself, Gemma. This is big sister speaking."

For a moment Gemma's eyes widened and she looked as if she might cry. But then she pushed back her chair and tossed her hair back. "Look at the time! I didn't bring the car and I just daren't walk back home through the park all by myself. So who's the lucky man to see me home, then?"

"Of course," said Patrick. "I'll get the car out, if you'll forgive the smell. I gave a lift to a hitch-hiker yesterday and I fear . . ."

Gemma shuddered and turned to Neville, who knew a fib when he saw one and gave Patrick a darkling look. But he responded in the manner expected of him.

"Of course I'll take you. We'll drop Minty off on the way back, look under her bed for burglars and all that."

"Burglars? What nonsense. I daren't be late back," said Gemma. "I have to pop in and see my great big daddy before he drops off to sleep. Sometimes he's so sleepy he just smiles and gives me a great big kiss, and sometimes we sit and chat for a bit. So perhaps Minty can make it down the hill under her own steam. You don't mind dear, do you?"

"Of course not," lied Minty, wondering if Gemma had visited her father at all recently. It didn't sound like it. If Gemma had lied about that, why? Did Gemma really not know about the "burglar"? Yes, of course she did. And that warning . . .

"I'll see Minty back to her place," said Patrick, which made Neville shake his fist at his host behind Gemma's back. Neville knew when he'd been stitched up.

"Nonsense, you've no need to stir yourself," said Gemma, laughing in her pretty, lively way. "Neville and I'll see her safely back and I promise we'll check the place out for burglars."

Minty carried the glasses out to the kitchen, hoping Patrick would follow her, which he did. "You were right," she said, low down. "Gemma really came to warn me. She says Miles might want to pay me back for what I did to Simon last night. I'll go in the front and out the back."

"Better still," he countered in the same low tone, "You let me in the back door when they've gone and I'll walk up the back way with you."

Minty nodded. In a louder voice she said, "What about the washing-up?"

"Leave it," said Patrick, also in a louder voice. "I put everything in the dishwasher and do it when I feel like it."

Gemma was fussing with a wrap, getting Neville to put it around her shoulders. "Yes, great evening, Patrick. See you tomorrow, right? Are you ready, Minty? No jacket? Well, it's a warm enough night, I suppose."

Patrick saw them off the premises. Neville led them up the street and carefully inserted Gemma into the front seat of his car while Minty slid into the back. Down the hill they went and piled out of the car at the bottom of the street. Gemma giggled, getting Neville to help her out. Minty sprang out with the key in her hand, wanting to get this over quickly. She opened the door and tested the air that smelt much as before. Dampish, dusty. She turned on the lights. She didn't think anyone had been in since she left. She drew the curtains.

"Is this the crime scene?" Gemma brought her familiar scent in with her. "I never liked this place. So poky and dull. I wonder you can bear to live here, Minty."

Neville rolled his eyes at Minty and said, "Shall I check upstairs?" He went up while Gemma tested the table for dust and didn't find any. "I suppose it really doesn't matter to you where you live, does it, Minty? How . . . quaint. Me, I'd just be stifled in here. Are you ready, Neville? No burglars? Well, that's a relief! Let's be off, then. Night, Minty!"

She swept out of the door.

Neville took her hand. "Come to the ball with me?"

"I'm sorry. My father's made other arrangements for me."

"Oh." He hesitated. "Where are you sleeping, Minty? I've just noticed that there's no duvet or blankets on the bed upstairs."

"With friends. Not with Patrick, if that's what you're thinking. Keep it to yourself, will you, Neville? And many thanks."

"Neville!" The bell-like tones didn't disguise that this was an order for Neville to attend her immediately. Neville gave Minty a hunted look and disappeared.

Minty shut the door and bolted it. Then she went to the back door and unlocked that. Patrick stepped in. "They've gone? I've got a timer switch here for the lights, which I'll fix up in the bedroom for you. It'll come on in two minutes time and go off in half an hour. This should make any watcher think you've gone up to bed and turned out the lights in the normal way. Only you won't be there. You and I will walk out of the back door, back up the alley to our respective beds."

"Neville suspects."

"He's no fool. Let's get on with it."

He moved past her and up the stairs. She considered his smell. A trace of good soap, a trace of good wine. No aftershave. One minute she thought the precautions they were taking were ludicrous and the next, she was glad she wasn't sleeping there that night.

He came down, leaving a faint glow from a light upstairs. She turned off the lights downstairs, he took her hand and they felt their way out into the back garden, locking the door behind them. The sky was overcast, hinting at rain.

They did not speak on their way back up to his place. He went into the bookshop garden with her and they made their way up the iron staircase to the French windows. Lady the cat was waiting for Minty on the staircase and plopped through the cat flap ahead of her.

Patrick stepped back a half pace, and suddenly there was an awkwardness in the air between them. Patrick's head was bent, turned away from her. His body language said he did not wish to get any closer.

Minty whispered, "Goodnight, and thanks!" She slid inside after the cat.

She was woken by a phone ringing . . . and ringing . . . and ringing. It was still dark. She put on the light. It was half past one in the morning and dark outside. Stumbling out of bed, she reached for her mobile, but it wasn't turned on, and it wasn't that phone which was ringing but Hannah's own phone in the sitting room. As she picked up the phone, she thought she oughtn't to have done so if she didn't want anyone to know where she was. But it was all right.

"Miss Cardale? This is Willy at the Chinese restaurant. Are you all right?"

Minty shook her head to clear it. "Why shouldn't I be?"

"We were woken by the noise. All the windows of Spring Cottage have been smashed and the police have been called. They will go into the cottage, looking for you. If you're not there, they may think all sorts of things. Will I escort you down there, to talk to the police?"

Was this what Gemma had warned her about? She shuddered.

"Miss Cardale? Shall I telephone Mr Patrick?"

"No. I'll meet you downstairs in a minute."

She pulled on jeans and a sweater and picked up her mobile. If Ms Phillips were sound asleep, she was about to have a nasty awakening. The phone rang and rang as Minty slipped down the stairs and let herself out into the street. There was a small knot of people down by the bridge and, even as she watched, a police car drew up and parked.

Willy was waiting for her and they went down the road together.

At long last Ms Phillips picked up the phone and Minty gave her the news.

Ms Phillips said, "It can't be Simon. He went up to London to see the Americans and he's staying overnight."

Minty was appalled by the damage. "Every window downstairs has been smashed in, and someone's used an aerosol to write the words 'Get out!' across the front door. Gemma warned me that Simon might get Miles to punish me for turning him down. I think it was Miles who did this, and I'll suggest his name to the police."

She ended the call as the police and bystanders turned to her with their questions. She said she'd been asked to stay with friends that night and had only just heard what had happened.

Then it was the bystanders' turn. "I saw it all!" claimed a man walking a dog. "He drove down the road so fast I thought he'd clip me as I crossed the road. He was wearing a hooded anorak, but I knew the car and I knew him, of course. He parked in the middle of the road outside the cottage, so I thought there was some kind of emergency. He squirted something at the door and then he got a garden spade out of the back of the car and smashed the windows in. I thought he might turn on me if I interfered, so I ducked into a doorway."

"I called the police," said a woman in a winter coat over pyjamas. "I live opposite and I saw it all. It looked like . . . well, I can't be absolutely sure, but I think it was Miles. I only got the first half of the car number, though, before he shot off over the bridge."

"He turned to the right over the bridge," said an elderly man, wearing an anorak over pyjamas. Minty recognised him as one of the holidaymakers in Riverside Cottage. "I thought it was our windows he'd smashed, and my wife said I shouldn't get involved, but I had to see what was going on. He threw the spade or whatever it was over the bridge into the river, got back into his car and took off. I tried to get the number, but I couldn't get my glasses on quickly enough."

Minty's phone trilled. It was Ms Phillips. "Miles has just returned. Drunk."

So Miles also lived at the Hall. In Gemma's flat? "What's his car number?"

Ms Phillips gave it to her. It matched.

The police asked the first witness. "You say you recognised the car and the man?"

"Miles, the estate manager. I think he was drunk."

Minty turned away from the crowd and spoke low into the phone. "Miles has been identified by two witnesses. Do you want to warn Gemma?"

Ms Phillips hesitated. "Yes, I suppose so." She disconnected.

Ms Phillips was waiting for her in the courtyard at one o'clock next day. As Minty parked her bike, Ms Phillips informed her that her father had had a poor night and a worrying morning. Miles was out on bail. His temper was savage, and even Gemma—who could usually manage him—was keeping a low profile.

Minty was distressed. "All this because of me?"

"Miles has a wicked temper and has overstepped the mark several times before. Simon's always been able to hush things up before, but this time he can't. Sir Micah thought he had done enough to warn Simon off you and was very angry when he discovered what Miles had done. Like you, he believes Simon was behind the attack. It is possible that no charges will be pressed, because technically Spring Cottage belongs to the estate and not to you. The windows have been boarded up and will be replaced tomorrow. The graffiti has also been removed from the door, but I don't think you should return there."

Minty shuddered. "Neither do I."

Minty was shocked by her father's appearance. He was propped up in bed with the oxygen mask on and barely managed to lift his eyelids to see who had come in. She sat beside him and took his hand in hers. For a while she stroked it, gently. He made an effort to smile.

She smiled back. "You'll never guess what I've been doing this morning. I didn't ask for the job, but I got landed with taking a Sunday school class." She kept her voice low and spoke slowly, ready to stop if he signalled he'd had enough.

"I took the children's group and we acted out the story of Noah and the Great Flood. I asked some of them—including the androgynous Becky—to mime bad behaviour, and then had to stop a fight between a couple of boys! I told them this was how everyone had been behaving before God intervened and ordered that good man Noah to build an ark."

Sir Micah listened, his mouth relaxed in a half smile.

"Then we had another fight about who was to be God, and who was to be Noah. I solved that by making Becky play at being God. As the others are all in awe of Becky, that worked out all right. Becky enjoyed herself, too. Noah was one of the biggest boys, and everyone else turned themselves into animals and walked around, pretending to be giraffes, or roaring like lions or mewing like cats. Then we all went into a circle on the floor that I'd marked out with chalk, and there we were in the ark.

"I showed them how to imitate the rain coming down, by pattering with their fingers on the floor. Becky made a screeching sound to represent lightning and it was a wonder there were no complaints from the congregation next door, because we were making so much noise!

"Everyone had to 'swim' in the rising waters, and throw up their arms and pretend to drown. We all enjoyed that, particularly me, who'd been landed with twins clinging around my neck, both screaming to me to save them.

"At that point I asked the youngest child—representing the dove—to 'fly' around the room and come to rest on the piano stool, to show there was now some dry land nearby. Then God—or rather, Becky—told Noah he wasn't going to destroy man in such a way again, and that as a sign he was giving the world a rainbow.

"At which time," said Minty, "we discovered we'd gone on longer than the service in church, and we had to scurry to get our own squash and biscuits. The children said they'd come again. Becky assumes she's always going to play God, so I'll have to think of something else for them to do."

He really was smiling now and his colour was better.

"The Reverend Scott thinks I'm an answer to his prayers for help in the parish, but I'm not so sure. At least he's stopped calling me 'Martha'."

His eyebrows were raised in query.

She explained. "The church has got this Mary and Martha window. Gemma thinks she's Mary and that I'm Martha. I suppose, to be truthful, that I really was a Martha in the old days. I worked hard but never took any joy in anything. Last night at supper we had a competition to say which character in the Bible we thought we resembled. I said I'd like to be Deborah, the Old Testament woman who was a victorious general in battle." She laughed. "Which was really silly, but made everyone laugh. Patrick said . . ."

She stopped, because he'd frowned at her slip of the tongue.

She folded her hands more firmly around his. "I'm sorry if it upsets you, but yes, Patrick and I are friends. In fact, we're going blackberrying together this afternoon. Very innocent. We'll probably not even shake hands, certainly not kiss. He's holding back. I don't know why, but I respect him enough to take it on trust. I suppose you could say that—to use a really old-fashioned term—we're 'courting'. It may go further. It may not. I don't know. What I do know is that he is both wise and kind. He's also devious, absent-minded, and forgets to eat when he's working. You don't need to tell me why I shouldn't be seeing him, but perhaps I need to tell you that he's a good Christian."

She smiled. "Probably Cecil wouldn't agree with me. I suspect Patrick is the sort of Christian who doesn't always get to church on time, who avoids committee meetings like the plague, but can be relied on for the dirty work of picking up the broken pieces when people's lives go smash. I doubt if he'll ever make much money, but that doesn't bother me."

He sighed and closed his eyes. Now she could see that he was very tired. His hand was lax in hers, so she let go of it, slowly, and palmed tears from her cheeks. *Big girls don't cry.*

Ms Phillips touched her shoulder and obediently Minty rose and followed her, not to the office, but into the cool green sitting room next door. Serafina was there, hovering just inside the door.

"He's worse," said Minty. "How long has he got? I'm so stupid. I hoped my coming might make a difference."

"It has," said Ms Phillips, closing the door behind her. "He wants desperately to live till your birthday, but he knows he may not make it."

"Simon's back," said Serafina. "Raging to get at his father. Apparently his latest meeting with the Americans went badly and they're still refusing to sign."

Ms Phillips soothed Minty's fears. "It's all right. The people in the office will see that he's not disturbed."

Minty rubbed her forehead. "Surely they can't keep him out? He's the heir."

"We don't know what will happen after Sir Micah dies."

Minty rounded on them. "Why did he want to come back here, when you two love him so much?"

"There's nothing like a child's love," said Serafina. "I should know, who have lost four. He remembered what it was like to have you love him. He'd long ago recognised that he wasn't going to get any loving response from Simon, but he still had hopes of Gemma. Unfortunately she's grown into a hard woman, only thinking of money. And now that she's engaged to Miles, she has no time for him."

"I don't understand Gemma," said Minty, thinking of her half-sister's very timely warning. "She's not all bad."

"She's tied her future to Simon and his minder, Miles. That was another reason your father wanted to come back here. He's always loved this place, and he didn't like what Simon was doing to it. Now he's discovered you, Minty, and he thinks you're worth it. Go and wash your face and hands."

Ms Phillips disappeared into the sickroom while Minty went to do as she was bid. Returning to the green room, she went to the mantelpiece and leaned her arms upon it, looking into the mirror. Her own image looked back at her, and then it changed. The woman in the mirror reached out her hand and touched Minty's lips . . .

Then Minty saw only her own reflection again.

Serafina reappeared with the hostess trolley. "Come and eat."

Minty tried to laugh. "I thought I saw my mother's ghost just then."

"You've been thinking about her a lot. Your imagination is playing tricks. That was her own mirror from her bedroom. Perhaps you remember it? I'll give you the key to her special place tomorrow. You'll like to see that."

Serafina vanished, leaving a tantalising odour of soup and hot rolls behind her.

Minty raced back to the bookshop on her bike, stowed it under the iron staircase, and just had time to change into T-shirt and jeans before Patrick started up his car outside.

As they passed the ugly botch of derelict farm buildings near the station, Minty turned to look at it.

"Who owns that?" she asked. "Looks like it's ripe for redevelopment. I hear there's a shortage of housing in the village. Wouldn't that be a good site for it? Right by the station, so commuters to the city might like to live there, too?"

"Mmm. So thought some locals, who bought it a couple of years ago. Problem: for years access has been over that small, stony field that lies between the buildings and the road. The farmer paid a nominal fee yearly to the Hall for this access, because the only other way on to his land was by an unmade track up and over the hill into a series of narrow lanes that eventually meander in this direction. It's too long a way round to get to the village or the station. The farmer was content to rent the field rather than buy it, because it's no use for farming purposes. Naturally the new owners wanted to buy the field. Miles agreed and they settled on a reasonable price. Then Miles changed his tune. He said he'd be delighted to broker a deal—for a fee. Unfortunately his fee was so outrageous that negotiations have stalled."

"How much did he ask for?"

"Three million pounds."

"What?" She couldn't believe her ears. "Is that the way Miles normally conducts his business? Why does Simon put up with it? No, that's the wrong question, isn't it? What sort of cut does Simon get? Does this explain why Gemma is marrying Miles? Is he getting rich quick or . . . does she know . . . ?"

"I don't know the answer to any of your questions and I must warn you they're probably slanderous. Off the record, I totally agree with you. His father was an excellent estate manager, but Miles hasn't a good reputation, and it has been Simon's least popular appointment." He shrugged. "They were at school together."

Minty frowned. "I'm told the Americans are refusing to go ahead with Simon's plans for the clinic. How did you manage to stop that?"

"I knew someone who could pass along a word of warning to the right people. I faxed them a copy of the scaremongering surveyor's report, and I also suggested that they checked to see if Simon had the right to sign a lease. I gather they were suitably appalled by what Simon had *not* told them."

"I appreciate your tactics. But . . . my father's much worse . . ." She bit her lip. "It's horrible. I think Ms Phillips and Serafina are the only people who love him."

He put his hand on her knee for a moment. "Apart from you."

Chapter Twenty-One

Patrick parked the car beside a gate leading into a steep field. Everywhere Minty looked there were mounds of blackberry bushes, glinting purple from the clusters of fruit that tipped every spray. The air was fresh and she was glad of the sweater Patrick produced from the jumble in his boot. He also produced containers for gathering blackberries, stout walking sticks and wellington boots.

Giant clouds moved across the landscape, casting shadows on the fields below. She clapped her hands and laughed. "You can see for miles!"

He smiled. "You're such a child."

"I need to be, sometimes. Being grown-up all the time is depressing. I had to grow up so quickly back in the city. There weren't many occasions on which I could be a child again. Perhaps only when playing with my cat. Now there's so much to take in, so much fresh grief to carry . . . let's have a holiday from it all?"

She thought then that he'd take her in his arms, but at the last moment he turned away. They started picking blackberries, close enough to one another to be able to talk.

He said, "I hear Mrs Collins didn't make it to the service. Exhaustion."

She giggled. "I hear that Mrs Chickward's flower arrangement was given pride of place by the altar."

"And looked very odd indeed."

"Broaden your outlook, Patrick. It was stunning. Modern. Stimulating. So you did make it to the end of the service?"

"In time to hear Cecil announce that Lady Cardale has graciously consented to present a new banner to the church, featuring—of course—Mary and Martha. The news was received with modified rapture."

Minty giggled. "How's Hannah?"

"I took Jonah to see her again, but it may have been a mistake. Hannah's set on moving in with her sister and never having to look at the bookshop again. Jonah finally got the message. He was uncharacteristically quiet afterwards and I wondered whether I was wise to leave him with Ruby . . . she's coped so well all these years, but . . ."

"Can't Hannah forgive him?"

"She forgives in her head but not in her heart. I worry about Jonah and I also worry about Ruby. How much more will she be able to take? She's been so good, first caring for her potty old father after her mother died, and then Jonah. I honestly don't think there's been anything sexual between them since that one flight of passion so many years ago. Jonah gives her his pension book in return for pocket money, but she has to carry the responsibility of looking after him. How did you get on with the children?"

They talked about Becky a little, and then Minty went on to tell Patrick about her own first Sunday school teacher and how she had made such a difference to Minty's life. And from there to discussion of Alice—whom Patrick said had been outside the church when he arrived, but refused to come in.

Minty popped another ripe blackberry into her mouth. "Oh, by the way, I think you dropped your prayer list in the garden."

"Was that where I lost it? Never mind. I was due to make a new one."

Minty thought, *These are safe subjects for discussion by good friends, but I'm hungry for something that's not at all safe.*

When they'd filled all their containers with blackberries, Patrick spread an old rug on a comparatively flat piece of ground and produced sausage rolls, a thermos of coffee, some cans of cold drinks, and packets of biscuits. They ate side by side, in companionable silence.

Minty asked, "What are you going to do with all these blackberries?"

"I give some away, keep some in the freezer. They're good with ice cream in the winter. It'll be my last opportunity to get them this year. They say blackberries are no good after Michaelmas, and they're right. They get too dried up and pippy. Anyway, I thought that as you've got apples at Spring Cottage, I could supply the blackberries and you could make us some blackberry and apple pies."

She inspected a purple thumb for a thorn. Michaelmas fell on September 25, which was her birthday. Was it also a Lady Day? Yes, it was. She'd forgotten that, living in the city. So her birthday fell on a Lady Day, and Patrick was going to ask her something on her birthday. Hmm.

His mobile phone rang and he answered it, saying "Yes, yes," at intervals. And then, "We'll be there."

He said, "We've been invited to the Woottons for supper because Mr Lightowler has asked for a council of war. What will you do if the Woottons ask you to move in with them?"

"Mmm," she said, snuggling down on the rug, eyes half closed.

Patrick drank some coffee, not looking at her. The air between them was no longer easy-going. He seemed tense. Perhaps he was regretting having invited her to come out with him. He lay back, pulling a disgraceful old hat over his eyes.

She leant on one elbow, looking at Patrick's prostrate body. He seemed perfectly relaxed. He'd probably gone to sleep. His breathing was gentle. His mouth . . . she considered his mouth, which was almost all that could be seen from under that awful hat. He was wearing scruffy old jeans and an even scruffier old shirt. Suitable for blackberrying, of course. Also they'd be good to touch, because they'd originally been very expensive clothes.

His mouth was wide, a little uneven, crooked at one side. There was a line developing down his left check, where it creased when he laughed. She wondered about his past love life. He must have had one. He was older than her . . . the words "five years older" crept into her mind.

He was certainly asleep. She was tempted to ... no, she couldn't. Too brazen! But wouldn't it be delicious just to touch his lips with hers? Just in the name of science, of course. Just to see how they felt. He wouldn't know.

She held back her hair and leaned over him. His lips were just as she had thought they might be, soft, but ... he gave a great start. His arms sprang up on either side of her and suddenly they were kissing one another without tenderness, with such hunger ... such desire! His lips were hard on hers, on her mouth, her eyes, her throat, her lips again ... he was gasping her name and she was clinging to him, kissing him back wherever she could, on his lips, his jaw ... his lips again, and again ... they were tumbling over and over ...

She had never experienced anything like it. Her body felt boneless and yet she was hot and in pain.

He threw her back down on to the ground and sat up with his back to her. "That was a rotten trick!" His voice was not under control.

She pressed both hands over her face and curled up on her side.

He staggered up the hill away from her.

After a while she got a can of cold drink from the car and drank it. He came down the hill more slowly than he'd gone up. He took a cold drink, too.

He said, "Feeling pleased with yourself?" The tone was sharp.

"I needed to know. I thought you might be holding back because you didn't fancy me."

"I fancy you all right. You think I'm slow, don't you?"

"Since I've arrived, I've had three offers to take me to the ball. I've been invited out for meals, twice—no, three times if you count Simon's invitation. I've been told that if nothing comes of it between you and me, I have only to lift the phone to acquire another suitor. I've found a man in my bedroom, assuring me that I'm hungry for sex with him, and I've had the word 'Get out' sprayed on my door for everyone to see. 'Slow', Patrick? You? Surely not!"

"There is a reason, but I can't tell you what it is, yet."

"Answer me one question. When I know the reason, will I think it a good one?"

"I hope so."

"Why have you never married?"

He threw up his arms. "You've had your one question."

She felt mischievous. "Go on. You can tell me."

His face went through a variety of expressions, but finally he grinned. "I've looked. Of course I have. Sometimes I thought I'd found a pearl of great price—usually when a girl was bright enough to laugh at my jokes. But none of them checked me when I said something unkind."

Oh. Minty remembered that she herself had checked him when he had been too sharp in his wit. Mmm. She liked that.

He started packing things into the car. "Yes, I suppose I am slow—compared to Neville—it was Neville, wasn't it? Who asked to be first reserve? Was it Cecil who asked you for supper? I suppose you think that a proper man would have taken one look at you, asked Norman Thornby where you were staying, and come round with flowers that night? Under different circumstances I suppose that's what I would have done, but I knew who you were straight away, you see. No, you don't see. You can't. Not yet. Just write me down as 'slow' for the time being. All right?"

"What happens on my birthday?"

He practically snarled at her. "Wait and see."

Minty put her head on one side. She liked playing games with Patrick. "Would you let me drive your car back?"

He was, predictably, horror-struck. "You impertinent child! Drive my pride and joy? You must be out of your mind!" He fought with himself, then fished keys out of his pocket and threw them to her. "All right, but you won't mind if I don't look, will you?" He got in the passenger side, adjusted the seat so that he was practically lying down and pulled his hat over his eyes.

She pulled her seat forward, checked over the controls and turned on the ignition. It was going to be tricky doing a three-point turn in that narrow lane. Maybe he'd relied on that, expecting her to give up at the first check. But she'd been driving in city streets since she was seventeen and knew what she was doing . . . though the Rover was a more powerful car and had stiffer controls than she was used to.

He lifted the hat off his eyes and said in tones of astonishment, "You can drive! You're not a qualified pilot as well, are you? Or a cordon bleu chef?"

She laughed, content that they were back on friendly terms. "Perhaps," she said, "you play chess to Olympic standard, or write learned tomes on tropical fish?"

"Oh, no. I'm very ordinary."

"*That* you are not," she said with conviction. "And don't go to sleep on me. I don't know whether to turn left or right at the T-junction here."

Venetia kissed Minty, and touched Patrick on the shoulder in a familiar gesture. "Go on in. We'll have a sherry and eat before we talk. Mr Lightowler is coming at eight."

Hugh assumed Minty would like a sherry. "Dry or medium dry for you?"

"Neither," she said. "If we're having a council of war, shouldn't you invite Mr Thornby, too?"

She felt the shock wave go through the room, though not a muscle moved on the faces of the Woottons or Patrick. Then both the Woottons looked at Patrick accusingly.

He threw up his hands. "Not me! Honest. She saw the potential of the site without my saying a word. I don't know how she got from there to Thornby, but of course she's right."

Minty said, "I was looking for a connection. Mr Thornby came to meet me at the station in case no one arrived from the Hall. He told me himself that he had fingers in all sorts of pies, and on the way from the station he nearly stopped beside the farm buildings. I think he wanted to talk to me about them, perhaps ask me to intercede with my father, but decided against it. Two and two makes four."

Venetia said, "I must see to the vegetables," and disappeared.

Patrick was fiddling with his mobile. "Hugh, may I use the phone in your study? My battery's going down. I think we should get Florence, not Norman. She's an incomer and knows what the village needs rather than wants. Also, she's got a sharp mind, which we natives seem to have lost." He disappeared, too.

Hugh gave a long, long sigh. "Minty, my dear."

"It's a consortium who bought that land," said Minty, realising the truth. "You're in it, too? That's why you've been so good to me?" The thought stung.

"Yes and no. For years Lady Cardale has refused to take any interest in the village, and I suppose that's understandable seeing that we didn't agree with her version of how Milly died. We hoped for a better rapport when she passed the estate over to Simon, but soon realised that all he was interested in was milking it for all he could get. Yes, we welcomed your coming and . . ."

"And you expect great things of me."

Hugh smiled. "Yes, but we've come to value you for yourself, too."

"What can I do? When my father dies . . ."

"I gather he's not expected to last long. Sorry, my dear. Didn't realise you had become so fond of the old . . . well, mustn't call names now, eh? So we must plan for the future. We deplored our empty buildings but blamed everyone but ourselves for them. You looked at them and saw the potential. Like Mr Lightowler. He wants to buy the shop and flat and start literary and music societies and book-reading clubs and all that. You two have brought fresh life into the village. That's what we must work on."

It was a tall order and she didn't think much of their chances. However, if they were willing to try . . .

She looked around. The room was furnished with comfortable old pieces of furniture. There were some good pieces of silver on display and a multitude of family photographs. One of these attracted her attention, and she picked it up. A lively, dark-haired girl laughed up at her. The same girl appeared in other photographs, as a teenager, as a baby, as a small child. Minty felt the tug of old memories. Had she played with this girl once? What was her name?

Then her brain zigzagged to another memory. Patrick had mentioned a previous girlfriend or friends and he'd used the word "pearl".

"Yes, that's our daughter Pearl," said Hugh, fondly. "We wondered if you'd remember her. She used to play with you at the Hall when you were both tiny things."

"I half remembered. She's in New Zealand?" Minty picked up a wedding photo with a hand that she ordered not to tremble. "Happily married?"

Hugh beamed. "Expecting, already."

Minty nodded and put the photo down. Patrick and Pearl. She was horrified at her reaction. *PATRICK'S MINE! How dare he go out with another woman!*

She turned her back on Hugh so that he shouldn't read her face. Of course Patrick would have known Pearl, and Pearl would have been attracted to him. How could she not have been? He was the most attractive man Minty had ever met.

She was ragingly jealous.

Another memory: Florence Thornby had lost her elder daughter to the city. She would be about the same age, so perhaps . . . had that girl, too, once been interested in Patrick?

She felt stunned.

She told herself that the Patrick she thought she knew wasn't necessarily the real man. These people had a history she didn't know anything about. She'd been plumped down in the middle of them, and they'd adopted her for their own purposes.

She thought, *How can I trust any of them?*

She was a little late for her appointment with Ms Phillips next morning.

"Sorry. So much to do! I haven't even had time for breakfast."

Ms Phillips relaxed. "Would you like some coffee and a croissant? Do you think you could call me Annie?"

"I'd be honoured. And yes, I'd love something to eat, but only if I'm not keeping my father waiting."

Annie Phillips spoke into her phone, and said, "Your father has someone with him now, so we have a few minutes to spare. Tell me how you've been getting on."

Minty hooked up a chair, tossed back her hair and obliged. "Well, to start with, I've decided not to go to the police about the money. My uncle sent me a cheque and a note saying he'd acted for the best. His reasoning defeats me, but the money's very welcome. I earned every penny of it. So now I have to find out what the buses are like to town, so that I can open an account."

"I have to go to town tomorrow morning and I'll give you a lift, if you wish."

"Why, thank you. I accept. Patrick's offered me a lift in, but then I couldn't get back. So yes, please."

Florence Thornby came in with a laden tray on which reposed not only coffee and croissants but also a selection of yoghurts and a plateful of thinly sliced cheese and ham. Minty cried out in delight. Florence Thornby returned the smile and withdrew, saying to Annie, "Remember Gemma's wanting to see her sister."

Minty tore the foil off a yoghurt. "I suppose she wants me to get Miles off the hook."

"It might be that," said Annie, cautiously. "I said you were busy this morning but might fit her in this afternoon. Do you know Florence well?"

"I know lots of people, though not well," said Minty, round a mouthful of yoghurt.

Annie Phillips poured coffee and pushed it towards Minty. "Tell me about the council of war last night."

Minty almost spilt yoghurt down herself. "Ah. Florence talked, did she? Well, you must be aware that the village feels threatened by Simon's plans. A number of us got together to prepare some sort of business plan for the future. Long term, I think we ought to have a proper information office, attract specialist food shops, antique shops, a cafe. The area is beautiful enough to attract visitors even without the Hall, though with the Hall it stands a better chance of surviving. If the Hall closes and we do nothing, then we'll soon lose our railway station, the bus service will be withdrawn, to be followed by the post office and the smaller shops. Am I making sense?"

"Most interesting. I'll check if your father is free, but in the meantime you might like to look at this."

Annie laid a manilla file on the desk and withdrew. Minty pushed the last piece of croissant into her mouth and opened the file, which had been compiled by a detective agency. It contained two sections: one dealt with Richard Sands, Patrick's father, and the other with Patrick himself.

She scanned the section dealing with Richard Sands first. She found a biography of a man respected both in the village and in his practice. Dates of birth, marriage, birth of only son, death of wife ... investigation of the gossip surrounding Milly Cardale's friendship with Richard Sands ... no grounds for suspicion. After Richard Sands lost most of his practice, he removed to ... and on his retirement bought a house at ... and so on. Nothing new there.

Minty turned to the report on Patrick Sands ... his date of birth, schooling ... yes, there was the break in his schooling that he'd told her about. Academic, not athletic. Prizes for this and that. University ... glowing reports. Opinion of college ... a good mind, could go far but lacks ambition. Taking up position in father's firm ... could have gone into something bigger, in the opinion of the writer. Had made quite a name for himself in boundary dispute cases, which he usually managed to settle out of court. Not liked by everyone as he could be sarcastic. Hardly likely to make a fortune, since he spent so much time doing pro bono work.

Gossip: name linked with ... and there it was. Not just the names she'd expected, Pearl Wootton, Trudy Thornby, but others as well. Ugh. She supposed it was only natural. Put him down in a room of nubile females and within ten minutes he'd have all the girls salivating over him. His combination of wit and sex would always attract.

Then came the killer. "The subject was the prime mover behind the scheme to acquire the land to the west of the railway station for development. Other partners: Hugh Wootton and Norman Thornby, who have each contributed a quarter of the purchase price. Patrick Sands provided half the money and will be a very rich man if the project goes through."

She set down the file, feeling dizzy. She thought, *This is totally out of character. He's not ambitious or money-minded. Even the report says so. On the other hand, what man could turn down a chance to become rich quick?*

Why hadn't he told her? Well . . . there could be various reasons and none of them particularly bad. He might have wanted her to love him for himself. She did, of course, love him for himself. Not that she felt particularly sure of him, but there it was. He had dragged her into loving him.

He was going to ask her for something on her birthday. It could be that he would ask her to help him get that all-important piece of land for access.

No, it couldn't. Whatever he was going to ask her then was tied up with marguerites, or a daisy chain. Some memory about daisies lingered at the back of her mind . . . something important. Something to do with butterflies?

Annie Phillips returned and locked away the file.

Minty said, "There's something else you could add to that file. Patrick spent two long hours last night trying to talk Jonah Wootton out of committing suicide. It's finally got through to the poor little man that Hannah's not coming back. Patrick called the doctor, saw Jonah sedated and safely in bed. That's the reason I was late this morning. I promised Patrick I'd look in on Jonah and Ruby on my way here. Jonah's sitting in his chair staring at nothing. His little feet don't even touch the floor. Ruby was fretting about not being able to open up the charity shop, but she couldn't leave him on his own. Sorry. You don't need to know all that."

"I'll get you some fresh coffee."

"No, I'm all right. Thank you for showing me the file. I knew most of it, but not about him being behind the development plan. Did you know why it's stalled?"

"It's really not my business."

"The Hall owns a small, stony field—useless for farming purposes, which the developers need for access. The original owner of the farm used to rent that field from the Hall at a nominal rent. Miles asked for three million pounds to arrange the sale of it to the developers. I don't know whether Simon is in it or not."

Annie raised her eyebrows and made a note on a pad. "I'll find out. Miles has been suspended from his job for the moment. Simon had to agree to that, though he didn't like it. Between you and me, I doubt very much if charges will be pressed against Miles, but we're not telling him that—yet. It was disgraceful behaviour."

The phone beside Annie rang. She listened for a while, nodded and said "We'll be right up." She replaced the phone, and said, "Your father's had Simon with him this morning and is in consequence very tired. He still wants to see you, but perhaps you can find something pleasant to talk to him about?"

Chapter Twenty-Two

A male nurse was on duty. Sir Micah was in bed and the oxygen mask was on. His eye sockets looked black and he was obviously exhausted, but he lifted his hand in greeting to Minty when she sat beside him.

She took his hand and stroked it. What could she talk about that wouldn't be controversial? Ah, he loved the English countryside, so she'd talk about that.

"We went blackberrying yesterday. Old clothes, wellington boots. Look, my hands haven't recovered yet. I've scrubbed the stains, but the blackberries were so ripe I had purple marks right up both arms and all over my mouth, I was horrified when I looked in the mirror. The blackberries are so ripe they squash in your fingers as you pick them. I got scratched, too. It was amazing up there on the hillside . . ."

She went on to describe the enormous stands of brambles, the heavy clusters of purple fruit, the softness of the turf beneath their feet . . . the wild flowers and the myriad butterflies. She said she didn't know the names of all the butterflies and the wildflowers, though Patrick did . . . and here a long-buried memory tugged at her consciousness for a moment. She intended to get a book on them, and find out. She spoke of the great shadows moving across the landscape as the clouds rushed across the sky, and the picnic, as she lay on an old rug in the sun.

There she fell silent, remembering the kiss that had sparked off such a violent reaction in Patrick. And smiling at the memory. She continued to stroke her father's hand. His eyelids were closing. Presently he would sleep. She was filled with pity for him.

She heard her voice say, "I wish you didn't find it so hard to say sorry."

His eyes opened wide and he looked at her. He shuddered, trying to speak, panting with the effort. Minty was alarmed. She looked around for the nurse. Her father withdrew his hand from hers and the nurse came forward to adjust the oxygen.

Minty scraped her chair back.

"Why did you say that?" Serafina was standing in the doorway.

"I don't know," Minty said. "The words just came into my head."

Serafina beckoned to Minty, who followed her into the calm green room. Minty went to the fireplace and looked in the mirror. She saw only herself, but a ray of light from somewhere caught the tiny gold cross she wore round her neck.

"What do you see?" asked Serafina.

"The cross round my neck," said Minty. "He needs to say he's sorry. Not to me. To God. Am I making sense?"

Annie Phillips had joined them. "He's dying. He's done many things that he regrets in his life, and you're quite right: he does find it difficult to say sorry. I've asked him several times if I might send for the minister, but he's refused. He says he's always lived as if there were no God, and he'll die that way."

"We have prayed about it," said Serafina.

"I'll pray, too," said Minty, gripping the mantelpiece and bowing her head. *Dear Lord and father, forgive our foolishness. Forgive him . . .*

But into her mind came the words, "Only if he wants to be forgiven."

She prayed, *Then tell me the words that will open his eyes to what he's rejecting.*

"I'll show you a better place to pray," said Serafina. "Only Annie and I use it now, but it's yours, really."

Minty followed the older woman through Sir Micah's suite of rooms till they came to the anteroom at the end. Serafina unlocked the door in the tower and stood back to let Minty enter.

Minty entered her mother's private place.

Long, long before, the tower room had been fitted up as a small chapel. The walls were panelled and had once been painted golden yellow, but were now cream. Lancet windows were let into the walls, except on the east side, where a small altar stood, backed by a cloth of cream and gold. On the altar was a cross of plain wood, and before it was a long kneeler, embroidered with flowers.

Fresh flowers had been placed on a small table, next to a much-used Bible. There was rush matting on the floor and three chairs stood like a trilogy, waiting for people to make use of them. Minty thought, *The low nursing chair belongs to Serafina, the one with the padded seat and back is for Annie, and the high-backed carved chair is for me.*

The atmosphere of the chapel was full of prayer.

As a child, Minty remembered she'd often run up the pretty stairs to find her mother, who would be sitting on the great carved chair with her hands lying idle in her lap, or sometimes reading the Bible. There had been only the one chair there, then.

Minty did not sit in a chair, but sank down on the kneeler. This was indeed the right place to pray. She could feel the weight of other people's prayers in the air around her, prayers spoken by many generations of her ancestors, by her mother, by Annie and Serafina. It was not an eerie feeling, but a comforting one. She looked at the cross, and it was as if someone had shouted a welcome to her. "Here you are at last!"

She held out her arms to the cross, bent her head and prayed as she had never prayed before. She praised God for all his goodness to her, for the love he had shown her. For his tremendous patience with her sins. She praised him for the sun and moon and the stars above, for all the flowers and fruit, for his goodness to the world.

She prayed for guidance, and to be worthy of his trust in her. She prayed for her long-lost father. She prayed for all those she had come to love, and she prayed for those she feared and distrusted.

She knelt with head bent and eyes closed, feeling the warmth of his blessing enclosing her. Finally, she rose and went out of the door, noting that the key had been left in the lock. Serafina was outside, waiting for her.

"That key is yours," said Serafina. "Annie and I have the others. Now I'll show you where her things are kept."

Serafina crossed the anteroom and unlocked the door opposite. This was a storeroom in poor decorative condition. Perhaps it had once been a servant's room? Minty did not recognise it, but she greeted with pleasure the furniture that had been stacked around the walls.

She touched the pieces one by one: her mother's workbox and dressing table, the carved wood cabinet with the many drawers in which the child Minty used to hide her treasures. She pulled open one drawer and found the carved nuts her mother had brought her back from the Far East. Still there! And the old wax doll her godmother had given her.

In a low bookcase were all her favourite books, the fairy stories, the Beatrix Potters, the pop-ups.

Suddenly she felt faint. The books! She let herself sink to the floor, and reached for her treasures one by one. Her hand was trembling. She felt her breathing shorten. The exercise book with her name printed on it in bold letters. An illustrated leaflet on butterflies. The Beatrix Potter *Peter Rabbit.* She opened each one at the flyleaf.

"This book belongs to . . . Patrick Sands."

These were Patrick's books.

On the first line of every page in the exercise book he had written words in big letters. Underneath were her first wavering attempts to copy the words he'd written. "My name is . . . Araminta Cardale. I live at . . . Eden Hall. I am . . . four years old."

Had Patrick taught her to read and write?

Her throat ached. She wanted to cry. The more she tried to remember, the more she hurt all over. At the back of her mind she could hear the swish of her aunt's belt, striking at her over and over again. "Forget it . . . forget . . . forget . . ."

Serafina hadn't noticed. She said, "Lady Cardale doesn't know I have the key. To tell the truth this key is from another room, but it fits well enough."

Minty looked up at Serafina, trying to make sense of what she'd just said. Serafina was turning a sheeted picture frame round to face the room. She pulled back the cover. "This is what you'll be wanting to take with you."

The portrait of her mother was by a master, but it would not sit easily in the Long Gallery. It would not sit easily anywhere. A woman looking like—and yet not like—Minty, was seated in the carved oak chair from the chapel. The chair was slightly turned away from the viewer, but the woman's head was turned towards the front. She had curly blonde hair and was wearing blue. One hand held on to the arm of the chair, and the other lay relaxed in her lap.

Minty thought her mother looked ill. There were greenish shadows beneath her eyes and she looked thin, yet gave the impression of being pregnant. She wore a wedding ring but no other jewellery except for a tiny gold cross on a chain round her neck. Her eyes looked straight at the viewer. They were steady, steadfast, enduring. Her lips looked as if she were trying to smile but not quite succeeding. Minty looked at the picture of her mother and the pictured eyes looked back at her. Minty moved to the right, and the eyes followed her.

Serafina's mobile phone trilled and she left the room, saying she was needed. Minty sat on, holding the books in her lap, staring at her mother's portrait. If only she could remember! Patrick had asked her twice if she remembered . . . but remembered what? "Forget it . . . forget . . . forget."

Annie Phillips came in and asked if Minty was all right.

Minty pulled her mind back from the past. She put the books back in the bookcase, stood up and covered the picture over again. "I can't take that away. It belongs here. Was she pregnant or am I imagining it?"

"I looked up the autopsy. She was five months pregnant and had gone into premature labour at the time of the crash. It would have been a boy."

Minty shuddered.

Patrick had called her father a "serial adulterer". Put it all together, Minty. The heavily pregnant woman finds her husband making love to . . . Lisa? In her distress she flees the scene. And crashes into the parapet of the bridge.

If it were so, then the husband had sinned, and being the kind of man he was, had neither been able to acknowledge that guilt, nor to deal with it. He had allowed all traces of his first wife to be swept away, including the child Minty. He had taken on board the lie that his wife was running away to a lover. Perhaps he had even come to believe it. Now he was dying, that old sin was coming back to haunt him.

What was Minty supposed to do about it? Ask him to say he was sorry? Yes, but look what had happened when she did just that!

Annie Phillips said, "Gemma is agitating to see you. She's in the east wing, directly beneath us. Down the stairs and to the right."

"The nurseries used to be on the first floor of the east wing—that's where Gemma is now?"

"She expected you ten minutes ago."

Minty sighed, running her forefinger over her mother's dressing table. And wasn't that her grandfather's cane over there? And yes, her grandmother's parasol?

Why can't I remember?

Annie was almost pushing her out. "Before you start worrying about Jonah Wootton, I've been in touch with the surgery and either his doctor or the practice nurse will call round to see him again this afternoon."

Minty tried to think straight. "Thank you, dear Annie."

A wintry smile. "Gracious! I don't need thanking for doing my duty."

"Wasn't that above and beyond the call of duty?"

Annie actually laughed. It wasn't much of a laugh, but it did show that she was still capable of it. She led the way down the twisting stairs to the first floor and knocked on the door to the east wing.

"Come!" Gemma shouted, opening the door to them. "You've taken your time, I must say!" She was in a bad mood, tossing her red curls, smoking in gasps, twitching at the neck of the perfect trouser suit she was wearing. She wasn't wearing any shoes or tights, and her toenails were painted bright red to match her fingernails. Although she was four years younger than Minty, she looked older. Yet her bare feet looked vulnerable.

"Sorry I'm late," said Minty, feeling uneasy in her half-sister's presence, remembering the problem represented by Miles, trying to push her recent discoveries to the back of her mind. To cover her embarrassment she went to the nearest window. Yes, this had definitely been the day nursery. Beneath her was the formal garden she'd seen from the terrace, but at this height the design made sense and she could see over the high hedge that surrounded it to the white pillars and domed roof of a small folly on the green hillock beyond. A folly. It meant something to her. But what?

The folly seemed to be beckoning to her. She wanted to climb that hill and stand in the little temple, because only there would she know . . . what? But Gemma was speaking. "Do you like my little den?"

The room was now a sitting room and had been decorated in modern taste. To Minty's mind, the angular furniture and strong colours didn't fit comfortably within the old walls.

"Did you do it all yourself?"

Florence Thornby appeared at the far door. "Lunch is served."

"I'm not eating," said Gemma, "but I suppose you'll want to feed your face. Come along through." She led the way through the angular modern furniture to a dining room done in a dark prune colour, with furniture made of steel and glass.

Florence was taking a delicious-looking cold soup, some chicken and salads from a dumb waiter and laying them on the table. Gemma lit another cigarette and tossed back her hair. "Help yourself," she said. "Everyone says I've got to look after you, though if you'll take my advice you'll go on a diet till you've lost a few pounds. It makes all the difference to the way a dress hangs. I'd offer to let you borrow something for the ball but I don't suppose you'd fit into anything of mine."

Florence rolled her eyes at Minty behind Gemma's back and withdrew. Minty defiantly took a helping of tomato and basil soup and a hot roll and started to eat. The soup was almost as good as Serafina's.

"I suppose you're wondering why I asked to see you," said Gemma, flicking ash carelessly on to a side plate and ignoring the ashtray on the table.

Minty was wary, remembering how Gemma had warned her about Miles, but remembering also that Miles was Gemma's fiancé. "Before you start, I wanted to say thanks for inviting me back."

"It's caused a lot of bother, though. Simon was absolutely livid with you yesterday. Miles too. I assume you won't be pressing charges, it being all in the family and that."

Minty noted that Gemma placed her concern for Simon before Miles. "It's out of my hands. Up to the police."

Gemma ground out one cigarette and lit another. "None of this was Simon's fault, you know. He's only trying to do his best for all of us."

Nothing was ever Simon's fault. Minty sighed and helped herself to some sliced chicken and salad. "And Miles? Was it his idea alone to break the cottage windows, or did Simon put him up to it? I'm amazed you want to marry him."

Gemma ground out the cigarette she had just lit, and stole a piece of cucumber from Minty's plate. Minty thought about that. It was the action of a bully, and bullies had to be outfaced or they would progress to worse.

Minty snatched up Gemma's pack of cigarettes and sat on it. Then returned to her plate of chicken and salad.

"How dare you!" said Gemma, reddening.

"Easily," said Minty, keeping calm.

Gemma threw back her chair and started to pace the room. "You've got it all wrong about Simon. Of course he was angry when you turned him down, but he soon got over that. Yes, he did sound off about it to Miles, but it wasn't Simon's idea that Miles should break the windows at the cottage. Miles has an awful temper and sometimes he goes off at half-cock. He's sorry now, of course. And half out of his mind with worry. Did you know he's been suspended from his job here? If he loses that . . . well, I don't know what we'll do. He couldn't afford the house I want. Simon's had to help us out on that. So if Miles loses his job, we've no hope of repaying him. Look, I'll show you a photograph."

She rummaged in a stylish handbag and produced some colour photographs of a Georgian house that looked almost as imposing as the Hall. "And these are the sketches for my wedding dress." Designer drawn, of course, and elaborate.

"Beautiful," murmured Minty, wondering if Gemma was marrying the house, or the man who was buying it for her.

Gemma said, "Look, it's important for all sorts of reasons that we all—you and me, Simon and Miles—see eye to eye and work together for the future. Now we know you're not the sort of girl to jump into anyone's bed without a wedding ring . . . well, we can build on that, can't we? I told Simon straight off that you weren't that sort, but he had to try. You've earned his respect now. He wants to start again, to be friends and to discuss the future with you. You don't understand yet—though you will when he explains it—but it's really important for all of us that the clinic comes in. Simon has debts. He needs the money. We all do. You've no money yourself, have you? So what if we cut you in?"

"It's nothing to do with me, and anyway, you know I'm against it."

"You don't understand how important it is. Simon's so afraid that . . . and Miles, too. He and Simon had another money-making plan, but it's got held up, and if they can't raise some money soon, I don't know what will happen. Me, too. I want to get out of here, but to do that, I need money. Mother doesn't care about anything except being made a Dame for services to charity. You've just got to listen to Simon. I mean it, Minty! I'm desperate. We all are."

Other scheme? thought Minty. Would that have been the matter of selling access to the derelict farm buildings? "Why are you tied to their chariot wheels, Gemma? Isn't the world at your feet? Don't you have beauty and money to spend? A fabulous home here? A loving brother and a fiancé?"

"Beauty? Yes, I have my looks. You'll never turn heads as I do when I walk into a room, but I saw last night that in your quiet way you've managed to corral two eligible men. Yes, I did try to prise them off you, and yes, I failed. You've got Simon so mixed up he doesn't know whether he's coming or going, and let me tell you, that takes a bit of doing. Yes, I've got my looks, but they don't help me with the sort of man I'd like to attract. And as for the rest, I've no money apart from my allowance, and that's not going to keep me in diamonds.

"Miles is exciting, though sometimes he frightens me. He's convinced that you're behind everything that's gone wrong for us lately. He thinks you've somehow stopped the Americans signing, and persuaded the developers not to pay the transfer fee for the farm up by the station. But you don't know anything about that, do you?"

Minty bit her lip. "I've heard about both. It's common knowledge in the village." With a stab of fear, she realised that if Miles suspected it was Patrick who'd been responsible for stopping both plans, he'd go after him, too. That must not happen. If necessary, she must draw Miles's fire on to herself. "I did get the sale to the Americans stopped, yes."

Gemma laughed uneasily. "You . . . what? No, no. You don't mean that, I'm sure. How could you have stopped it? You must let Simon explain things to you and, meanwhile, I suggest you keep out of Miles's way. He can be a bit . . . well, impetuous. And I wouldn't like you to get hurt."

She seemed to mean it. Minty thought Gemma was like a seesaw, teetering between good and evil impulses. "Why are you marrying him, Gemma?"

"He wants to marry me and I'm damaged goods. Who else would have me?" She stood over Minty. "Give me a cigarette. Sorry I pinched your cucumber."

Minty replaced the cigarettes on the table. "Damaged goods?"

Gemma lit up and attempted an airy tone. "To celebrate my sixteenth birthday, Simon arranged for me to go along with him for a weekend in Cannes on a friend's yacht. I got drunk and slept with—I don't know how many men. I got pregnant. I had an abortion and it went wrong. No more children. End of story."

Minty wanted to throw her arms around her sister and hug her tight. There were definitely tears in Gemma's eyes, but Minty was beginning to realise what a clever actress her half-sister could be. Was that a hint of calculation in those large green eyes? With sadness, Minty saw that there was.

She said, "I'm so sorry." And meant it. "So what are you going to do with the rest of your life?"

"Have a good time, of course. Which is where you come in. Father's taken to you in a big way. If you and Simon make it up, then everything will be all right."

"I'm not sure I can trust Simon after what's happened."

"Of course you can. He just misread you at first; that's all. I'll tell him that you've agreed to kiss and make up, shall I? Maybe it will all turn out for the best, my calling you in."

"I hope so," said Minty.

When Minty reached the courtyard again, she found her bicycle was being ridden round and round by the burly man who had brought her Alice's pay packet. At that time he'd been in chauffeur's uniform, but today he was in sweater and jeans. The restaurant and shop were closed today as the Hall was not open to visitors.

"You'd got a puncture, miss. Thought I'd mend it for you. I'm taking the car up the road for a run. Like a lift?"

Minty was too distracted to do more than thank him and say she'd be all right on the bike. She was thinking hard. Praying hard. For her father. For Simon and Miles and Gemma. For Patrick. *Forget him . . . forget . . .* For Jonah above all. There must be some way of giving hope to poor Jonah. For dear Ruby, putting up with so much all these years.

She was nearly at the bridge before she heard a car coming up fast behind her. She drew to one side, thinking that she must make out a proper prayer list . . . when she felt a shock go through her and was flying through the air . . . off the road and down the bank towards the river . . .

She went under. The shock of it . . . she was drowning . . .

She surfaced, gasping, spitting out water. The recent rains had swollen the brook to twice its previous depth. She was only thigh deep but the current was strong, tearing at her. She staggered. She could feel weeds tangling around her legs. She was being forced back. Couldn't reach the bank. There was nothing to cling on to. She heard the car accelerate and drive off and she hadn't even caught a glimpse of it.

Something hard and angular thrust against her. The bike was threatening to push her under water. She was going to go down and then . . . was this the end? *Lord, save me!*

Chapter Twenty-Three

Someone crashed down the riverbank and grasped one of her wrists as she was about to be swept away. He wrestled the bike toward one side and heaved her to the bank.

"Up you go!" With an effort he pushed her halfway up the bank. She scrabbled for a hold and found one. Hung there, panting, unable to move, dreading that in a minute she'd slide back into the brown flood water. He climbed up beside her, kicking footholds into the bank with his strong shoes. He got his arm round her waist and, pushing and pulling, managed to force her up the bank and on to the road.

He followed her up, moving her arms and legs to make sure nothing was broken. "Are you hurt?" It was the burly man she'd seen before in uniform, who had just offered to give her a lift.

She shook her head, gasping out water. She was dripping: hair, dress, sandals. Shocked. "He ran me down!"

"I'm ringing the police. It was that something Miles!"

He had his phone out. Minty collapsed on to the bank and closed her eyes. Shivering. Praying for strength, for courage. Praying for guidance to do the right thing. Praying for Gemma, who had tried once again to warn her. Thinking that at least this time Simon had not been involved. But even so, this attack was going to make life complicated. Yet right was right and wrong was wrong, and Miles had twice attacked her . . . and possibly had known what he was doing when he'd taken Gemma away and left Minty alone with a drunken man intent on rape.

"Come on. I'll get you back to the flat." The man had his arm around her, urging her to get into the car. Her father's car? Was he her father's chauffeur? He said, "The bike's ruined. I ought never to have let you ride. He'll have my guts for garters."

Minty pushed the wet hair out of her eyes. "You're a bodyguard? My father asked you to watch out for me?"

"Reggie's the name. Fine bodyguard I make, eh? Chauffeur, odd jobs, that's me. Straight to the bookshop. Hot bath. Hot drink. Change of clothes. Make a statement to the police. Can do?"

She nodded. "The bike belongs to the Thornbys."

"I'll attend to it. Don't you worry."

But she did worry. Patrick was away in town today. Jonah was in distress. Gemma was desperate. What a mess all round!

Hot drink, hot bath, bruises and grazes attended to, police. She mustn't ring Patrick in office hours, though she desperately wanted to do so.

Mr Lightowler hovered. "Well, that settles it. I'll move into the flat above the bookshop and keep an eye on you tonight."

She gave him a hug and tried to stop shivering. To prevent herself from thinking about that awful moment when she'd nearly drowned, she kept herself busy, though she felt as if her limbs were made of paper. She checked on supplies at the housekeeper's hut and slowly made the rounds of the holiday lets, replacing items as required. She emailed Annie with the usual report. She kept looking at her watch. Surely it had stopped? How soon could she expect Patrick to be back?

Virginia and Hugh were up in London seeing one of their children, and wouldn't return till late. She couldn't go to them.

Mr Lightowler insisted on treating her to an early supper at the pub and she agreed. He wasn't about to force drink on her, and the landlady had been kind to her on the night she'd found Simon in her bedroom. Besides, she was too tired to cook for herself.

Steak-and-kidney pudding went down well. She tried to concentrate on what Mr Lightowler was saying, because it was important. He was talking about signing up with a good wholesaler for the bookshop and getting in a special computerised system, which meant they could access information about the availability of books and order them for delivery the following day! Wasn't that good? It meant Minty would have a permanent job with him until such time as she moved next door . . .

Minty blushed. She looked at her watch again. No, Patrick wouldn't be home yet.

"There's one thing," she said. "Jonah's been tending that garden of Hannah's for years and for all that he talks about Hannah a lot, I think he might miss the garden even more than he misses her. Do you think you could keep him on?"

"Gracious heavens, I never thought of him going! I'm hopeless with plants. I thought that sometime we might open up the back door, put a conservatory out there with tables and chairs, serve teas. I'll tell him he must stay on."

The landlady came and sat down with them, uninvited. "Listen up, my dear," she said to Minty. "We think, us here in the village, that you're a good thing, going to make life a lot livelier and that can only be good for the bank balance, know what I mean? My man and I were wondering if we might have to up sticks and move somewhere with a bit more going on, but now we've decided to stay on, see what happens.

"We think you ought to move in with us, spare room, use of bath. No one will get at you there, my man says, and it's no good you thinking you can go back to living over the bookshop, because that back staircase is an invitation to any burglar—never mind someone as determined as that Miles . . . whom I can't abide to tell the truth, though he's spent enough money here over the bar, that I will say for him. So just you get some night things together and I'll show you where to sleep, all right?"

"That's very good of you, and I appreciate it, but Mr Lightowler is moving into the flat to look after me."

"I'll bet he sleeps as sound as anything, and snores, what's more."

Mr Lightowler admitted he did sleep heavily and yes, he did snore, but—

"That's settled, then."

Minty's phone trilled, and it was Patrick. "Minty, are you all right? I've just heard. Where are you?"

"At the pub just above Spring Cottage."

"Give me five minutes."

He was there in four, ordering food for himself on his way in. Mr Lightowler tactfully made his way to the bar and left her alone to talk to Patrick. Surprisingly, Patrick also thought it a good idea for Minty to sleep at the pub. The Woottons wouldn't be back till late, and someone had moved into the spare room above the Chinese restaurant.

"What would my uncle and aunt say?" asked Minty, torn between laughter and tears. "They consider a pub to be a haunt of Satan."

"But you aren't your uncle or your aunt."

She sighed. "No. And everyone's so kind to me here."

His steak-and-kidney pudding arrived, and he tackled it as if he hadn't eaten for days. She thought, but did not say, *Patrick, I missed you today.*

She said, "Patrick, when we were children, did you teach me to read and write?"

"You've remembered?" His face was transformed with happiness . . . which slowly faded as she shook her head. He turned his head away for a moment, and pushed his plate aside. She could feel his disappointment. She wished she could remember whatever it was that she'd forgotten, because it obviously meant a lot to him.

"No, not really," she said. "I found your books up at the Hall today. *Peter Rabbit* and the others. How did it happen that you taught me to read?"

He pinched the bridge of his nose. Put himself back together again. No one would have guessed that a moment before he'd looked heart-stricken. He even managed a smile. Stoical, that was Patrick. "*Tom Kitten* was your favourite. You loved that book so much you tore it to pieces one day. Was I annoyed! Well, it was the summer term before you were to go to school. Your mother was away travelling with your father. Simon liked to play with one of his friends after school and Nanny liked to visit one of her cronies for a cuppa and a gossip. She needed somewhere to park you for an hour or so. My mother offered to look after you, but somehow you always used to find your way on to the chair beside me while I was doing my homework. You wanted to do homework, too. So I'd stop for a bit and read to you. You learned quickly."

He looked at his half-empty plate. She could see him thinking that even if he wasn't hungry, he ought to eat. He picked up his fork and took a mouthful. "How is your father?"

"Not well. I try to divert him, but . . . I think you should know that Gemma warned me about Miles. He blames me for stalling the Americans and for holding up the sale of the field that gives access to the farm buildings up by the station."

Patrick stared. "But you weren't even here, then."

"I told her that it was I who'd stopped the sale to the Americans. I didn't want him coming after you. Reading between the lines, Miles is desperate for money. He's buying a mansion for Gemma, but had to get Simon to help him out on the downpayment. If he loses his job, and doesn't get that money from the redevelopment plan, I don't know what he'll do."

Patrick blinked. "You're right to be afraid of him. He kicked a man half to death once. It's not the first time he'd attacked someone, but it was the first time anyone had gone to the police. He got a suspended sentence. So you put yourself in the target area instead of me?" He drew a deep breath. "I shan't have a minute's peace till he's under lock and key."

Mr Lightowler insisted on moving into the bookshop from his digs. He said this was so that he could look after Lady the cat, but Minty felt he was staking his claim to the place. Patrick and Mr Lightowler stood over Minty while she gathered up what she needed for the night, took her keys off her and escorted her back to the pub. She fell asleep in the spare bedroom over the bar even before last orders were called and the customers filed out into the night. So it was that she missed Miles breaking into the flat above the bookshop from the garden, and his rampage through the rooms, looking for her and startling Mr Lightowler out of his bed.

Next day—the day of the charity ball—Miles's car was found abandoned at the railway station. Minty's burly bodyguard was livid. He'd taken a room over the Chinese restaurant opposite to keep an eye on her, and had run across the road when he'd seen lights come on in the flat above the bookshop. Unfortunately, by the time he'd got round to the back, Miles was in his car and away, leaving Mr Lightowler to ask where he could get a shotgun for protection!

Everyone agreed it was a good thing Minty had moved out. Gemma was reportedly fit to be tied, as not only was her fiancé missing, but she now had no escort to the ball. "And I bet," said Venetia, on the phone to Minty, "I bet she keeps that socking great emerald ring, no matter what happens to Miles! Oh, and I've got the spare room ready for you tonight, OK?"

Mr Lightowler insisted he could manage at the bookshop by himself for one day or so. Feeling as if she were travelling in a runaway train, Minty allowed herself to be picked up by Annie Phillips and driven to town to open an account at the bank. Annie insisted on buying Minty a pair of pretty blue and gold sandals to go with her dress for the ball, together with some fine silky tights and new underwear. "An early birthday present, my dear," said Annie.

"Everyone's so kind," said Minty, feeling rather daunted. She was looking forward to the ball, of course. But suppose no one wanted to dance with her, or even talk to her? She'd never been to such a big function in her life. Suppose she made some hideous gaffe and made all her friends ashamed of her?

Annie said, "We are looking forward to seeing you all dressed up."

Minty giggled. "War's broken out over who's to help me dress. Ruby's been asked to look after the cloakroom in the bowels of the Hall from eight till midnight and has arranged for a friend to sit with Jonah till then. She assumes she's going to dress me. Did you know she's provided the dress and found me a tiny beaded evening bag to go with it? Only, Serafina's announced that she's going to be responsible for getting me ready, as well. I can see myself being torn apart between the two of them."

❧

Late that afternoon Reggie, the burly bodyguard, escorted Minty and Ruby through the park and up to the spare bedroom in Sir Micah's suite. Then Serafina took over, with Ruby acting as assistant. Minty had never been so pampered in her life. After a bath in soft-scented water, her hair was washed with a special lotion—provided by Serafina—and the ends trimmed. Her fingernails were manicured and given a colourless varnish. Her hair shone with brushing, curling over her shoulders.

Pale blue pants and bra—hardly more than a wisp of each. The very finest of tights.

Minty stepped carefully into the beautiful dress and Ruby zipped it up the back and attended to the tiny hooks and eyes that made the seam lie flat. Serafina knelt to fit on the blue and gold shoes, while Annie held up the opals, wondering aloud whether the drop earrings would be best by themselves, or with just one bracelet.

The bodice glinted with every breath Minty took, and she took many breaths because she was so excited.

"I look amazing!" she said, twirling in front of the full-length mirror. "Oh, look at me! Don't I look beautiful tonight?"

Her three attendants laughed and clapped their hands, agreeing that she did indeed look beautiful.

Ruby glanced at her watch. "I'm on duty in five minutes."

"Thank you, dear Ruby," said Minty, kissing her. "I'll come for you just before midnight and we'll vanish together."

"Not without an escort," warned Annie.

Minty kissed her, too. And Serafina. Then she tiptoed in to see her father, who was awake . . . just.

"Don't I look beautiful tonight?" She bent to kiss his cheek. He held her hand to his cheek for a moment and his eyes said yes, she did look beautiful tonight, and that he was glad to see her. Then his mouth tightened and a glittering, hard expression came into his eyes.

"What is it?"

He made an enormous effort to speak. "I'm sorry . . . sending you away!"

She stroked his cheek with one finger. "Don't be. It was tough at the time, but it's made me what I am. It isn't me you should say sorry to, you know." She pressed his fingers to her lips. His eyes were still registering distress. She pondered this, wondering how much to say, wondering if it would do any good to speak of God.

"So . . . much . . . to regret!"

"Can't you say that to God, who loves you so much?"

He made a violent movement of his head, turning from her. The nurse replaced the oxygen mask on his face. He closed his eyes, shutting her out.

With sorrow, she felt his rejection.

From below she could hear the sounds of an orchestra. There were lights set in the park, fairy lights in the trees, lights on the terraces . . . delicious food and drink in the marquees . . . the bustle of people arriving . . . all the excitement, the anticipation of a ball.

She hesitated. Ought she to stay with him for a while? No. He'd turned from her, effectively throwing her out of the room . . . and below they were beginning to dance.

Annie Phillips came into the room, every hair in place, dressed immaculately in midnight blue lace. Serafina made shooing motions. "You must both go, quick, quick! What a night it's going to be! You mustn't miss a minute!"

Annie and Minty came to the head of the grand staircase and looked down into the hall. A master of ceremonies was announcing guests to the reception line at the foot of the stairs. Lady Cardale looked magnificently chilly in black and silver. Simon's blond beauty looked too good to be true, as if he were a male model posing for evening wear. Gemma was in brilliant, flaunting red, wearing her giant emerald ring on her left hand. Felicity Chickward was standing a modest half pace from Lady Cardale, ready to supply information or helpful introductions as required.

Annie whispered that it might be tactful to avoid the reception line, so led the way back along the gallery and down to the ground floor. All the doors and windows were open on to the cloisters, and people were using the courtyard to pass from one side of the Hall to the other. Though the fountain was not working, its basin was floodlit and filled with plants.

Minty wondered if she were in a dream. The ropes that normally kept the public away from the furniture had been removed, and the rooms were being used as they were originally intended; not as showpieces. Stands of flowers were banked in the fireplaces and on side tables, matching the style of each room. In the Chinese room were arrangements featuring bamboo. There were red roses in the red drawing room, the flower arrangements in the music room were in cool blues, and there was a great stand of lilies in the library.

What, no daisies? thought Minty, and for a moment had a flash of memory . . . of the white-pillared folly above the formal garden?

Waiters and waitresses were everywhere, proffering trays of drinks. Minty took a glass at random, sipped it, didn't like the taste but continued to hold it, to give her hands something to do.

Annie said, "Everything's been arranged by a London firm, specialists in this sort of corporate hospitality. They tell me there's to be modern dancing in the first marquee, the sort where no one touches their partner and is always looking over their shoulders to see if there's a better prospect in sight. The music—if you can call it that—is by one of these popular groups of unshaven teenagers, whom I'm told have sold millions of records. There's a cabaret, too, of course. I shan't attend any of that.

"The second marquee is serving a sit-down meal at large round tables, and an early breakfast with champagne to those young and strong enough to see the dawn break."

The rooms were already crowded with people and yet more were arriving every minute. Minty was overcome with stage fright.

All these people knew one another. She knew no one. If only she'd accepted Patrick's offer of an escort!

Annie saw that Minty needed encouragement. "You look beautiful. Why don't you join the dancers in the marquee?"

"Too noisy. I don't know anyone."

"Well, there's proper ballroom dancing in the Gallery. Perhaps you'll find some old friends there."

The Gallery had been stripped of its fragile tapestried chairs, while more banks of flowers—this time multicoloured—filled the two marble fireplaces. Halfway down the long room, a dais had been installed to accommodate an old-time, old-fashioned group playing smooth music to dance to. Minty blessed the youth club helper who had insisted on teaching a ballroom dancing class. Her feet wanted to dance, but would she ever be invited on to the dance floor?

She saw Mrs Collins, surrounded by a chattering throng of friends and relatives. She saw a sea of faces she didn't know.

Minty's hand was caught by the Reverend Cecil, looking rather more red-faced than usual. "Minty, you look wonderful! I hardly recognised you. Dance with me?" Minty put down her drink and stepped into his arms, not caring that as a dancer he was a little on the clumsy side. She was actually dancing at a ball!

"Minty! I've been looking everywhere for you. Dance?" Roly-poly Neville, light on his feet and light-hearted enough to flirt with anyone. "Minty, you're the most fabulous creature I've ever seen . . . another dance?"

Mrs Chickward, looking pleased to see Minty dancing with Neville.

Mrs Collins, introducing a distant cousin of hers, who asked to dance with Minty. He had damp hands, a title she didn't quite catch and was slightly out of time with the music . . .

Where was Patrick?

She caught sight of Lady Cardale, looking horrified at seeing Minty dance along with her guests . . . or perhaps that was just her normal expression?

Minty danced with Hugh Wootton, stately in tails. He knew how to dance the foxtrot, though. Venetia swung past in Mr Lightowler's arms. Hugh introduced her to another older man, who hummed as he spun her around in a waltz. And then to another elderly man, who pumped her hand up and down out of time to the music.

She danced with Mr Lightowler, in evening dress enlivened with a bright red cummerbund.

She danced with Neville again, who wanted to take her off to eat in the marquee. She agreed. Where was Patrick? Hadn't be been able to get a ticket?

Neville and Minty joined a rowdy table in the marquee. They were all youngish and lively and the sort of people Minty felt she would like to know better, though perhaps a trifle on the boisterous side for her. She wanted Patrick so badly that it hurt.

Neville took her into the first marquee to dance, but she only lasted ten minutes in that noisy venue before she smiled and made her excuses. Because where was Patrick?

"Back to the Gallery, then?" said Neville. "I'd rather dance with you in my arms, anyway. Otherwise, you might just float away from me."

As they were passing back through the library on the way to the gallery, Simon caught her hand and with a bare word of excuse to Neville, drew her over to the fireplace. Although people were now and then passing through the library to reach the gallery, the room was large enough to allow them to talk in privacy.

It was quiet in there, lit only by one standard lamp. The gold titles and tooling of leather-bound books were warmly reassuring. The furniture gleamed from much polishing, and the stand of lilies by the fireplace laid a powerful scent over all.

"Minty, Gemma told me you were willing to listen."

"Of course," said Minty, gravely. She wondered how she'd feel if she could see Patrick and Simon standing side by side. Simon had a charismatic presence. She could feel it, even while she remembered the bad things she knew about him—particularly his taking so little care of the sixteen-year-old Gemma.

He took her hand in his. "My, you are fine tonight! Quite the belle of the ball. Which is how it should be, isn't it? With you at my side, what couldn't we do together? Pretty Araminta, my almost-but-not-quite sister. I'm very glad you're not my sister, and I hope you are, too."

"I would like us to be friends, yes."

"If you could be a little more than that? It's all in your hands, you see. It's up to you to decide the future of the Hall."

She tried to withdraw her hand but he held on to it. "What do you mean?"

"An alliance between us. Your pretty ways with people. My brains and know-how. You must know that I'm at your feet. Oh, I handled things badly. I was wrongly advised: I thought you were a woman and not a frightened little girl still. Well, that's all forgiven and forgotten, isn't it? I'm offering you my hand and my heart. What a marvellous lady of the manor you will make! You can take over the Hall and the estate, save the little people's jobs if you want to, or sell out to the clinic and fly with me to join the beautiful people in Bermuda. Whatever you choose, I know that the Old Man will give you whatever you ask for."

He pressed her hand in both of his. "Come, now. What do you say? Shall we announce it at midnight?"

"I'm not sure what you mean. What exactly is it that you want?"

His mouth curled, and then straightened. "To marry you, of course. We make a fantastically handsome couple, you must agree. And I'm prepared to be a very loving husband."

She stopped breathing. She felt dizzy.

"If you want separate bedrooms, then of course I'll agree to a civilised arrangement—provided you don't make scenes if I take someone else to share my bed. You persuade the Old Man to come through with the money, and give me a child to inherit, and in return I promise you'll see me as little or as much as you wish."

The scent of lilies was overpowering. She felt faint. Was he making fun of her? He couldn't possibly mean what he was saying. She tore her hand away and escaped to the window, drawing back the curtains, thrusting open the glass to catch a breath of fresh air. The sound of the orchestra came faintly to her ears. The lights glittered on the terrace outside. A girl laughed, running along the terrace, pursued by two men who were also laughing. A group of elderly people passed through the library on their way back to the gallery. And left them alone again.

Simon ran a hand over her back and she stiffened.

He nuzzled her ear through her hair. "Think about it, my dear. Unlimited power over the lives of all the little people. Money to burn. The Hall your very own toy to play with."

With Simon as her husband? Impossible.

"Think about it. Think how much good you could do. Think how everyone would bless you. Don't you owe it to them? Think about that for a minute."

She thought about it. If he was serious . . . what he had offered her . . . wasn't it all and more than she had ever dreamed? To become Lady of the Manor! She didn't know how to open fêtes and sit on charities, but she could learn. She could reorganise all those aspects of the Hall that had become run-down. She could save Gloria's job and Florence's. She could fill the Hall with fresh flowers and have new booklets prepared about this wonderful old place. They could be distributed throughout the county, attracting more tourists. She could revitalise the village. The empty shops would be filled, the holiday lets refurnished . . . and Alice could be given a house and a good job. Then she must start a crèche, which was badly needed. And a playgroup. And perhaps even an adventure playground in the park.

She could do . . . what could she *not* do! All that was required in return was a small sacrifice. She'd be marrying the handsomest man she had ever seen. That was something, wasn't it?

Simon had said he wouldn't bother her if she didn't wish it, and indeed she did not wish it . . . though of course it would be good to have a child or two to love.

She smiled, thinking of taking her place ahead of Lady Cardale in church on Sunday mornings. Perhaps wearing a hat? Though, of course she didn't usually wear a hat. The Reverend Cecil would be unhappy about her elevation to lady of the manor but he'd soon get over it.

Then she would take the Communion cup and . . .

No. She couldn't do it. At the back of her head a voice was whispering some old, old words to her. As she listened, the words became more and more clear.

" . . . the devil took him to a very high mountain and showed him all the kingdoms of the world and their splendour. 'All this I will give you,' he said, 'if you will bow down and worship me.'

"Jesus said to him, 'Away from me, Satan! For it is written, "Worship the Lord your God, and serve him only!"'"

Slowly the triumphal vision faded from her mind. No, she could not do it. She could not sell herself for what little good she might be able to do for others.

And then—she couldn't think how she had forgotten—there was Patrick.

If she was married to Simon, then every time she saw Patrick, she would regret what she'd done.

No, she couldn't accept Simon's offer. She turned away from him, resting her head against the ancient greenish glass of the window, closing her eyes on the dream.

Well, life was tough, wasn't it? She was never going to be Lady of the Manor or have much money. She was going to work in the bookshop and live goodness knows where, and eventually she would marry Patrick and they would work together, doing what they could for others. That would be a good life. A life lived Jesus' way. The thought warmed her.

Some sound made her turn. Someone was standing in the open doorway. Patrick. Looking at her. She smiled at him, but he didn't smile back.

Simon twisted round to see whom she was smiling at. Both men were tall. Simon had the broader shoulders, but Patrick was elegant in tails. One was very dark, the other very fair. Handsome is as handsome does, she thought. No contest. Goodness wins every time.

Simon ignored Patrick. "Well, my lady—shall we go?" He offered her his arm.

"Thank you, Simon. But no to everything. This is our dance, isn't it, Patrick?"

A trio of young men swept through the anteroom from the gallery, laughing loudly, linking arms with Simon and taking him with them out into the courtyard. Simon tried to resist, but they carried him away. A passing waiter offered Patrick champagne, but he declined, as did Minty.

The band was playing the "Gay Gordons" in the Gallery. Patrick closed the door behind him, cutting off the noise. He was very tense, not looking at her. "Minty, what was all that about?"

"He offered me the Hall in exchange for a wedding ring and my influence with his father."

He drew in his breath, his face expressionless. "The clever . . . ! It's not his to offer."

"That's roughly what Jesus said when Satan tempted him with dominion over the earth."

Patrick was taking this badly. He walked away from her to lean against the mantelpiece, eyes down, thinking hard. One part of her mind registered the fact that he looked perfectly at home in that splendid room. She thought, *He's comfortable in himself, wherever he is. In his own home, in a Chinese restaurant, a church hall, on a hill-side. Here. I like that in him.*

He was still tense. "If you'd agreed . . . !"

"You told me never to sign anything, or agree to anything until after my birthday. Though, come to think of it, I'd forgotten that when I turned him down."

He did not seem reassured.

She smiled. "I said no, Patrick."

"Minty, if I could say what I want to . . ."

She went close to him and put her fingertips over his mouth. "On my birthday. You'll tell me on my birthday?"

He took her wrist very gently in his hand. He kissed first her fingertips and then the palm of her hand. "You're so beautiful! I can hardly believe you're real."

"You look magnificent."

Colour tinged his cheeks. "Don't make fun of me."

"I don't. You look absolutely right, whatever you're wearing, wherever you are. Tails suit you to perfection."

He let out a slow breath. "I underestimated Simon, didn't I?"

"Never mind that now. Why were you late? Was it Jonah?"

"I went to offer him the care of my courtyard, but Mr Lightowler had been there before me, and he was happily burbling away about Hannah's garden being turned into a conservatory, with you serving home-made cakes in a milkmaid's costume or some such. I kept wanting to get away, thinking that you needed me, but he wanted to talk so—"

She touched his arm. "Can we forget all that for a while, Patrick? You may be used to going to balls in grand houses, but I'm not, and I want to remember this night for ever. I've only ever danced in church halls on worn lino before, to the smell of disinfectant and stale food. I've never before waltzed in a fairyland of lights hanging from trees, or dined on oysters and lobster in a marquee hung with pink silk. I've never danced with men wearing evening dress, or seen so many women's beautiful gowns and jewellery. I've never worn such a pretty dress myself or such beautiful shoes. I want tonight to be perfect, and I want to dance with you till midnight strikes . . ."

He smiled. "Why midnight, Cinderella?"

"Because that's when Ruby has to be back home to take over her charge again. I said I'd walk her back and then take a taxi up to the Woottons. So will you dance with me?"

"I can only do the old-fashioned sort of dancing. I'm afraid I'm rather old-fashioned all round."

"I like old-fashioned. Breathing and eating, trusting in God, praying. If those things are old-fashioned, then I'm old-fashioned, too."

The band had been taking a break in the gallery, but were now preparing to start up again. He took her in his arms, holding her firmly but lightly. She could float away from him at any time, or stick like glue.

He danced well. Not showily, but taking good care of her and in perfect accord with the music. She liked that in him, too. Now and then some man tried to cut in on their dance, but Patrick would twist his shoulder and she would frown at the man and they would dance away together ...

Sometimes she almost closed her eyes, trusting him to lead her safely through the dance. Sometimes she let herself look up at him until he smiled down at her, and she smiled back. She thought, *I can dance away the hours ... this moment will go on for ever ... I want to dance like this till dawn comes ...*

Then she caught sight of another man's watch as he pushed a giggling matron around the floor. And came back to reality.

Chapter Twenty-Four

"Twenty minutes to twelve," said Patrick. "One more dance?"

She looked around. "I have to find Ruby. And Reggie—that's my father's bodyguard person—because he's supposed to escort us back through the park."

"Won't I do?"

Dear Ruby, unearthed from the cloakroom, was very ready to go. "You still look lovely, Minty. Doesn't she, Patrick?"

"Yes," said Patrick. "She does." His eyes shone with a silvery light as he looked at Minty, and she thought, *I'll remember this moment all my life.*

They stepped out of the Hall into the starry night. Minty sighed. "It's been perfect." She looked back at the lights, the dancers, the couples wandering around with their heads together, the conflicting sounds of the two bands.

Would she ever have such a wonderful experience again? Perhaps not. Such occasions were not very likely to come her way in the future. It didn't matter.

She was filled with elation. She ran down the drive ahead of the other two, singing, "I could have danced all night . . ."

Patrick and Ruby laughed, indulging her. She swung around a tree, laughing, too.

"Wait for us!" cried Patrick, helping Ruby along.

Ruby was half laughing and half annoyed with herself. "These shoes! I should never have worn them. They've rubbed my heel."

Minty ran and ran, her skirts streaming out behind her. She held her arms wide, glorying in the warm night air. She reached the bridge and climbed on to the balustrade.

"Look at the stars! Look how high I am! I'm going to dance all the way home."

"You mad creature!" cried Patrick. "You'll fall and hurt yourself."

"Catch me, then!" She raised her arms wide and launched herself from the bridge, trusting that he would leap forward to catch her, which he did. She put her arms about his neck and buried her face in his shoulder. She could feel his heart beating against her.

Someone came pounding along the road behind them. If it were Miles . . .

Patrick swung her behind him, but it was only Reggie. "Miss Minty! Your father! They sent me to find you. Come, quick!"

Minty put both her hands over her face. "I guessed something was wrong, but I didn't want to know. I wanted to dance and be carefree for once. Dear Lord, forgive me."

Patrick took charge. "Reggie, can you take Ruby back home? I'll see Miss Cardale back to the Hall."

Ruby kissed Minty. "I'll be thinking of you, my dear."

Patrick and Minty walked swiftly back through the park. The lights, the music, and the dancing continued, but now they had no part of it.

Minty said, "I must get hold of Cecil. I'm hoping against hope that my father will agree to see him now."

"I'll find him for you. Have you your mobile?"

"I think so. I left my ordinary clothes in my father's flat."

"I'll find the Woottons and tell them where you are. Ring me?"

They did not rejoin the party-goers, but turned into the first courtyard, where they saw lights on in the reception room.

Annie was just lifting the phone. "I was going to ring the Woottons, see if you'd got there already. Sir Micah's worse."

Minty lifted her hand to Patrick. He nodded, and left. Minty ran along the corridor behind Annie and they went up in the lift together.

Annie said, "I don't know why I went back to check on him. I don't usually at this time of night . . ."

The outer office was deserted. The sickroom was very quiet. The lights had been dimmed, but the two women could see that the nurse was looking tense.

Sir Micah was propped up in bed, wearing his oxygen mask. His eyes were open, staring. He looked tortured. His fingers strayed over the sheets.

Annie stifled a cry and turned away, but Minty sped to the bed and took one of his hands in hers. Did he know her? She wasn't sure that he did.

Then he did know her. He fought to speak, pulling weakly at the mask on his face.

Minty stilled his hand. "It's all right. He's on his way. He's not as big a fool as he looks and he is a man of God."

Annie did cry out, then. "Are you sure? Oh, Micah! Will you listen to him, now? Oh, praise be!"

"It's all right; it's all right," Minty murmured, over and over. "He's coming. Just hang on a little while. Just a few more breaths, calm and quiet. Think how good God is, how much he loves us, all of us, rich and poor, strong and weak. He knows all about weakness and temptations, doesn't he? He knows and he understands. He loves you, more than you think possible. More than anyone can understand, he loves you. He's waited so long, so patiently, so lovingly, for you to turn back to him . . ."

"So much . . . to regret . . ."

"Yes, I know. We all have. But he can take our burdens from us. He knows the cost, he's born it for us. He loves us. He loves you. Just hang on a little while . . . breathe deeply, that's it, that's it. You're doing fine. Just a few more minutes and the battle will be over, and you'll be able to rest in peace . . ."

Annie was crying.

Minty said, "Annie, Patrick is trying to find Cecil Scott. Neither of them will know the way up here. Can you get someone to show them?"

"I'll go," said Serafina, materialising from the gloom and then disappearing.

"Annie, ought Lady Cardale to be called? And Simon and Gemma?"

"No!" It was a voiceless shout from the man on the bed.

"All right," soothed Minty. "Just the people around who love you."

His eyes closed but his breathing eased. The nurse mouthed the word "Doctor?" at Annie, who shook her head.

They waited. Minty had taken off her watch because it hadn't looked right with her dress and the opals she was wearing. There didn't seem to be a clock in the room. She was sitting awkwardly. She tried to ease her right leg, but instantly the man on the bed opened his eyes, startled.

Annie was standing at the foot of the bed, her hands gripping the rail. She seemed to be willing Sir Micah to keep breathing.

There was a stir at the door and Cecil Scott stumbled into the room. His head and shirt were wet, the collar undone and his tie missing. There was what looked like panic in his eyes, but that might have been a trick of the light.

Minty vacated her place by the bed and steered Annie into the green room. Serafina followed them in. "Your young man found him and dunked his head in cold water in the loo. I think he's sober enough now."

Minty suppressed hysterical laughter. How efficient of Patrick! And what a story to tell about Cecil . . . not that she would ever tell it.

"Coffee all round?" asked Serafina, steady as a rock.

"How can you?" said Annie, twisting her handkerchief.

"It'll be a long night and maybe a night and a day," said Serafina. "I've watched enough dying men to know."

"You can't tell!" cried Annie. "He may rally."

"Don't fool yourself," advised Serafina.

Minty sank into the nearest chair. "Will you let me stay? If so, I'd love some coffee, Serafina. Thank you."

"No one outside this room cares enough to sit with him," said Serafina. "I'll fetch you coffee and a shawl, Minty. Annie, pull yourself together."

Minty asked, "What about the doctor? Can't he do something?"

"She," said Annie. "She was here this afternoon, but said she didn't expect any change for a while."

"Should we get the doctor back now?"

"What for?" asked Serafina. "To say he should be in hospital? To pull and push him around when all he wants is to die in peace? He's made a living will to say he must not be resuscitated, but if they get him into hospital they'll put him on life machines and pump him full of this and that. No. Leave him in peace."

Cecil was with Sir Micah for what seemed a long time and when he left, he promised to return to give the dying man his last Communion.

Sir Micah seemed more peaceful after Cecil had gone, drifting between sleep and semi-consciousness. Serafina, Minty, and Annie took on the watching, two of them with him at a time. He seemed to know them and moved fretfully when they exchanged positions.

The party went on below. Some people left, but those behind became more raucous. Cecil returned, very sober, at a quarter past three, to administer the last rites. Sir Micah came back to full consciousness for a short time, smiled at them, and lapsed into unconsciousness.

"We must tell Lady Cardale," said Minty.

Annie sighed. "She'll send you away if she finds you here, and he needs you."

Minty sighed. "Nevertheless, we must tell her. I'll go next door while she's with him."

Serafina said, "You do that. Lady Cardale has the right to be informed. I'll fetch her."

The two women and the nurse waited, treasuring every breath the dying man took. His fingers had ceased to play across the sheets and he lay still.

The music from the bands finally ceased down below. A chorus of farewells. The sky turned from black to grey and the stars lost their brilliance. There was a clatter of cutlery and plates as the last of the revellers abandoned the tent in which breakfast had been served, and the weary cooks and waiters began to stow away the hundreds of dirty dishes and glasses that remained.

The sun came up. Time passed slowly. The dying man lay like a waxen image. Annie brought a clock into the room, and told Minty to go and rest for a couple of hours.

Minty dragged herself into the green room as a bustle at the far door announced Serafina's return.

Minty thought, *What Lady Cardale doesn't see, she won't fret about.* She fell on to the settee and tried to relax. Found she couldn't relax. Prayed a bit. She slipped into a half-waking, half-sleeping state.

Annie roused her. The sky was overcast with drifts of mist obscuring the trees in the park. Lorries were creeping on to the site and men were working to dismantle the marquees, trundle away the ovens, the dirty dishes, the crates of empty bottles.

"Serafina's sitting with him now. Lady C stayed ten minutes, very annoyed that he hadn't been removed to hospital to die. I tried to find Simon and Gemma, but Simon's gone off with some of his cronies; no one seems to know where. Probably taken off in his aeroplane. His mobile's switched off and so is Gemma's. She's gone off with a party of her friends, too. Those people down there don't know the master of the house is dying," said Annie, looking down at the workers outside. "No one seems to know, or care."

Annie had changed into her everyday clothes, and looked—almost—as usual.

Minty looked down at herself. Her dress looked tawdry in this light. Her hair was tangled, her shoes—her beautiful shoes—were the worse for wear.

"Have a shower," said Annie. "Serafina's put you in the spare bedroom and freshened up your clothes for you. She doesn't seem to need to sleep at all. Breakfast in half an hour."

Minty nodded. She showered and changed into her old clothes, which had miraculously been washed and ironed since she took them off to dress for the ball. She found her mobile and got Patrick's answerphone.

"Patrick, I'm going to stay. He needs me. He's dying and they say it can't be long now. Please pray for him. There's a little chapel here at the top of one of the towers. My mother used it a lot, but it was a chapel for many, many years before. It's . . . helpful. I'm going there now to pray for him."

She didn't know what else to say, so she sighed and switched off. She went into the chapel and sat on the kneeler, praying . . . and drifted off into a doze again.

Annie woke her and told her to eat and drink. She couldn't eat, but drank a glass of orange juice. Then took Serafina's place at Sir Micah's bedside. Even in the few short hours she had been away, his face had altered. It was serene, now. Only occasionally did he half lift his eyelids, or move a finger.

She sat. And prayed.

Once she found herself singing a lullaby. At times she lapsed into a half-waking, half-sleeping state, but the moment her grasp on his hand slipped, he stirred. She thought of the peace of the park, when it would be returned to its usual quietness. She thought of the little green hill, with the white-domed folly on top.

She thought of Patrick's silvery gaze on her, and his half-declaration of love. She puzzled what daisies meant. Daisies and the folly on the hill. They were connected, she was sure of that now. What was it she had forgotten?

Annie came in to take her place.

Serafina served Minty a light lunch in the next room.

Minty tried to eat, but couldn't. She hadn't thought she'd be so badly affected by the death of a man she had known for such a short time . . . or all her life.

Serafina sat opposite Minty, a cup of espresso coffee in front of her. She said, "Eat, and I'll tell you a story. Pick up your fork."

Minty did as she was told, but couldn't face putting the food into her mouth.

Serafina said, "As I expect you've guessed, I was not born in Britain, but my people were wealthy and I was educated here. I married straight from school, had four children, and servants who did everything for me. My husband was much older. He indulged me and bored me. I lost two children from a fever, one year apart. Thinking of my figure, I said I didn't want any more. My husband was furious. What were women for, but to bear children? Go on. Eat."

Minty put the food in her mouth and chewed.

"Perhaps I would have stayed if my little boy hadn't been run over in the street. Perhaps. His sister ran out to save him and a following car caught her, too. She died a week later. That was a bad time. I was dead, inside. Religion? Hah! It meant nothing to me.

"Fifteen years ago I met Micah and he was different. He really looked at me, into me. He saw . . . what? A rebellious spirit? He said he was separated from his wife, that she'd only married him for his money. I didn't believe him at first, but after I met her, I saw he'd spoken the truth. I left my husband to go with Micah on a business trip to the States. We had fun. Go on, eat up.

"On our return my husband, my father, and my brothers came looking for me. I was no beauty by the time they'd finished with me. I ended up in hospital, needing a number of operations. My family disowned me. My husband divorced me. Micah paid for the operations and offered me a place in his household. I've been with him ever since."

Serafina took away the half-eaten plateful of food, and slipped a dessert of puréed fruit and biscuits in front of Minty.

"Of course he took more women to his bed after that, but I tell you this: he never cared for any of them as he cared for me . . . or for Annie. Now don't go thinking the worst of Annie, because it's not so. She's never been to bed with a man in her life, for all that she loves him with the devotion of a spaniel. Annie and I got on from the beginning, though I can't think how she managed to put up with me. I was so bitter. I couldn't accept it was all my own fault—or most of it, anyway."

She poured Minty some coffee. "Sir Micah paid a decorator to do up these rooms at the top of the Hall for his own use, but I found them cold and unwelcoming. Like a hotel. He said I could alter anything I wanted, to take my pick of the old pieces of furniture in storage on the top floor and in the basement. So I did. A chair here, a table there. Some good stuff, eh? Lady C didn't like it, but didn't dare say anything while he was paying for her to swan around being Queen Bee for her charities. One day I was poking around as usual, trying keys, when I stumbled upon the chapel. It was just as your mother had left it, with dead flowers in the vases, dust everywhere, and the Bible on a chair, open at one of the psalms.

"It was Psalm 88, beginning, 'O LORD, the God who saves me, day and night I cry out before you. May my prayer come before you; turn your ear to my cry.'

"I sat down and read that psalm all the way through. I'd heard about your mother and the rumours about the way she died, and I knew enough by then to suspect it was all lies spread by the present Lady C. She never used the chapel, of course. Catch her going on her knees in private! Her devotions are for display purposes only. Go on. Drink the coffee. Keep your strength up. So I started to read the psalms through and think about them. It's easy to think in that room, isn't it? After a while I started praying. I cleaned the place up, and went there every day till Annie found out and said she'd like to come, too. Sir Micah was amused, but he didn't stop us. He knew we prayed for him."

It was raining now. The last of the marquees came down in a flurry of canvas. The men toiled on, clearing the site. The lorries took away all evidence of the ball. There were a few scars on the turf, but not many. Soon they would heal over.

Minty went to sit in the chapel again for a while. It rested her. She still didn't sit in the carved chair for some reason, but half knelt and half leaned on the kneeler by the wall. She even fell asleep for a few minutes. In her sleep she dreamed of the white-pillared folly on the green hill, and woke to the patter of rain on the windows.

Then Serafina came to fetch her, and she returned to sit with her father. The male nurse was on duty today. The doctor came, shook her head, and said he ought to be in hospital.

Annie said, "He wants to die here."

Serafina took Minty's place, and Annie went with Minty into the green sitting room. Annie was tense. "The press have heard. The phones keep ringing. I wouldn't put it past Lady C to hold a press conference, saying how much her dear husband will be missed. Which he will be, but not by her. She knows you're here, by the way. She told me to tell you to get out, but I didn't hear that, and you haven't, either. Oh, and Simon finally turned his mobile phone on again. He's staying with some friend or other on one of those millionaire's islands in the West Indies. He's flying back tomorrow."

Minty pressed her forehead against the window. It was still drizzling outside. She wanted to get out there, to run and run and run. Run away from all this grief. But she knew she couldn't. She thought of ringing Patrick, but decided not to. Somehow it was not appropriate.

Serafina had left a hostess trolley with coffee, sandwiches, and soup. Annie helped herself to coffee, put it down and forgot to drink it.

She said, "You'll be amused to hear that Miles is back. He came back early this morning and met Gemma, who was just returning from her latest sleepover. Sounds carry in that enclosed courtyard. Everyone from the kitchens and the restaurant came to see what the row was about. Apparently bets were being placed on her throwing her ring back at him. Of course she didn't. But she did say she was finished with him, so he attacked her car . . . and dear Florence Thornby came out of the kitchen with a rolling pin—yes, really!—and tried to give him what for. So he socked her one, and finally Reggie—why is it that man always turns up late? Anyway, Reggie laid him out cold. By which time the police had been called . . ."

Annie sat down and started to laugh and cry at the same time. "I wish I'd seen it! Apparently they had to take Miles off to hospital to have his head stitched, and he was vowing to sue Reggie for assault!"

She sobered up. "Oh yes. Venetia Wootton left a suitcase of clothes for you—Reggie's put it in your bedroom here. Also your young man has been ringing the office here, saying that if you don't switch on your mobile, he'll personally storm the fortress. Can I have got the message right?"

"It sounds right," said Minty. "I'll ring him again soon. I can't think about the outside world at the moment."

Annie said, "I saw you two dancing together. He couldn't take his eyes off you. Everyone could see it. Are you lovers?"

Minty thought, Serafina wouldn't have needed to ask. She'd know. She rubbed her forehead. "No, Annie. He's not that sort, and neither am I."

"Go for a walk in the park," said Annie. "It'll do you good. It's almost stopped raining."

Ever since she'd caught sight of the pretty little building on the mound, Minty had felt it tugging at her mind. Mist still hung over the far reaches of the park. She pulled on her old jacket and trainers, and walked out through the courtyards to the terrace above the formal gardens.

The grass, the plants, all dripped from the recent rain. The earth smelt sweet and fresh. She descended a flight of steps into the formal garden and took the path between the beds. The box edging to the beds needed trimming. The tall laurel hedge that bounded the garden looked unbroken, but she knew that there were—or had been—openings cut into it in the corners. And yes, one was still there, though much overgrown.

She pushed her way through, ignoring the shower of raindrops from the leaves. Now she was in the park proper, facing the gentle rise up to the Temple of Apollo. Yes, that was what it had been called. It was not very grand, as classical follies went, being just a circle of white marble pillars holding up a dome. She seemed to remember that there were marble seats inside and the marble floor was laid in geometric patterns, radiating out from a star in the centre. A pretty place, though now neglected and forlorn.

Gazing up at it, she thought—though she might be mistaken, for it was all a long time ago—but hadn't there been baskets of flowers hanging from the roof between the pillars? And brightly coloured cushions on the seats?

And . . . a picnic?

A voice far back in her mind shouted, "Forget him! Forget all that nonsense . . ." And then came the swish of a belt against her legs. Minty drew in her breath sharply. Forget? Yes. She had done. But now . . . ?

The grass beneath her feet had not been cut recently. Perhaps this tourist attraction was avoided because there was no gravel path up to it? Only the gentle slope of green, starred with a few late daisies.

Daisies?

She plucked one and twirled it in her fingers. She looked up at the folly again. Forget? No. Remember. She was so tired, so short of sleep . . .

Pictures and words came back into her mind from years before. She had gone up there with her mother and . . . and . . . a friend. Two friends. Her mother had been sad that day, though trying to laugh, trying to talk to the man, and yet sparing time for her little daughter as well . . .

Her mother in a blue dress with a daisy pattern on it?

No. The daisies were in the grass, and the child Minty was being shown how to . . . ?

She remembered.

Her mother was wearing a blue dress and laying cushions on the seat, while a man—a nice man, she knew him well—unpacked a picnic basket. Minty was carrying another cushion for her mother up into the folly, but the boy was still on the slope, weighted down by the collapsible table he was carrying, watching a butterfly in the sky above him.

He shouted, "Look, Minty! It's a Blue. I haven't seen one of those here before."

Her mother took the cushion from her and said, "Minty dear, why don't you go down and play with Patrick for a bit? Make me a daisy chain or something?"

Minty didn't know how to make a daisy chain. She put her thumb in her mouth and looked down at the boy. He came to play with her now and then in the holidays, and she often went down to the village to have tea with him in term time. He was teaching her to read and write.

He went to school with Simon, but he wasn't like Simon at all. Patrick was nice. As she went down the slope, she heard her mother say to the man, "I don't know how much longer I can . . ."

Patrick would show her how to do it, if she remembered to say please and ask him nicely.

He showed her how to pick daisies with a longish stem—not too short and not too long. He split the stem of one for her and she tried to do the same, but tore the stem right across. He was much older than her, of course. She got it right eventually, and when he'd helped her complete the daisy chain, he crowned her with it.

She always liked being with Patrick. He was patient—unlike Simon. And he made jokes just for her. She knew he liked her, too. She made a crown for him as well and put it on his head. He laughed and said it tickled his ears, but he didn't take it off. Then together they made a crown for her mother and took it up to her.

Her mother had a cold and was blowing her nose. The man was patting her hand. He was a nice man. The man liked her mother, too. He was like a grandpa to Minty and her mother.

"How clever of you, darling!" said her mother.

"Patrick showed me," she said. "I'm going to marry Patrick when I grow up."

Both her mother and the man laughed.

Patrick didn't laugh, and neither did Minty.

As they were returning to the house, Patrick said to Minty, "I'm only five years older."

Minty considered that. Nanny had said children grew up at different rates. Minty was a big girl at four, nearly five, and Nanny didn't expect her to whine when she wanted something, while a boy of Simon's age was still young enough to do so. Nanny said that was because girls grew up faster than boys. It was all very odd. She asked Patrick, "How long will it take for me to catch up?"

And he'd said, "I'll wait . . . wait . . . wait . . ."

Minty came back to the present with a little jump. The daisy was still in her hand. Daisies. Marguerites. Patrick.

He had remembered, and she'd forgotten.

He'd hinted at it, time and again. Waiting for her to catch him up.

Well, he was five years older, and had waited . . . even if he had dilly-dallied along the way once or twice.

She thought of Lucas, of Neville, and of Simon, and pulled a face. She had looked elsewhere, but nothing had happened. For which she was now very grateful.

Thank you, Lord.

She replayed the scene in her mind's eye. Her mother had been crying; she realised that now. Her mother had confided her unhappiness to Patrick's father, who had comforted her, but not in any loverlike way. Her mother had sent Minty off to play with Patrick while she talked to his father, and the two children had made a pact together because they had liked one another more than anyone else they knew.

Minty wondered how long afterwards it had been before her mother ran off the road in her car. Minty could now guess what it was that had caused her mother so much distress.

And then . . . and then when she'd been driven away to the city and had called out for her mummy and daddy and Patrick, and would not stop, her aunt had grabbed the child by her hair while she beat at the back of Minty's legs . . . "You can forget all that, little miss! There's no one coming to take you home . . ."

And there hadn't been. She hadn't wept, even when the beating became so severe that her uncle had to intervene. He, too, had said, "This is your life now. Forget what happened in the past. Forget . . ."

A movement in the great house caught her eye. Someone was pulling down the blinds along the windows of the Gallery on the ground floor. Well, the stewards usually pulled down the blinds to keep the sunlight out of those rooms. But the sun wasn't shining.

Gemma's rooms faced her across the garden. The big windows there were wide open and pop music was banging away, assaulting the ears of whoever might be listening. Suddenly the noise ceased.

Minty understood that her father had died, even as she stood there, holding the daisy in her hand. She opened her fingers and tried to shake the daisy from her palm, but it clung.

Desolation. There were too few daisies on the slope now, to make a daisy chain.

Chapter Twenty-Five

The three women who had loved Sir Micah stood at his bedside. He looked serene, Minty thought. He had a noble head. He'd had a fine mind, lived hard, laughed a lot . . . founded a charity, married twice, sired two children, been knighted. He'd made mistakes. But then, don't we all? She didn't altogether understand why he'd rejected her for so long, but he'd said he regretted it and that was good enough for her.

She reached out her hand and touched his lips for the last time.

Annie put her arm around Minty's shoulders and guided her through to the sitting room, leaving Serafina and the nurse to make Sir Micah ready for his last journey.

"Did you have a good walk, Minty?"

Minty pressed her fingers to her forehead. Must they behave as if nothing at all had happened? "Yes, I did. Have you been out at all? Would you like to go now?"

"I've been in the chapel. It's restful there. Cecil Scott rang. I didn't realise it, but the village holds—held—Sir Micah in some esteem. They want to ring the passing bell for him. Once for each year of his life. I thought all such customs had died out."

Minty nodded. Yes, she could see that people like Ruby and Willy at the Chinese restaurant, and Doris-of-the-gift-shop, and the publican and his wife, and all the stewards and the people who served in the kitchens and cared for the gardens—they would think it a fitting tribute. The tourists wouldn't care one way or the other, of course, but would wonder what all the fuss was about and ask when the Hall would be open again.

Annie said, "He gave me a list of instructions for his funeral, even down to the hymns and the readings. He wants—wanted—a very simple service, family flowers only, followed by a cremation.

His ashes are to be interred next to his first wife's. Lady C would have preferred a big funeral up in London with maximum press coverage, but we'll do it his way. She can arrange a memorial service up in London later, if she wishes."

Minty nodded.

Annie said, "Have you got a black outfit, Minty?"

Minty shook her head. "I'll buy one." She opened her fist. A crushed daisy sat there. She would press it in her mother's Bible in a minute, but first . . .

"Annie, I'm worried. Not about me; I'll be all right. I can go up to the Woottons, back to the bookshop, anywhere. But you and Serafina. Will Lady C want to turn you out? Because if so, perhaps I can ask the Woottons to let you stay there for a bit and then perhaps, if I can get my job sorted out at the bookshop, perhaps I can rent a cottage here for you . . . or no. Perhaps you'd rather leave the village altogether?"

"My dear, how like you to worry about us. I am a trustee of the Foundation, and the Foundation pays rent for this suite, including the offices and our living quarters. The Foundation pays our salaries and those of the office staff as well. She can't turn us out."

"Silly of me," said Minty. "Of course he'd have thought of it."

"You know very little of the Foundation and its work—as yet. There's time. Now you'd better get on that phone to that man of yours or it'll be pistols at dawn."

Minty stared after Annie's retreating back. Had Annie actually made a joke?

She got out her phone and tried Patrick's number. She felt dizzy, disorientated. She couldn't think what day it was, or even whether it was morning or afternoon. Or—she looked out at the darkening landscape—evening. Patrick answered.

"Patrick, he's at peace . . . and I'm so tired."

"Tell me about it."

The world turned itself right way up again.

Venetia fetched Minty from the Hall and installed her in the bedroom that had once been their daughter Pearl's. It took some time for Minty to remember where all her belongings were around the village, and it took a couple of days of rest and a couple of nights of good sleep before she felt anywhere near herself again.

Now Mr Lightowler had asked for another council of war. Hugh said it was too early to make plans, but Mr Lightowler insisted, saying he'd asked Patrick to come up to the Woottons, as well. Mr Lightowler arrived early, so Venetia gave him a sherry while they waited for Patrick.

Patrick was late, having been in court all day. Minty sped into the hall when she heard his car and flung open the front door to let him in. She'd thought she would be able to run into his arms, and he would hold her tightly and kiss her.

Instead, he held her at arms' length, and his face was grave. Minty felt chilled. She heard Hugh come into the hall behind her. Hugh said, "Whatever's the matter, Patrick?"

"Miles is out on bail. I think he's mentally unbalanced myself, but Simon got him a good brief who said tipping Minty into the stream was an accident, so he's out again. I gather Gemma's told him to get lost, and he certainly hasn't gone back to the Hall. No one seems to know where he's gone, and I don't like that. He's blaming everyone but himself for his troubles: you, Gemma, and Simon. I don't know who he wants to hurt most. Whoever he comes across first, I suppose.

"So I think for that and other reasons Minty ought to go back to her aunt and uncle's until the funeral. Next Friday. Lady Day. Her birthday." He shot Hugh a glance that made that worthy narrow his eyes and massage his chin.

Minty was shocked. "Why do you want me to go back to a place where I was so unhappy?"

Patrick looked at her and she saw pain in his eyes. "For your own safety and for closure," he said. "Settle your accounts. You left in a hurry, and don't tell me you didn't leave any unfinished business behind. Brown Owl, weren't you? How is your Brownie pack getting on without you? Parish secretary? Can your replacement cope with your filing system? Your uncle's church accounts: who's preparing them for audit? Your aunt: does she need steering to a consultant for her aches and pains?"

She gasped. How did he know all that about her? She reddened. Was he right? Had she been evading her responsibilities? The thought of going back there was horrendous, but was he right in thinking she should do so?

He looked directly into her eyes. "Lucas. Do you have any unfinished business with him?"

She didn't understand why he was holding her off like this. He couldn't be jealous of Lucas, surely? "Lucas means nothing to me." she said, sharply for her. "I'd rather stay here and help Mr Lightowler get the bookshop sorted."

His eyes were telling her one thing, but his voice was steely. "There'll be time for that later, when Miles has been dealt with. If you're going to make a fresh start here . . ."

"If!" Minty exploded. "You know I want to live here more than anything!"

"All right, but it's early days yet and you may change your mind. Women do." He put his hands in his pockets and then took them out again. Only later did she realise he was nervous.

"You are the most disagreeable . . . !" Minty stopped herself from continuing. She tossed back her hair and turned her shoulder on him. She said, "I'm counting ten. See? I'm quite, quite calm again. I take your point, Patrick. It's my aunt's birthday on Sunday. I'll go back then, just for the day."

"Reggie said he'd drive you back there tomorrow, Saturday. Pick you up at ten o'clock."

Minty told herself it did no good to blow off steam at Patrick. None whatever. She would, of course, like to chop him into tiny pieces with a meat cleaver and strew the bits on the lawn for the birds, but she wouldn't give him the satisfaction of showing how angry she was.

Patrick addressed the ceiling above her head. "Reggie's got a week's leave coming to him and wants to see the sights of the city. He wondered if you could find him somewhere to stay, perhaps even at the vicarage. Perhaps show him around a bit?"

"Did Annie suggest my returning to the city?"

"She agrees with me that it's a good idea. Reggie will drive you back here in time for the funeral, which practically the whole village and most of the county will attend, plus grandees from the Foundation in London—"

"He wanted a simple affair."

"To be followed by a massive reception at the Hall, and the reading of the will. Some codicils too, I shouldn't wonder. It should be an interesting occasion. I hope you can find yourself a really fetching hat to wear, and a classic black outfit. Something subdued, modest, and in good taste but showing a certain amount of leg."

"Patrick!"

Patrick didn't even wince, concentrating on some agenda he'd set for himself. "Oh, and there's something wrong with my mobile phone, so you won't be able to get me for the time being." He yawned. "I was up early. Nasty court case. Read all about it in the papers tomorrow, Hugh." Patrick opened the front door and went out.

She would have followed him, but Hugh put his arm around her shoulders and steered her out into the garden through a side door. "Leave him be. Let's go look at the garden. Favourite time of the year, this. Colour. Lots of it."

She went with him in a daze. He ushered her across the lawn to a door in a walled garden. Within was a well-tended kitchen garden plus a herbaceous border that was a sight to see. The border was ten feet deep. At the back, sunflowers and wigwams of sweet peas and potato vines grew taller than Hugh's head. There were mounds of busy Lizzies and eschscholtzias and lobelia and petunias at the front. In the middle were stands of phloxes and penstemons and asters of all colours, with the brilliance of huge dahlias between. And great clumps of white Michaelmas daisies.

Minty was amazed. So this was Hugh's secret passion?

He waved his hand at the flowers. "God: proof of. If you see what I mean. All's right with the world. Not clever, me. Venetia's clever. Me, I'm just steady. Patrick's both clever and steady. Man of honour. Must have cost him, to do that to you. Even forgot his manners, didn't he? Do you like dahlias? Some people don't. Venetia says they're over the top. I like them, though."

She winced. It had cost her, too. "Does Patrick think my father left me some money? And that that will make any difference to the way I feel about him?"

"Something like that, yes. Got to hand it to him, holding back, giving you a free hand to make your own choices. Sweet peas are going over. Sad, that. Need a lot of manure. Going to try canna lilies next year. Ordered a couple thousand daffodils of all sorts for the lawn where it slopes down to the stream. Help me plant them, eh? Should look a treat."

He took out a large penknife, opened the blade and started cutting dahlias. "Take them to your aunt, eh?"

"I thought Patrick loved me." She heard herself sounding like a child.

"He does. You'll understand soon."

Silence. "Hugh. About Pearl and Patrick."

"Pearl's like me. Steady. They had a lot of fun. Venetia thought . . . hoped. I didn't. Knew it would end in tears. Not up to his weight, not like you. To see you two dancing together . . . anyone could see you're a pair! Pearl, not his fault. Always kept it light. Warned her, but . . . can't tell the young anything. Only thing, pick up the pieces." He sighed. "New Zealand's a long way. She's expecting. Thought we might move there. No go. Nothing to do. Came back. Empty house. Empty life. Even prayed a bit. Pathetic, what?"

He piled more flowers into her arms, moving gradually along the border.

She said, "Didn't you have any other children?"

"Two. Boy, information technology. Out of work now. London. Girl, architect, Midlands. Not happy, either of them. But what to do, eh?"

"Get them back here, of course," said Minty. "We've got masses to do here, and not enough hours in the day to do it in."

He gaped at her. "That's your grandfather speaking. Well, well. Could be you're right. You won't let us down, now? You will be back?"

"Count on it."

The fiery glow of the dahlias was the brightest spot in the room. Uncle Reuben had cancelled a meeting—unheard of!—to talk to Minty. Reggie was out somewhere, enjoying himself. Aunt Agnes used a stick to get across the room into her chair. Uncle Reuben looked a trifle more stooped, a little more worn than she remembered. One arm of his glasses was broken and mended with Sellotape.

Minty felt impatient with them and with the evident poverty and poor taste of the room. Why didn't they upgrade the light bulbs at least? And throw away the stack of free newspapers and junk mail that had accumulated in the fireless hearth?

She sat in her usual chair by the table on which rested piles of parish mail. It had been one of her jobs to sort and deal with this. Had no one touched it since she left?

"You look well, Minty," said her aunt, easing her bad knee into a new position, "though I can't approve of your wearing jeans."

"Positively blooming," said her uncle, hands braced on knees. Minty looked for a likeness to his brother and found hardly any. Perhaps a similar strong nose and chin?

"Lucas is looking forward to seeing you again," said her aunt, nodding.

Minty leaned forward. "Well, before he comes . . ."

Her uncle exchanged glances with her aunt. "Yes. The money. We knew we'd have to tell you one day, but we hoped you'd have grown up enough by then to understand.

"Micah and I were born only two years apart. We were fortunate in that our parents were wealthy and gave us a good education. At university we joined the set of the aimless rich, rejecting our parents' Christian values, but a chance meeting with an old friend who'd entered the church set me on the right track. I dropped out of university and retrained in the church. Micah and I kept in touch but at increasingly rare intervals.

"I met Agnes. We got married . . ." and here he smiled at his wife. "Micah made his millions and his name was associated with many different women, though he seemed to care for none of them. When he met and married your mother out in Australia, we were surprised. She was so much younger and from a very different background. We hoped it might be the making of him.

"We met your mother a couple of times up in London. I thought her a pretty child, hardly able to comprehend a man of Micah's ferocious intelligence and willpower. It was about that time he started his charitable Foundation, even asking me to be a trustee. I refused: what did I know of such things? But I was touched. Every now and then Micah invited Agnes and me to join him and your mother for lunch up in town. The Foundation has offices there, too, you know.

"It would have been about a month before your mother died. We were all due to meet up for lunch. Your mother, Agnes, and I met up in the foyer at the Foundation offices and went up in the lift together. There was no one in the outer office, so your mother opened the door to Micah's. His then secretary was on his desk with her skirt up and Micah was, well . . . there's no need to spell it out, is there? Your mother fled, but Agnes and I . . . we just stood and gaped.

"Micah laughed it off. He said if his wife had seen, then it was just tit for tat, as she'd been having an affair with some solicitor or other. He showed us a photograph of him that he'd taken from a local newspaper."

"It wasn't true," said Minty. "Richard Sands was a family friend, much older. Lisa spread the rumour deliberately."

"Well, of course it's more comfortable for you to think so. It wasn't long after that we heard your mother had been killed, but it was clear she'd been running away to be with her lover . . ."

"Again, not true!" said Minty.

Her uncle shrugged. "That's what we were told. We went to the funeral, of course. We could see that his secretary was pregnant. It was no great surprise to hear that Micah was going to marry her and leave the Hall. His wife to be was desperate to get rid of you. Micah asked if we'd take you in. We talked to your nanny—a hard woman, we thought—who seemed to be making a favourite of the secretary's son by a previous marriage . . . if indeed there ever had been marriage, which we rather doubted.

"We talked it over, Agnes and I. Agnes was not a well woman even then, and it was not an easy decision to make, but we'd seen what wealth allied to a rejection of God had led to in Micah's case . . . adultery, pride, lies, deceit. The whole sordid business reinforced our conviction that it was the wrong way to bring up a child. We could see exactly what would happen to you if you were left in that moneyed but godless household. We prayed about it, and it seemed that God was telling us that it was our duty to take you. So we did—under certain conditions."

"I wasn't to have any money?"

"Micah was to resign you to us completely, to let us bring you up as a Christian, to work for love and not for money, to be chaste and humble. Micah was not to have any contact with you until you were twenty-five, by which time we hoped you'd understand the value of a life devoted to God. The legal people didn't like it, but we overruled them. Our argument was that if you knew of your expectations, you wouldn't make any effort to earn your own living."

"What happened to the money my father sent?"

"We tried to make him pay as much for you as for any rich man's child. We didn't want the money, of course. It went into a charity account. I signed a direct debit for the bank to pay it into the Foundation once a year. I have now closed that account and the money I sent you the other day was some interest that had accrued."

Minty started to laugh. So the money had gone back to her father? Well, why not!

Aunt Agnes shifted in her chair, "It was no laughing matter. You were headstrong and needed curbing at every stage."

Uncle Reuben excused her. "Minty missed her parents and her friends . . ."

"Minty's sort coasts through life on pretty clothes and flirting. It's cost me many a grey hair keeping you out of trouble, Minty. Your uncle wanted you to go away to university when you finished school, but I couldn't have managed without your help in the house by that time, and anyway we'd promised to teach you the proper value of money. So it was best you learned it under our roof. The men I've had to warn off, to keep you safe! And look at you now! A fortnight away and you're flaunting your body in clothes to show your cleavage, and letting your hair down to attract the men. Didn't you come back with a man in tow?"

"Men . . . warned off?" said Minty.

Uncle Reuben said, "Whenever we thought a man was becoming too interested in you and might lead you astray, your aunt felt it her duty to warn him off, saying you were unofficially engaged to our dear nephew Lucas."

"Which I hope she will be, very soon," declared Aunt Agnes.

"There was one man," said Uncle Reuben, steepling his fingers, "that we feel we must warn you about in particular."

"Cecil Scott, I presume."

"No, no. The son of the man who led your mother astray."

Minty shot up out of her seat. "Patrick? He's been here? When?"

"Twice. We recognised him from the cutting Micah showed us. Luckily Agnes was able to intercept him before he had a chance to charm you to destruction, as his father had charmed your mother."

Aunt Agnes sniffed. "He tried to gatecrash your eighteenth birthday party in the church hall. I told him you were perfectly content and about to go to college. Then I spotted him in church the day you were twenty-one. Luckily it was a parade Sunday and you were occupied with the children. I took him on one side and told him that you were engaged to Lucas. He didn't come again."

Minty closed her eyes, trying to take in what her aunt had been saying. So Patrick had known where she was all these long years? He'd come to see her, to satisfy himself that all was well? Wondering, perhaps, if she would remember him. She hadn't even caught a glimpse of him. If she had . . . yes, she would have gone with him, without a backward look . . . and what would that have done to the terms of the agreement? Would she have been able to cope with that life at eighteen or twenty-one? Or would she have been corrupted by it, as Gemma and Simon had been?

Perhaps her aunt had had good reason to be wary, but not—surely not—to lie to Patrick. If they had only allowed Patrick to see her, to visit her now and again . . . what bliss that would have been, what fun! But of course that would have interfered with their plan to marry her to Lucas.

There was a bitter taste in her mouth. She pushed her hair back from her face with both hands. For years she had resigned herself to the idea that she simply wasn't attractive to men.

She now began to understand why Lucas had treated her so cavalierly. Aware of his aunt's hopes for their union, he would have thought that Minty could be his any time he liked. Wrong!

Patrick didn't seem to care about her looks. He liked her for herself. She wondered what he had thought of her aunt. She shook her head. Not much, perhaps.

Her uncle eased his back. In the poor light Minty saw that Aunt Agnes had lost weight. Suddenly she saw what their future was going to be like. Ill health and loneliness. She didn't think Lucas was going to become less selfish or look after them properly in the future, and she herself would never come back . . . she hoped.

She couldn't bear to look at them any longer, but fled to the kitchen. It seemed a dreary place now, without her little cat for comfort.

Her uncle followed her. "This must have come as a shock to you, but you do see how it was? We acted in your best interests all along. I'm glad that it's all out in the open. It's been a heavy burden for us to carry. We're not getting any younger and your aunt's on the waiting list for a knee replacement. We're retiring from the parish at Christmas and looking around for some sheltered accommodation."

Minty struggled to see their side of the matter. Was it possible that they had done their best, as far as they were able? Perhaps they had, according to their limited understanding. If they had removed her from an unsuitable environment—and considering what had happened to Simon and Gemma, they might well have been right to do so—they had failed to give her the one thing that would have made all the difference, and that was love. They hadn't had it in them to love her.

Her aunt had whipped her till the blood ran on more than one occasion. And Uncle Reuben had condoned his wife's behaviour.

Telling her to forget . . . forget . . .

Upstairs her tiny, shabby room awaited her, without so much as a bolt or a lock on the door . . . and Lucas down the corridor. She shuddered. No, she couldn't stay here even for one night, never mind the six that had been planned.

She had made a few friends during the years she had lived here. One in particular, whom she'd met at college. Carol's family was chaotic, noisy, loving. They'd put her up and maybe even find a corner for Reggie, too.

She went to look for a telephone book in her uncle's study. He followed her. "What is it, Minty? Say something."

"I'm phoning a friend to see if she's a room for me."

"What? But now you're back, surely you'll be staying here with us. We need you. Surely, now we've explained . . ."

"Understanding doesn't necessarily lead to forgiveness. I think I understand your reasoning about the money, but I don't understand how Aunt Agnes could abuse a child as she abused me, and I don't understand why you let her do it."

"She was very fond of you."

"No, she wasn't. I think you were fond of me, a little, but she hated me." She shuddered. She could dimly remember the way her aunt had swung her round and hit her, again and again and again. Perhaps they had been right, and it was best to forget what you couldn't alter. They had told her to forget her past, to put it out of her mind, because she was never going back. They had told her to forget her mother and everyone she had ever loved. They had told her to forget Patrick . . .

And to survive, she had forgotten.

"Aunt Agnes still doesn't realise what a terrible thing she did, does she? Have you ever talked to her about it? Perhaps with God's help I might manage one day to forgive you, but not yet."

Lucas burst into the room, seized Minty by the neck and planted a big kiss on her mouth. "Welcome back. I've missed you. Have you eaten? I've got the car outside, thought we'd go to a little place I know, eat, drink, and be merry, what? Oh, and the new girl I've got in the office is no good at all, so you can start on Monday."

Her uncle nodded approval. "Yes, yes. Good idea."

Minty was amazed. Did they really think she could slip back into Marthadom so easily? She'd changed since she left such a short time before. Every trial, every test she'd had to meet in Hall and village, from Mrs Guinness to Mrs Collins to Simon, had made her stronger. She'd been in good hands, of course. Patrick had looked after her well, teaching, guiding, encouraging her until he'd cut the umbilical cord and set her free to go on by herself. She thought, *Just you wait, Patrick . . . !*

She could even feel sorry for Lucas now. A little.

"I'm not staying here, you know. Tomorrow I'm going to take you all out to lunch to celebrate Aunt's birthday, and on Monday I'm going shopping."

Carol's house was warm and welcoming, with bright lights everywhere. Carol and her family were delighted to see her, and wanted all the news. Carol even said she'd get time off to go shopping with her.

Now for Patrick. He'd said his mobile was out of action, but that might not be true. His mobile was switched off. She left a message on the voicemail, and texted a message. "I remember. Ring me."

He didn't reply till Sunday evening. Then it was a text message, which read, "Remember what?" She pictured him hunched over his mobile, carefully considering all his options. He would want to be absolutely sure what she meant.

Monday morning she rang his office, before she went shopping. "Please ask Mr Sands to ring me this evening." Nothing happened, so she texted the word "Daisy".

He understood that reference all right. On Tuesday he texted back, "2 young."

Wednesday she texted, "Not 2 young on Friday."

Thursday evening he rang her. "Minty, I'm trying to be sensible for both of us. You must not make any commitments yet."

"I'll see you on Friday, though? My birthday. Lady Day."

"Yes. I'll be there." He disconnected.

Chapter Twenty-Six

It was the morning of the funeral and her birthday. Oh well, she'd never had a fuss made of her birthdays and didn't expect this one to be any different. She'd had two birthday cards before they left the vicarage: a restrained country scene from her uncle and aunt, and a large splashy one with red roses on it from Reggie. Nothing from Patrick. The journey back to the village seemed interminable.

Reggie was wearing his chauffeur's uniform today, but had to park the car in a back street behind the church because the Green and the High Street were already full of cars. Sir Micah's funeral would be well attended.

Minty slid out of the car with a flash of expensively shod feet. She thought Patrick would be pleased with her appearance, as she'd aimed for the apparently-simple-but-actually-costly in every item she wore. She had on the stud opal earrings and one bracelet. She turned to help her uncle and aunt out of the car and handed a stick to her aunt. Lucas drew up behind them in his car and scrambled out, adjusting his coat collar.

The bell was tolling as they joined the sombre crowd passing into the church. The organ was playing something difficult, a trifle beyond the organist's capabilities. There were flowers everywhere. Minty's sheaf was of red roses, while Uncle Reuben and Aunt Agnes had sent a donation to the Foundation instead of sending flowers.

Annie Phillips, also in tailored black, came to Minty's side and directed them down the aisle. Minty saw and acknowledged tiny greetings from Serafina, the Woottons, Ruby and Jonah, Mr Lightowler, Mrs Chickward and Mrs Collins ... Nanny Proud, Mrs Guinness ... the Thornby family ... Willy and his wife from the restaurant ...

Half the village seemed to be there. Annie ushered Minty, her aunt and uncle into the second-from-front pew, behind the large black hats of Lady Cardale and Gemma. Simon turned his head to acknowledge Minty and then turned to the front again. He looked well barbered and his tan was deeper than ever. Neither Lady C nor Gemma turned to greet Minty.

The printed service sheet had been expensively produced. Hymns . . . readings by . . . names Minty didn't recognise. People from the world of finance, of business, of the Foundation? There were some grave-looking people sitting opposite. Most of them wore three-piece suits, including the women. Minty thought she'd glimpsed two of them in the office at the Hall.

She hadn't seen Patrick.

She'd told herself she was not going to cry.

Big girls don't cry.

She wept for her father as she would never weep for those who had brought her up.

Ample refreshments had been laid out in the Great Hall. Half the county seemed to be there. Lady Cardale held court at one end, while Annie steered Minty to the other.

Minty was kept busy as Annie Phillips and the Woottons kept bringing people up to be introduced to her. Several of them had brought birthday presents for her. Minty was surprised and touched, putting them down on a window seat to open later.

She shed her hat and jacket. It was going to be a fine day.

Serafina materialised at Minty's side with a plateful of sandwiches. "Eat."

Gemma drifted up, made as if to speak, shook her head at herself, took another glass of sherry from a passing waiter, and departed.

Gloria, Ruby, and Alice were among the waitresses serving drinks and canapés. Minty made sure to speak to them all. Alice said she'd heard there was going to be a crèche opening in the village and, if so, and there was an opening in the bookshop, she'd like to go for it. Would Minty bring her influence to bear to let Alice have Spring Cottage, even in its present state? Minty didn't know what to say to that, so just smiled. She hoped Alice was wrong about a job going at the bookshop.

Ruby said Jonah was just fine, out and about all day long, drawing up plans for a conservatory at the bookshop.

Venetia said they'd asked Patrick to draw up a lease for Mr Lightowler to take over the shop and flat, that Lady the cat had Mr Lightowler firmly under his paw, and that Hannah was going to a convalescent home before settling in at her sister's. Patrick never came near her. She thought she'd seen double once, but realised that the other Patrick was not a reflection in a mirror, but a much older man. She looked and thought, *Yes, Patrick's father is a lovely man, a courteous, kindly man, but he doesn't have steel in his backbone like Patrick.* Then she thought, *Whatever is he doing here? And come to think of it, why is Norman Thornby here, in a good suit that he probably only wears for weddings and funerals?*

Mrs Collins . . . Mrs Chickward . . .

Simon caught her arm and pressed her back against the wall. He'd been drinking. Well, drink was flowing freely enough, and the funeral and cremation had been a strain. "Well, my lovely? This is your last chance. Will you marry me, and take over the running of this place, and the village, too, of course?"

"Thank you, Simon. But no, thank you. Your mother is looking for you."

Lady C was, indeed, staring at them across the room. Simon frowned but removed himself. Someone brushed past Minty's back and deposited a long, official-looking envelope on the pile of presents behind her, said Happy Birthday and removed himself. Minty stiffened. She would know Patrick's voice anywhere. This was one birthday present she would open immediately.

She tore open the envelope and scanned a couple of pages of legalese. It looked as though . . . could it be true? Could he have done something so quixotic? He had deeded his shares in a company . . . other directors Norman Thornby and Hugh Wootton . . . to Araminta Cardale.

If the development near the railway station went through, then these shares would make her a rich woman. What a birthday present! She could buy a house in the village and be independent. She was stunned. She looked around for him so that she could protest, but he'd gone again. Had he planned this all along? She'd thought it was out of character for him to become a developer. Perhaps this was the answer, that he'd done it for her? Was this his way of apologising for his behaviour the night before she left the village?

People were making their farewells, leaving by the great front door to resume their lives. Others were being shepherded through the stately rooms to the library where the will was to be read. Serafina led Minty to a chair to one side of the fireplace, while Lady C and her children took centre stage on a long settee. Minty frowned. Why had Norman Thornby and Hugh been asked to stay? Also, Patrick and his father, who had been seated on the opposite side of the room to Minty?

Several important-looking people clustered around the large double desk near the fireplace. Minty assumed these were people from the Foundation. Above the fireplace was a portrait of her father, next to one of Lisa. They looked down on everyone in a haughty manner. Minty wondered what she ought to do with the portrait of her mother.

Her uncle and aunt were being seated at the back of the room, with Lucas. Ah, Lucas was probably hoping for something under the will?

Reggie and some other members of Sir Micah's staff filed in and took seats at one side, leaving the door to the music room open. Annie Phillips looked around, mentally checking off that everything was in order, and nodded to one of the grey men. A solicitor? A trustee of the Foundation?

The other people from the Foundation seated themselves, and the grey man began to read from a document with many pages.

Minty's mind began to drift as the legal terms regarding disposal of assets, and so on, passed over her head. A sharp exclamation came from Simon, "Get on with it, man!"

The grey man looked at Simon over the top of his glasses. "Very well. In simple terms for Simon Cardale to understand . . . certain assets are to be realised in order that the following bequests may be given. All Sir Micah's staff who were still working for him at the time of his death, to receive a year's salary. Serafina Sforza to receive one million pounds sterling, and Ms Annie Phillips—for long and faithful service—to receive two million pounds sterling."

Good! thought Minty.

"To my brother, Reuben, the sum of ten thousand pounds sterling with the proviso that it is spent on himself and not given away to charity. To Richard Sands and his son, Patrick Sands, an unqualified apology for any distress and loss of business caused by the regrettable misunderstanding regarding my first wife Millicent, and my good wishes for the future."

The grey man looked up to address the room. "Sir Micah added a codicil to his will before he died, a recommendation that the heir to the Hall and estate lease the field called the Lytchett to Patrick Sands and his partners at a peppercorn rent."

Wow! thought Minty. *That's some apology!*

Norman Thornby and Hugh grinned. Patrick's face was in shadow and Minty couldn't read his expression. She thought, *This means the development can go ahead and Patrick will still gain by the deal . . . and me, too? Although . . . can I really accept those shares from him? I'm not sure that I can.*

Simon jumped up. "But Miles said . . . !" So Simon *had* been in on the scam to sell the access at an inflated price. Several people turned surprised looks on Simon, who subsided, muttering.

The grey man waited till all was quiet again. "Now as to the affairs of the Foundation . . . I fear Simon will find them confusing . . ."

Minty smiled. The grey man didn't like Simon much, did he?

"So we will deal with those later, when we can have a meeting with those whom Sir Micah wished to be involved with the Foundation in the future . . ."

"As a director of the Foundation," said Lady Cardale. "I shall naturally attend that meeting and I give you warning that I shall once again—and this time I trust my wishes will be observed—I shall be nominating my son Simon as a director."

"That is your prerogative," said the grey man, with a bland look Minty interpreted as "Over My Dead Body". "Now we come to Sir Micah's personal fortune . . ."

"How much do I get?" Simon, being sharp.

"Please bear with me, Simon. Lady Cardale is to have the choice of whichever one of Sir Micah's houses and flats she prefers, together with any contents that did not originally come from Eden Hall, or that were bought with Sir Micah's money to be placed in Eden Hall. There is a proviso that she leaves Eden Hall as soon as practicable."

"I am to leave the Hall?" Lady Cardale was not amused. "Well, I suppose I can make do with the London flat."

The grey man bowed. "Sir Micah has always been fond of Eden Hall, and he has therefore left ten million pounds sterling in trust for the upkeep and development of Eden Hall. The trustees are . . ."

Simon leaned forward.

The grey man lifted his eyebrows. "It appears that Simon does not wish to know who the trustees are. Very well. Now we come to something that will interest him, I think. Fifteen million pounds is to be divided equally between Sir Micah's second wife Lady Lisa Cardale, his daughter Gemma, and his adopted son Simon . . ."

Nothing for me? thought Minty. She shrugged. *Oh well. I can manage.*

"Only five million pounds?" Simon sprang up. "That'll hardly cover what I owe."

"Sir Micah was aware of that. He suggests you leave the Hall and the estate at once and get yourself trained to earn your living. Oh yes, and if you contest the will, you are to lose the money Sir Micah has left you. Now, please let me finish. Another five million is to go to the Foundation . . . and the residuary legatee is . . . Sir Micah's daughter by his first wife, Araminta."

Simon reddened. "Do you mean she gets everything else? How much is that going to be?"

"When everything is settled, about five times as much as you," said the grey man, smoothly.

Minty felt as if she'd been turned to marble. Her father had left her twenty-five million pounds? Twenty-five . . . ! She could hardly believe it.

Lady Cardale was on her feet, too. "The Hall. The estate. He's left it to Simon, surely?"

The grey man took a step back and gestured for Patrick's father to take the floor. "Perhaps Mr Sands would care to explain?"

He's like and yet not like Patrick, thought Minty, trying to think on two levels at once. *All that money for me? Doesn't Simon get the Hall?*

Patrick's father took centre stage, as it were. His dark hair showed white streaks at either temple and he leaned slightly—possibly for effect?—on a cane. Otherwise he looked like his son, and like his son he seemed thoroughly at home in that great room. "Sir Ralph Eden's last will and testament has been in the common domain for twenty years, but as I drew up the will at the time . . ."

"Who's Sir Ralph Eden?" asked Simon, wildly.

"Millicent Cardale's father. Or rather, Millicent Eden as she was before her marriage to Sir Micah. As you probably know, Sir Ralph died shortly after Araminta was born. Sir Ralph was not consulted about the marriage, but by the time his daughter returned to this country with her husband, Millicent was already pregnant. Enquiries made by Sir Ralph about Sir Micah led him to suspect that the marriage might not last. He did not wish Eden Hall to become just one more asset in the portfolio of an international financier, something that might be sold off to provide Sir Micah with extra cash in an emergency.

"Sir Ralph therefore stipulated that his daughter would inherit the Hall and estate, but that if she died before her husband, it would be held in trust and pass to her daughter Araminta on her twenty-fifth birthday. If said child were to die before he or she were twenty-five, the estate would pass first to any other child of that union, or failing another direct heir, to a distant branch of the family. When Millicent died, Sir Micah became trustee for his daughter's inheritance. He could administer the property as he saw fit, but he could not dispose of it. Therefore, Araminta Cardale now inherits the Hall and the estate."

There was a cheer from the music room, where some of the staff must have been listening. Several people in the library clapped and made "Well done!" noises. Minty got to her feet, hesitantly. She felt stunned. The Hall was hers? But . . . She didn't know what was expected of her, or what she ought to do next. Or feel.

She looked at Patrick. He had known, and that was why he'd turned himself into a mother hen, teaching her what she needed to know, encouraging her to be independent, causing her to feel responsible for the future of the village . . . loving her but holding back. A man of honour, as Hugh had said.

Hugh Wootton had known, but had played fair. She didn't think he'd even told Venetia, because otherwise Venetia would have smothered her.

Norman Thornby had known, which was why he'd gone to the station to meet her . . . and then decided to play fair, too.

Annie Phillips probably hadn't known at first, but being the kind of woman she was, she would have checked over all the records and discovered exactly who was to inherit the Hall. Annie would always play fair.

Sir Micah had told Simon, which was the reason his tactics towards Minty had changed. First he'd tried to seduce her, then to intimidate her, and finally offered to marry her. The skunk!

Lady C hadn't known, and neither had Gemma. They both looked stricken.

Uncle Reuben had known. He was looking serene. Aunt Agnes looked spiteful. Lucas looked shattered.

The men and women of the Foundation looked pleased, in a temperate sort of way.

Patrick's father concluded, "I was executor of Sir Ralph's Will, of course, but felt I must resign as trustee for Araminta when scandal linked my name—quite wrongly—with that of the first Lady Cardale. Sir Micah has been a faithful trustee on his daughter's behalf. Before we leave this room, however, I suggest that Araminta Cardale sign a will—a temporary measure purely—to continue the safeguards put in place by Sir Ralph. I am sure she understands the necessity for this, in view of recent—ah—incidents. As my son took over the practice when I retired, I have asked him to prepare this will."

Without looking at Minty, Patrick produced a legal-looking document and laid it out on the desk. He produced a pen and laid it on one side, saying, "If there is anything that isn't clear . . ."

Minty found herself being shepherded by Annie Phillips towards the desk. She looked at Annie, who nodded and smiled. Annie would have read the document first, of course, and Minty could trust Patrick. But she would still have to read it herself.

She bent over it. It was quite short. It did what it said it was meant to do. Patrick's pen rolled off the desk, but there was a huge glass inkstand on the desk with a quill pen beside it. It amused Minty to think of using the quill. As she reached out her hand for the quill, she was shot forward across the desk, winding her. Someone screamed . . .

A hoarse voice in her ear. "Everyone keep back!"

Miles! He must have come from the courtyard via the anteroom. Minty felt the prick of a knife at her throat. She was bent forward over the desk, couldn't move. Could hardly breathe.

Patrick's voice. "Everybody keep still. Miles, what do you think you're doing?"

"I want what's mine, what she's cheated me out of!"

"What would that be?" Patrick's voice was conversational. Minty saw a drop of blood plop on to the desk. Miles's hand was on the back of her neck, pressing her down to the wood. He was half lying across her, one hand holding her left hand clamped to the desk, his whole body's weight on her right arm and shoulder.

She tried to see where Patrick was. He'd been standing close to her, at the side of the desk. The knife bit into her neck. More blood dripped on to the wood. She tried to breathe lightly. How was this going to end? She wasn't afraid, much. No. But she was getting angry. How dare Miles do this to her?

"A million pounds. And my job back. A public apology for all she's put me through."

"It wasn't Minty who put a stop to your schemes," said Patrick, still in that conversational tone. "It was I who did it."

The pressure on Minty's neck eased and she tried to lift her head, only to have the pressure renewed. Her cheek was being ground down into the wood.

"Then you'll give me what I'm due, or else she gets it!"

"No, Miles. No!" Gemma's voice, with a tremor in it. "I don't want you to do this."

"You, you stupid cow! What do you know about anything?" He shifted his feet to look at Gemma, and in doing so moved his weight so that Minty could breathe more easily. His grip on her left wrist was so tight she was losing all sensation there, but as he shifted he released her right arm. If she could just kick his feet from under him or . . . perhaps Patrick could . . . she concentrated on Patrick, standing almost within reach.

Gemma's voice came nearer. "Yes, but Miles . . ."

Then everything seemed to happen at once. In the split second before Minty drove her spiked heel at Miles, she felt him jerk.

The knife wavered away from her throat.

Minty grasped the heavy inkstand and twisted hard under Miles, bringing it round in one swift movement, risking the knife, catching Miles on the side of his head.

The knife fell to the floor as Patrick twisted Miles's right arm behind his back and Gemma seized his left. Reggie—always a second or two late—threw himself full length on Miles and they all fell to the floor in a scramble.

Minty set her beautiful black court shoe over the knife.

Miles began to scream, his face ugly.

Gemma fell away from him. Crying.

Patrick groped for the edge of the desk and hauled himself to his feet, dabbing a cut on his cheek.

Even a short time ago, Minty wouldn't have known what to do. But now she did. "Gentlemen," said Minty. "Black ties off and hand them to Reggie. Mobile phones out! Ambulance and police!"

Patrick handed Reggie his tie. His father flicked open his mobile, and spoke into it.

Minty helped Gemma to her feet and hugged her hard. Gemma's tears were very real. She must feel the end of her world had arrived.

"Thank you, Gemma," said Minty. "Now please would you consider giving the man back his ring?"

Reggie hauled Miles to his feet and dragged him out of the room. "The knife stays where it is until the police get here," said Minty. "As for the ink on the carpet, I think we'll leave it. The tourists will love seeing evidence of the attack. Now, Patrick. Where am I to sign?"

Two hours later Minty saw off the last of her guests, saying she needed to be quiet for a while, but if anyone wanted her, they could come and find her in about an hour's time. She went up to her father's suite—now hers, apparently—changed into a white T-shirt and jeans. The scratch on her neck was covered with a band-aid. She let herself into the chapel and fell into the first chair she came to. She had been holding herself together in front of the others, but now she began to tremble. To shake. The encounter with Miles had made her angry, but that was all over and done with. Now she was suffering from reaction.

If she could only cry, she would feel better. But big girls don't cry, and she was a big girl now, with more responsibilities than she'd ever dreamed of.

The Hall was hers? And all that money?

The grey men from the Foundation expected her to become a trustee. What did she know about such things? How on earth was she going to manage?

The people in the village looked to her for a lead, for jobs, for money.

Lady Cardale had icily requested an interview as soon as possible; Gemma had wept; Simon had raged.

Everyone wanted something from her, and she had no idea how to answer them.

"Dear Lord, grant me wisdom!"

The words burst out of her, and gradually she felt the calm of the room, of Jesus' love, enfold her. The surface of her mind was still in turmoil, but below that she felt the stirring of a new thought. If she trusted in Him, if she took all her perplexities to Him, He would help her.

There was a knock on the door, and Serafina entered, carrying a trug full of Michaelmas daisies. "Hugh Wootton said you'd asked him to send you over some flowers."

Minty pushed her hair back from her face. She might be reeling from everything that had happened to her, but she understood that the dear Lord had set some good people in her way to help her. "Serafina, I know you and Annie will have enough money to live wherever you want in future, but would you stay on to look after me for a while?"

"Annie told Sir Micah she would stay on if you asked her, and I said I would even if you didn't ask. No one's to know where you are for the next hour or so, is that right?"

"Well, there is one person who . . ."

"He left with the others, but took a walk in the park and is coming back now. Shall I tell him which tower you're in?"

"He'll find it by himself."

Serafina left, and Minty looked about her. She was amused to note that there were now four chairs facing the altar. One for Annie, one for Serafina, the carved chair in the middle, and the one she had fallen into, which was a cane-seated upright. So her mother's carved chair was not meant for her? How very odd.

She seated herself on the kneeler and started making a giant daisy chain from the Michaelmas daisies. She had almost finished when Patrick tapped on the door and entered.

He seated himself in the high-backed chair her mother had used for her portrait. The cut on his cheek had stopped bleeding. He looked perfectly at home. Minty thought, *So that's why I didn't sit there. I'll have him painted sitting in the carved chair and hang the portrait opposite my mother's in the library.*

He rested his hands on the arms of the chair and placed one knee over the other.

He said, "Simon's running through the house looking everywhere for you. Gemma's wandering around like a wraith. Lady C has locked herself in her rooms. Annie's hiding behind her computer screen, and Serafina said she'd have supper ready for you in Sir Micah's suite in an hour. But really, all this cloak and dagger stuff. It's absurd. We can't get married just because you thought it was a good idea when you were five years old. Anyway, those are not the right kind of daisies."

And attack, she thought, *is the best method of defence.*

Patrick had known that she would inherit the Hall. He had coached her to an understanding of the responsibilities involved and, fearing she might have no money to stay on at the Hall, had devised a means of giving her a substantial sum of money. He'd then tried to cancel her debt to him, so that she could go forward into her new life without ties to the past.

She could appreciate his problem. He wanted her, but his pride was protesting. Instead of his being able to give her money, it was going to be the other way round. Given half a chance, he'd swear blind he didn't love her. But, he had still come to find her.

She slipped one daisy stem through another. "It's too late in the year for wild daisies, so I improvised. Of course we won't get married just because we liked one another as children. I know *that!* Tell me: did you come to see me when I was eighteen out of curiosity?"

He frowned. "I'd just joined the firm. Yes, I was curious. I wondered how you'd grown up. You were wearing a ghastly pink dress—"

"Charity shop."

"And dancing with a boy of perhaps twelve. You had your hair tied back in a pony tail and looked about twelve, yourself. Your aunt said you were going to college and that sounded all right, so I left."

"You came back when I was twenty-one."

"You were in the middle of a pew full of Brownies, with your hair all scraped back and up. I thought you looked thin and pale, as if you could do with a square meal, that you needed to feel the wind on your face, perhaps take a holiday by the sea."

Concentrating on pushing one daisy head through the stem of another, she said, "If that were all you thought, why did my aunt react so strongly?"

He uncrossed and recrossed his legs. "She could probably see that I also wanted to take you outside and tear the clothes off you. And . . . well . . . she told me you were engaged to Lucas. I was angry. I took one look at Lucas and thought that served you right. So I left."

"To come back and cut a swathe through the local girls?"

"What was I supposed to think? Then you knocked me off my feet in the street, weeks before you were supposed to return."

"By which time you'd worked out how to give me a fortune, in case I was left the Hall without any money to run it. Can you draw up a lease for the Lytchett field, at a peppercorn rent? Let us say, one Michaelmas daisy plant a year?"

"I can't act in the matter. I suppose I could get my partner to do it." He drummed long fingers on the arm of his chair and looked away. He was nervous. Good.

She picked up the daisy chain she'd made. "This is for the three of us." She took the chain to the altar, and put it over the cross as some people put the crown of thorns in Lent. "For my five-year-old self, about to be torn away from everything she loved. For you, a ten-year-old boy, about to be driven from his home with his family, and for my poor unhappy mother. I give this to God. For closure. Let the past rest in peace."

She turned to face him, and he stood, too.

"So now we start again," she said. "Shall we start from the moment I knocked you over in the street, knowing all that has passed between us since then? The result would be the same, wouldn't it? Perhaps we start from this moment on. Me looking at you and you looking at me. Knowing the sort of people we have come to be, and the sort we hope to become."

For a moment she lost her nerve. "Have I got it completely wrong, Patrick? You do love me, don't you?"

"As God is my witness, I do. I think I've loved you all my life. But Minty, you could do better than a poor country solicitor. You are Miss Cardale of Eden Hall, with millions in the bank. You must look around you for an equal match."

"Look for someone else with your wit and intelligence, your loving kindness? Someone who is also a Christian? Who would you recommend? Simon? Cecil? Neville? Neville's the best of the bunch, but he'd never check me if I did anything stupid."

He made a sharp movement but did not speak.

She said, "Someone who is as far-sighted as you? Do you see anything in the future for us that would be against God's will?"

"I do see problems, yes."

"Are they insurmountable? Have you prayed about us?"

"I've hardly done anything else since you returned. Minty, are you sure?"

"Yes. This is Lady Day and I've made you your daisy chain. It's time for you to ask your question."

He looked beyond her to the cross. Then back at her. He took both her hands in his and said, "Araminta Cardale, will you marry me?"

"Before God," she said, "I will."

The future frightened her still, but with this man beside her, with Serafina and Annie to help her . . . and, above all, with God to guide her, she wouldn't go far wrong.